the french house

Also by Nick Alexander

The Case of the Missing Boyfriend
The Half-Life of Hannah

The 50 Reasons Series
50 Reasons to Say Goodbye
Sottopassaggio
Good Thing, Bad Thing
Better Than Easy
Sleight of Hand

Short Stories
13.55 Eastern Standard Time

the french house

nick alexander

CORVUS

Published in paperback in Great Britain in 2013 by Corvus,
an imprint of Atlantic Books Ltd.

10 9 8 7 6 5 4

A CIP catalogue record for this book is available from the British Library.

Paperback ISBN: 978 0 85789 635 3
E-book ISBN: 978 085789 634 6

Printed in Great Britain by CPI Group (UK) Ltd, Croydon, CR0 4YY

Corvus
An imprint of Atlantic Books Ltd
Ormond House
26–27 Boswell Street
London
WC1N 3JZ

www.corvus-books.co.uk

ACKNOWLEDGEMENTS

Thanks to my friends and readers and to those that are both, for being so constantly enthusiastic and supportive – you make it all worthwhile.

Thanks to everyone at Corvus for making this book a reality, to Jerome for his help with the French text, and to Rosemary for being my touchstone.

THE BIG SKY

When I get to Nice airport, I am expecting my new boyfriend to be ready and waiting, pulling faces at me through the glass as I watch for my suitcase to appear on the carousel.

I'm already in a heightened state of anticipation about this trip because, however it goes, it will influence our future. If I like it here as much as Victor seems to, then we could end up together in France. If I don't . . . well, that hardly bears thinking about.

When he still hasn't appeared by the time I drag my suitcase out into the arrivals hall, I feel a spike of anxiety.

I scan the crowd a few times, walk around the big fish tank – twice – and even read the names people are holding up on their scraps of cardboard, before doubtfully following the smokers outside.

I switch on my phone and adjust the clock to local time – 2 p.m.

It's a crisp January afternoon and the sky is deepest blue, the light low and yellowy. It's exactly the same weather as the last time I came to Nice and I wonder if it is always this way. I check my mobile and start to compose a text message asking Victor where he is but am interrupted by two hands slipping around my waist from behind.

'Hello, sexy lady. Don't turn around,' he says in a dodgy French accent.

I giggle and attempt to turn but Victor hops around and manages to remain behind me.

'What are you *doing*?' I ask, starting to laugh and finally pulling free before spinning around to face him.

Victor raises his hands to cover his grinning mouth. My own smile fades.

'I know,' he says. 'I'll get rid of it as soon as we get back.'

I have had a phobia about men with beards for as long as I can remember. I even saw a shrink once, and we pretty much traced it to the fact that my father had one. But, sadly, knowing the origin of a phobia doesn't seemingly make it go away. Such are the limitations of therapy.

I swallow hard, and pull his hands away from his face. 'Jesus, Victor!' I say. 'You look like Osama Bin Laden.'

'It's why I was late,' he says. 'They wouldn't let me into the airport until I could prove I wasn't a terrorist.'

'Really?'

'No,' Victor laughs. '*Not* really.'

I pull a face in spite of myself.

'I *know*!' he says. 'Honestly, I was going to shave but the pipes froze.'

'They froze?'

'Yeah. It was cold last night and both the tank in the van and the standpipe froze. But I'll do it as soon as we get back, I promise.'

I nod and just about manage a smile. 'You will!' I say.

'Anyway,' Victor says, moving in. 'Any chance of a kiss from my little Chelsii?'

I shake my head. 'None,' I laugh. 'And calling me Chelsii definitely won't help your case. You know I hate it.'

'Sorry. CC. And just a peck then?' he says. 'To say hello?'

I close my eyes and lean in, trying to push my phobia from my mind. Our lips meet, but then his straggly beard tickles my top lip and I suddenly feel sick. 'That's it!' I say, covering my disgust with a false little laugh. 'Sorry but . . .'

'Hey,' Victor says, serious now. 'It's OK. You told me all about it. I know. I'm sorry.'

He starts to drag my suitcase towards the car park and reaches for my hand. 'So how was the flight?'

'Fine,' I say. 'Orange.'

'On time, anyway.'

'Yes. Unlike someone I could mention.'

'Yeah, the roads were bad,' he says. 'So I had to take it easy. Have you eaten?'

'A sandwich. Horrible but filling. And what do you mean the roads were "bad"?'

'Oh, icy. Slippery.'

'Eek,' I say. 'Should I be scared?'

'No. Well, maybe just a bit. Later on, I'll tell you when.' He squeezes my hand tight. 'God, it's good to see you.'

'You too,' I say. 'Well, it will be when you get that doormat off your face so that I *can* see you.'

Once Victor has negotiated the traffic and merged onto the motorway, I ask, 'So we don't go through Nice, then?'

'No,' Victor says, leaning forwards to look in my wing

mirror before changing lanes. 'No, we're, um, west, so . . . But if you want to go down and visit, it's only an hour.'

'Is it hard having a right-hand-drive?'

Victor shrugs. 'You get used to it. But ultimately I'll end up swapping the van for a French car. As soon as I don't need to live in it any more, I suppose.'

'It's freaky sitting here,' I say. 'I feel a distinct need for a steering wheel.'

'We'll get you one,' Victor says, casting me a wink. 'One of those stick-on kid's ones.'

We sit in silence for a minute or so and I steal a glance at Victor's bearded profile. Surprisingly, I think it suits him. He looks rugged and sexy. It's just the sensation of it against me that I can't stand.

After only a few minutes on the motorway we turn off and immediately start to head up into the hills. 'I had no idea that the coastal towns ended so abruptly,' I say, watching the clichéd tableau of French Provençal life sliding past the windows.

'Yeah,' Victor says. 'It's great, isn't it? And this is still town compared to where we're going.'

The road winds past stone cottages and along tree-lined country lanes and then up and over a small hillock and through a copse of dense trees. When we come out on the other side, a majestic mountain range comes into view – bleak and grey and stark against the blue sky.

'Wow,' I say. I point to a raggedy village clinging to the side of the mountain. 'Is that us?'

'No,' Victor says with a laugh. 'No, we're right over the other side of that mountain.'

4

We continue on and up, and around each bend there is another bend, and over each peak there is another peak.

'So many hilltop villages,' I say.

'Yes. And all empty.'

'Really?'

'Pretty much. Most of them have twenty or thirty old people living in them. When they're gone, I think that will be it.'

'Incredible views, though,' I say.

And they are. As we round another bend, suddenly we can see the road before us. It is a simple ledge carved from the side of the mountain winding around its contours, gradually heading towards the peak. To the south I can see the Mediterranean Sea in all its turquoise glory, and in the distance I can see huge, white, snow-capped peaks.

'They're like *proper* mountains,' I say.

'They are, they're the Alps.'

'They're not, like, the *actual* Alps, though, are they? Not really.'

'Yes,' Victor says, glancing at me. 'They are. Really.'

'It's not snowing where we are, is it?'

'No. Not yet at any rate.' He glances at me. 'Are you scared?'

I look down at the sheer drop below and say, 'No, not yet. Is this where I should start to be?'

'No,' he says, slipping one hand onto my knee. 'Not of my driving, anyway. You should maybe be scared of the facilities.'

'The facilities?'

'The bathroom. In particular.'

'Right.'

'It's cold.'

'Nice. I love a cold bathroom.'

'Very, very, very cold,' he says.

'OK,' I say, pulling a face. 'I shall prepare myself for that.' I turn back to look out at the scenery. 'I'm in awe. I had no idea the Riviera could look like this.'

'No,' Victor says. 'It's surprising, isn't it?'

'It's just so *big.*'

'You said you've been here before, though?'

'Yes, but just to Nice. And along the coast a bit.'

'On a date, you said.'

'Yes.'

'You didn't want to tell me about it.'

'No,' I say.

After a full minute of silence, Victor laughs. 'OK then. I'll just try to imagine it, shall I?'

'If you want,' I say.

As we bump over the numerous potholes in the final stretch of 'road' to La Forge, the hamlet in which the house is located, I check the time on my phone. Though the drive has taken almost an hour, the torturous road and the setting sun make it feel like more.

'You have reception?' Victor asks, glancing over at me.

'On and off, yes. I was just looking at the time. It's hard to believe that it's not even four, what with the sun setting and everything.'

'Well it's not really setting, is it?' Victor says. 'It's just dipping behind the mountains.'

'Sure ... God, this road's bad!' I exclaim as the van bumps around.

'Ha! You think *this* is bad? You just wait!' And as if to prove his point he turns off down a dirt track – in fact, even dirt track would be overstating it. It's a muddy wheel-stain which crosses a field.

'Don't you worry about getting stuck?' I ask. 'I mean if it rains ...'

Victor shrugs. 'It doesn't really matter if I can't get home, this *being* my home,' he says, gesturing about the van.

'No,' I agree. 'I suppose not.'

When we finally pull up in front of the farmhouse, words fail me. 'Gosh!' is the best I can manage.

'Gosh?' Victor repeats, pulling on the handbrake and releasing both of our seat belts.

We climb down from the van and Victor slides one arm around my waist. 'Home!' he says.

The farmhouse is a large single-storey building of the same grey stone from which all the drystone walls around the property are made. It is set into a niche carved from the hill behind. The building has only two tiny windows on the visible side and a gaping hole in the roof. To the right and left of the main house are two outbuildings, each about two-thirds the size of the main house, neither of which has any roof whatsoever.

The three buildings enclose what must once have been a gravelled courtyard, only most of the gravel has long since been driven into the mud. Vast amounts of junk sit in piles strewn around the courtyard: a rusty bike, a half-burnt settee, an almost entirely decomposed oil drum over there; a broken lawnmower, a garden chair, an old gas cooker and a toilet seat over here.

The sun is dipping behind the mountains now, the whole ensemble sliding into grey and, to be perfectly honest, I'm struggling to see the potential. The overriding ambience is cold, derelict and rather sinister.

'You have to use your imagination,' Victor says, pulling me tight. With his free hand he points as he describes what I'm apparently failing to imagine on my own. 'This whole area nicely gravelled. Roses growing up the walls. No, um, hole in the roof. That cherry tree in blossom.'

I nod at the gnarled skeleton of a tree. 'Is that really a cherry tree?'

'Yep,' he says.

'It looks dead, though.'

'You'll find trees do that in winter,' Victor says. 'Come! I'll show you the house before it gets dark.'

He leads me across the desolation zone to the front door and then pushes and kicks it until it opens. The inside isn't as bad as I expected. That is to say that it actually looks like a house, albeit one that has never heard the words 'interior design' or 'cosy'. With the exception of the gaping hole above our heads, it looks like a basic, old-fashioned Provençal farmhouse. It looks like someone lived here once.

'Nice range,' I say, nodding at the huge iron wood stove.

'Yes,' Victor says, releasing my hand and crossing the room to stroke it. 'It's rusting because of the roof. I wonder if it will clean up?'

I follow him across the room and look up through the hole. 'It's not going to fall on us, is it?'

'What, the sky?'

'The rest of the roof, silly!'

Victor shakes his head. 'No, I went up there to check it. It all seems pretty solid. The hole is a bit of a mystery, actually.'

'Yes,' I say, thoughtfully. 'It's not like there's anything to fall on it.'

'Big bird?' Victor says in an ironic tone.

'Bloody big bird,' I laugh. 'Meteorite, more like.'

'Maybe.'

'When are they fixing it?'

Victor shrugs. 'I can't get anyone to even come and have a look. They all say it's too remote.'

'Well, we need to get it covered,' I say, 'even if it's just with a tarpaulin.'

Victor grabs my hand and squeezes it. 'You have no idea how nice that "we" sounds,' he says.

'Actually, I have,' I say, bumping his hip. 'It felt nice to say it, too.'

Victor looks up at the darkening sky again. 'I thought about fixing it myself,' he says.

'That's dangerous.'

'Nah, not really. It's just that the roof is made of these corrugated sheets and I can't even lift one. Anyway.' He pushes me towards the hallway. 'So you've seen the lounge-cum-kitchen-cum-dining room.'

'Have I?'

'Yes. Here's the rumpy-pumpy room,' he says, steering me into the next room.

'Hmm,' I say. 'Needs some work before it'll be seeing any rumpy-pumpy.' The walls are bare stone. The floor is peeling vinyl. The hole in the roof extends over a rusty metal bed.

'Indeed,' Victor says, already leaving the room. 'And then this is the second bedroom or office or—'

'Cupboard,' I say, peering into the gloomy, windowless box room.

'Probably need to put a window in here.'

'Yes.'

'And then, *finally* ... *La pièce de résistance* ...' He grabs my hand and pulls me excitedly through to the final room. 'The facilities.'

'Jesus!' I exclaim. For though comfortably sized, the 'bathroom' is absurdly basic, comprising a toilet bowl in one corner, a rusty yellow sit-up bathtub, and a stone sink.

'All mod cons,' Victor says.

'Yes, I can see that.'

'Madame will note the complete absence of a flushing mechanism,' Victor says, sliding his hand across the wall behind the toilet bowl.

'How lovely!'

'And ... wait for it ...'

'Yes?'

'No hot water.'

'Jesus, Victor.'

'I know.'

'Can't we get that working?'

'It's not that it doesn't work. It's that there isn't a hot water system in the house.'

I frown and scan the room, then peep back down the hall. 'I also just noticed – no heating.'

'Other than the range, none.'

'God, whatever happened to the French *art de vivre*?'

'I know. But I can imagine it finished,' Victor says, heading back outside. 'Can't you?'

'Sure,' I say. But it's a lie. Maybe I'm just too tired to imagine anything this evening.

Back out in the yard, the light is fading fast and, with it, the temperature is plummeting.

Aware that I'm sounding like a real killjoy, I try to think of something positive to say about this tumbledown farmhouse he has inherited. I'm a terrible actress, so any outright lies about finding the place appealing are only likely to make things worse.

'I bet you can see masses of stars up here, can't you?' I finally offer.

'Yes. It's amazing.'

'I love that,' I say. And it's true. 'I'm actually quite good at spotting all the constellations. Waiine had a telescope when we were little.'

'Waiine? Oh, your brother. Sorry, I forgot. Sorry.'

'It's fine. Even I forget sometimes,' I say, clearly a lie. 'It was a long time ago.'

I stroke Victor's arm and then add, 'But yes, I'm sure it will be brilliant up here for star-spotting. God, it's going to be cold, though. I can see my breath already.'

'Yes, as soon as the sun goes behind the hills. Still, it is January. And we are eight hundred metres above sea-level.'

'Right,' I say.

I turn to look back at the house and shiver. Victor wraps his arms around me and slips his hand into the pocket of my jeans. 'It's *bad*, isn't it?' he says.

I sigh deeply. 'It's a lot more work than I thought. If you want to make it nice, I mean.'

'Is it a mistake, do you think?' he asks. 'Do you think I've bitten off more than I can chew?'

I shrug and gaze at the buildings. 'To be honest, I'm not sure,' I say. 'Can you ask me again tomorrow?'

'Sure,' Victor says.

'I'm freezing.'

'Me too. Can I tempt you with an aperitif in Château Volkswagen, Madame?'

'Does the heating work in Château Volkswagen?'

'Oh yes.'

'Then that would be a pleasure, sir,' I laugh. 'But it's *mademoiselle*, thank you very much.'

Drinking gin and tonics in the van is cramped but rather lovely. Victor produces chilled tonic and even ice cubes from the mini-fridge and a bag of Japanese rice snacks from a cupboard, then we settle on the bench seat, my back against his chest, his knees either side of me.

Slowly, beyond the windows, the sky flames red and then gradually fades to black.

'You hate it all, don't you?' Victor says after a long

silence, during which the only sound is the clinking of ice cubes against the side of the glass and the hiss of the gas heater.

'What? This?!' I exclaim. 'You're joking! I *love* being here with you like this. It's fun.'

'But you hate the house.'

I reach up and stroke his head until my hand reaches his beard. 'I hate this thing,' I say, tugging on it.

'Oh, God!' Victor laughs. 'I nearly forgot. I'll shave in a minute. But don't change the subject.'

'I don't *hate* it,' I say. 'It's just, well ... it's a far bigger project than I imagined. I'm a bit daunted, I guess.'

Victor takes a few sips of his drink before replying. 'Can I tell you a secret?' he asks.

'Of course.'

'I'm not very proud, but, so am I.'

'You're what?'

'Daunted.'

I arch my back so that I can look up at him. 'I'm not surprised,' I say.

'It *is* too much, isn't it?'

I think about this for a while, and it slowly dawns on me that what Victor needs most from me, what he is silently begging me for, is to *not* agree with him.

'It'll be OK,' I tell him, struggling at first for authenticity. 'Projects always feel like that at the beginning. You just have to get stuck in. Do one thing at a time.'

'But I haven't got stuck in, have I?' he says.

I smile. 'I wasn't going to say anything, but I did wonder what you've been doing.'

'It's not that I'm lazy or anything. I just can't think where to start. I've just been sitting, staring at it mostly.'

'Well, that's easy,' I say. 'You start with the hole in the roof.'

'Yes, I know. That's what I thought. But when I tried ...'

'You couldn't lift the sheets of stuff.'

'Yes. I drove down to buy them. All the way to Nice. But when I couldn't even get them into the van, I realised that there was no point.'

'They're really *that* heavy?'

'Well, about forty kilos. It's more the size. They're pretty unwieldy.'

'So it's a job for a proper roofer.'

'Only I can't get one. I phoned at least ten but they're all busy or they say it's too far, or ...'

We slip into another less comfortable silence, and then Victor squeezes me between his knees. 'You're not regretting this, are you?' he says. 'Because I can drive you to a hotel tomorrow. I can drive you to a hotel *now*, if you want. You are on holiday. We can still make this into a nice one.'

'No,' I say, thinking as I speak. 'I think we need to get this whole project under way. I think that's why I'm here.' As I say this, it strikes me as a mini-revelation: this *is* why I am here. Because that is what love is – giving the person you love whatever they need at that moment in time no matter how uncomfortable it is to do so. And right here, right now, what Victor is silently begging me to be – even without realising it – is a roofing partner. So a roofing partner I will be. And strange as that may seem, it feels like the most amazing opportunity to turn our relationship into something real. It's not that is isn't real, of course. But being so recent – we only got together a month ago, after all – it all still feels rather fragile and new.

'We could do it together,' I say.

'You think?'

'Or are they too heavy? I mean, I'm not that strong, but I can lift one of those thirty kilo bags of soil. Well, just about ... Could two of us lift your roofing thingies if we put our backs into it?'

'You don't want to spend your holidays roofing.'

I laugh. 'You know what? It's *exactly* what I want to spend my holiday doing. I'm funny that way.'

'We could try, I suppose,' Victor says, his tone superficially doubtful, but already I can hear the first spark of hope breaking through.

'I'll tell you what else I'm itching to do.'

'Hmm? *Yes?*' Victor says sexily.

'Well, that too, of course. But I meant get rid of all of that junk in the yard. The place will feel much better then.'

Victor sighs deeply and then puts his drink down and slips his arms around me, pulling me tight. He's wearing the same Aran jumper he had on the day he left England, and the hug feels no less magical than the one we had then. 'Thank you.'

'Any time.'

'Can I tell you another secret?' he asks.

'Yes?'

'I think you're the bee's knees,' he says.

'Well, good,' I reply. 'Because I think that you're the bee's knees too.'

*

While dinner cooks, Victor shaves. We eat spaghetti for dinner and drink a bottle of wine, then simply fold out the bed so that we can lie side by side and look up at the night sky.

The stars, when they appear, are astounding in number and clarity, so we stare at them and talk quietly about everything and nothing: about my best friend Mark and his new boyfriend Iain, and France and Victor's missing aunt, who supposedly lives next door but hasn't been spotted yet. And when we have seemingly caught up on the gossip, I begin the far more soothing job of pointing out the constellations.

Just as I am describing Orion, with Victor's head squashed against mine so that I can point out the individual stars, I am overcome by a deep sense of belonging, an overpowering and rare sensation of being in exactly the right place at the right time within this vast universe, and, for once, of being with the right person too. It hits me unexpectedly just how improbable this is in this infinite space, how stunningly lucky we are to have bumped into each other, and the realisation is so moving, so humbling, that my voice cracks and my vision blurs, and I have to wipe away an unexpected tear before I can continue stargazing.

'You and me in the middle of all this,' Victor whispers, and I know that he is feeling it too.

NOT A HOT TORRENT

When I wake up the next morning, Victor is attempting to make coffee, something which is fairly challenging in the confined space left when the bed is folded out.

'Hello,' he says, grinning, presumably at my sleepy head. 'I tried to be quiet, but . . .'

I stretch and yawn. 'It's fine,' I say. 'God, I slept so well! What time is it?'

'Nine,' Victor says. 'The sun's just coming over the mountain now. Check out the frost before it vanishes.'

I blink to clear my eyesight and sit up, pulling the heavy quilt around me. 'It looks like snow,' I say.

'I know. Beautiful, isn't it?'

'Yeah, but it must be cold out there.'

'Oh it is. Good job Le Château has heating, huh?'

'The range?'

'No, I meant, Château Volkswagen.'

'It works well. What's that smell?'

'Smell?'

'Yeah. Toast or something.'

Victor grins and nods over at the cooker. 'They're only long life croissants, but grilled, they're fine.'

I yawn again. 'They smell fabulous.'

'Hey, look out the other side.'

I shuffle around to face the other way and stare as the sun creeps down the front of the farmhouse, bouncing off ice crystals as it hits each frosted item of junk. 'Beautiful,' I murmur.

'The frost melts almost instantly,' Victor says, and I see the sparkling reflections fading even as he says this.

'It's lovely,' I say, thinking as I say it that it will be all the lovelier once all the junk has gone.

Victor lights the stove underneath the coffee pot and then joins me on the bed. He slides his legs around me, cradling me in his arms, and together we sit and watch the advancing sun.

When I was single – which went on for a very long time – I remember having wished for a man who was capable of sharing the simple pleasures of life with me. I remember imagining a virtual boyfriend lying on a lawn with me, watching ants dragging breadcrumbs through the jungle of blades – a childhood memory, no doubt. Watching the sparkle and melt of the frost until the smell of coffee joins the buttery burn of the croissants is close enough for me.

The rest of the day is, though, less idyllic. I am saved from the ignominy of having to refuse an icy shower by the fact that the water is frozen again.

'It'll be thawed by this afternoon,' Victor promises.

'But not warm.'

'No,' he laughs. 'No, it really *won't* be warm.'

'We need to find a solution for that,' I say.

'We do,' he says. 'But until I can get a plumber to redo the whole system, I'm at a bit of a loss.'

On my insistence – Victor seems to be lacking the *efficiency* gene – we load the van with a first batch of junk before heading off. We stop first at the nearest village – a ten-minute drive – and drink coffee in a tiny bar-tabac, mainly so that we can ask where the nearest dump is. Most of the locals seem to be starting the day with wine rather than coffee.

Victor chats fluently to the bar staff in French. Though I knew he could do this – he is, after all, French, even if he did grow up in England – it still comes as a bit of a shock. Everything about him is different in French, from the timbre of his voice to his body language, to the way he moves his hands; it's like watching a stranger, which is a little unnerving, but also rather exciting. It's like having two boyfriends for the price of one.

The half-hour detour to the dump completed, we head back through the village, past La Forge, and back down the same stunning road as yesterday.

'It looks totally different with the sun coming from the other side,' I comment.

'It's jaw-dropping, isn't it? I suppose you must get used to it eventually. I bet the locals don't even notice any more.'

I stare out at the crazy rock formations, at the deep blue sky and the white-tipped mountains. 'I somehow doubt that,' I say.

Eventually we reach the industrial outskirts of Nice and

Victor swings into the car park of a DIY superstore. 'There,' he says. 'Don't say I never take you anywhere nice.'

I laugh.

'You said you wanted to go to Nice.'

'Not *quite* what I had in mind.'

'No, sorry about that. I have to load the roofing stuff over there,' he says, pointing to an outdoor building supplies section. 'Do you want to come with me, or look around inside?'

'I thought you needed my help?'

'Not for loading. They have staff there. It's at the other end I have a problem.'

I shrug. 'I don't . . .' I'm about to say that I have no great desire to visit the French version of B&Q, but then I think about using their bathroom to at least wash my face.

'Actually, yes. I would like to have a look,' I say.

'Meet you here in half an hour, then,' Victor says. 'And don't go spending a fortune on jewellery.'

'Copper bracelets, anyone?' I laugh, climbing down from the van.

Once inside the bathroom, the hot water gushing from the taps feels heavenly. And it gives me an idea. Somewhat excited at the idea of being able to demonstrate my resourcefulness, I head into the store.

Though the front of the store is big, it doesn't prepare you for the crazy size of the inside. This is truly a cathedral of DIY.

When I eventually find the plumbing department, I think that my problems are solved. Three salesmen are leaning on a counter joking amongst themselves, clearly bored.

Forcing myself to remember that French was once my best subject, I launch myself into it. '*S'il vous plaît, est-ce que vous pouvez m'aider?*' I ask. *Please, can you help me?*

The older, more senior of the guys sighs deeply, stands, and straightens his body.

'*Bonjour,*' he says in a strange, questioning tone.

'*J'ai un problème,*' I continue. *I have a problem.*

'*Bonjour,*' he says again.

'We have just bought a house,' I tell him, in what I'm pretty sure is perfect French.

'*Bonjour!*' the man says again.

I start to frown. I feel like I'm stuck in a time loop.

'We have no hot water,' I say, deciding to simply plough on.

'*Bonjour,*' he replies again, causing his mates to snigger. I frown.

'*En France on dit, "Bonjour",*' he explains. *In France we say, 'Bonjour'.*

I blush. Have I been rude? I try to retrace my words. Surely I said, '*S'il vous plaît.*' Is that not enough?

'*Bonjour,*' I stammer, still unsure if this is the key to making progress here.

'*Bonjour!*' he says yet again, but in a happier tone of voice. This time, he continues, '*Qu'est-ce que je peux faire pour vous?*'

I take a deep breath. I feel like I'm in an adventure game and have only now unlocked the right to proceed to the next level.

But the salesman remains surly and recalcitrant as I explain, in very dodgy French – I seem to lack a number of useful technical terms, such as 'heater' and 'pipe' – that we have just bought a house with no hot water system, and that we urgently need a temporary solution. He frowns and wrinkles his nose throughout. He resists my attempts at humour, refuses to cave in to my most coquettish attempts at charm and, finally declaring what I think means, 'You need a plumber, not a salesman,' he turns and walks away.

'*Au revoir!*' I say, annoyed now. '*En France, nous disons au revoir!*'

Quietly fuming, I start to head back towards the exit, but a voice behind me says, in a plummy home counties accent, 'Do you have electricity, dear?'

I turn to see a tiny, red-faced man who looks not unlike Ronnie Corbett.

'I'm sorry?'

'No, *I'm* sorry,' he says. 'But I couldn't help overhearing your dilemma. Do you have electricity? Because if you do, there is a terribly simple solution, despite what that rude man would have you believe.'

When I get back outside, the van is parked opposite and Victor is leaning on the window staring straight at me. Some croony French music is playing on the radio. 'I thought I'd lost you,' he says. 'Lord, what have you been buying?'

'My gift to you,' I say, somewhat proudly.

He opens his door and climbs down, then reaches out to take the huge bag from me. 'And that would be?'

'A hot shower!'

'Really?' He frowns and peers into the bag. 'What ...

Oh! How obvious. I never even thought of that. I had one of those in my first London flat.'

'That will work, won't it?' I ask, watching him pull the electric shower heater unit from the bag.

'Kind of. Except there are no power points in the bathroom.'

'Oh. I thought there were. There's a light.'

'Yes, there's a light, but you can't run an instant water heater off that. The amperage isn't high enough.'

'Oh,' I say, disappointed.

'But it doesn't matter. I can run a long temporary cable to the fuse box. It won't win any safety inspections but ... yes ... With a couple of bits of extra tubing. Actually, that's a brilliant idea. Thank you.'

'Thank God for that,' I say. 'I thought you were going to make me attempt a refund in French.'

On the way home, we stop at a different bar-tabac and sit in the winter sunshine to eat the only thing on offer: ham and cheese sandwiches.

Whether it's the crisp mountain air, the quality of the ingredients, or simply the joy of being on holiday I couldn't say, but that sandwich is the finest meal I've had in a long time.

Back at the farmhouse, we drag the roofing supplies from the van – I have serious doubts whether we will be able to get them onto the roof – and then in less than an hour Victor manages to screw the Daffy Hot-Torrent shower heater to the bathroom wall and run a long length of wire to the fuse box.

'I'll go first,' Victor says, 'just in case I get electrocuted.'

I laugh and watch him strip and climb into the tiny sit-up bath. But just as he reaches for the unit to switch it on and says, 'Here goes . . .' I shout, 'Stop!'

'What?' Victor asks, looking alarmed.

'Can you tell me the number for an ambulance? Because I wouldn't even know who to call.'

'I'm only joking,' he says. 'It'll be fine.'

'OK!' I say, raising a hand to stop him continuing. 'But just in case something happens, what is the number?'

'One-one-two works,' he says.

'OK,' I say. 'Do your worst, Mister Dodgy Electrician.'

He turns the switch and water starts to flow.

'Hot?' I ask.

'No,' he says, running one hand under the spray. 'Hang on. Give it time . . . ooh, it's lukewarm . . . getting warmer . . . Yes!'

The second I see steam rising, I start to strip. 'Make room!' I shout.

'In here? Are you joking?'

'Nope. Love is never claiming that the bathtub is too small for two.'

Victor laughs. 'Come on, then,' he says, momentarily pointing the shower head at me and wetting the floor.

They should probably have named the Daffy Hot-Torrent the Daffy Warm-Spray instead. The jet from the shower is barely enough to keep us both warm at the same time. But being the first shower in thirty-six hours, not to mention the first shower in five years where I have had my back soaped by someone else, it feels brilliant.

THE GREAT
CONTRACEPTION DEBATE

The process of fixing the roof turns out to be far more elaborate than either of us had imagined. Motivated we may be, but roofers we aren't.

We first have to remove all of the red earthenware tiles from around the hole. Victor clambers around precariously on the roof, and I climb up and down the ladder a hundred times to ferry them to the ground, all the while reciting the emergency number – one, one, two – like a lucky chant. Once the tiles have been removed it transpires that the top edges of the underlying sheets are concreted into place, so Victor spends half a day smashing that to pieces whilst I build a huge, incredibly satisfying bonfire from everything that will possibly burn. Bits of wood that will fit inside the range I move to a covered area beside the entrance.

It all ends up being dirty and physical and tiring, but it's so far from the purely mental stress of my job in advertising that, surprisingly, I find myself enjoying it all. Whether it's carrying tiles or burning old sofas, I find myself somehow lost in the process of it all, and that is strangely restful.

Every now and then I become aware of myself and notice that I'm humming, or singing, or simply that two hours have passed, and I realise that in some way, this process of being physically *busy* is precisely the thing that I sensed, but couldn't name – precisely the thing that has been missing from my London life. A change, as they say, really does seem to be as good as a rest.

By the end of the fourth day, the new panels have been manoeuvred up onto the roof, screwed and concreted into position, and the tiles replaced. Though the ceiling is still damaged, the house is, in theory, watertight and – from the outside at least – looks whole again.

Victor climbs down and we stand side by side to stare at it, and I feel incredibly proud, as proud, in fact, as I have ever felt.

'I didn't think we'd manage it,' I say.

'Nor me,' he laughs, slipping one arm around me. 'It can rain now.'

'I'd still rather it didn't.'

'Me too. But at least then we'll know if we're any good as roofers.'

'A gynaecologist and an advertising exec,' I say. 'What a team!'

I look down at my hands. Despite gloves, in only four days they have started to look like farming hands, and I'm not sure how I feel about that. 'So what are we doing tomorrow?' I ask.

'I think we deserve a day off,' Victor says. 'Maybe a trip to the coast?'

'Ooh,' I say. 'Are you taking me to the DIY store again?'

'You make me sound like a slave driver,' he says. 'No, I was thinking more of a wander round the shops and a nice restaurant. A nice, *romantic* restaurant.'

I lean into him and he kisses the top of my head. 'That sounds fabulous. You are clever, you know. I mean, gynae-cologist, electrician and roofer . . .'

'So are you,' he says. 'Advertising exec and builder's buddy.'

'We can take another load of this shit on our way down, can't we?'

Victor laughs. 'You see,' he says. 'You're worse than me.'

That night a wind gets up, buffeting the van enough to make it creak on its suspension. My back aches from too much unaccustomed lifting and, combined with the full moon and the fact that my camping approximation of spaghetti carbonara spends the entire night repeating on me, I end up having a thoroughly lousy night's sleep.

In the morning, when Victor wakes me by sliding one arm over me and pulling me against his ready-for-action dick, the only thing I'm in the mood for is more sleep.

I doze for what seems like a few more minutes but could be much longer, and then hearing the door to the van slide open, I roll onto my side and watch Victor climb in.

'Morning,' I say.

'Morning,' he replies. His voice sounds unusually flat and lifeless.

'Jesus, I slept badly,' I groan. 'Did you hear the wind last night?'

'No,' he replies, loading coffee into the espresso pot.

I sigh and stretch, and then realise that he hasn't caught my eye yet. 'How are you this morning?' I ask, suspicious now.

'Fine,' he says, in a tone of voice that leaves no doubt that he isn't. Something knots in my stomach. The first inkling of tension reaches my slowly wakening mind.

'*Victor*,' I say.

'Hmm?'

I wrinkle my brow and sit up. 'Victor!'

'Yes?'

'What's wrong?'

'Nothing.'

I rub one hand across my face and glance outside. 'God it's all grey outside, is it early?'

'No. The weather's changed,' he says, still without glancing my way. 'All grey.'

'Something *is* wrong,' I say. 'What's up?'

He finally turns towards me and his eyes look, for the first time since I have known him, cold and unsmiling.

'Come here, babe,' I say.

'Just let me *do* this,' he says, sounding irritated now.

I watch him light the stove with a match, and then he turns to face me again, sighs and forces a tight approximation of a smile. 'Right,' he says, flatly.

I pat the bed and he crawls towards me, rolling his eyes. He lies beside me with his head on one hand, a definite frown creasing his forehead.

I lean forward to kiss him, but because he doesn't in any way facilitate this, it ends up being nothing more than a peck.

'Something *is* wrong,' I repeat. 'Tell me.'

Victor sighs, and I'm reminded of how little I know him. I have absolutely no idea what is wrong, or how this is likely to pan out.

'It's nothing,' he says. 'I'm just being an arse.'

'OK,' I say. 'But unless you tell me ...' I reach out and stroke his hair.

'I'm just being a twat,' he says. 'Because you pushed me away.'

I frown. 'I pushed you away?'

'Yes.'

'When?'

'This morning.'

I shake my head. 'I'm sorry, I don't even remember that.'

'I tried to cuddle you and you elbowed me in the stomach.'

I try to remember but it's hopeless. 'I was asleep,' I say. 'And I slept so badly, I probably just wanted to stay that way.'

Victor nods. 'OK,' he says, his voice cold.

'I'm sorry. But sometimes you're just asleep and ...' I shrug. 'It doesn't mean anything.'

Victor shrugs back, as much as his position will allow. 'Sure,' he says. 'Well ... sometimes I get in a hump about nothing. It doesn't mean much, either.'

'You're sure?'

He nods and his features soften a little. 'I'll be fine in a bit.'

'Would a cuddle help?'

'It might, I guess,' he says, sulkily.

'Come,' I say, beckoning him with a sideways nod of my head.

Victor swallows. 'I can't,' he says.

'You can't?'

'I'm too stubborn.'

I laugh. I have never heard anyone explain so clearly that universal, but oh-so-destructive mechanism of pride. Such self-awareness strikes me as unique and refreshing.

I shuffle towards him and I see him fighting the desire to smile. 'Is that better?' I ask.

'A bit,' he says.

I kiss him lightly on the forehead. 'And that?'

'Yes,' he says. 'That's definitely heading in the right direction.'

And then he inclines his chin towards me slightly and I kiss him on the mouth.

'See,' he says. 'Stubborn.'

'Too stubborn to make up, but not too stubborn to be made up to.'

'No.'

'I'm glad about that. That was almost a row.'

'Yes. Almost.'

'Come here,' I say, linking one arm behind him and pulling him with me as I roll onto my back, a manoeuvre that he allows but doesn't exactly contribute to. 'You can stop that now.'

He pulls his head far back enough to look at me. 'What?'

'That *I'm-all-rigid-so-you-can't-cuddle-me-properly* thing.'

'Oh, *this* thing?' he says, turning his body into an uncomfortable plank of wood.

'Yes. Stop it!'

Victor laughs in spite of himself, and then collapses against me.

His weight is hurting my back – still sore from yesterday – but I decide that it probably isn't the moment to mention that, so I grin and bear it, and kiss him until I can discreetly roll over and swap positions. We kiss and cuddle for a moment, and then I nod over at the condom box on the side. 'Go on then,' I say. 'Do your enveloping business.'

'If you don't want to, that's fine,' Victor says.

'Of course I want to!' I say, reaching for the packet myself.

The blanket grey sky darkens as we eat our croissants and then shower in the freezing 'bathroom'.

'Are we really going to Nice today?' I ask, as I energetically attempt to dry myself on a damp towel.

'Sure,' Victor replies from the bathtub. 'Unless you want to go somewhere else?'

'It'd be good to see the sea,' I say.

'Nice, Antibes, Monaco, Cannes,' Victor says. 'They're all pretty close. They're all by the sea.'

'Somewhere new, then,' I say. 'Somewhere I have never been.'

'Somewhere you have never been on a mysterious date that you won't tell me about?' Victor says.

'It was a bad date with a pervy guy. That's all you need to know.'

'Hmm,' he says, soaping himself. 'Pervy. Now I *really* need to know more.'

*

31

By the time we have loaded the van, *unloaded* the van at the dump, and driven back past the track leading to our house it is already twelve, but we agree to wait and have a late lunch rather than delay our departure any further.

Victor takes a different route down today and the roads are even steeper, even more precarious than before. The mountains today are swathed in mists – low clouds, in fact – and look like Japanese prints.

'Do you think it's going to rain?' I ask as we pass a sign saying *Villeneuve Loubet Village*.

'I don't know,' Victor replies. 'There have been a few days when I thought it might – before you arrived – but so far I've been lucky.'

'We're lucky it didn't rain when we were doing the roof.'

'Very lucky. Look!' Victor says, pointing. 'Blue sky!'

'Is that where we're going?'

'It is now,' he says.

We continue south until we hit the coast and then head west, chasing better weather, fleeing the dark clouds over Nice. We drive past scrappy industrial zones and vast stretches of empty pebble beach and on through the outskirts of Antibes, which Victor promises we will visit another time.

'I want to show you the Cap,' he says. 'It kind of starts here.'

And suddenly we're in millionaire land, where the crinkling coastline has been preserved for the coastal gardens of isolated villas and their gleaming jewel-like swimming pools.

'Wow,' I say, pointing up at a vast rectangular window overlooking the bay. 'Imagine waking up to that every morning.'

'Imagine cleaning the salt off the windows,' Victor says, leaning over the steering wheel to peer up at it.

'I think they can probably afford a window cleaner.'

At Juan-les-Pins, we park the van and manage to find a pizzeria still willing to serve us despite the late hour.

'I wanted to treat you,' Victor says. 'I was thinking of something a little more sophisticated than pizza.'

'A pizza in the sun on a beach in January? Are you joking?'

'Cheap to run then!' Victor says. 'As well as being beautiful, easy-going and good with building materials.'

'I wouldn't count on it.'

'Which?'

I shrug. 'Any of them actually.'

The pizza when it arrives is entirely average, but it being two-thirty, I'm ravenous, and with the sunshine, the sound of the sea and the gulls swooping overhead, it feels like a perfect holiday moment.

'I'm sorry the holiday has been so full on,' Victor says, clearly not picking up on my sense of contentment. 'I do realise that it's probably not the best way to seduce you into coming back.'

I fork a huge lump of pizza into my mouth as cover for not replying immediately. Because what I want to say is that what we have been doing – building a home together – feels so special that I can't think of a single thing that I would rather be doing. I want to say that because of the fact that we have worked together and sworn together, and even good-humouredly sworn *at* each other and got over it, I feel like I know him a thousand times better than when I arrived four days ago; that with manoeuvring around each other in the cramped van and eating long-life croissants, I now have a real sense that this *can* work, that we *are* good together – good enough to negotiate the humps and bumps that life inevitably brings. And I want to tell him that for so many reasons, including my past, my aching desire for a child; the fact that I'm running out of time, that my friends in London are moving on and my career is floundering as the recession bites; and because, quite simply, I really, *really* like him, he no longer needs to seduce me. It's a done deal.

But I know men or, at least, I think I do. I know that their desire for flattery is proportional to their fear of entrapment. So now is not the moment to say all of that. Even a tenth of that would have half of the men on the planet throwing themselves from the nearest cliff.

'I'm loving it,' is all I finally say. 'Every minute.'

After lunch we walk along the deserted beach for a mile or so. I'm aware that with the dipping sun to the west, we must look like some absurd cliché from a romantic comedy, but it feels no less wonderful for that.

We sit for a while behind a permanent windbreak belonging to a closed-for-winter restaurant and watch cormorants dive-bombing the waves for food. And then Victor glances at the setting sun and says, 'We should head back. Before the roads freeze up.'

'It's so easy to forget we're in January, what with this sunshine.'

34

'It's getting cold already though,' he says, holding out a hand.

I take his hand and he pulls me upright. 'Take me to your château,' I declare.

'I need to go to the pharmacy quickly,' he says as we start to walk back along the beach.

'What do you need?' I ask. 'Because I have half a hospital in my suitcase.'

'Condoms,' Victor replies. 'We're almost out, and we can't have that, can we?'

For ten steps, I say nothing. As we walk on in silence I even stop breathing, desperately trying to calculate whether now is the right time for *that* conversation. And then I stop walking and grab Victor's arm. He spins to look back at me and grins quizzically.

'Can't we?' I say simply.

Victor frowns. 'Can't we what?'

'Have that?'

'Oh. Well, no ...'

'You're sure?'

'Oh,' he says. He coughs. 'Well, that's quite a big conversation, isn't it?'

I shrug and smile. 'Is it? Or is it a simple one?'

Victor smiles vaguely. 'Unless you've gone on the pill or something?'

'I haven't,' I say.

'Right ... then ...'

I purse my lips and blow out through them. 'God, this is harder than I thought. This is where I want to be. You know?'

'Here?'

'No, not *here*. With you, silly.'

'But you're going back. You're just on holiday.'

'Yes, but I don't *want* to go back. I want to be *here*.'

'So . . . You're coming back then? Is that what you're saying?'

'If you'll have me. Yes.'

'Are you saying that you want to come back . . . *permanently*?'

'I'm not sure about *permanently* but . . . as long as, you know . . .' Victor looks confused, so I continue. 'As long as we both want to be here.'

'I see. Well, I *think* I do.'

'So do we really need condoms?'

Victor shrugs and takes my hand as we continue along the beach, me waiting for him to say something, he, presumably, trying to decide what to say next.

When we reach the van, we climb aboard and he inserts the keys into the ignition but doesn't start the engine.

'What's up?' I ask.

'Well, it's a big thing,' Victor says. 'I just feel that there are things we need to discuss, things we need to say before we go down that route.'

I release my seatbelt and turn to face him. Behind his head, a palm tree is flapping against the reddening sky, making it the perfect romantic moment for what needs to be said. 'Like "I love you?"' I ask. 'Neither of us has said that yet.'

'For instance,' Victor says, turning fully to face me now and grinning in a way that makes him look young and somehow rather dorky.

'OK,' I laugh. 'You go first.'

'But I can't,' he says. 'That's the thing.'

My smile fades. 'Oh,' I say.

'It's not ... It's just ...'

I sigh and wonder if this is that strange unexpected moment when everything crashes to the ground. Because history teaches that you never know when that might happen.

'It's just, well, it's like this morning,' he says.

'This morning?'

'Yes.'

'I'm sorry, I don't ...'

'I'm too stubborn.'

'Too *stubborn*?'

'Yes. You have to go first.'

I slip back into a confused smile. 'I just said it,' I say.

'No, you said that "I love you" is something we haven't said yet. But that's not *saying* it.' He looks amused, but deadly serious as well.

'I do,' I say, reaching out to touch his arm. 'I love you.'

'How much?' Victor asks.

'Masses,' I say.

'Me too,' he says.

'No, no, no!' I say, laughing.

'No what?'

'You can't get away with "Me too".'

Victor rolls his eyes, licks his lips and takes a deep breath. 'I love you too. I don't want you to go back to London. I want us to have this adventure together.'

'Me too,' I say.

37

Victor smiles and shakes his head. 'You said that "me too" doesn't cut it.'

'I *do*!' I insist. 'I want to come back. I want us to have this adventure together. And loads of others, too.'

'Gosh,' he says, taking my hand and squeezing it, and I wonder briefly if have crossed the line and erred into the danger zone of entrapment. 'How lucky am I?' he declares.

I lean in and we kiss. 'How lucky are *we*?' I say.

And then a shadow crosses his features.

'What?' I ask.

'Well, there's another conversation people usually have before they, you know ...'

'Oh. Right.'

Because the other conversation is of course marriage, and having already been married, it's such a complicated one for me that I get into a pickle even thinking about *thinking* about it. Right now it's a subject that can only spoil what was promising to be a perfect moment.

'Have I said the wrong thing?' Victor asks.

'Are you talking about ... Do you mean marriage?'

Victor's eyes widen. 'God, I wasn't *proposing*.'

He looks so scared that I can't help but laugh.

'What?' he asks, his expression shifting from scared to confused.

'You just looked so worried,' I say.

'Did I?'

'Yes.'

He shrugs. 'Maybe marriage does scare me a bit.'

'And maybe I've already been married and I'm not at all sure that I want to do it again.'

'Right.'

'Actually, it's not even that I *don't* . . . It's just that having taken all of those vows, and broken them . . . I don't know. I suppose the truth is that I don't have a view on marriage any more.'

'Right,' Victor says.

'You look disappointed,' I say.

'No,' he says. 'I'm not. It's just . . . well . . . I'm not sure where that leaves us. In the great contraception debate.'

I sigh deeply. 'The only way I know how to do this is to be honest.'

'Honesty is always good.'

'Not sure about the always. But, well, I want a child, Victor.'

'I know.'

'You know that I had an abortion when I split up with Brian. I told you about that.'

'Yes.'

'I was worried that I'd missed my chance. I was even thinking of doing it, alone. I told you that when we met.'

'Yes.'

'So getting pregnant doesn't scare me at all.'

'No. No, I suppose not.'

'And I'm quite in love with you.'

'Quite?'

'Quite a lot.'

'Me too,' he says, then sniggers and adds, 'I am in love with you too. Quite a lot.'

'So I want things to work out.'

'But even if they didn't . . .'

39

'Exactly.'

Victor turns and looks out at the sea for a moment, then says, 'So are we sure we don't need anything from the pharmacy, then?'

I release his hand and stroke his back. 'What do you think?'

'I think that I quite like kids,' he says. 'And I hate condoms.'

I laugh. 'Well, there you go then. We agree.'

Victor nods, and smirks and reaches down to start the van.

As we drive inland and the road begins to wind, the weather darkens. For some reason, I start to feel nervous. At first I think that it's just the steep drop and the menacing sky, but then I realise that it's because I'm feeling nervous about making love tonight. We have done it tens of times already, so it seems silly to suddenly be feeling apprehensive, but it somehow seems different and important.

We stop at a tiny roadside supermarket and stock up on supplies. As we pass a rack sporting packs of condoms, we both look at it, glance at each other, and move on around the store without saying a word. I am starting to feel like a teenager who has decided that tonight is the night. For the first time ever. With all of the anticipation, and all of the excitement, and all of the fear that that entailed.

As we load the shopping into the van, the first spots of rain start to fall. By the time we reach La Forge, it's a deluge.

Victor parks right next to the front door of the farmhouse. 'I want to see if our handiwork is holding up,' he explains.

We run the three yards from the van and burst into the dark, cold space of the kitchen. We peer up at the broken ceiling and listen to the sound of the pummelling rain.

'It looks OK!' I comment.

'It does,' Victor agrees, bumping me with his hip.

'It's ever so damp in here though,' I say.

'It's just the rain I think,' Victor says. 'We're kind of in the clouds up here.'

'Maybe we could try to light the range tomorrow. We have all that wood I put aside.'

'Exactly what I was thinking,' Victor says. 'Now, can I tempt you to a little salmon in white wine sauce at Le Château?'

'Do you think it's defrosted?'

'It's boil in the bag,' Victor says. 'I don't think it matters.'

'Then that would be lovely.'

'Little' turns out to be the operative word. The meal is surprisingly delicious, but the packet, which says, *serves three-to-four people* is, even for two, ungenerous to say the least. But after bread, cheese and half a bottle of wine, I'm feeling warm and satisfied.

We tidy away the dishes and fold out the bed, and there, in a camper van, with the drumming of rain upon the roof, it happens.

Victor hovers over me and says, 'Are you sure about this?'

I nod mechanically and reply, 'Yes, I think so, are you?'

And then, with a humorous wiggle of his eyebrows, he's pressing at the gate, now slipping inside me.

'Oh God!' I say quietly. 'God, it feels so different.'

41

Victor nods, and lowers himself gently onto me. 'It does,' he says.

'Just . . . stay . . . like that . . . for a while,' I say.

And so we lie, with Victor seemingly deeper inside me than he has ever been, and I hug him tight and think how much difference the absence of three microns of latex makes.

A shudder passes through my body.

'What was that?' Victor murmurs, amused.

'It's . . .' I say, surprised that he could feel it too. 'I don't know.'

'Are you cold?'

'No. Not at all. I think it's . . .'

And what I think it is is *love*. A ripple, a wave of love.

I'm shocked to discover that only now, for the first time, are we *making love*. I had thought that was what we were doing every night. But this is so different. Maybe we were just having sex before.

Victor starts to move gently against and into me and I gasp. Is it really just the missing latex, or is it because we have now said those magical words, because we have now declared our love? Is the fact that our feelings are out in the open the reason that I am suddenly able to feel them with such force?

Victor moves gently, then with increasing gusto until he is thrusting into me, building almost to a climax, and then – because neither of us wants this to end yet – freezing, waiting a terrible, wonderful, tremble-inducing moment, and then starting all over again. This is not aerobics. It's slow, gentle, rhythmic heaven. It's a quasi-spiritual experience, and by the time Victor and I gaspingly collapse into orgasm

42

almost an hour after we started, I feel as if I have been dragged through a sea of chocolate and licked clean by angels.

We sleep, sweatily interlaced, and I have floaty, gorgeous dreams of underwater swimming and tadpoles chasing Easter eggs, but when I wake up, my first thought is that we have perhaps made a terrible, terrible mistake, and that it might already be too late.

I lie there in an unexpected, sweaty panic, wondering if somewhere inside me a sperm has already met an egg and if we should go and find a pharmacy which sells morning-after pills, pronto.

And then Victor wakes up and the second he kisses my neck and wraps his arms around me, the fear is replaced with a feeling of everything being just perfect, of this all being no more, no less than destiny.

MEETING TATIE

We spend the next day in the dank interior of the house, dragging the rotting remains of furniture out into the rain, creating a fresh pile of rubbish in the space we had just cleared. I clean out and then attempt to light a fire in the wood burner, but smoke just billows back into the room and eventually we have to throw water inside to extinguish the flames.

'Chimney must be blocked,' Victor says.

'Maybe birds have built a nest in it. That's what always used to happen at home.'

'I'll climb up and check it later.'

'But not in this rain?'

'No, not today.'

Mid-afternoon, lacking supplies and tools, or even a coherent plan of what to do next, we retire to the van. The bed is still in place from this morning, and so Victor lies back and I put my head on his chest and feel the vibrations as he speaks.

'What do you think we should do tomorrow?' he asks.

'Me?'

'Yeah,' he says. 'You seem quite good at all that planning malarkey.'

I shrug. 'Unblock the chimney?'

'Sure. But after that?'

I sigh. 'I don't know. It depends what you intend to do to the place.'

'Everything.'

'The ceiling, I suppose.'

'Right. Well, I need a plasterer for that.'

'Maybe we should fix up the smallest room, just so you can sleep there comfortably.'

'The ceiling's down there too.'

'Oh yes. Of course. The bathroom then. Pull up that horrible lino, see what's underneath. Put in a flushing toilet. A new bath. Heating . . .'

'Which requires a plumber.'

'Then I guess that's your answer. Finding a plumber and a plasterer is what to do next.'

'I *have* tried,' Victor says. 'But it's like the roofer. Incredibly hard to get people to come up here even to look – even to provide a quote.'

'Maybe it's because it's January.'

'Sure. Maybe. But if I have to wait until summer.'

'Till spring maybe. Hey, look!' I say, pointing at the closest house, some hundred yards away. 'There's a light on.'

'I can't see,' Victor says, lifting my head and sitting, 'you'll have to move. Oh! She's home!'

'You reckon?'

'There was no light there yesterday,' he points out.

'But wouldn't she have come and said hello? She knows that it's her nephew moving in here, right?'

'Of course. Shall we go see her?'

'I suppose we had better,' I say.

We pull on our fisherman's macs and squelch across our yard, and, to avoid the track, now a sea of mud, climb the wall and cross his aunt's land as well. The rain is torrential, and when it starts to hail huge, painful, gob stopper sized balls of ice, we begin to shriek and laugh and run.

From the porch – which is so tiny, it only just shields us from the hail – we can see a rusty four-wheel-drive Lada parked behind the house.

Victor knocks politely, then raps harder, and finally hammers on the door.

'Maybe she's in bed,' I say, stepping briefly back into the hail to peer up at the yellow-lit window shining weakly from the dark stone frontage of the house.

'Not at six,' Victor says.

'Maybe she can't hear us with all the rain,' I offer.

'Maybe.'

At that instant, there is a flash of lightning, followed by a delayed clap of thunder. 'It's like a horror film,' I laugh. 'Maybe we should split up.'

'Split up?'

'Yeah,' I shout, having to raise my voice as the intensity of the rain increases. 'They always split up in horror films so the zombies can pick them off one by one.'

Victor laughs. 'I never watch horror films.'

'I like them,' I say with an embarrassed shrug.

'OK,' Victor says. 'So, we split up for the zombies?'

'That's the rule.'

'OK. You stay here, I'll check around the back.'

I squeeze myself into the corner of the porch and watch the hail bouncing off the step, and within seconds I start to feel nervous and wish he would return.

When he does, he simply says, 'Nada,' and so we return, running and laughing at the absurd downpour, back to the van.

As we run I glance back and think that I see a curtain twitch, but I nearly trip and have to look back to where I'm going. I decide that I probably imagined it – all part of my horror film scenario.

We're so wet that the van steams up the second we close the door, creating an unpleasant, stuffy feeling of being in a sauna, only fully clothed.

'Maybe whoever was there just didn't want to answer the door on a dark evening in the middle of a storm,' I volunteer.

'My *aunt* lives there,' Victor says.

'You know that for certain?'

'Yes.'

'That's definitely the house, then? Not the other one round the bend?'

'No. That's *hers*,' Victor says. 'Maybe she's just really tired from driving or something.'

Or maybe she isn't very nice, I think, admonishing myself for the thought even before it is fully formed. But after all, if I came home to find my nephew and his girlfriend camping in a van in a muddy field in the midst of a vast storm, the first thing I would do would be to say, 'hello.' And the next thing I would do would be to invite them into my big, cosy house. But maybe that's just me.

The biblical deluge continues all through the evening and on into the night.

By the time we have eaten breakfast the next morning, I'm feeling distinctly stir-crazy from the crushing confinement of the van, made worse by the fact that the windows now seem to be permanently misted up.

'Let's go and do something in the house,' I suggest.

'But it's all cold and damp in there,' Victor reminds me.

'I know,' I say, 'I just can't stand another minute cooped up in here.'

But the house *is* cold and damp, and we're at a loss to know what to do next.

Victor sighs deeply as he sinks into one of the tatty dining chairs.

I drag another chair across the room and sit and take his hand. 'It will all be OK in the end,' I say. 'It's always depressing at the start.'

'Sure,' he says.

We sit for a moment, staring at the curtain of water gushing past the window from the blocked guttering above.

'And everything's always worse in the rain,' I point out.

'I'm fine,' he says. 'But this *is* horrible, isn't it?'

I nod. 'I'm quite cold as well,' I say. 'We need to find something to do, some way to get moving, or do something else instead.'

Victor sighs again. 'Let's fuck off to a hotel for the night, eh? Let's treat ourselves to a nice room with a big hot bath.'

I start to smile. 'That sounds fabulous,' I say. 'Down on the coast somewhere?'

Victor nods and winks at me.

'Maybe we should try your aunt again first,' I say.

I shriek. An embarrassing, girly, squeak of a shriek. Because beyond the window, a face has appeared, nose squashed against the glass as the figure peers in at us.

Victor jumps too and then bounds to the front door to wrench it open.

Silhouetted against the grey daylight outside, it's hard to see if the mac-wearing figure is a man or a woman.

'*Bonjour*,' Victor says, upon which the figure steps inside and lowers her hood.

'*Tatie?*' Victor says. *Auntie?*

I'm not sure how I imagined Victor's aunt to look, but I'm convinced enough that this lank-haired, dirty-looking old crone *isn't* her to momentarily doubt Victor's sanity.

The woman frowns and wrinkles her nose slightly as if she finds the sight of us a little distasteful.

'*Tatie?*' she repeats doubtfully. '*Mais vous êtes qui? Et qu'est-ce que vous faites, ici?*' Which I understand to mean, *Who are you? And what are you doing here?*

'It's me,' Victor answers in French. 'Victor Ynchausty. Evelyn's son.'

The woman opens her eyes wide and rolls them in a wide sweep, taking in every corner of the room and ceiling. I'm not quite sure what the expression means, but I think it's a manifestation of surprise. She holds out her hand. 'Distira,' she says. 'Distira Dalmasso,' and I think, *Aha! She isn't your aunt, you twit!*

They shake hands and Victor beckons me over with his free hand.

'*CC – ma tante Distira.*'

I try not to frown as I shake her cold, wet hand. '*Bonjour*,' I say. '*Enchantée.*'

'CC?' she repeats.

'*Oui, CC*,' I say.

'*CC* . . .' she says again, then, turning to Victor, '*Elle est Anglaise?*'

'*Oui*,' Victor says. '*Elle est Anglaise.*'

'Um, Irish, if you don't mind,' I remind him.

Distira performs the same wide-eyed roll once again and then pulls her hand free.

'*Elle ne vaut rien, vous savez*,' she says with a nod, which I think means, *She's worthless, you know.*

I silently stand as they talk and attempt to decode the conversation, but it's machine gun speed and within seconds I have no idea what subject they are talking about. So instead I muster a vague smile and try not to stare at her rotten teeth or dirty fingernails as I wonder if she really could have just said that I was worthless. Since Victor seems unfazed, surely not.

Once she has pulled her hood back up and vanished into the rain, Victor closes the door and wide-eyes me.

'Tell me she's not your aunt!' I say.

He nods slowly. 'Afraid so.'

'And *who's* worthless, anyway?'

'Worthless?'

'Yes, she said, "*Elle ne vaut rien*", didn't she?'

'The house.'

'Oh, *the house*! Of course. I forgot that houses are feminine. Anyway, which house? This house?'

'Yeah. She says it's badly built. Damp and cold in winter. Too hot in summer.'

I pull a face. 'Oh,' I say. 'That's not very encouraging.'

'No,' Victor agrees.

'Does she understand that you're her nephew?' I ask. 'Because I couldn't see much family love leaking out there.'

Victor shrugs. 'I don't know, to be honest. That was weird, wasn't it?'

'Very,' I agree.

'I haven't seen her for about thirty years. I think she's just been very isolated.'

'All the same.'

'And I think they're dubious about newcomers in places like this.'

'Right. Except that she's your aunt.'

'We'll have to win her over this evening,' Victor says.

I frown. 'This evening?'

'Yeah. You heard that, didn't you?'

I shake my head. 'Not a word. She could have been speaking Swahili for all I understood.'

'She invited us to dinner.'

'She *what*?'

I pull a face. I'm thinking about her dirty fingernails preparing dinner, imagining the state of her kitchen, and suffering over the excruciating attempts we will have to make to communicate all at the same time.

'You said yes,' Victor says. 'I looked at you and you nodded.'

'But you said we were going to a hotel,' I protest.

'Yeah, but . . .' Victor whines.

'But?'

'Well, one, she's my aunt. Two, she's our only neighbour. Three, she just invited us to dinner. Four, she's going to try to get me the number for a plumber and a builder. And five, I looked at you and you nodded.'

'So, no hotel?'

'Tomorrow,' Victor says. 'I promise, OK?'

I sigh deeply. 'You'll have to translate for me,' I say, aghast at the idea, but clever enough to know when a battle has already been lost.

'Her accent is pretty bad, I know.'

I shake my head.

'What?'

'I can't believe that she's your aunt.'

'I don't think she can either.'

'Your mother's sister?' I ask. 'Or your father's?'

'Mum's. Dad's side is where the money was. But they disowned him for marrying her.'

'Well, yes . . .'

'And no, my mum didn't look like her. Actually, Distira looked pretty different when I was little.'

'Maybe it's living here that does that to you.' I give a playful smile.

'Don't!'

'Would you still love me?' I ask. 'Even if I ended up looking like your aunt?'

'No,' Victor says.

'Scary thought.'

Victor performs the wide-eyed ceiling roll.

'Don't you *ever* do that again,' I tell him. 'Or I'll divorce you.' I wonder why I have used the word 'divorce' and what I shall reply if Victor questions it.

'Do what?' he asks innocently.

'This,' I say, imitating the eye-roll.

Victor starts to smirk, and I realise that he has done it on purpose. 'I knew you'd like that. My mum used to do it too.'

'It looks completely mad,' I say.

'Oh, totally,' he agrees. 'Anyway, you'd have to marry me first, if you want to divorce me.'

'Yes, um, anyway ... You're quite sure that she's your aunt?' I say, desperate to change the subject.

'Yep. She's *really* my aunt.'

It rains all day without letting up, so we just lounge around as much as the cramped van will allow – me reading, Victor playing sudoku.

At 6 p.m., as requested, we don our macs and head through the drizzle to the house next door.

'I *am* sorry about this,' Victor says. 'But I swear I thought you said yes.'

'Oh, it's fine,' I lie. 'Genuine French country food. It'll be something to tell people about when I get home.'

When we reach the house, it looks as cold and uninviting as before. This time, though, a second car – a small red Twingo – sits next to the rusty Lada. 'Maybe she wasn't even here before,' I say, nodding at the car. 'Maybe the Lada's dead. Maybe *that's* her car.'

When the front door opens, it is not Distira's face that appears, but the drawn features of a pale, wiry woman with wispy blonde hair.

'*Bonsoir*,' she says. 'Carole.'

'*Bonsoir*,' Victor replies. 'Victor.' He leans in and kisses the woman on both cheeks.

'Hello,' she says to me, smiling unconvincingly, as if it somehow hurts her face to do so. 'I am Carole, the friend of Distira. You are English, yes?'

'Irish,' I say.

She shrugs, as if to imply that it amounts to the same thing. Copying Victor's lead, I lean in to kiss her as well, but she extends a hand instead and so, blushing due to the apparent *faux pas* of having attempted to kiss her, I step back and shake hands instead.

'She is in the *cuisine*,' she says, ushering us into the lounge. 'Please, sit. I go get drinks.'

Victor hands her the bottle of wine we brought and she grimaces strangely and performs an even weirder curtsy as she backs out of the room.

Victor sinks immediately onto the monstrously ugly brown vinyl sofa, and I stand and look in wonder at the walls. 'Come sit down,' Victor says, patting the sofa beside him. 'You look like a Dalmasso.'

'A Dalmasso?'

'Yeah,' he says, doing his wide-eyed room sweep again, which makes me snort.

'Have you *seen* the pictures?' I ask, taking a seat beside him and watching as he scans the walls. They are plastered with photos of random animals cut, badly, from newspapers.

'I guess she likes dogs,' Victor says, smirking.

'And llamas,' I say, pointing to a faded clipping in the corner of the room, and struggling not to laugh.

'Great wallpaper, though,' Victor says.

'It looks like one of those interiors from an Almodóvar film,' I say, taking in the vast orange swirl of the underlying paper.

'Here,' Carole says, entering the room with a tray. 'Aperitif!'

She lifts the four glasses and an old wine bottle full of a green soupy herb concoction from the tray and then sits opposite us. She must notice me staring at the bottle, because she catches my eye and says, '*Génépi. Eau de vie.*'

I nod and smile.

'*Fait maison?*' Victor asks.

'*Oui.*'

'It's home-made,' he translates for me.

'Yes,' I say, struggling to muffle the irony in my voice. 'I spotted that.'

'*Alors!*' Distira says as she walks into the room. Actually, Distira isn't a woman who walks. She is a woman who trudges. Wearily. But in all fairness, she has scrubbed up reasonably well. She is wearing a tartan skirt and a big grey jumper. Her hands, if not her pinafore, look clean now, and her hair is washed and bouncy. If I can just avoid looking at those teeth . . .

She slides a plate of petits fours onto the table. They look incredibly professional, and I wonder whether she is a master baker, or simply a good defroster. She kisses Victor *bonsoir* and, in an attempt at avoiding my previous error, I hold out a hand for her to shake. She grabs it and uses it to pull me towards her, then kisses me twice, while holding me in a surprisingly powerful embrace.

When she releases me, I see that Carole is staring at us. We sit again and Distira says something, apparently addressing both Victor and me, and Carole starts to slop the green liquid into the glasses. As before, I don't understand enough of what Distira is saying to even work out what the subject is.

A couple of hours, I think. *You just need to get through the next couple of hours without upsetting anyone. They're his family.*

Distira pauses in whatever she is saying and looks at me. I smile and shrug blankly. '*Je suis désolée,*' I say. *I'm sorry.*

'Distira is saying that Carole here is an English teacher,' Victor says.

'Ahh!' I exclaim. 'So *that's* why your English is so good.'

'It could be good,' Carole says. 'I am teaching for twenty years.'

I frown and then belatedly understand. 'Oh! It *should* be,' I say.

'I'm sorry?'

'Nothing ... I was ... agreeing,' I splutter, realising that correcting the English teacher isn't going to make me any friends here tonight.

Distira pushes my serving of *eau de vie* towards me and lifts her glass. With some trepidation, I raise my drink. Victor catches my eye, sniffs his own and almost invisibly raises an eyebrow. The liquid smells like Deep Heat rub.

Distira raises her glass a little higher and says something.

'She toast your holidays,' Carole explains.

'Chin chin,' Victor says, so I copy him and pretend to sip my drink. The liquid barely touches my lip, but even that's more than enough. It tastes like stinging nettles soaked in petrol. I'm pretty sure you could run the Lada on it.

'*Mais nous ne sommes pas en vacances,*' Victor begins to explain. *We're not on holiday.*

Because I can't understand Distira's half of the conversation, I study her face for clues. And though I may not know what her lips are saying, I can read her expression perfectly. When Victor says that we will be living here full-time, I see horror hidden behind a dishonest smile. And when Victor explains his dream of rearing goats and making cheese, I see disbelief and not a little amusement hidden behind both women's nodding encouragement.

Carole offers me the plate of petits fours so I take a vol-au-vent stuffed with prawn mayonnaise and bite into it. The centre is still frozen, so to disguise my inability to eat it, forgetting myself, I sip at my *eau de vie*. This results in such a disastrous coughing-fit that Victor, thinking that I am choking, has to put his own glass down in order to pat me on the back.

'You're not use to then,' Carole says, nodding at the glass. 'The real *eau de vie.*'

'No,' I splutter, my eyes watering. 'No, not used to that at all.'

'So,' she says. '*Tu parles un peu Français?*'

'*Oui! Un peu.* But it's not very good yet. Not as good as your English.'

'It's good for me to hear the accent,' she says. 'I don't meet so many English people up here.'

'I'm sure. But my accent is a bit Irish. My dad was Irish, and I grew up in Ireland, so I still have a bit of an accent. It comes and goes.'

Carole nods and frowns. 'British . . . English . . . Royaume-Uni . . . It is complicated for us.'

'Sure,' I say. 'I live in London now, but I'm not British at all. Or English. Or from the United Kingdom, even. I'm Irish.'

'I see,' Carole says, but I can see that she doesn't.

'You know Ireland?' I say. 'The island of Ireland over here?' I draw the British Isles with one finger on the table.

'Of course,' she says.

'And it's divided in two? The top bit, Northern Ireland, is in the UK – the United Kingdom. And the rest of it is Ireland. A completely different government, no queen, we have the euro . . .'

'Oh, you have the euro in England now?' she says. 'I didn't know this.'

'No, we . . .' I sigh. 'Actually, you know what, it doesn't matter.'

'I see a film recently,' she says. 'The history.'

'A history of Ireland?'

'Yes. With the Australian. Mel Gibson. I like very much.' I shrug. 'I don't know it.'

'*Braveheart*, perhaps?' she says.

'Oh, no, that's Scotland,' I tell her.

'Yes,' she says.

Victor, who has been having a parallel conversation in

French, nudges me and says, 'Distira is asking if you like the *eau de vie*.'

'Oh, it's unbelievable stuff,' I say, knowing that only Victor will spot the irony in my choice of adjective.

'I'll tell you how she makes it later,' he says, and I can hear laughter in his voice.

After our frozen *petit four* and Deep Heat aperitif – is the one designed to thaw the other, I wonder – we move through to the big kitchen-cum-dining room for dinner. Despite the fact that the oven is on, the room – barely more modern than our own kitchen next door – is still about five degrees below comfortable.

The big, rather lovely farm table, which looks as if it has been hewn from a tree with an axe, is part covered with a yellow olive-branch motif tablecloth. A huge, and rather scary-looking dog – a Rottweiler, perhaps – is asleep on an armchair in the corner of the room, but it merely opens one eye, checks us out, and then falls back to sleep.

Any hopes of traditional French farm food vanish entirely when Distira serves the starter: a factory-made quiche served straight from the aluminium tray with pre-prepared salad tipped unapologetically from the bag. But at least there is no pretence that the food might be home-made; when Victor politely comments how good it is, Distira even gets the box from the bin to show him what brand he needs to buy.

After this, she serves us boiled potatoes and salmon in white-wine sauce. The salmon is so similar in taste and quantity to our boil-in-the-bag meal from a few nights ago, I suspect that it probably came from the same supermarket.

The dessert is probably the best part of the meal – the

first Viennetta I have tasted since the eighties. Who knew they still existed? And in France! At the first bite, child-hood memories come flooding in.

'Well, that was top-class nosh,' Victor says as we walk home.

'Huh,' I laugh. 'It was indeed!'

It is Victor who wakes up first. I become aware of him moving around in the van and struggle to open my eyes, and then to focus properly in the weak moonlight. I feel cold but clammy at the same time. I shiver violently then ask, 'Where are you going?'

Pulling a jumper over his head, he replies, 'The loo. I've got gut-ache.'

He slides open the door to the van, letting in a blast of freezing air, and then closes it behind him with a thud. I listen to him crunching across the gravel and take in the sensations within my own body. I touch my forehead with the back of my hand – I'm sweating. I shiver again from the cold. I feel as if I have caught the flu. And then a wave of cramp sweeps through my insides making me gasp in surprise. I roll onto one side in the hope that this will feel less uncomfortable – it doesn't.

I try lying on my front, my back, rolled up into a ball, and then, with a sigh, I switch on the light and start to pull on my jeans.

Waiting for Victor to return and free up the 'facilities' is excruciating but, just in time, I hear the front door to the house creak open. I slide open the van door and sprint across the frosty gravel.

'You too?' Victor asks, reaching out to brush my arm as we pass each other in the moonlight.

'Uhuh!' I groan.

'I'm sorry,' he says, 'but I couldn't ...'

'Jesus,' I say, when I reach the bathroom. Because, of course, the bloody pipes must be frozen again, and what Victor hasn't been able to do is *flush*.

And thus the night from hell passes. We take it in turns to run knock-kneed to the bathroom. I eventually discover that the kitchen tap still works, so at least we are able to ferry buckets of water for flushing purposes. But the combination of stomach pain, cold and lack of sleep make it truly one of the worse nights of my life. I feel shattered, feverish and irritable.

The temperature outside the van is, Victor reckons, about minus-five and the horrid bathroom isn't much warmer. It's like sitting in an industrial deep freeze. And with the constant opening and closing of the van door, even the Volkswagen's little heating system struggles to maintain a reasonable temperature.

Our cramps finally subside at 9 a.m., just as the sun comes over the mountain top and finally starts to warm the van. Lying rigidly side by side, our only contact Victor's hand lain over my own, we finally start to doze.

At some point I must truly fall asleep, because suddenly it's midday and the van is as bright and warm as a tanning machine.

'Croissants,' Victor says when I open my eyes. He waves a small bag at me and then drops it onto the counter. 'Distira must have left them. They were tied to the door handle.'

I groan. Even if I *could* eat something this morning, it wouldn't be croissants. And even if croissants *were* what I fancied, food from Distira would definitely not be my first choice. 'So is *she* OK then?' I ask.

Victor shrugs. 'I guess,' he says. 'She's been into town for these. They're proper ones, from a bakery.'

'How can she not be ill?' I ask. 'We all ate the same thing.'

'Maybe it was something else. Maybe it was . . .' he says.

'We had baked beans for lunch; it's hardly going to be that. That horrible *eau de vie*, more likely.'

'I reckon that *kills* germs,' Victor says.

'Yeah. You're probably right. The frozen prawns, then.'

'Frozen prawns?'

'In the vol-au-vents.'

'Oh God, yeah. They were *bad!*'

'Did she eat any? She didn't, did she?'

'No, Carole brought them in,' Victor says.

'Well, there you go, then. God, I feel rough.'

'Me too,' Victor says. 'A lazy day, methinks.'

'I'm dehydrated. Do you think the water's safe?'

'I could boil it.'

'Ooh, make tea,' I say. 'That's what I need. A gallon of tea.'

'Sure,' Victor says. 'And then I need to shower. I feel dirty.'

'Do you think the pipes work yet?'

'Yeah,' he says. 'They thawed almost the second the sun came out this morning.'

'Anyway, why don't you just leave a tap running?' I ask.

'What for?'

'To stop it freezing.'

Victor shakes his head in dismay. 'Now, why didn't I think of that?' he says.

We dedicate day six of our 'holiday' to recovery, and by the time the sun sets again, I'm finally starting to feel human.

There is no sign of movement over at Distira's place; in fact, once the sun goes down, we can see that there aren't even any lights on at her house.

'Do you think she's ill?' Victor asks when I point this out.

'She wasn't too ill to head out for croissants.'

'Maybe I should go check though,' he says.

'No,' I say. 'You shouldn't do anything that might result in a dinner invitation.'

'No, I guess not.'

'If she does invite us to dinner again . . .'

Victor looks up from his sudoku. 'It's a "no",' he says firmly.

'God, I'm getting hungry. I'm a bit scared to eat anything, though.'

Victor puts down the magazine and peers into one of the cupboards. 'Pasta and cheese?' he says. 'Should be safe enough.'

I pull a face. 'I don't think I even want to risk cheese.'

'Pesto?'

'From a jar?'

'Of course from a jar.'

'I mean, from a new, unopened, sterilised jar well before its sell-by date?'

Victor grins – the first smile of the day. 'Yes,' he says, pulling it from the cupboard and waving it at me. 'January 2016,' he reads from the lid.

I nod. 'OK. Let's try that.'

It's not until we have eaten, and waited long enough to be sure that our bodies are coping with food once again, that I start to accept that the ordeal may be over and relax enough to read. Victor grunts and groans as he struggles with a crossword.

After a while, he strokes my cheek and I look up at him. He raises one eyebrow. 'That was *bad*, huh?' he says.

'The meal or the aftermath?' I ask.

He shakes his head. 'Well, both. But I actually meant the meal.'

'I thought it was going to be hearty French fare,' I say. 'Farm food.'

'Yeah,' Victor says.

'The company wasn't fabulous either.' I pull a face as I realise that's probably the kind of truth that should never be spoken about a family member.

Victor bites his lip to hide a smile. 'Don't,' he says. 'She is my aunt.'

'Yeah,' I say, performing a Dalmasso wide-eye-sweep of the van. 'Yeah, she is.'

Victor snorts and struggles not to spit out a mouthful of tea, and I realise that this too we have survived: dreadful relatives, awful food, frozen pipes, and a night of illness ... If we can get through all of that and still be in good humour, well, compatibility-wise, we're pretty much there, aren't we?

TOURIST HEAVEN

The next morning, I wake up early. I gently reach for my phone so as not to wake Victor and see that it is just after 7 a.m. I lie there listening to the birdsong and Victor's gentle snoring, and take in the fact that I no longer feel ill. When you have been ill, that first morning when you realise that you're back to normal feels wonderfully optimistic.

I lie quietly for half an hour, but then I can resist it no more – I shuffle across the bed and lay one hand upon Victor's chest.

He groans, blinkingly opens one eye and yawns. 'Mmm . . .' he mumbles.

'Good morning.'

'Mmm. What time . . .?'

'Nearly eight. How do you feel?'

He rubs his eyes, and then focuses on my face. 'OK, I guess.'

'Good.'

He frowns at me. 'What?' he asks, laughter in his voice. I slide one hand down his stomach.

'Someone's full of beans.' He winks at me and then closes his eyes again.

I give him a squeeze. 'We didn't do it yesterday,' I point out.

'Oh, you think we have some catching up to do, do you?'

'I do.'

And so catch up is exactly what we do.

'So what now?' Victor asks later. 'Down to the coast?'

'I think we deserve a treat,' I say, 'after yesterday's ordeal. But if you want to get on with the chimney or something, that's fine too.'

'I thought maybe I'd buy some chimney brushes, to try to unblock it from the inside. So how about we go have lunch in Nice, wander around, do some tourist stuff, and then pick them up on the way back?'

'That's a plan,' I say. 'Can we have pizza?'

'Pizza? Again?' Victor laughs.

'I had the best pizza ever the last time I went to Nice. If I can just find the same place . . .'

'I could do with some meat,' Victor says. 'A steak or something.'

I shrug. 'I really have this craving for pizza. They did other stuff too anyway.'

'Well, we can have a look. Do you remember where it was?'

'Sure,' I say. 'In the old town.'

'Do you remember who you were with?' he asks.

'Of course,' I say. 'I was with Ch—' I interrupt myself and shake my head. 'You! No! I'm not telling.'

Victor smiles and stands, pulling change for the coffees from the pocket of his jeans.

As we drive down to Nice, we pass a seemingly constant stream of cars going the other way, many of which have skis and snowboards on their roofs. 'Can you ski up here?' I ask. 'I didn't realise.'

'*I* can't ski anywhere,' Victor says.

'You know what I mean. Can *one* ski nearby?'

'In Gréolières,' Victor says. 'It's just over the other side of that mountain.'

'I love skiing,' I say.

He turns to look at me and grins. 'Are you hinting?'

'Only if there's time,' I say coyly. 'I'm quite happy to spend all my holidays ripping up rotten lino and freezing my tits off in an ice-box-cum-bathroom if that's what's required.'

'But if there *was* time for a day's skiing, you wouldn't say n—' He is interrupted by a blaring horn, and we both look back at the road. My heart leaps into my mouth. We have drifted to completely the wrong side of the road, and are facing a huge 4x4, headlights blazing, horn blaring, and now less than twenty yards away. With the van being right-hand drive, the SUV is coming straight at *me*.

Victor yanks the wheel, violently correcting our trajectory, and then, disaster averted, says, 'Fuck! Sorry about that.'

'Um, I think it's best if you keep your eyes on the road now,' I say, my voice trembling.

After a few minutes my heart stills. When we pass another ten cars with skis, I comment, 'So why today? Why are they all going skiing today?'

Victor shrugs. 'Maybe it snowed when we had all that rain. Shit! It's Sunday. That's why! Damn!'

'Damn, *because* . . .?'

'Well, the shops are closed, aren't they?'

'The DIY place?'

'Everything.'

'God, I forgot about that. Is France still like that?'

'Yep. Some food shops are open on Sunday morning, but that's about it.'

I shrug. 'So no DIY.'

'Nope. And God sayeth unto them, thou shalt not fixeth anything on the Sabbath.'

'He dideth. So a whole tourist day then.'

Victor glances over at me and smiles, but snaps back when I shout, 'Road!'

'Sorry,' he says. 'And yes. Day off. Looks like it.'

Because I'm a little nervous of distracting him while he drives along the edges of the ravines, I remain silent for a while. But then I forget myself and ask, 'Was Distira ever married?'

'Yes. To a guy called Paul. He died, though.'

'Kids?'

'None. He died pretty young.'

'Of?'

'I'm not sure, to be honest. A heart attack, maybe. The funeral was the last time I saw her.'

'Your mum didn't keep in touch with her, then?'

'Not really. Distira came down a few times when she had to, but they never got on that well. I think they had a falling out. About inheritance from their mother.'

'Was there much to fight about? I mean, not being funny, but they don't seem to be exactly loaded.'

68

'No. But Gran ended up with three properties all the same. None of them were exactly palaces, but there's the house in Perpignan, and the farmhouse here.'

'Your place?'

'*Our* place.'

'Right.'

'And Distira's house, of course.'

'I suppose that is quite a lot of property.'

'Well, Gran was an only child. Which was pretty unusual then. So she inherited places from both her parents. They were only peasant farmers, I think, but they had houses.'

'And Distira wasn't happy with her end of the deal?'

'Well, Mum got two places, and Distira got one. Even if on paper Distira's place was worth more than the other two put together ...'

'So what's the place in Perpignan like? You still own that, right?'

'Sure. It's much smaller. Pretty but small. I'll sell it at some point, I suppose. When the French tax man catches up with me, probably.'

'You never lived there, though?'

'To start with, yes. Afterwards I went back for holidays sometimes. It's really tiny. And no land because it's in town. But Mum loved that place, so ...'

'There were fights in our family too. About some rings.'

'Yeah?'

'Yes, when my gran died – on Dad's side – apparently his brother was in the house taking all the jewellery virtually before she was declared dead.'

'Yuck,' Victor says.

69

'Well, that's how the story went, anyway. You never know with families. But they never got over it.'

'You never saw your uncle?'

'Never. Not after that.'

'Well, there you go. Same sort of story.'

'Maybe that's . . .' I begin. But then I think better of it. I had been about to suggest that that was maybe why Distira doesn't seem to like him much.

'Why what?'

'Look! Hang-gliders!' I say, pointing at the sky, grateful for an excuse to change the subject.

'Para-gliders,' Victor says. 'Hang-gliders have a rigid frame, like kites. Those are like big parachutes, hence para-gliders.'

'Have you ever done it?'

'No. But I wouldn't mind having a go.'

'You wouldn't get me up there,' I say.

'Spoilsport.'

'So Distira has been single for what, twenty years?'

'Yeah. I think so.'

'That's tough. Especially living where she does.'

'Yes. It is,' Victor says. 'I bet she's really glad that she's going to have neighbours.'

'Mmm,' I say, thinking that she didn't strike me as *that* glad. 'Still, she has friends. Or at least one.'

'Carole.'

'Yes.'

'D'you think . . .' Victor starts.

'Yes?'

'Nothing.'

'No, go on.'

'I think we'll try this route today. It's a bit longer but ...'

'What were you saying?'

'Sorry, I forgot,' he says.

'Something about Distira and Carole.'

Victor shrugs. 'Nope ... It'll come to me.'

I wonder if what he was about to say was what I was wondering myself – whether Distira and Carole are more than just friends.

'They seem very close,' I say.

'Yes,' Victor says. 'They do.'

I wait for a few moments to see if he is going to explore the subject any further, but he doesn't say a word.

When we hit the Promenade des Anglais, I'm stunned once again by the turquoise brilliance of the sea. A gentle breeze is moving the flags that mark each of the beach concessions.

'This really is an amazing place. I mean, when you think about it, there can't be that many places in the world where you can ski, paraglide and sit on a beach on the same day.'

I turn to look at the joggers on the promenade, at the rows of blue bicycles to rent, at the flapping flags and white-capped waves. Everything looks fluorescent due to the clarity of the light.

'Yeah,' I murmur.

'Yeah?'

'Oh, I was just wondering if I could really live here ... I reckon I could bear it.'

Victor glances at me and smiles. As we pass the Negresco hotel, he follows my gaze. 'I wonder how much it costs to spend a night *there*,' he says.

'The rooms aren't that impressive, really,' I say, only real-ising once I have said it where that conversation is going to lead.

'You've been there?'

'Yes. The communal bits, the lounges and the halls are pretty amazing. They have this stunning lounge with blood red walls and frescos all over the ceilings. We can go look, if you want. As long as you walk in with enough panache, no one even questions you.'

'You *stayed* in the Negresco?' Victor asks. 'Or is that part of the secret story that shall never be told?'

I sigh. 'I'll tell you if you want,' I say, aware that not talking about it is becoming worse than caving in. 'But don't judge me, that's all.'

'Of course not.'

'So . . . I stayed there two nights. I met this guy on a plane.'

'On a *plane*?'

'You see,' I say. 'There you go.'

'I'm not *judging*,' Victor says. 'I'm just surprised. Go on.'

'I met a very nice guy on a trip back from New York. He invited me to Nice for the weekend.'

'*OK*.' Victor sounds dubious. 'Jeez these lanes are narrow,' he says.

'You're right,' I say. 'They are. You only have a couple of inches on this side.'

'So you met a guy on a plane.'

'It was pissing down in London. I was depressed about going home all alone. I had been single forever. And all my friends encouraged me to let my hair down and just go. I had

72

my own room, so it was nothing sleazy. It wasn't that impressive, really. Though it did have clouds painted on the ceiling.'

'Right.'

'And that's about it.'

'Only that isn't "it", is it?' Victor says. 'Otherwise you wouldn't have been so mysterious about it.'

'Well, the guy turned out to be a bit weird,' I say. 'A bit pervy. So it didn't really go anywhere.'

'Pervy?'

'Yes. You'd never believe me, even if I told you.'

'Try me.'

'He had a balloon fetish. His thing was making love in a room full of balloons.'

'God,' Victor says. 'Now that's specialised.'

'Indeed.'

'And you said no.'

As soon as he has made this assumption, the only thing I can do is go along with it. Figuring that he's unlikely to ever find out the truth, I say, 'Of course I did. But other than that, it was a really nice weekend. I had my own room, and we went out to a lovely posh restaurant . . .'

'You said it was a pizzeria.'

'God, it's like the Spanish inquisition,' I say.

'Nobody expects the Spanish inquisition,' Victor says in a silly *Monty Python* voice.

'So yes, we had a pizza on the first day, and we went to an expensive fish restaurant in Villefranche on the second night. With a horrible snobby waiter who kept cleaning crumbs off the table every ten seconds. And that's it. Anything else you want to know?'

73

Victor pulls up at a set of lights, puts the van into neutral and lays one hand upon my knee. 'I don't think so,' he says, 'except, maybe, did you stay in touch with this charming chap?'

'Of course I didn't.'

'So I don't need to feel jealous?'

'Absolutely not.'

'OK,' Victor says. 'I won't then.' And then he squeezes my knee and puts the engine back into gear.

Even in January, it's impossible to park the van anywhere near the town centre, so we end up driving beyond the port and walking all the way back. But it's a lovely breezy day for a walk and, after the confinement of the van, the exercise feels good.

'There's definitely something special about the light here,' I say, looking at the luminous fishing boats bobbing up and down. 'It makes everything glow.'

'It does.'

It takes almost forty minutes to reach the main beach. We lean on the railings beneath a flag that says *Castel Plage* and watch a ferry heading out to sea. 'It goes to Corsica, apparently,' I say.

'Yes,' Victor says. 'I know.'

'Have you ever been?'

'No.'

'Me neither,' I say. 'Maybe we could go sometime, if I move here. *When* I move here.'

'Maybe.'

'Did you know that it used to be a fishing village here?' I tell him. 'They had photos in the Negresco from the twenties, and this beach was covered in boats and fishermen mending their nets. Not a single tourist in sight.'

'I'm sure.'

The terse nature of Victor's replies is starting to concern me, so I stroke his hand and ask, 'Are you OK?'

'Sure,' he says. 'Why wouldn't I be?'

We cross the main road and head through some arches to the vast Cours Saleya. A huge colourful food market is in full swing. 'Now that's the way to do your shopping,' I say. 'We should get some veg.'

'Maybe after lunch.'

'Yes. Let's do lunch first.'

It's only just twelve, but we decide to hunt for my restaurant straight away. By the time we have walked through the old town, taken a number of wrong turns, finally located the Gésu, only to discover that it is closed on Sundays, it is half twelve and I'm quite certain that Victor is *not* OK. I wait until we have found another restaurant before I attempt to find out why.

Once we each have a glass of rosé, I say, 'So, go on. Out with it.'

'Out with what?'

'Oh come on,' I say. 'You haven't said a word since I told you about Charles.'

'Charles?'

'The guy I went to the Negresco with.'

'So his name's Charles?'

'I shouldn't have told you,' I say. 'I knew this would happen. But you kept asking.'

Victor shrugs. 'It's nothing to do with that,' he says.

'God, you're a sulker,' I say. 'Just tell me, and maybe I can help.'

Victor sighs and sips his drink. 'I'm not sulking at all,' he says softly. 'I'm actually worried about you.'

'So tell me what you're worrying about.'

'It's just that ... well ... since this morning ... you've been kind of talking about how nice it is here.'

'Yes?'

'About skiing and the beach and the Negresco, and posh restaurants in Villefranche ...'

'Right. And that's bad?'

'And going to Corsica.'

'Yes?'

'Well, I can see that tourist heaven is quite attractive.'

'Well yes. It is.'

'I'm just worried you're not going to like life up *there*.'

'In the hills?'

'Yes. Because that life has nothing to do with this one, really.'

'I see,' I say.

'I mean ... this is all lovely ...' He waves his glass to take in the surroundings. 'But it's a different thing to down-sizing and living simply and farming ...'

'I know that,' I say.

'I doubt we'll even be able to *afford* to eat in restaurants any more. Let alone go skiing. And as for trips to Corsica ...'

I nod slowly and sip my drink and stare at Victor as he fiddles with his fork. 'But I *know* that,' I say again, even though, in truth, I'm only just starting to follow his logic, only just beginning to imagine how different that life will need to be. Stupidly, I haven't even attempted to work out how much a goat farmer might earn, or what a goat farmer's life might be like. When I now do try to picture it, I imagine myself living Distira's life.

Something of this thought process must show because Victor raises one eyebrow and says, 'You see?'

'Yes.'

'I'm not even sure that *I* will be able to cope living like that. So is it really fair for me to expect someone who likes shopping and—'

'I am *not* someone who likes shopping,' I cut in. 'You have me all wrong.'

'OK. Skiing and posh restaurants then.'

'The restaurant wasn't very nice, either,' I point out. 'Well, the food was, but the service was awful.'

'But you get my point,' Victor says.

'I do, but . . .'

'But?'

I shrug. 'I don't know. I haven't had time to think about it, really.'

'But you do see what I'm saying?'

I stare into his eyes and smile weakly as my brain makes the adjustment from a roses-round-the-door image of me baking pies and Victor coming in from a hard day's graft to something much, much grimmer.

'I do get what you're saying, but . . . I mean, we won't have to live like Distira, will we?' I sound a little like I'm pleading. Maybe I am.

Victor shrugs. 'It all comes down to money in the end, doesn't it?'

'Well, then, we won't,' I say, thinking on my feet. 'I'll have some income from my flat – if I rent it – or interest or something on the capital if I sell it. You have the place in Perpignan to rent or sell or whatever . . .'

'Yes,' Victor says. 'But that won't make much. And even that won't last forever.'

'The thing will be to use that to set things up so that they make more money. Maybe I'll set up a business.'

'I was thinking we could convert the outbuildings and rent rooms out,' Victor says doubtfully.

'Exactly! You see. Like a *gîte* or something. And that's something I'd be happy to do.'

'Yes.'

'Run it, I mean, not rebuild it. Though I'm happy to help, even with that.'

Victor laughs. 'Of course,' he says, squeezing my hand. 'You're really quite brave, aren't you? I don't think I realised.'

'No,' I say. 'No, I don't think I did either.'

After lunch, we climb what seems like a thousand steps to the top of the Park du Château where we ask a Japanese tourist to take our picture with the sweeping bay of Nice in the background. I suddenly realise, as Victor slides his arms around me for the photo, that this will forever be the first photo taken of us together, so I wriggle my bottom against him which, as expected, makes him laugh and protest, 'Stop it!'

I want us to look at this photo and remember laughter, not the very real worries that have surfaced today. Because though we have done our best to reassure each other that everything is going to be fine, a fresh set of less idyllic images are now playing on both of our minds.

I simply hadn't thought enough about the whole adventure to create a realistic image of what it was going to be like. But now that I *have* started to analyse it, the only thing I know is that what's on offer is so alien and new, that I won't really know if I like it until it happens. For Victor, I suppose it's the fact of trying to imagine his partner, and potentially a baby, in the middle of this mayhem that has made everything that much more challenging, that much more real.

We meander down the other side of the hill which the park occupies, and on through the narrow streets of the old town to the market, where, it turns out, we are way too late to buy anything – the stalls have been folded away, the square hosed down. Instead, we buy a few essentials and as much bottled water as we think we can carry from an old-fashioned corner shop and head back around the port to the van. I wouldn't say that the atmosphere is tense, exactly, but an onlooker would definitely be able to spot that we have things on our minds.

Halfway home we pass a farm with a sign that says *fromage de chèvre*.

'You have competition, then,' I say.

'Oh, there are a few,' Victor says. 'But not loads.'

'Can we go get some? At least see if I like the stuff. I mean, I've obviously had goat's cheese before, but not home-made goat's cheese. Plus they sell eggs, and we didn't get any.'

'I'm worried it might scare you off,' Victor says, slowing the van and swinging into a lay-by to start turning around. 'It might be worse than Distira's.'

He turns down the track to the farmhouse and parks up in a scrubby courtyard not dissimilar to our own. We walk through a group of scrappy-looking chickens. The shop entrance is signposted around the side of the house, so we follow the track until we reach the door. I ring the bell.

'It's quite quaint, really,' I say, looking at the low sun cutting across some rusty farm machinery. 'They could do with a few trips to the tip, though.'

'They could,' Victor agrees, and at that moment a woman appears around the side of the house with a baby slung over one shoulder.

She is younger than I would have expected – about thirty. She is slim and pretty with shiny black hair pulled tightly back and a ruddy country complexion. '*Bonjour!*' she says in a sing-song voice. '*Vous voulez du fromage?*'

Victor tells her that, yes, we want to buy some cheese. He asks her if they have something called *tome* and she laughs and says that, no, they only have fresh cheeses, that the *tome*, whatever that is, arrives late summer. I worry a little about how much Victor actually knows about making cheese.

She opens the door to a spotless room with a simple scrubbed wooden table, a set of scales and a big glass-fronted refrigerator. And then, with a simple, '*Vous pouvez?*' and before I can even reply, she hands me her baby.

I'm a little surprised by this, but the baby, who must be six to eight months old, is sleeping, so I simply lay it against my own shoulder in the same way the mother did and it continues to sleep. There is something a little unsettling about the smell of milk emanating from the baby, here, in the midst of a cheese shop.

Victor catches my eye, glances at the baby, and then bites his cheek, clearly suppressing a chuckle.

The woman washes her hands and produces three different trays of cheeses, which, as far as I can understand, differ only in how old and hard they are.

We taste all three – they range from a creamy cottage cheese texture to the hardness of parmesan – and then Victor, rather extravagantly it seems to me as they aren't particularly amazing, buys three of each and asks for a dozen eggs as well.

'*Vous êtes en vacances?*' she asks as she wraps the cheeses in greaseproof paper, and Victor explains that, no, we're not on holiday, that we're moving to La Forge, and that he's thinking of getting a couple of goats.

'You will talk to Georges,' the woman tells him. 'He will help you.' No conditionals here. You *will* talk to him. He *will* help you. I reckon that she has spotted a business opportunity. She has that kind of face.

Once the cheeses are wrapped, she washes her hands again, and steps outside to shriek her husband's name, and Georges comes running. He's a tiny man with a kind, weathered face and prematurely grey hair swept back Einstein-style. He looks a little dazzled and I guess that we have woken him from his siesta.

'They want eggs,' she says, and Georges starts to move back outside to go and fetch them. '*Non!*' she shouts. 'Stay and talk! I'll get them. He wants to keep goats!'

As she leaves, she startlingly wrenches the baby from my arms.

And so Victor and Georges start to discuss goats. Unlike Distira, I can, for some reason, understand most of what they are saying quite easily. Perhaps my French is getting better as my ear becomes attuned, but I think Georges and his wife actually have a different accent. They speak in a similar, sing-song way, but far more slowly, almost pedantically.

Victor makes his project sound like a hobby. 'Just a couple of goats,' he says. 'Try and make some cheese, just for the fun of it . . .'

And Georges, unthreatened by any competition from such a tentative project, seems keen on the idea of selling Victor a few goats and giving him some tips on looking after them. He even suggests that his wife could give me some tips on cheese-making!

By the time we leave with our eggs and cheese, the men have swapped phone numbers and whacked each other on the back.

As we pull away, I say, 'Why did he assume that *I* was going to be the one making the cheese, then?'

Victor snorts. 'It's what girls do, isn't it? You look after babies and make cheese.'

'Cheeky bugger.'

'You don't fancy it, then?' he asks.

'I wouldn't mind,' I say. 'But only if you help out too. I'm not going to get landed with cheese-making duties forever more, simply because you weren't there when madame was giving lessons.'

'You were cute with the baby, though,' Victor says, and I suddenly feel a little flushed. I suspect that I am blushing. 'The ROAD!' I shout, when Victor starts to turn to look at me, and he snaps back to the front.

'Did you see how she bosses him around, though?' Victor asks.

'Yes! Now that's something useful I might get her to teach me.'

'I think you're already there,' he says.

'Ooh, you're cheeky today.'

'The ROAD!' he shrieks.

'Well someone has to keep us alive!'

By the time we get back to La Forge, the sun has set and the temperature is falling fast once again. Victor parks the van and I head to the bathroom to open one of the taps.

Despite the sunny day we have just had, the interior still feels dank and icy cold, and as I am about to leave, I pause to stare at the kitchen, try to visualise it finished.

Hearing footsteps on the gravel approaching the open door, I say, 'You know we really *must* get that range li—' I jump when I realise that it's not Victor behind me, but Distira.

'*Bonsoir*,' she says, grinning and flashing her dodgy gnashers at me.

'*Bonsoir*,' I reply, unsure if we are now meant to kiss or shake hands. She attempts neither.

She says something else and I realise for the first time that the problem with understanding her is not just her accent but that she also has some kind of speech impediment, which seems to result in her swallowing her words. It could well be something to do with her teeth.

'*Pardon?*' I ask.

'*La maison est foutue,*' she says. '*Elle est mal faite.*' Which I understand to mean that the house is badly built.

'*Oui, mais Victor va l'améliorer,*' I say. *Victor's going to improve it.*

She frowns at me as if I am speaking Chinese rather than French, and then thankfully Victor appears behind her.

'*Bonsoir,*' he says.

She kisses him on both cheeks and then nods at me. '*Qu'est-ce qu'elle dit, elle?*' she asks. *What's she saying, that one?*

Victor looks at me, smiles and raises his eyebrow.

'She was saying that your house is crap,' I tell him, making the most of the fact that she won't understand, 'and I said that you were going to improve it.'

'Yes,' Victor tells her. 'The house will be wonderful – *merveilleuse* – once it's finished.'

'That I doubt,' she replies drily, in French.

'I think I might go start dinner,' I mumble, nodding respectfully at Distira as I edge around her. Because the truth is that she gives me the willies.

As I squeeze through the gap between her and the door, she grabs the sleeve of my sweatshirt and says, '*Vous ne serez jamais heureuse ici, vous savez,*' which sadly I understand. *You'll never be happy here, you know.*

I stick a false grin on my face and flash the whites of my eyes at Victor as I escape, leaving him to deal with her. As I crunch across the gravel, I hear him reply, 'But why

84

are you saying that, Auntie? You have to be positive about these things ...'

Safe in the van, figuring that we will be better protected against a dinner invitation if I can get things moving, I put water on to boil for the pasta.

But when Victor returns to the van, it is with Distira in tow. I silently pray to Him/Her/It for Distira *not* to invite us to dinner.

Victor slides the side door open and she leans in and performs her trademark wide-eyed scan of the van. '*C'est chouette*,' she says. '*C'est comfortable.*' It's cute. It's comfortable.

'*Mais petit*,' I say, hoping that emphasising how small it is will make her less likely to join us. I peer at the water, willing it to boil quicker, and wonder if I should drop just enough pasta for two into the pan right now.

Distira unexpectedly starts to smile, and then she laughs out loud. She points at the eight bottles of Volvic lined up and asks why we have bought water.

Victor hesitates and looks at me and I realise that, of course, he doesn't want to tell her that we have both been ill.

She says something else about water that I don't catch, and claps her hands, and then, still chuckling and talking to herself, she starts to wander back towards her own house.

Victor blinks exaggeratedly and shakes his head, then climbs in and closes the door.

'What's she saying?' I ask, as her voice fades into the distance.

'She's laughing at us buying water,' he says. 'I think it's the funniest thing she's ever seen.'

I snort and shake my head. 'Well, if she defrosted her *vol-au-vents* properly ...'

'She said that our tap is connected straight to a spring. That we have mountain water on tap. That it's the same stuff.'

'Except that this is filtered and sterilised by Danone,' I say, turning one of the bottles and examining the label.

'Well, quite,' Victor says. 'Though I'm sure she's right. I'm sure it *is* fine.'

'Oh look,' I say, 'me too. But just for a few days I want to play safe. I don't think my body could cope with another round of dengue fever.'

'That's caused by mosquitos.'

'Well, you know what I mean.'

'It cheered her up, anyway,' Victor says.

'It did! She doesn't like me, though, does she?'

Victor shrugs. 'I'm not sure she likes *me*.'

'And she certainly doesn't like the house.'

'No,' he says. 'No, I'm getting that too. She's a proper little prophet of doom. You're cooking early.'

'Yeah,' I say, glancing over at Distira's and seeing a light go on. I reach out and switch off the gas. 'It can wait a bit, actually. It was just to avoid being invited over.'

Victor laughs and moves towards me, slipping his arms around my waist. 'I asked her about plumbers and stuff,' he says.

'And?'

'She said no-go. Says there's no way anyone will come up here in this season.'

'That's crazy,' I say, leaning into him and now looking over his shoulder towards her house in the distance. 'I mean, people up here *do* have plumbing. It must have got here somehow.'

'Judging from this place, they don't have *much* plumbing,' Victor says.

'What will you do then?' I ask.

I feel Victor shrug against me. 'Get a book on plumbing, maybe.'

'Eek. That sounds like a recipe for disaster. Couldn't you ask Goat-Man?'

'Georges? I doubt he does plumbing.'

I sigh. 'Ask him for an address, silly. He must have a plumber.'

'Now that . . .' Victor says, gripping my shoulders and leaning back so that he can look at me, 'is a very good idea.'

As Victor paces up and down outside, speaking into his phone, I pour a bowl of nuts and serve myself a glass of wine. I watch his breath rising in little steam-train puffs.

'Sorted!' he declares when he clambers back in.

'Really?'

'Yep. He has a guy who does plastering *and* building *and* electricity *and* plumbing!'

I pull a face. 'Mixing plumbing and electricity sounds even more dangerous than you doing it.'

'*And* he's invited us to dinner tomorrow.'

I grimace.

'Oh, come on. They seem really nice. Plus he's going to try to get the amazing DIY superhero over for the aperitif so we can meet him.'

87

'But it'll be frozen prawns and lettuce-in-a-bag all over again,' I say. 'Followed by a night of vomiting. You mark my words.'

'They're farmers,' Victor says, grabbing my waist and giving me a peck. 'I bet you it won't.'

'Oh yeah? How much?'

'Um . . . washing up.'

'Ooh, I hate washing up here.'

'Exactly.'

'OK. For how many days?'

'Till you leave.'

I sigh. The sudden reminder that I'm leaving in less than a week is sobering. I had almost forgotten.

'OK, just for two nights, then,' Victor offers.

'No,' I say. 'No, the whole week is fine. And when is the dinner from hell happening? Tomorrow?'

'Yes.'

I pull him tight. 'Yippee!' I say, sarcastically.

The next morning, we head out early. Victor wants to buy various DIY bits, and we decide to make this our final day of sightseeing before getting stuck into some serious renovation tomorrow.

Just as we reach the main road, we cross paths with Distira and Carole coming the other way in the Lada.

Victor brakes hard and slithers to a halt, and I wind down my window so that they can talk.

'*Bonjour!*' Victor shouts enthusiastically, and I follow suit, albeit more quietly.

Distira, looking directly past me at Victor, shouts something back, cackles, and then accelerates immediately off up the track. Carole, for her part, doesn't even turn her head.

'What did she say?' I ask, once the window is back up.

'She asked if we were going to buy some water,' Victor says. 'Cheeky bugger.'

'She didn't look at me once. She totally blanked me.'

'Hmm, well . . .' Victor says vaguely.

I turn to look at his face, but it's giving nothing away. 'Hmm well, what?'

'You don't want to be getting paranoid, that's all,' he says, shooting me a small smile.

I think about this for a moment. 'I'm not *getting paranoid*,' I say eventually. 'She blanked me.'

Victor laughs. 'Oh, they're just . . .'

I wait a moment and then prompt him with, 'Just what?'

'Dunno . . . *rustre*,' he says.

'Which doesn't help because I don't know what *rustre* means.'

'And I don't know how to translate it. I'm not sure that we have a word in English. It's kind of . . . wild . . . untamed . . . but more personality-wise.'

'Abrupt?' I say.

'Not quite. It's that special sort of abruptness that people have when they're not very well-educated. No, that sounds snobby. When they're not very socialized, maybe,' Victor says. 'Or does that sound worse?'

'Like rustic?'

'In a way, yes.'

'Yes, well, she's rustic all right.'

'Yeah.'

'And I'm not paranoid.'

Victor glances over at me and pats my knee. 'No,' he says, 'of course you're not.'

In another industrial zone, this time in a town called Grasse, we buy various tools, lots of reels of cable that Victor says are half the price of anywhere else, and a bathroom heater.

We then head into the gritty (and poor) mediaeval centre of the town, populated in this season, exclusively it seems, by aged Arab men sitting around in groups, chatting happily and smoking. After coffee, we take the van again and head along another nerve-racking mountain road towards a town called Gourdon, which Victor promises is spectacularly beautiful.

As we drive, my mind drifts onto the subject of what Victor used to do for work, something we have never discussed in detail. 'What's it like being a gynaecologist?' I ask.

Victor pulls a confused face, then smiles and glances at me. 'Where did that come from?' he asks.

'Not sure,' I say.

'It's like anything else, I suppose. You get used to it. It becomes quite mundane. There are only about ten procedures that take up ninety-nine per cent of your time, so …'

'Right,' I say thoughtfully. 'But it *is* kind of intimate.'

'It seems it for patients,' he says. 'But that's because they don't come that often. When you're doing that all day … Well, it becomes pretty routine.'

'But you must fancy the women who come in sometimes, right?'

Victor wrinkles his nose and changes gear.

'Oh, I bet you do!' I tease him.

'Honestly, not really,' he says. 'It's kind of a different part of the brain, if that makes any sense.' I remain silent for a minute as I think about this, but then he continues. 'Often there's some infection. Thrush or warts or discharge or whatever. None of that's very sexy.'

'Yuck!'

'I suppose sometimes you open the door and think, *Wow, what a cracker*. But as soon as you get down to the nitty-gritty, well, it's just plumbing, really.'

I nod. 'OK, but what about me? You already liked me when I stumbled into your surgery.'

My mind flashes back to the moment we met and I remember how shocked I was to discover that Mark's friend Victor – who I still assumed was gay – was my new gynae-cologist. Who would ever have believed that we'd end up together, here, in France?

'You thought I was Russian!' Victor laughs.

I smile. 'Yes. SJ was calling you Doctor Yinkchovsky instead of Ynchausty. That was funny.'

'But yes. I liked you, but . . . It's just work. It's different.'

'So what about *out* of work?' I ask. 'Does it change how you feel about sex, for instance? Being that *au fait* with so many women's bits?'

'It makes you pretty wary of STDs,' he says. 'Hepatitis, HIV, syphilis . . . But other than that, how would I know how other men feel about sex? And if they feel any different to me.'

'You never discussed it? Or don't guys talk about sex the way girls do?'

'About what they get up to, maybe, but even then – other than a bit of boasting – not much. But they definitely don't talk about how they *feel* about it.'

'You never asked *me* about STDs.'

'I didn't need to,' Victor laughs. 'I had your file. I gave *you* the results of all the tests.'

'Of course,' I say, suddenly aware that the conversation is making me uncomfortable, but not sure why.

'And I know I'm all clear, too,' Victor says, 'so it's not really an issue.'

I look over and see a village perched on the farthest edge of a rocky outcrop. 'Is that it?' I ask, grateful to change the subject.

'Yep.'

'What is it called again? Gordon?'

'It's G-O-U,' Victor spells. '*Gourdon.*'

'It's pretty.'

Gourdon, it transpires, is famed for glass-blowing, so the tiny main street is stuffed with tourist shops selling glass knick-knacks of every imaginable shape and size. Even today – on a Monday in January – a busload of tourists are milling through the streets.

'Nice, huh?' Victor says.

But the truth is that although Gourdon is undeniably pretty, the tourist takeover has left it all feeling a bit like a Disneyland version of itself. It's just too quaint for its own good. Too aware of its own quaintness, perhaps. I prefer the gritty reality of Grasse.

Once we get to the far side of the village, though, the view – stretching from Nice to Cannes – is spectacular.

'God, it's beautiful,' I say, and Victor makes the moment even better by nuzzling my neck.

'It is, isn't it?' he says.

He points out Nice airport, sticking out on reclaimed land into the sea, and Cap d'Antibes, where we saw the millionaires' houses just a few days ago.

And then we wander through the tiny streets until we get back to the van, where we pull out the map.

'Are those lakes?' I ask, pointing to a patch of turquoise.

'Dunno,' Victor says. 'I was wondering about that.'

'They look big.'

'D'you want to go see?'

'It looks a long way,' I say, 'but, lord knows, I like a lake.'

'We have all day,' Victor says, 'Let's do it.'

We head back to Grasse and on towards the lake. It takes, in fact, less than an hour to get there. We park the van in the scrubby car park of an out-of-season restaurant and descend the ten steps from the car park to the water's edge. From here, the water stretches almost as far as the eye can see. All around us are hundreds of tarpaulined pedalos.

'I bet it's heaving in summer,' I say. 'Look how many pedalos they have.'

'Yes,' Victor says. 'I reckon you're right. It's lovely today though.'

'A shame all the restaurants are closed. I would have liked to eat here.'

Victor looks around and then says, 'One of them is open.'

'Are you sure? They all looked pretty closed to me.'

'Chez Victor is open,' he says, pointing at the van.

'Of course!' I say. 'How perfect!'

Victor heats up some vacuum-packed boiled potatoes and fries some salmon steaks while I pour two glasses of rosé, then we carry it all down to one of the picnic benches. With the water lapping at our feet, we eat our simple cooked meal.

It's a perfect moment, in fact it's so perfect that I dare not say anything for fear of getting weepy.

A duck glides up to the river bank and I say, 'No bread, Mister Duck, sorry.' Then, to Victor, 'Do you think they like potatoes?'

'I bet they like salmon.'

'Only I don't want to give it my salmon,' I say.

Victor stands and jogs to the van. He returns with a croissant, which he rips in half so that we can both throw crumbs to the solitary duck.

As the sun sinks lower, its reflection twinkles on the surface of the water. The duck eventually glides away and the sun sparkles even more dazzlingly where the wake creates ripples.

'This is heavenly,' I say quietly, feeling tears welling.

Victor hears the emotion and reaches out for my hand. 'Are you OK?' he asks.

I nod and wipe a tear from the corner of my eye. 'Of course. It's just . . .' I shrug. 'Sometimes you feel so happy, it feels almost the same as sadness. Do you know what I mean?'

Victor blinks at me slowly and smiles. 'Of course. But it isn't the same, is it? It's much nicer.' He leans over and kisses my forehead. 'Now this,' he says, 'is the kind of thing we can do.'

'I'm sorry?'

'This we can do even when we *don't* have any money.'

'It's enough for me,' I say.

He nods, with meaning. 'Yes,' he says. 'It's enough for me too.'

DIVINE INTERVENTION

As we drive back from the lake, the VW roaring throatily up the hills, I watch the countryside slipping into shadow as the sun fades and try again to imagine what our lives would be like here. Though I know that life will be harsher and more physical, I imagine us enjoying these simple pleasures: spending a Sunday at the lake, driving to the sea for an occasional swim. And then I try to imagine bringing up a child here and think of picnics and pedalos and the whole thing starts to seem romantic instead of frightening.

We drive past Georges' farm on the way up but because it's too early and because I want to shower and change into warmer clothes, we carry on towards La Forge.

As we pass the farm, I say, 'You know you told Georges that you only want one or two goats, just as a hobby?'

'Yeah,' Victor says. 'I didn't want him to think I was going to steal his business.'

'I got that,' I say, 'but how many goats would you need?'

'I'm not sure,' Victor says. 'When I did my course in the Lake District, the guy had sixty.'

'Sixty?!'

'But goat's cheese is more expensive there, so maybe I'll need even more here. I'm hoping to find out how many Georges and Myriam have and how they sell their cheese.'

'Georges and Myriam? Is her name *Myriam*? God, that's almost George and Mildred.'

'George and Mildred?'

'Did you never see that? Dodgy seventies sitcom.'

Victor frowns. 'I don't think so,' he says.

'You didn't miss much ... But if you're going to pump them for information, they're going to want to know how *we're* going to live too,' I point out.

'The B&B,' Victor says. 'I thought that we'd say that the B&B was our main project. And you never know, that might end up being true.'

'Sixty goats ...' I say. 'That must be a lot of milking.'

'I'm not even sure the whole thing is feasible, to be honest. And I probably *will* start with two or three, just to see if I can do it.'

'You have to *sell* the cheese, too.'

'I know. Although I have no idea where. Not yet.'

I sit in silence for a while thinking about all of this.

'What?' Victor asks, as if my silence is in some way a rebuke.

'Nothing,' I say, 'but I must admit, I thought you would have had this all, well, better planned.'

Victor looks at me, shrugs and grins. 'It's all a bit of fun though, isn't it?'

Despite myself, I laugh. He looks about eighteen, and I suddenly want to be eighteen again too. I suddenly want to have unfeasible, youthful dreams and live them anyway because I simply don't know yet that they *are* unfeasible. 'I suppose if you look at it that way, it is,' I concede. 'But if it all goes wrong and you run out of money, it won't be a bit of fun any more.'

'If it all goes tits up, I can always go back to gynaecology. But I really don't want to have to do that.'

'Was it that bad?'

'Not really. But I've been living this safe life for so long, you know? I really needed to give myself this adventure. Do something a bit scary and challenging.'

'I understand that.'

'Mark says it's a mid-life crisis.'

I laugh. 'Well, that I can certainly understand.'

Frost is already forming by the time we reach La Forge. We step from the van and I glance west at the thick band of cloud obscuring what would normally be the setting sun.

'It's colder tonight,' Victor says, following my gaze and lightly stroking my back.

'It is,' I say. 'The air smells of snow.'

'How can snow smell? It's just ice. Ice doesn't smell.'

I shrug and start to follow him towards the house. 'I don't know, but it does. It's a sort of metallic smell.'

Victor unlocks the door and then sniffs at the air. 'Nope. Anyway, I hope you're wrong.'

I look around the desolate kitchen again and struggle to resist the wave of depression that hits me every time I step into the house – the house where Distira says I will never be happy.

'Can we sort out—' I start to say, as I follow Victor through to the bathroom.

'The range?' he finishes.

'No, well, *yes*, that too, but I was thinking about the—'

'The bathroom heater?' he volunteers.

'Yes.'

'Sure. I'll get on it tomorrow morning. I promise.'

After another lukewarm spray in the freezing bathroom, we dress in our best jeans and cleanest jumpers, then drive back down to the farm. Random wildlife leaps out in front of the van unnervingly every time we turn a bend. In fact, after the first few miles, there are so many that we start to keep tally. 'How come there are so many out tonight?' I ask.

'I don't know,' Victor says. 'I guess we're not usually out and about this late.'

By the time we reach Georges's place, I have counted three wild boar, five hares, two foxes, a bat, and bizarrely, in the middle of nowhere, a Siamese cat.

As we swing around to park the van, the front door to the house opens and Georges steps into the strip of light streaming across the courtyard.

'*Bonsoir,*' he says loudly, crunching across the gravel, opening my door and chivalrously holding a hand to help me down.

We kiss twice and then have a moment of confused pantomime where Georges tries to kiss me a third time and I miss the cue. I then attempt to lean in for the third kiss but Georges has already given up.

'*T'as raison*,' Georges says, '*C'est que deux fois par ici.*' *You're right, it's just twice around here.* '*C'est chez nous, à Toulouse, qu'on s'embrasse quatre fois.*'

I turn to Victor and say, 'Can you translate? I missed the second half.'

'He says he's from Toulouse. They kiss four times there,' Victor tells me.

'Yes, four time,' Georges says.

Georges shakes Victor's hand, and then heads back towards the house, saying, '*Venez, venez! Il fait froid ce soir. Ca sent la neige!*'

'Did he just say it smells like snow?' I whisper as I trot beside Victor towards the house.

Victor looks at me and rolls his eyes.

'I'll take that as a yes, then,' I laugh. 'I *told* you so.'

The property has a similar layout to our own: three buildings forming three sides around a courtyard area. The only real differences are that their main house has two storeys and their outbuildings, of course, have roofs.

The inside of the house is warm – I stroke a radiator as I pass by – but decor-wise it is almost as bleak as our own. The floor is covered in worn mock-tile lino, and the walls with chipped, swirly artex. The furniture is an eclectic mix of hand-me downs: a knobbly Louis VII buffet next to a chipped formica mock-wood wardrobe, and a metal serving trolley acting as a telephone table. It's not, frankly, a good combination.

Georges leads us into the lounge, which has the same lino as the hall, an almost identical sofa to Distira's brown monstrosity, and bare, picture-less walls.

'Please . . . sit,' Georges says in English, before vanishing, presumably to the kitchen.

'Déjà vu,' I say to Victor, who grins at me and pulls a face.

'I just hope we get some frozen *vol-au-vents*,' I laugh, but this time Victor frowns at me, a silent rebuke, and I think that I probably am sounding, and perhaps even *being*, a bit snobby.

'*Elle dit de venir là-bas*,' Georges says, reappearing in the doorway. *She says to come through.*

And so we stand and follow him down the junky hallway to the kitchen. A big tabby cat flashes by in the other direction and climbs the stairs behind us.

The kitchen also is almost an exact replica of Distira's place – worn formica kitchen units along one wall, a vast scrubbed farm table in the middle of the room, surrounded by random non-matching chairs.

But there are two differences here and these change everything. The first is that at one end of the room is a crackling log fire throwing heat and an orangey glow throughout the room. The second is the incredible smell of herbs and spices coming from the stove. This is not the smell of a shop-bought quiche in a microwave.

I cross the floor to embrace Myriam and note another difference, the many signs of life scattered untidily throughout the room: a pile of CDs next to an old hi-fi, a shelving unit stacked two deep with a mixture of spices and books, and a tobacco tin and three packs of king-size rolling papers.

'*C'est plus cosy ici, et comme ça je ne passe pas ma soirée toute seule*,' Myriam says, turning to kiss me while still stirring her stew. *It's cosier here. And this way I don't have to spend the evening on my own.*

Victor plonks the wine we have brought on the table and nods discreetly at Georges, now seated at one end of the table rolling a joint. Victor winks at me and I break into a grin. Warmth, wine, wonderful food and a joint. I reckon it's going to be a good evening.

The meal is a surprisingly relaxed affair. For some reason I imagined the French to be more formal about their dinner parties, but I suppose these are younger people with different rules. We simply push all the junk covering the table to one end and throw a folded tablecloth over enough of the table for the four of us to sit down.

Georges serves aperitifs; thankfully of factory-produced alcohol. Vodka and tonic for me and pastis for everyone else. And then, without a hint of embarrassment, he hands out one of the hugest joints I have ever seen.

'*On le fait pousser au grenier sous le Vélux,*' he explains. *We grow it in the attic underneath the Velux.*

Georges explains that it's dangerous to grow it outdoors as there are rumours that the helicopters that fly overhead are dope-spotters. Myriam lets it be known that she thinks this is utter rubbish, but they both agree that it's better to be safe than sorry.

The food, when it arrives – and the smoking of the joints does slow this process down somewhat – is simple but sumptuous. Goat's cheese on home-made bread dribbled with local honey and served on a salad, followed by their own chicken in red wine sauce with potatoes and French beans. It's simple fare, but the fact that every ingredient except the wine comes from their own farm changes everything. The goat's cheese, once toasted and gooey, tastes rich and tangy; the honey, from a guy down the road, tastes of lavender; and the chicken is so rich and meaty, it tastes more like pheasant. Dessert is a home-made tarte tatin with apples from their own orchard topped off with a squirt of cream from a tin – the only shop-bought ingredient I spot.

Mellowed by fabulous food, wine and the dope, the conversation flows easily. Myriam asks why we chose to move here, and Victor explains about his family links to the region. I don't think I have ever heard him speak for so long in French, and I notice again how different he seems, almost like someone that I don't know at all. He explains his idea of converting the outbuilding into accommodation, and both Myriam and Georges state in a very no-nonsense way that it will be hard to fill rooms in such a remote location.

And then, oh so subtly, Victor gets them to talk about how *they* make a living.

It turns out that Georges has about thirty different sidelines, including growing and bailing straw for local dairy farmers, cutting and selling firewood from a large chunk of forest they own, rearing and selling goats, milk and cheese. He sells to a number of small local supermarkets, and sets up a roadside stall on the tourist trail in summer. He sells cherries, apples and pears from his trees via a friend who goes to market in Nice. And as far as we can tell, all of this combines to *just* about allow the three of them to get by. Looking around, there are certainly no visible signs of material wealth here.

Victor glances at me, smiles weakly and raises an eyebrow, and I nod, acknowledging that I know what he is thinking and agree. His own plans are half-baked and need to be far more comprehensive if they are ever going to work. Making a living from the land is as hard today as it ever was, and we're not even halfway to understanding what is required.

Georges picks up a bottle of wine and attempts to fill Victor's glass for the third time but I pointedly ask him who is driving home and he thankfully – because I don't much fancy driving the van – declines the refill.

And then Myriam says, 'Shhh!' and points at the glass bay window at the far end of the room and we all turn to look. There, just two layers of glass away, an adult doe is standing. She is looking straight at us, chewing slowly and sniffing the air.

My mouth falls open. 'My God!' I whisper. 'How beautiful.'

Georges slowly stands and passes behind me. When he comes back into view, he is carrying a shotgun and my joy at seeing this beautiful creature turns to fear and revulsion at what might now happen.

My skin prickles with outrage as Georges loads the gun and edges out into the hallway.

I open my mouth to beg him not to kill it, but Victor grabs my leg beneath the table and I'm not sure if he is simply letting me know that he is here with me and understands, or if he is silently asking me to say nothing.

And so we sit in silence, watching and waiting for Georges to appear behind the doe and a shot to ring out. I stop breathing and my heart starts to race. At the precise moment that the air inside the house moves due to the opening of the front door, the deer sniffs the air, looks right and then left, and bolts into the blackness of the night. Secretly, silently, I will her to run like the wind, as far from Georges and his horrible shotgun as possible.

Georges returns with a half smile and leans the gun back against the dresser before slumping into his seat. '*C'est quasi impossible*,' he declares. '*Le temps que t'ouvres la porte ils sont partis.*' *It's just about impossible. By the time you open the door, they're gone.*

'Do you get a lot of deer?' Victor asks him as I slowly start to breathe again.

'Not here. Not in the farm. It's what, the third?' he asks, looking to his wife for confirmation.

'Yes, the third. In ten years,' she confirms. 'But they get them when they go hunting, don't you?' She turns to Victor. '*Tu chasses, toi?*' *Do you hunt?*

'No,' Victor says. 'No, I don't think I could.'

And I think, *Thank God for that.*

Georges then starts to talk about how many meals you can get from a deer and how good venison tastes, and so that they can't see my expression, I cross the room and peer out into the night.

Surprisingly, Myriam stands and crosses the room to join me. She lightly touches my shoulder and says, 'It's hard, but you'll get used to it,' and I reply that I suppose that I will and suddenly warm towards her for having understood what is going on in my head and coming to comfort me.

'It's very dark tonight,' I comment quietly.

'Yes,' she agrees. 'No moon. That's why all the animals are out. They feel safer.'

I tell her that we saw three wild boar on the road and she laughs and says that it's a good job Georges wasn't with us as he would *definitely* have shot them.

And then something catches the corner of my eye and I turn to watch a fleck of something drifting down. And then I see another, and another, and Myriam says loudly, startlingly, '*Ça y est, il neige.*' *That's it, it's snowing.*

Georges asks us if we have chains and Victor replies that no, we don't, but that we have snow-tyres.

'*Ça ne suffit pas,*' Georges says categorically. '*Il faut des chaînes.*' *It's not enough. You need chains.*

'But we'll be OK tonight, won't we?' Victor asks.

'If you leave now, you should be OK,' Georges says.

So, in a panicky fluster of thanks, goodbyes and promises to do this again soon, we're crossing the whitening courtyard then accelerating off through a snow-globe of drifting flakes.

'Are you OK to drive?' I ask. 'You're not too stoned? Or drunk?'

'No,' Victor says. 'I'm fine.'

'I love snow,' I say, aware that the dope is making it look even more magical than usual. 'Isn't it beautiful?'

'It is,' Victor agrees.

'But what happens if we get stuck?'

'We won't.'

'And if it snows a lot overnight and we can't get out tomorrow?'

'I don't think it will,' Victor says. 'But we can always get Distira to get us some supplies in her Russian tank.'

'I suppose,' I say.

'Georges and Myriam are really nice,' Victor says, squeezing my knee. 'I'm glad we met them. A real stroke of luck.'

'They are,' I agree. 'I couldn't believe it though when he started rolling joints. I mean, how could they know we wouldn't mind? Or call the police or something?'

'He asked me first. Georges asked me man-to-man if you'd mind.'

'But how did he know *you* wouldn't mind?'

Victor shrugs. 'Maybe I just look like a cool dude,' he says.

'And presumably I look like an uptight bitch?'

'Presumably,' he says, so I punch his arm.

'And what happened to the DIY superhero?'

'He couldn't make it, but he's going to call.'

'I missed that,' I say. 'I think I just zoned out on whole chunks of the conversation. It's quite tiring trying to listen in French.'

The snowflakes are huge now and their downward drift, combined with the motion of the van, makes them look surreal and ghostly as they spin past the headlights.

'God, I *love* snow!' I say.

'I'm not so keen on driving in it,' Victor says.

'No,' I say. 'But it isn't half pretty.'

'You're stoned,' Victor says.

'And so are you,' I snort. 'So just, you know, concentrate on driving!'

'I'm not stoned, actually,' Victor says. 'I only had a single drag at the beginning of the evening because I knew I was driving, so there.'

The next morning when I wake up, the first thing I notice through my dope-induced hangover is that the light in the van is different. Even through the orange curtains of the van, the interior seems somehow flashlight-bright. I then notice that it seems to be even more silent than usual this morning. No bird noise, no wind noise, no chainsaws or cars in the distance.

I listen to Victor's steady breathing, and then I remember the snow from last night and prop myself up so that I can peer beyond the curtain.

'Jesus!' I gasp, and I hear Victor groan beside me. Our muddy field has been transformed overnight into a Swiss ski station. The ground, the track, and every bit of junk are coated in a crisp coat of whiter-than-white snow.

I shuffle across the bed so that I can look out at the house, exhale deeply and smile. With a coating of wedding cake icing covering every horizontal surface, it looks incredibly pretty, amazingly romantic.

'Victor,' I say. 'Look! Just look!'

He groans again and reluctantly opens his eyes, then rolls onto his side and says, 'What is it? Snow?' He pulls back the curtain. 'Wow!' he says. 'I thought it was bright in here.'

'Isn't it beautiful? But we can't drive in that, can we?'

'Nope.'

'And if it doesn't melt, what do I do on Friday about getting to the airport?'

Victor pulls a face. 'I suppose we'd have to ask Distira

or Georges to take you. But my guess is that it will melt by then.'

'You're gonna need a Jeep or something to live here full time.'

'I know,' Victor agrees. 'I was thinking that last night.'

We're incredibly slow to start moving this morning, which I think is in part because we're tired and hung-over, but also because we're so in awe of the reborn landscape that all we want to do is lie side-by-side and stare out at the sparkling freshness of it all.

Victor manages to make coffee without folding the bed away and so we lie and sip and stare and occasionally chat. It's a beautiful moment.

'Last night was great, wasn't it?' Victor says quietly.

'Yes. They're really nice. I was pretty shocked when we got there though. The interiors are just so sixties.'

'I don't think they care,' Victor says.

'No. It's an entirely different mindset, isn't it? It wasn't until that deer appeared that I really got it. I mean, you could live in London and cover your walls with lovely paintings, and fill the house with Italian furniture, but you'd never see anything your whole life as beautiful as that deer peering in.'

'I think Georges saw it more as a free meat delivery,' Victor laughs.

'I'm so glad he didn't manage to shoot it. I don't think I could ever kill something that lovely. Could you?'

'I'm not sure,' Victor says. 'Maybe your point of view changes when you live somewhere like this.'

'But they're so gentle. They don't kill anything, they don't cause any harm. Why would you *want* to kill one?'

'Nor do cows,' Victor says. 'Or pigs, or sheep. But we eat them.'

'I suppose.'

I point towards the house, where a huge cat is jumping comically as it tries to cross the field without sinking into the snow. 'Look at that stupid cat. Whose is it?'

Victor shrugs. 'Distira's, maybe. Or a wild cat perhaps.'

'She looks pregnant,' I say.

'In winter?'

'I think cats can get pregnant any time. We should put some food out for her just in case.'

'If you want. I wanted to fix the chimney and get some heat going, but look at all the snow up there.'

'We could still put the electric heater in the bathroom.'

But neither of us want to leave the cosy warmth of the quilt, so for the moment we continue to lie there and watch the stillness of the landscape.

Just after 1 p.m., I am forced to leave the warm security of the van for the bathroom. I pull on my clothes and step down into the snow, which squeaks beneath my feet like clean hair. 'It's not even cold out here,' I declare, shouting as I close the van door, 'the sun's really warm!'

When I get back, Victor has folded the bed away and is making tuna melts for lunch.

'Can you save me a bit of tuna?' I ask. 'I want to put some outside for the cat, see if she takes it.'

Victor forks a lump of tuna onto a saucer, which I take and put outside the door.

'It's OK out there, isn't it?' Victor comments. 'Almost T-shirt weather.'

'In the sun it is,' I say. 'But you should try the bathroom.'

'Is it bad?'

'There was ice in the loo,' I say.

'You're joking.'

'It was only a thin crust on the top. But yes, there's actual ice.'

'Wow, I had better install the heater then,' Victor says.

'It is kind of urgent, I think.'

It only takes an hour to screw the new bathroom heater to the wall and run a cable to the fuse box. But even an hour in there is an hour too long. By the time we finish, my nose is running and my feet have gone numb from cold.

Victor switches the new heater on, and we stand and watch as it starts to glow. And then we both step forwards and pause, mere inches away.

'This isn't going to cut it, is it?' Victor says glumly.

'It'll be OK once the rest of the house is heated, but I don't think you can expect it to do much when everywhere else is minus five.'

'I can't face showering in here. It's too cold. If we could get that range lit . . .'

'I don't think you're gonna be able to get up there with all the snow on the roof.'

Victor sighs and shakes his head then says, 'Fuck it! We need heating now. I'll just have to be careful.'

And because there's something bold and manly about his sudden determination, something that secretly I have been worried might be missing from his psychological make-up – something absolutely necessary for a project such as this – I don't talk him out of it.

'I'll help you,' I say simply.

'Tuna's gone,' Victor comments, when he opens the front door.

'Poor thing,' I say. 'She must be starving.'

Fixing the chimney is a far easier task than we imagined. We carry a long but slightly rotten wooden ladder from one of the outbuildings to the side of the house, and I hold the base while Victor climbs. From the top it turns out that he can easily reach the top of the chimney stack, and when he, pulling a disgusted face, reaches inside to see what might be blocking the hole, his hand reappears holding a mass of balled chicken wire, presumably inserted to prevent birds nesting, but now completely clogged with soot.

'Let's hope that's what the problem was,' he says, casting it to the ground.

With the chimney unblocked, the range lights easily. It is such a vast mass of cast iron that it takes two hours and frequent restocking with wood before it starts to make any impression on the temperature in the kitchen, but we find ourselves sitting up against it to drink our tea, and then slowly moving back into the room.

By the time the sun sets, we are sitting at one end of the vast farm table drinking hot chocolate, and it suddenly dawns on me that we are, for the first time, living inside the house. Heat changes everything.

Victor loads more wood into the crackling fire, before

returning to sit opposite me. He takes my hand and says, 'This is nice. This is the first time I haven't wanted to return to the van.'

'I know,' I say. 'I was thinking that too.'

'I don't think we can get down to the shops tomorrow,' Victor says. 'So what do you think we should do?'

I look around the room and then sigh. 'I'll tell you what I *really* think we need to do.'

'Yes?'

'I think we need to fire up the laptop and do a spreadsheet of what we need to spend on this place, what money we have coming in, and how we think we might make a living.'

Victor pulls a face.

'You know on *The Apprentice*, or *Dragon's Den* or whatever, you'd have been fired by now for not having done that.'

Victor wrinkles his nose in a childish gesture of resistance.

I laugh. 'Why are you so loath to plan any of this?'

He shrugs cutely. 'I suppose the truth is that I don't really see how it can work. So I'm scared to work it out in case I have to give it up as hopeless.'

I nod. 'I can understand that. But I'm not sure burying your head in the sand is the answer.'

'I thought about it a lot before I left, but I just felt that if I looked at it too closely, I would realise that it was impossible, and I just ...' He swallows and grips my hand tightly. 'I really want this, CC. And I really needed to get out of London.'

I grip his hand in return and smile. 'I get that,' I say. 'And

I'm with you. But I still think a proper plan is the way to go.'

Victor slowly nods. 'OK. Get the laptop.'

Because we can't get out to any shops, we spend the next two days eating bizarre combinations of whatever food we have left, working on our spreadsheet, which isn't looking very optimistic, and improving the interior of the house in any way we can without supplies. This limits us to dragging any remaining junk from the house into the snow outside, and scrubbing every surface with bleach. Despite the fact that what the house really needs is gutting and refurbishing, at least this, combined with the heat from the range, removes the all-pervading smell of damp from the space. By now, we have pretty much moved into the kitchen and are using the van as no more than a bedroom.

When, on Thursday morning, the snow still hasn't melted – it seems, in its whiteness, impervious to the heat of the sun – I start to panic about getting to the airport.

'Yep, you're right,' Victor says, when I mention this. 'I'll go ask Distira if she can take you.'

'Are you sure that old banger can handle it?'

'They were designed for Siberia,' Victor says. 'I think it can cope with a bit of Mediterranean slush!'

I can think of few things I want less than to spend an hour in a car with Distira, but as one of those few things is missing my flight home and having to buy another one, I acquiesce.

Just as we are about to leave the house to go and ask her, a small white van appears, labouring its way along the track towards us. It pulls up in front of the house and a pot-bellied man gets out.

'*Bonjour*,' he shouts. '*Je cherche Monsieur Victor. C'est ici?*'

'*C'est moi*,' Victor says. '*Bonjour*.'

Monsieur Clappier doesn't look much like an angel but his appearance transforms so many things that it's hard to imagine that some higher power isn't involved. Firstly he informs us that the roads are totally clear from the end of our track down to Nice and that we'll have no trouble getting down in the van, thus sparing me the trip with Distira.

Then he wanders around the house in a matter-of-fact way, listing everything that needs to be done to the house and in what order. 'Well, we need to get this ripped out, replaster that and run the pipes for heating and hot water before anything else,' he says. Something about his manner, probably the fact that he seems totally unfazed by the project, is entirely reassuring.

Then our DIY superhero gives Victor the verbal quote of eight-thousand euros and two weeks for ripping out the kitchen and bathroom, installing wood-fired central heating, a basic bathroom suite and replastering the ceilings. Victor um's and ah's about this, but I can tell by his suppressed smile that he considers it to be something of a bargain.

And for his fourth and final act, Monsieur Clappier announces that he doesn't need Victor around for the work as he has a boy to help him. And this leads to the best surprise of all.

'You know what?' Victor says, once Monsieur Clappier has gone.

'Yes?'

'I might come to London with you.'

I close the front door and turn to face him, my expression a mixture of surprise and mounting joy. 'Really?' I say.

'He says he doesn't need me here for the next two weeks. I could come back with you, tie up all my loose ends, and return to a lovely stripped house with a bathroom and heating in two week's time.'

I stride across the room, grab Victor's head between my hands and kiss him full on the lips. 'That would be absolutely brilliant,' I say. 'I've been dreading going back alone.'

'Then it's settled,' Victor says. 'If you give me your flight details, I'll try to phone for a ticket.'

'Are you sure you don't need to be here? I mean, to check stuff, like what kind of bathroom suite he chooses, what kind of boiler ...'

Victor shrugs. 'I told him white and basic for the bathroom stuff. Bath, sink, toilet – hard for him to go wrong, isn't it?'

'I suppose,' I say. 'And the boiler?'

'He says he can add a back-boiler to the range, which will run radiators and hot water. Sounds perfect to me. I was worried we would have to rip it out.'

I nod, thinking that although I understand that this is an entirely normal point of view for a bloke – that a bathroom is a bathroom, that central heating is central heating – I'm not sure that it's one that I agree with. Realising that if I convince Victor of my point of view he won't come home with me, I rather dishonestly pretend to agree.

*

The next day goes by in a flurry of activity. We wake up early and move the contents of the van into a corner of the kitchen, then drop the key with Distira before nerve-rackingly slip-sliding our way to the end of the track. As predicted by Monsieur Clappier, the second we reach tarmac the roads are entirely clear though, which is a huge relief.

We drive into Nice so that Victor can withdraw half of the cash before meeting Clappier on the port to hand it over. Victor and he have a succinct discussion about the work Clappier is going to do in our absence, but I still fear that letting someone do such major works based on such lightweight instruction is a recipe for disaster. In addition, the handover of the cash – in a carrier bag – feels more like a drug deal than a prelude to any renovation work, and it's a struggle to avoid revealing my suspicion that we will never see Clappier or the money again.

We drive to the airport, where Victor buys an outrageously overpriced plane ticket and then retire to an airport restaurant for dodgy pizzas and expensive glasses of rough wine as a cushion for the elbow-jostle that is the easyJet boarding experience.

It's 5 p.m. when we get to Gatwick but it's already dark, and this combines with our tiredness and the drizzle to leave us both feeling more than a little grim.

We take the Gatwick express to Victoria and then, on my insistence, a cab to Primrose Hill. Victor suggests that the tube would be more economical *and* ecological, but I point out that as someone who has just spent £300 pumping the atmosphere full of carbon, he's not in the strongest position to force a public-transport-hater like myself into the tunnel-of-gloom. He capitulates immediately, which cheers me up. There was no way I was going to take the tube today, and I do like a man who knows when he's beaten.

As I attempt to insert my key into the flat door, it opens to reveal Mark grinning broadly and holding my recalcitrant cat, Guinness. On seeing me, the cat meows angrily, jumps from his arms and vanishes through to the kitchen.

'That cat is such a Friskies junkie,' Mark says, giving me a quick hug, then, 'Hello! They let you back in then?'

Something about his tone of voice catches my attention – something melancholy lurking behind the humour. I'm going to say something but he reaches to shut the door to the flat and is so startled when Victor, following behind, pushes it back open, that he actually shrieks. This makes us all laugh.

'Shit, you made me jump!' he says, leaning in to hug Victor as well. A hug that I can't help but notice lasts at least three times longer than my own.

'God, I didn't know you were coming,' Mark says, sounding almost love-struck. 'I haven't seen you for ages.'

In the end, it's rather lovely that Mark is here to meet us. Over glasses of wine, he excitedly interrogates us about the house, the snow, the nearby villages ... He wants to know every detail *in detail*. And through telling him, our own enthusiasm, previously dampened by tiredness and travel, is rekindled.

And then Mark turns to me and says, 'So? What have you decided?'

Mark is the only person who I have told what this trip is really about. He's the only one who knows that my whole future depends upon it. I glance at Victor, who looks at me intently, then nuzzle Guinness, to give myself thinking time, before saying, 'I think I'm going.'

'Really?' Mark looks at me wide-eyed.

'Yep. Don't sound so surprised.'

'I thought you'd come back and chicken out.'

I shake my head. 'No,' I say, reaching out for Victor's hand, and then feeling embarrassed about the gesture and withdrawing my hand again. 'No, I think it'll be fun. I think I need a change. And I want to be with Victor and, for now at least, that's where he is, so ...'

I glance at Victor again and he grins broadly before looking away in embarrassment.

'So when?' Mark asks.

I shrug. 'As soon as I can get everything sorted.'

'And Guinness?' he says, nodding at the cat, now leaving the room.

'Well ... Guinness is one of the things that needs to be sorted,' I say vaguely.

'You'll bring him, won't you?' Victor asks.

I sigh. 'I'd like to, but I think he'd hate the journey more than human language can express.'

'I could ask Iain,' Mark says. 'I mean, if you're really leaving him behind. If you're looking for a new home for him.'

I laugh. 'I hardly think Iain will want cat fur all over his minimalism,' I say.

'Iain's minimalism went out the window when he met me,' Mark says. 'And anyway, I love Guinness. And I wanted another cat since Madge died. I might not even give him the choice.'

Again, something in his voice, a cold edge, makes me wonder what's been happening in my absence.

'Are you OK?' I ask him. 'Or is there trouble at mill?'

'Yes, I mean no. I'm fine,' Mark says, but he glances at Victor as he says this, and I think I understand that whatever is happening, he doesn't want to discuss it in front of Victor.

'Anyway,' he says, standing. 'I should go and leave you two to do whatever loving couples do.'

'Like you don't know,' I say.

Mark ignores this comment and scoops his backpack from the floor. I spot some satiny material peeping out and identify it as the corner of a sleeping bag. Mark has been staying here in my absence.

'You can stay the night on the sofa if you can't be bothered to go home,' I offer.

'Nah, time to go home and sort stuff out,' he says with meaning.

'All *I* want is a bath. A hot bath in a warm bathroom and then bed.'

'Me too,' Victor says. 'I'm shattered.'

'So that's what loving couples do, is it?' Mark laughs.

After he has gone, Victor says, 'What's wrong with Mark?'

'I don't know,' I say. 'But I think I need to find out.'

SNUGGLING

It rains constantly for the entire weekend, but neither of us mind one bit. The luxury of being in a large, clean, warm space – of having hot water and a dishwasher and an amazing electronic device one can speak into to request pizza and a side of garlic bread – is quite simply heavenly.

We lie in bed till late, take baths that last so long that we have to empty half the water and top up with warm halfway through, eat, drink, and make love. Sometimes the love-making lasts ten minutes, and sometimes it takes hours. But as the rain lashes against the windows in a way that would have left me suicidal when I was single, this turns into one of the best weekends of my life.

Come Monday morning, the mental shock of having to wrench myself from our love-nest, of having to leave Victor's warm body beneath the quilt and head out into the gloom and hail (hail!) could hardly be overstated. After two weeks spending every moment with Victor, the wrench of being alone at 8 a.m. on dark, rainy tarmac – of having to fight my way through the polluted streets of London – feels like a torture plan devised by the CIA's top interrogator, a plan devised specifically to make me crack.

When I get to Spot On, the advertising agency I work for, I prop my dripping brolly in the stand, hang my drenched overcoat with all the others and cross the large open-plan floor before sliding into my seat. A couple of people look up at me and their expressions register a vague acknowledgement that I'm back after a break. As the computer starts up, I try to remember what I usually do here. Actually, what I *used* to do here feels more like it.

My mail program starts to download three hundred and seventy messages, and I watch them as they pop up and see that they are virtually all spam and that those that aren't are semi-spam – emails from agencies we use, begging for work. And then, unable to face an hour of deleting emails right away, I head to the kitchen for a mug of coffee before heading upstairs to see my friends in Creative.

When I walk in, Jude is holding a pantone colour chart up against a black and white poster of a yoghurt pot, apparently choosing a colour for the spots on his cow.

'Hello!' he beams as I walk in. He crosses to peck me on the cheek and then flicks through his pantone samples until he gets to the flesh tones. '4745 EC,' he says, holding one up against my cheek. 'Looks like someone has been somewhere sunny.'

I laugh. 'If only you knew.'

'You look well, anyway,' he says. 'How was it?'

'I feel well,' I say. 'Well, I did until I had to come back to work.'

'Post-holiday blues?'

'Yep.' I glance over at Mark's desk. 'Where's that other bloke who works here?'

'Oh, what's-his-face?' Jude mugs. 'He's up with Stanton and VB. And anyway, it's *worked*, not *works*.'

I frown. 'He's with both of them? What's he done?'

'Nothing,' Jude says. 'It's his last day.'

'You're joking,' I say. But as I say this, Mark enters the room, waving an envelope like a fan.

'P45,' he says, before pecking me on the cheek.

Though I knew that Mark was leaving the sinking ship that is Spot On, I had no idea that it was so soon. 'You didn't say,' I protest. 'You didn't say anything on Friday about this being your last day. Not one word.'

'I know,' he says, looking glum. 'I didn't want to bring anyone down.'

I glance over at Mark's empty desk. 'I thought your desk looked tidy for once.'

'D'you want to move up here?' Jude asks me, touching my arm imploringly. 'Keep me company? I don't think I want to sit here on my own.'

'I can't,' I say, catching Mark's eye, and realising that Jude doesn't know yet that I too have decided that I am leaving. Decided that I *may* be leaving. I frown as I internally struggle to work out which tense is the right one. 'You should move downstairs,' I say, to distract my brain from the question.

I turn to Mark again, who is sliding his P45 into a box on the floor that apparently contains the rest of his things. 'You're not leaving right now, are you?'

''Fraid so,' he says. 'Well, once I've been to Foyles and

back. I need a book on PPM. It's what they use at Archimedia.'

'PPM?'

'Progressive Project Management. And don't ask – I don't know. I haven't read the book yet.'

'But you're coming back here after Foyles?'

'Yeah.'

'So we can do lunch?'

'A last supper?' Mark says.

'All three of us?' Jude asks.

'Of course,' Mark says. 'Just don't get soppy.'

'Soppy?'

'Yeah. Don't make me cry.'

When I get home that night, Victor has prepared dinner. It's admittedly only two aluminium trays of M&S cauliflower cheese cooking in the oven, but walking through the door to a hug, a ready-made gin and tonic, a bowl of olives and the smell of melting cheese really does feel special.

'How was your day?' he asks me once my wet coat is off. I sit and sip my drink, then tell him about my dull day processing emails, about my funeral-like pub lunch with Mark and Jude, about asking Mark while Jude was at the bar if he had slept here, if he was having problems with Iain, (the answer to both questions was 'no') and about trying to talk about my holiday without telling Jude that I have decided, too, to quit our foundering ad agency.

'Have you had any thoughts about that?' Victor asks. 'I mean, the actual *when*?'

I shake my head. 'Give me a few weeks,' I say, 'and I'll start to get my head around it all.'

Victor nods vaguely. He looks unconvinced.

'I will!' I protest. 'I know you don't believe me but—'

'Hey, hey!' he interrupts, moving behind me and crouching down so that he can wrap me in his arms. 'I *believe* you,' he says, nuzzling my neck.

And I wonder at how amazing it is, that it doesn't really matter how dark or cold or rainy it is outside, it doesn't matter how boring or depressing your day might have been, if you have someone to snuggle with at the end of the day, someone like Victor, well, it's all all-right really, isn't it?

When I get home the next night, Victor has dinner waiting once again — this time a Waitrose chicken korma.

'Is that OK?' he asks, holding the packet up.

'Perfect,' I say, taking the gin and tonic from his hand, 'but I do worry about how you're going to cope without a ready-meal chill cabinet around the corner.'

'I can cook,' Victor protests. 'I'm just enjoying the convenience of it.'

But in truth I'm ragging him only to disguise just how much I'm loving coming home to drinks and food served by my own personal butler. This, I think, must be what having a wife used to feel like before the women's lib movement happened. And who could blame men for making *that* system last as long as it did?

Victor asks me about my day and so I tell him in detail about my meeting with Stanton and my business lunch, and he listens surprisingly intently.

It's not until I ask him about his own day and he replies that he went to the bank and Waitrose that I realise that he is living vicariously through me, that the dull role of house-husband has suddenly made *me* seem, sound, and indeed, feel, rather exciting by comparison.

'What about all of those ends you said you had to tie up?' I ask.

Victor shrugs. 'There aren't that many to be honest,' he replies. 'I went to the bank today to get them to send my statements overseas. I had to do that in person. And I have an appointment at the tax office on Friday. But other than that . . .'

I pull a confused face. 'You said you had *masses* of things to do,' I point out.

Victor grins at me, gormlessly, cutely. 'To be honest, I really just wanted to be with you,' he says.

He tells me that he wants to see his friend Jeremy one evening, a rather boorish college friend I briefly met over a Christmas pint.

Because I have no real desire to see Jeremy ever again, and because I honestly don't think that I can sit through another of his micro-brewery-rules-and-lager-is-poison monologues, I phone my friend Sarah-Jane so that Victor and I can coordinate our nights out to happen at the same time. SJ tells me that Thursday night would be perfect as they have made an offer on a house and we should be able to celebrate the acceptance of their mortgage deal.

As Victor phones Jeremy in the other room, I tidy the kitchen and think about these friendships – Jeremy and SJ and Mark – and wonder how much we will miss them once we are living six hundred miles away. In a way, Mark and SJ have been edging out of my life for a while now, caught up in their own relationships, driven to different locations by their own housing issues. I suppose that there isn't much that anyone can do to fight that. It's called getting older.

I move to the kitchen sink and stare out at the garden – at the now entirely dead Leylandii – and wonder if it now needs to be cut down before it rots and falls on someone's house. I stare at it swaying in the breeze and try to guess which way it would fall if it did.

'You OK?' Victor asks, making me jump at his sudden proximity. He slides his arms around me and I squash myself back against him. 'You look deadly serious,' he says, so I half-turn and smile up at him.

'Not at all,' I say. 'I was just miles away. Thinking about how things have changed. Thinking about that tree and wondering how long it will be before it rots. I suppose it needs to be cut down, now that it's dead.'

'Yes,' he says, leaning his head on my shoulder and looking out. 'Yes, I suppose it does.'

SEPARATE NIGHTS OUT

When I get to SJ's house, it is George, her husband, who opens the door.

'Ooh,' I say, stepping inside and handing him two bottles. 'I didn't know we were going to be graced with your presence.'

'Yep,' George says with a bemused expression. George always looks slightly embarrassed and it's really rather attractive. 'My travelling days are over now,' he explains.

He leads me through to the front room where SJ is lounging in a slovenly manner on the sofa while holding her bump and managing to look distinctly uncomfortable.

'Don't move,' I say, leaning over her and giving her a peck.

'Two bottles?' she says. 'You know I can't drink, right?'

'One of them is Appletiser,' I say. 'Anyway, you said it was a celebration.'

SJ smiles unconvincingly and glances over at George.

When I follow her gaze he sighs and raises an eyebrow. 'I'm in the dog house,' he says.

'Oh? How come?'

'They turned us down,' George says.

'The mortgage people?'

'Bloody banks,' SJ says. 'The cunts!'

'What happened?'

'I'll get a corkscrew. You'll need a drink for this one,' George says, heading off to the kitchen.

I sit next to SJ and take her hand in mine. 'So what happened?'

She shrugs. 'They changed their minds and withdrew the offer. That's all.'

'It's my fault,' George says, re-entering the room. 'I let slip that SJ is going to stop work after the baby arrives.'

SJ shakes her head in despair at her husband's ineptitude. 'All the paperwork was on the table,' she says. 'It was on the bloody table. All he had to do was keep quiet and sign the thing.'

'The guy asked how long it takes to commute from Amersham ...' George explains.

'The paperwork was right there,' SJ says, pointing to an imaginary desk just above her pregnant belly. 'There!'

'And I told him that it didn't make much difference, because I'm working from the High Wycombe office now, and SJ ...'

'I kicked him,' SJ says.

'She did. But I didn't get what she meant.'

'So he told them that I won't *need* to commute because I won't be *working* any more.'

'Ouch,' I say.

'By the time Big Mouth here had closed his gob,' SJ says, 'the guy had dragged all the paperwork back to his side of the table.'

'Because, what? The mortgage application was based on both your salaries?'

'Got it,' SJ says.

'But would you have been able to manage the repayments?'

'Course,' SJ says. 'But you know what they're like now. 'Getting a loan is like trying to get inside a nun's knickers.'

'So what happens now?'

'We've appealed,' George says.

'But it will be refused,' SJ adds. 'We know it will be refused.'

'SJ pointed out that they wouldn't even exist without all our taxpayer's money to prop them up.'

'I bet that helped,' I laugh.

'Exactly,' George says.

'Hey, I'm not the one who fucked it up,' SJ says with a mixture of sarcasm and real anger.

'I'm not sure that telling the guy that there's a reason why *wanker* rhymes with *banker* exactly helped though,' George says.

I turn to SJ. 'You didn't?!'

'Well . . .' she says. 'I was so fucking angry.'

George pours a glass of wine and starts to hand it to SJ but then withdraws it. 'Sorry,' he says, giving it to me instead.

'Can I have one?' she asks. 'Just one glass? It is exceptional circumstances.'

George shrugs and looks at me.

'Hey, don't ask *me*,' I say. 'That's your decision.'

'You *are* dating a gynaecologist,' SJ says.

'Ex.'

'He's your ex?' she says, her eyes widening. 'When did that happen?'

'No, he's an ex-gynaecologist. And despite what my mother would say, you don't absorb people's knowledge by simply spending time with them.'

'No, I suppose,' SJ concedes, holding out her hand for wine.

George reluctantly serves her with half a glass.

'So what happens now?' I ask. 'You just stay here?'

SJ shakes her head.

'It's too late, we've given notice,' George tells me.

'Then withdraw it!' I say. 'Surely you can withdraw your—'

'Too late,' SJ interrupts. 'It's already been re-rented. We have to be out by the end of the month.'

'Jesus!'

SJ pulls a face and tips her wine into my glass so that she can switch to apple juice. 'I don't want this after all,' she says. 'So yeah, looks like we'll just have to find a new flat to rent.'

'God, I'm sorry,' I say. 'I wish I could help, but I don't know any bankers. Except mine, and they're useless.'

SJ shakes her head violently as if to dislodge the whole sorry story from her mind. 'We'll sort it. Somehow. Anyway, enough of all that. How was France? How's it all going with the *lurve* machine?'

'He's fine,' I reply.

She pulls a face at this, and I suddenly wonder why I'm understating it. It's not as if SJ and George are lacking anything in the love department. It's not like they're going to be jealous.

'Actually, he's bloody brilliant,' I admit. 'I love him a bit more each day.' And so I start to tell her about the farmhouse and Distira, and Georges and Myriam ... I tell her about the holes in the roof, and the holes in Victor's half-baked plans, and about the snow and the icy bathroom.

Both she and George, as believers in love, are wonderfully enthusiastic about all of this and leave me in no doubt whatsoever about what they think I should do, but when they ask me how I am going to organise all of this, when they ask me when I am leaving, I subtly change the subject.

I do this not just because I don't know the answer to those questions, but also because I suddenly realise that I can turn their housing misery into something positive for all of us. It's a solution of such simple elegance that I can hardly believe it. But I don't say anything just yet. I need to run it by Victor first. And I can already imagine the grin on his face when I tell him.

It's just after midnight when I get back to Primrose Hill, and Victor isn't home yet.

I sit in the lounge, lit only by the orangey street-lamps outside, and sip at a cup of tea while stroking Guinness. I think about the ambience of the silent flat, a flat I have lived in for years. It feels safe. It feels reassuring. It's hard to believe that I might soon be moving.

After a while, I glance at the clock and feel a vague pang of unease that Victor isn't home yet, but immediately order myself to snap out of it. He's a fully-grown man, and I am not his mother. It's hard to remember sometimes that life isn't a film; that happiness doesn't always have to crash upon the rocks of misfortune for added dramatic effect.

I move Guinness to his favourite cushion, dump my cup in the sink, head to the bathroom to brush my teeth, and then gratefully slip under the covers, where I fall instantly asleep.

I'm woken by a heavy thud. I lie in bed, holding my breath and listening. Silence. And then a groan, a muttered 'fuck', and the sound of the kitchen door being opened with so much force that it whacks back against the cupboard behind it.

I yawn, climb out of bed and shrug on my dressing gown. The clock display reads 3.57 a.m.

In the unlit kitchen, I find Victor at the kitchen sink with his back to me. He is drinking water from my discarded mug.

'Are you OK?' I ask, and he turns to look at me, spilling his water in the process. His face looks swollen, as if it has been pickled in beer.

'Drunk. C'm'ere,' he slurs, opening his arms, again slopping water from the mug. But I don't move. I once dated an alcoholic, and it didn't end well. Ever since Ronan, drunks have made me nervous.

I rub my eyebrow and watch as he sips at the now-empty mug, peers into it in confusion, and then turns back to the sink for a refill.

Guinness is weaving around his legs in the hope of an extra serving of food.

'Did you have a good time?' I ask, a conscious attempt at being OK about this, a conscious attempt to fight my rising, if inexplicable, anger.

'A-one,' Victor says, turning the tap the wrong way before managing to close it off.

'I have to be up in three hours,' I say. 'So, I'll just head back to bed. You, um, sort yourself out and then come in when you're ready.'

Victor lurches in a strange way that I understand was meant to be a nod, had his hand not lost grip of the countertop. As he does this, he manages to stand on poor Guinness's tail. Guinness wails and runs from the room. I shake my head in dismay and follow him.

I try to sleep but there is too much adrenaline pumping through my system: a strange mixture of seething anger combined with real concern that he might hurt himself. And so I lie there and listen as he knocks a chair over, trips on the fallen chair and then stumbles against the wall. Finally, saying 'Shhh!' to himself, he staggers into the bedroom and then falls, face first and fully clothed, onto the bed beside me.

He lays an unbearably heavy arm across the small of my back and then shuffles to my side of the bed so that his head is against my neck. 'You're gorgeous,' he says. 'You know that?'

'Thanks,' I say, pulling a face at the pure ethanol stench of his breath. 'Don't you want to get undressed?'

But Victor is already snoring.

I lie like this for a few minutes before I realise that I don't want to sleep next to a fully clothed man with his shoes on, so *I* am going to have to undress him. Turning him over takes me three attempts; he seems twice as heavy as normal – the weight of the beer, perhaps.

Because I position him on his back to pull his trousers off, he starts to snore again, so I have to sit up one more time in order to pull him towards me so that I can roll him onto his side. This makes him smile in his sleep.

It takes me ages to get back to sleep, but at some point I must drift off, because the next thing I know it is morning.

I spend all day worrying about Victor's drinking. I reflect on the fact that it takes a very, very long time before you can truly say you know someone, because who can say how often Victor feels the need to get legless. Of course, I argue with myself, he just had too much to drink – that's all that happened here. And a guy is allowed, occasionally, to get drunk. Right?

But I know where dating a drunk can go. I know where that road can lead. I've had the bruises to prove it. So I'm allowed to feel uptight about it, too.

At 6 p.m., as I walk the last few hundred yards to the house, I decide that there is only one explanation for the fact that Victor hasn't phoned – he has plumped for the Big Gesture. I am fully expecting, as I insert my key in the door, to find bunches of flowers and piles of gifts on the other side.

Yet I find the flat in semi-darkness. I head through to the kitchen and find Victor sitting and nursing a mug of tea at the kitchen table. He looks up at me and smiles half-heartedly. 'Hiya,' he mumbles.

I don't answer. I hang my coat up and cross the room

so that I can lean against the countertop and glare at him.

'How's the hangover?' I say coldly.

Victor wrinkles his nose. 'Pretty bad.'

I only just restrain myself from saying, 'Good.'

'I bet,' I say instead.

'I had way too much to drink,' Victor volunteers, looking into my eyes with a vague air of puzzlement. 'They had a lock-in.'

I nod. 'Nice.'

'You look like you're a bit angry,' Victor says.

'Not really angry,' I say. 'More concerned.'

Victor nods slowly, and then starts to look less contrite and more annoyed. 'Look,' he says. 'Please don't give me a hard time here. I had too much to drink. It happens. I spent the whole day with a hangover.'

'You were blind drunk,' I say.

'Did I . . . say something horrible? Did I upset you?'

'No,' I say. 'It just . . . well, it makes me uncomfortable. I had a boyfriend once. He drank a lot. It got nasty.'

Victor nods. 'I didn't get nasty though, did I?' he asks.

I shake my head. 'No,' I admit.

He bites his lip and suppresses a smirk.

'I'm not laughing,' I say, but I realise that I soon will be, and that it's probably the only way to move beyond this.

'No, no, I see that.' But in spite of himself, Victor starts to grin and it takes all my effort not to smile back. 'Look, I'm sorry,' he says, standing, crossing the kitchen, and wrapping his arms around me. 'I'm really sorry.'

I sigh. I'm not giving in just yet.

'You're all rigid,' he comments.

136

'I know. I'm still angry.'

'I thought you weren't angry. I thought you were concerned.'

'Then I'm still concerned,' I say.

Victor pulls me tighter and nuzzles my neck. 'Still really concerned, or just a bit concerned? Or just pretending to still be concerned for maximum pain-infliction?'

'Pretending for maximum pain-infliction,' I confess.

'Well, that's your right,' he says. 'But I am sorry. What can I do to make up for it?'

'You could start by making dinner, I suppose. I'm starving.'

'I was thinking fish and chips,' he says. 'I'll go get it if you want.'

'Too right you will,' I say. 'And you can get a piece of fish for Guinness, as well. You owe him an apology. You stood on his tail.'

'Oops. Three bits of cod coming up.'

From that point on, everything is officially back to normal with Victor. I say officially, because in truth, it isn't.

I'm sure those who have never been in a relationship with an abusive alcoholic would think that I'm exaggerating, being absurd even, but as the days go by and as Victor's return to France inexorably approaches, I find myself watching him from the corner of my eye, looking for signs, suddenly, unexpectedly, suspicious.

And I find myself *not* telling him about my idea of renting the flat to SJ and George. And this *not* telling him really is a new thing for us, because it feels like a lie.

It indisputably becomes a lie as we are leaving the house for a final meal out on Saturday night.

I'm hunting around the flat for the keys that I have mislaid, and Victor asks, 'So have you had any thoughts? About this place?'

'Umm,' I mutter distractedly, pretending to be too lost in my key-hunt to hear him.

'Have you had any thoughts about whether you want to sell this place or rent it out?'

'No,' I say. 'Not really.' You see? A lie.

To distract both Victor and myself from this dissimulation I say, 'Do you think you could stop standing there like a big wet lump and help me look for my keys?'

Victor raises an eyebrow, sighs, and starts to half-heartedly lift the cushions on the sofa so that he can peer beneath.

Once the keys have been found – they had fallen from the kitchen counter into the vegetable rack – I lock the flat door and then catch Victor's arm as he starts to head down the hall.

'Sorry I was grumpy,' I say.

He pauses and turns back to look at me, both frowning and smiling at the same time.

'Grumpy?' he says.

'When I lost my keys. Losing things drives me insane.'

'I didn't notice, to be honest.'

'Don't say that,' I laugh. 'Anyone would think I spend all my time calling you a wet lump.'

'Oh, *that*,' Victor says with a shrug. 'Didn't even register.' And then he pecks me on the cheek and heads for the front door.

FAST TRACK

When I get home on Monday night, I have spent most of the day wondering how it will feel to be back home without Victor's presence. It feels exactly the same as the last time I was here without him. It feels awful.

And so I sit, suddenly too miserable to even step out of my work clothes, and stare out at the dark garden and wait for Victor to phone.

Eventually, just before nine, hunger snaps me from my reverie, so I check the freezer and am pleased to find that Victor has left it stocked with his trademark ready-meals. Even that vague presence, that proof of his existence, feels like something to cling to.

I have just dumped a tray of prawn madras in the microwave when the phone rings.

I run to the phone and answer breathlessly, 'Hello? Victor?'

'Darling!'

'Oh, hi, Mum!'

'Don't sound so disappointed, dear. It's rude. Especially when someone's phoning long distance. And even more so when that person is your mother.'

It's proof of how distracted I have been these last weeks that I haven't thought about Mum for weeks. Pre-Victor, my mother, and more importantly her romance with a twenty-three-year-old Moroccan called Saddam (who she has rebranded Adam when in Europe, for obvious reasons) was pretty much the only thing I could think about.

'Sorry, Mum, it's not ... It's just that I thought it was Victor. I was waiting for him to call.'

'Is he back in France? I wasn't sure if you were back home yet yourself, but I suppose normal life has to resume at some point, doesn't it? Or maybe it doesn't. Anyway, I'm not sure when we last spoke. Had I been to Imsouane yet? I hadn't, had I? Well, it was ever such fun to start with, dear. We rented a Jeep thingie and drove cross-country. They had cooked a big chicken tagine and all of Saddam's relatives came. There were eighteen of us all together. And a cousin was there and he was playing an instrument. A sitar, I think it is. Maybe not actually. Anyway, Saddam was just about to announce that we were going to get married when it all went horribly wrong, dear. You'll never believe it.'

This is the first sign of discord that my mother has ever let slip, so it snaps me right back into the moment. I even forget that she's hogging the line and potentially preventing me from talking to Victor. 'What went wrong?'

'Well ... Saddam's uncle Ilias – a terribly good-looking chap, the spitting image of Saddam, only older, of course – he took me to one side to talk to me.'

'He didn't make a move on you, did he?'

'No. I did wonder myself, but no. He asked me if I intended converting to Islam ...'

'You're not, are you? Tell me you're not converting to Islam, Mother!'

'Well, of *course* I'm not, darling. What do *you* think?'

'I don't know with you; these days anything's possible.'

'I spent half my life with a Catholic, darling, and I still don't subscribe to all *that* mumbo-jumbo. Do you really think I'm going to start wearing a what-do-you-call-it, a burka?'

'No, OK. I don't think you *have* to wear a burka, but anyway, what happened?'

'Well, I told him that I wasn't going to. Convert, that is.'

'Right.'

'And he asked me why. And I told him the same thing I just told you.'

'What? You didn't tell a Muslim that Islam is a load of mumbo-jumbo, did you?'

'Yes. Of course. I'm too old to beat around the bush, dear. You know that.'

'And what did he say?'

'Well, he didn't understand what I said, but luckily, or rather *unluckily*, Saddam's brother did, so he translated for him.'

'And?'

'Ilias punched him.'

'He *punched* him?'

'Yes.'

'He punched his own brother for translating?'

'Yes.'

'Talk about blaming the bearer of bad news.'

'Well, quite. It was all very *Carry On*. They seem to be a bit like the Italians, dear. It reminded me of Rome.'

'The Italians?'

'Yes, you know, lots of arm-waving and shouting. And then Saddam got involved and things got really nasty. Ilias punched him, too.'

'He hit Saddam?'

'Yes. He split his eyebrow. And then Ilias stomped off down the track and his wife and children all got up from dinner and ran after him, and then Saddam's mother ran after *them*. She's a lovely woman. She should have used a bit more face cream over the years, really, as what with all that sun she's gone a bit like a prune, but I suppose it's too late now.'

'Yes, Mum. And?'

'And what?'

'Well what happened next?'

'Well, I took Saddam off to the car because I had some plasters in my bag, and then, well . . . we just sort of decided to leave.'

'You left?'

'Yes, we just drove away and left them all to it. We had to drive through them all, fighting and arguing, but they were so busy shouting, I don't think they even realised that it was us.'

'God, that's awful, Mum. Is Saddam OK?'

'Yes, absolutely fine. He's a brave little soldier.'

'Right,' I say, grimacing at this poignant reminder of their age difference. My mother used to call Waiine a 'brave little soldier' when he was sick as a child.

'So what happens now?' I ask.

'Well, I don't think we'll be visiting Ilias in a hurry.'

'No.'

'What do you *mean* what happens?'

'Well are you going to call the wedding off?'

'Of course we're not calling the wedding off.'

'You'll have to at least postpone it, though, won't you?' I say hopefully. 'At least give them time to get used to the idea.'

'Saddam says it's best if we don't tell them about the wedding.'

'How can you get married without telling his family? Seriously, Mother!'

'Well, Saddam is very zen, dear. He likes to take the easy path. Which is terribly relaxing after your father, I can tell you.'

'But you can't get married and just not tell anyone, surely?'

'We'll see, dear. We haven't really talked about it. Anyway, enough of me. How was France?'

I'm a little shocked at this sudden switch, because, for once, I would rather talk about her. 'France?'

'Yes. Sandwiched between Spain and Italy and ...'

'Oh, lovely. A bit rustic.'

'You don't know what rustic means, darling!' she says. 'You know they only had one tap in that whole house ...'

Once Mum has finally finished telling me about Saddam's mother's house, and rerun various juicy events of that day past me one more time, I hang up and check my voicemail for messages from Victor, but there are none.

I have just tipped my dinner on a plate when it rings.

'Ahah! So who were *you* on the phone to?' Victor asks.

'My mother.'

'Your *lover*?'

'My *mother*. I thought it was her again, phoning back for round two.'

'You were arguing?'

'No. Not really. I always feel like I have been through a few rounds of boxing by the end of a conversation, though.'

'How is she?'

'Oh, you know. Mad. She ... Actually, you know what, I don't want to talk about her.'

'OK.'

'How is the house? Is it all toasty and warm?'

But the news from France is depressing. Distira, it seems, lost Victor's keys and was unable to let the workmen into the house.

'So the stuff's all just piled outside the door with plastic sheeting on it,' Victor explains glumly.

'Clappier didn't do *anything*?'

'Nothing. But he's starting tomorrow.'

'God, that's awful! And did she find the keys?'

'Nope. I had to break a window to get in myself.' Victor sighs deeply and his breath rattles against the mouthpiece.

'But you tried to phone him. If he had answered ...'

'I know. He said his mobile was flat and he forgot to charge it.'

'That sounds like bullshit.'

'I know.'

'But he's definitely starting tomorrow?'

'Yep.'

'So come back. Come back while he does the work.'

'I can't. There's too much to do here. And I want to make sure it all happens.'

'Of course,' I say. 'I just feel so miserable when you're not here.'

'I know you do. But it's not forever, is it? Anyway, how was your day?'

'Boring,' I reply. 'And I felt depressed all day knowing that you weren't going to be here when I got home.'

'So what does that tell you?'

'I know, I know. That I need to get my finger out, but . . .'

'But you need time,' Victor finishes. 'And that's fine,' he adds, sounding vaguely patronising. 'But if you need time, then at least try not to feel miserable about it. It's all down to you. You're doing exactly what you want. No one is imposing anything on you. So enjoy it. Because I don't want to think of you all miserable on your own, do I? That doesn't help anyone.'

It's my turn to sigh. Because the truth is that I can't enjoy it, because it *isn't* what I want to do. Which of course raises the question of why I'm doing it. Sometimes trying to understand your own motivations is as challenging as understanding a complete stranger's.

A silence ensues and then I surprise myself by saying, 'I've had an idea, though.'

'Yes? What's that then?'

And so, ten days after it first occurred to me, I finally tell Victor about SJ and George and my flat solution.

*

I barely sleep at all that night. I lie in bed staring at the ceiling, listening as the central heating creaks and Guinness, apparently untouched by the drama, snores.

I try to control my thoughts, but fail. I think about Victor in the van in France and wonder if he is sleeping, or if his own mind is racing. I wonder if he feels hopeful, or excited or scared about the possibility that I might be able to join him sooner than planned. And I think about just how soon this could happen if it works out. Because SJ and George need to be out of their flat by the end of the month. Which would push the rate of change well beyond my comfort zone.

I wake up at 4.45 a.m., which means that I have slept for less than three hours. I try to go back to sleep, but at 5.30 a.m. I give up and force myself to get up instead.

Breakfast and a shower provide a brief boost to my energy levels. But by the time I get to Spot On, I feel as if I have spent the night drinking and been dragged to the office backwards, through fields.

Our newest anorexic, would-be-supermodel receptionist – they change often, but always look the same – greets me with, 'Victoria is looking for you.'

'Morning, Sheredeen,' I say. Where do these girls' names *come* from, I wonder.

'Sorry. Morning,' she says, holding out a wodge of post for me.

'VB is already in?'

'Yep. Got here before I did.'

'Right,' I say, taking my post and turning towards the stairs. 'Thanks.'

Meetings with the aggressive Victoria Barclay are generally about as pleasant as a weekend visit to Guantanamo Bay. This morning, after three hours sleep, I wonder if I can cope with it at all.

I grab a coffee, down it, and then pour another one before returning to my desk. I start to sort through the weekend delivery of spam sitting in my inbox – pheromones to attract men and fifteen different diet/weight-loss/girdle solutions – but I have barely started the important business of reading about the Shrink-Me Waist-Witch™ when my phone rings.

'Good morning, CC,' VB says. 'Can you come upstairs? We need to talk.'

When I get to her office it's empty, so I check our MD Peter Stanton's office and find them both sitting on the far side of his desk.

'You wanted to see me?' I ask.

Peter Stanton looks up and claps his hands enthusiastically. 'CC!' he says.

VB simply points at the seat and says, 'Please. Sit!' Her expression is a mixture of hungry anticipation and hatred – she looks as if she's about to wrestle me to the ground so that she can drink my blood.

'Victoria and I have been thinking,' Stanton begins.

'About the workload,' VB continues.

'Yes, it's bad, I know,' I say.

'And it's not getting any better,' Stanton says, wringing his hands. 'We lost ManIn to Archimedia.'

'The razor people?'

'Yes. The news just came in.'

I wonder if Mark is responsible for that particular

defection, and I wonder if Stanton and VB know that Archimedia is where Mark went.

'What we *have* got, potentially, is a much bigger deal with Unibrand.'

'I didn't know we were even talking to Unibrand,' I say, 'Unless, of course . . .'

'Yes,' VB says. 'They're buying Cornish Cow.'

'Oh, I see.' Cornish Cow is the only client that Spot On have had that I have ever refused to work for. Disguising their horrible factory farming methods as 'the next best thing to organic' – the chosen tag-line – is just one step too far for me.

'They're rebranding their entire Dairy-Lite range to Cornish Cow,' she continues. 'That's over one hundred product references that will need redesigning and readvertising.'

'Gosh. And we've got that in the bag?'

'It looks like it. But you see our problem,' VB says, forcing a smile which looks more like a death rictus.

'Yes, I see your problem,' I say.

'Only it's become more *your* problem than ours now, hasn't it?' she says, with more than a hint of menace.

VB goes on to explain that the only project they need me to run right now is Cornish Cow, and that, although she understands my concerns about their farming methods, she is surprised at how little concern I have been showing for my fellow workmates, their wives and children, and, indeed, the health of the business.

By the time I leave the office, their alternate good-cop/bad-cop routine has made things pretty clear. Either I contribute to disguising Cornish Cow's misery-farms as pseudo-organic or leave my desk to someone who will. The whole thing feels like a conspiracy to eject me from my life.

The first thing I do on returning to my desk is to phone SJ at her workplace – the Macmillan Cancer Trust.

'Hiya,' she says, the second she realises that it's me. 'Guess what! We've found a flat! Just in the nick of time.'

My heart performs a strange flutter, no doubt the combination of its sinking due to the fact that my instant solution has just been trashed, and a strange relief that this phone call isn't going to be the final push on the button that launches the ejector-seat after all.

'It's only one bed,' she continues. 'And it's in the wrong end of Peckham, but . . .'

'Is this to buy, or to rent?'

'Oh, rent. I would never buy in Peckham. But it's only seven-fifty a month. We don't have time to buy now.'

'Right,' I say.

'Don't sound like that. I know it's Peckham but it's good news. I thought we were gonna have to stay with George's mum! Imagine!'

'No, that's great,' I say.

'What's wrong?' SJ asks. 'You sound funny.'

'No, everything's fine.'

'Has Vicky-Vick gone back to France? Is that it?'

'Yes,' I say. 'Yes, that's it.'

'Why did you phone? You phoned for something, didn't you?'

'Never mind,' I say. 'It doesn't matter now. So! New flat. Have you signed yet?'

'George is on his way to the estate agent's with a bank cheque thingy now.'

'Right.'

'CC!' SJ says. 'Tell me what's wrong. I know you like I made you, and something is wrong.'

And so I tell her what I had been about to suggest. When I finish, she is so silent that I wonder if the line has gone dead.

'SJ?'

'Hang on,' she eventually says. 'I need to call George. Now.'

I sit staring blankly at the Shrink-Me Waist-Witch email for seventeen excruciating minutes, until finally SJ phones me back.

'Sorry,' she says. 'He was in the tube. Why they can't make phones that work in tunnels is a mystery to me. They work in the Paris metro. All the Frenchies were blabbering away when we were there. Anyway, he's outside the estate agent's right now. He wants to know if this is definite.'

'Yes,' I say. 'Yes, I think so.'

'It needs to be, like, definite-definite. Not I-think-so definite. Because he was just about to hand over the cheque.'

'Yes. OK. It is. It's definite-definite.'

'And the rent?'

'We could call it the same.'

'What? Seven-fifty? Your place is in Primrose Hill. You could charge well over a thousand. More like two, probably.'

'I know, but it's you. And I could leave a bit of stuff there. And you could look after Guinness for me, couldn't you, so he wouldn't have to move.'

'Oh, that'll be a clincher for George. He wanted a cat, but I said no.'

'And you'd let me sleep on the sofa from time to time, if I come back?'

'Of course! But you know we need to move by Monday night?'

'Monday? You said the end of the month.'

'Well that *was* the deadline, yes, but because the new place was free and George is on holiday next week, and because the landlord of our current place wants to repaint it, Monday suited everyone.'

'Jesus, SJ! Monday?'

'That's too fast for you, isn't it? I know how you like to plod.'

'I do *not* like to plod.'

'You so do.'

'But yes. It's fine. I have to check something first, though. Can you ask George to wait five more minutes?'

'He's already late,' SJ says. 'He needs to get into work.'

'If he wants a flat in Primrose Hill with a cat for seven-fifty a month, tell him to wait. SJ, you do want this, don't you? You're not doing it just for me?'

'Don't be daft!' SJ says. 'Where would you want to live? Peckham or Primrose Hill?'

'So tell George to wait for ten minutes.'

'You said five.'

'I'll try to be quick.'

And so it comes to pass that by eleven on Monday morning, I have not only rented my flat out but also resigned from my job, negotiated early departure and booked a collection of 'up to three cubic metres' of my stuff by a storage company.

As I pick up the phone to call Victor, I notice that my hands are shaking. That could be lack of sleep, or too much coffee, or a combination of both. But it isn't. It's the sheer terror of having things change too quickly. For a plodder like me, this is way too fast.

But Victor doesn't pick up. When he still hasn't responded to my message by the time I get home, I phone his aunt's house and leave a message in dodgy French that he should call me as soon as possible.

And then I start walking around the flat, followed by about-to-be-abandoned Guinness, as I make a list of what to take, what to leave behind, and what to put into storage. And I try to ignore the rising quell of panic provoked by the realisation that there's no going back now.

It's not until eleven the next morning that Victor and I finally get to talk.

'Hey, sexy lady,' he says, in tone that indicates he has no idea what I'm about to tell him.

'I stayed up late last night waiting for you to phone me back,' I say, my tone harsher than I intended.

'Sorry, my mobile's out of credit,' he says. 'And it doesn't even let you check the messages unless you have credit. Tight bastards, French phone companies.'

'I left a message with Distira, too,' I say.

'Really?' Then I hear Victor in French, presumably to Distira, '*Est-ce que CC a laissé un message hier?*' *Did CC leave a message yesterday?*

Distira's reply is too distant for me to hear, but Victor eventually says, 'She forgot. Sorry about that.'

Losing keys, forgetting messages ... I think. And, as if to answer the thought, Victor whispers, 'She's getting old. Anyway, the good news is that Clappier—'

'Victor!' I interrupt. 'If I called you on your mobile *and* on Distira's phone, it's because I have some urgent news myself!'

'Oh, OK,' Victor replies, sounding put out. 'I thought you'd be interested to hear how—'

'I am, but for once my news is more exciting. Because I'll be able to see the progress you've made with my own eyes, and sooner than expected.'

'You're coming back?'

'Yep.'

'When?'

'Tuesday.'

'Next Tuesday?'

'Yes. Tuesday.'

'Wow, that's good,' Victor says, sounding less thrilled than I had hoped. 'How long for?'

'As long as you want.'

'As long as I want? I don't get it. Oh! SJ and George want the flat, do they?'

'Yes, but they have to move by Monday, so it's brought everything forward a bit. We're all going to have to share for one night, then I'll be leaving on Tuesday.'

'What about your job?'

'I quit my job. My last day is Friday.'

'Wow.'

'Sound happy,' I say. 'Please try to sound happy, because you're scaring me.'

'Oh, I am, I'm just a bit shocked. What about your notice period and all that?'

'I negotiated a quick departure. And I have two weeks' holiday to take, so ...'

'Are you sure about this?'

'Of course I'm *sure* about this,' I say, aware that I'm starting to sound angry. I need to try to get a handle on that.

'Well, it's a big decision. That's all I mean. I'm just a bit stunned, that's all.'

Victor's tone is so far from the enthusiasm that I envisaged that I'm momentarily lost for words.

'Hello?' he says after a few seconds.

'I'm still here,' I say.

'And now I've upset you.'

'No. No you haven't. Well you *have* ... But look – and I mean this – if you're having second thoughts about wanting me there, then now is the time to say. Actually, yesterday was the time to say, before I quit my job. But now is still better than next week.'

'CC ...' Victor begins.

'But if you don't want me there next week ...'

'CC.'

'Then please just say so now, and I'll try to cancel ...'

'CC!' Victor shouts.

'What?'

'You aren't pre—'

'What?'

'Nothing.'

'Pre-what?'

'Really, nothing.'

But I know what he was going to say. He was going to ask if I am premenstrual. And what's really bloody annoying is that I am.

'You're getting hysterical,' he says. 'So just stop for a second.'

'I am *not* getting hysterical! And it's got *nothing* to do with my period.'

'No. Sorry. You're getting upset then. Your voice is wobbling all over the place.'

Even I can't deny that.

'You need to listen to me,' Victor says. 'You're just not hearing me.'

I take a deep breath and then sigh. 'OK, I'm listening,' I say.

'I am over the fucking moon that you're coming so soon. I'm just concerned that it's too soon. Not for me, but for you. You said you needed time. So I'm worried that you're pushing this too fast for my sake, when you don't have to.'

'But it's not just for you. That's not the reason it's all so sudden. SJ needs the flat now, and it's a perfect solution for me, and for Guinness. And at work they basically told me to work for Cornish Cow, that company I hate, or resign. So it's like a perfect storm.'

Victor laughs.

'What? Don't laugh at me,' I say. 'So perfect storm isn't the right simile or whatever, but—'

'I'm laughing, you stupid sausage, because I'm happy,' Victor says. 'People do that when they're happy.'

'Did you just call me a stupid sausage?'

'I did.'

'I'm not sure how I feel about that.'

'About the same as I felt about being called a big wet lump.' Victor laughs again. 'Oh, hang on.' In the background I hear him addressing Distira. *Tu vois, Tatie? Elle vient! Mardi prochain.*

'What was that?'

'Just telling Distira that you're coming.'

'It sounds like she didn't think I would come.'

'No, she didn't, as it happens.'

'Why?'

'How would I know? You can ask her when you get here.'

'I will,' I say.

'CC!' Victor says. 'Stop picking fights.'

'I'm not,' I say. 'Am I?'

'A bit.'

'Oh.'

'Everything's good. So calm down.'

'You're right. I'm sorry. I didn't sleep much, that's all. So are you sure you're happy?'

'Yes.'

'Should I drive or fly?'

'Fly. Definitely.'

'But I can't bring much stuff if I fly.'

'There's nowhere to put "much stuff" yet.'

'OK. So I just fly down and then come back for the rest later on.'

'God, I can't believe it,' Victor says, laughing again.

'No,' I say, attempting, but failing, to laugh myself. 'No, nor can I.'

My period comes the very next morning. Though far lighter than normal, it brings with it the usual sense of relief. That this feeling of calm manages to dominate despite everything that is going on in my life, is proof, if any were needed, of the power of hormones.

For the first time in years comes sadness at the realisation that I'm not pregnant. I reason with myself that with everything that we need to do, later is probably better, but it seems that the hormones are shouting almost as loud as reason.

My last three days at work pass in a whirlwind of activity, much of it admittedly more my own personal arrangements than anything to do with Spot On. But between having to organise a hundred things for myself, take trips to the shops to buy sensible winter clothes, three months supply of make-up and a huge wheeled suitcase to carry it all, *and* say goodbye to every client, I hardly have time to worry whether I'm doing the right thing. The wide-eyed jealousy of my work colleagues, when I tell them, helps erase any remaining doubt.

On Friday night, seven of us meet for a goodbye drink at The Ship in Soho. It's all very low-key, and, to be honest, a bit frigid, so I phone Mark to see if he's in the neighbourhood. As he is in Compton's, just down the road, he comes to join us, but even with him present, the contrast to our wild Friday nights of old times couldn't be more marked.

Despite the fact that some of us have worked together for seven years, within an hour every one of my work colleagues, except Mark and Jude, has headed elsewhere to their own Friday night rendezvous.

When Mark receives a text from Iain informing him that he has arrived home, he too starts visibly pining to get away and the fifth time he checks his iPhone, I kiss him on the cheek and tell him, 'Just go!'

With Jude not drinking because of a cycle race on Sunday, there really doesn't seem to be any point continuing, so we too say our goodbyes.

And the truth is that all of this suits me fine. My work colleagues already feel strangely like part of the past, and Mark has fallen so far into coupledom these days that there's barely enough of him left sticking out for me to grab hold of. And even I would have to admit that a crazy night of drinking – which was pretty much all we ever used to do – is now the last thing on my mind. All that I want to do this evening is sit in my lounge with my cat and make the most of everything that, so very soon, will be hundreds of miles away.

It's amazing how, at certain times, life moves on in a leap and you find yourself looking back at everything you had only to discover that it was all about as important, all about as substantial, as candy-floss.

On Saturday morning, the storage trailer is delivered. Annoyingly, the nearest parking space is about one hundred yards away, so I have to trudge back and forth through drizzle as I remove all of my worldly possessions and stack them in the lockable trailer. As I do, the flat rapidly ceases to be mine in any meaningful way. It's astounding just how little you have to remove from a place for this to be so. Once the books and knick-knacks have gone, it feels like little more than an empty shell, a memory of a flat I once had, a place where my life once happened.

On Monday, SJ and George turn up with a van and start to refill the void with their own mixture of eclectic ethnic objects, every item of which Guinness sniffs thoroughly. I wonder what image his mind creates from the deeply lodged odours of the African earthenware pot he seems so obsessed with. Whatever it is, it makes his tail go all bushy.

Their previous flat being furnished, SJ and George don't have many large items, so within two hours we have finished.

SJ can barely believe her luck at being able to live in Primrose Hill, and George is starting a fresh love affair with Guinness, who doesn't seem to know what has hit him. They are both, in short, on fine form.

And despite the stresses and strains of everything that is going on here and everything that is happening tomorrow, it all feels fabulously funky. It's all impromptu and youthful, and I wonder if shaking everything up and cutting away all of the trappings was, in fact, all that I really needed these past years. I wonder if, perhaps, it was even more important than finding a boyfriend.

That Monday night, spent eating pizza amid a sea of boxes, turns out, unexpectedly, to be a wonderful moment of friendship, the kind of moment in fact that you truly never forget. It's the type of scene that, hopefully, when you get to the end of your life, flashes back past you.

COLD AND GREY, BUT IN LOVE

I spot Victor the second I get through passport control. He is pressing his nose against the plate-glass wall and waving his arms comically.

My bag is one of the first out and with the help of a seven-foot German guy, I manage to manoeuvre it from the carousel and set it upon its wheels.

'Jesus!' Victor says as I appear in the arrivals hall. 'Couldn't you find a bigger suitcase?' And then he wraps me in his thick, warm, sheepskin-clad arms and says, 'Howdy, partner!'

We hug for a moment and I breathe in the musky smell of him. When we finally separate, I glance down at my shopping trolley-sized case and say, 'And no. It's the biggest one they do.'

We cross the hall and head out into the gloom. 'I was hoping for the magical blue sky of the Côte d'Azur,' I tell Victor, nodding at the falling rain.

'Yes, sorry about that,' he says, grabbing my hand and starting to lead me and the crazed, swerving suitcase towards the car park. 'I did order it for you but they must have got the days mixed up. It's dry up in the hills, at least. So how was it leaving your place to SJ and George?'

'Kind of weird. By the time my stuff had gone and theirs had arrived, it seemed more like their place than mine. They hung those horrible African rugs of theirs on the walls. It looked a bit like a drug dealer's house! The worst thing was giving up my keys. I don't have any keys any more. Not one.'

'Nor do I,' Victor says. 'Well, except these.' He lets go of my hand and pulls the van keys from his pocket.

'Did Distira ever find the others?'

'Nope.'

'How do you do that?' I ask. 'I mean, how could she totally lose a set of keys?'

Victor shrugs and drags the case to the side door of the van. 'Dunno,' he says. 'She's a strange old bird.'

'Yes,' I say. 'Yes, she is.'

The drive up to the mountains feels totally different today. The grey sky, the falling rain, the sound of the windscreen wipers all conspire to make Provence feel quite British.

'So how is the house coming on?' I ask.

'Slowly. The ceilings are fixed but not painted yet. The kitchen is gone but not replaced. Same for the bathroom.'

'There's no bathroom?'

'Not for a couple of days. I've been using Distira's.'

'God,' I say.

'It won't be for long, though.'

'So is Clappier good?'

'Yeah,' Victor says.

'You don't sound that convinced.'

He laughs. 'No, he's good, but you have to maintain constant pressure. Otherwise he doesn't turn up.'

'He doesn't *turn up*?'

'He goes to other jobs. I think he works for whoever is nagging the loudest, to be honest.'

'Right.'

'So it's kind of hard being his mate and working with him and managing to nag him enough to keep things moving.'

'Maybe we need to do good-cop/bad-cop. I'm quite happy to nag. I do it a lot at work. Well, I *used* to do it a lot at work.'

'And how does *that* feel, giving up work?'

'Very strange. I don't think it's sunk in yet. Or maybe it's just one of those things where you keep waiting for it to hit you and it never does.'

'Because it wasn't as important as you thought it was?'

'Exactly.'

'Anyway,' Victor says, glancing at me and smiling, 'if you want to keep your nagging skills finely tuned by using them on Clappier, that would work for me.'

The snow from last time has all but vanished now, and as we bump along the final track to La Forge, the muddy slush and the grey sky make the house look vaguely hostile.

'Do you see much of Distira?' I ask, that thought somehow leading to this one.

'Not much,' Victor replies. 'When I shower in the evening, she's usually around. So is that friend of hers, Carole. But she never says anything. Actually, Distira doesn't say much, either.'

'How does she earn a living?'

'A pension, I suppose,' Victor says.

We pull up outside the house and together wrestle my case across the gravel to the front door.

'God!' I exclaim when Victor pushes it open.

'Bad, huh?'

Bags of plaster are spilling onto the floor. The farm table is covered with bits of copper pipe and random DIY equipment. The kitchen has been ripped out, leaving clean patches of wall that throw into sharp relief just how dirty the rest is. The range has been pulled from the wall too, and soot from the open chimney has blown a black arc around its base.

'It has to get worse before it can get better,' Victor says. He points up at the ceiling. 'Look at that though.'

I nod. 'He's good at plastering, I'll give him that.'

'It's really hard, too,' Victor says. 'I had a go and I couldn't even get a square foot of it smooth.'

'He's not obsessively tidy though, is he?' I comment sarcastically, glancing around at the desolation.

'No,' Victor laughs. 'No, I knew you'd say that. Come see through here, though.' He grabs my hand and leads me through to the bedroom.

'Wow!' I say. 'Now that's an improvement.'

'Clappier fixed the ceiling, but I did everything else.'

'Nice floorboards, too,' I comment.

'I know. That lino was a bitch to remove, though. It took me about three days to scrape it off.'

'And a radiator!'

'It doesn't work yet, but soon. Maybe even Friday, Clappier said.'

'God, it's lovely, Victor.'

'I thought you'd want it painted a different colour eventually, but I just wanted to make everything white first.'

'Clean and bright. It's good. All it needs is a bed and some heat and we could sleep here.'

'Not just sleep,' Victor says, nudging my hip with his.

'No.'

'I thought we could do that tomorrow,' Victor says.

'What, shag?' I giggle.

Victor laughs. 'Go bed shopping. If you're up for it.'

I cross the room so that he can fold me in his arms again, and then we turn, as if slow-dancing, as I continue to take in how hard he has worked on this room. 'Go bed testing with you?' I say. 'I can't think of anything nicer.'

'I'm sorry it's all so grey and cold,' he says, his voice making my chest vibrate. 'I was hoping to have the heating on by the time you got here, but, well . . .'

'You didn't have much warning,' I concede. 'It doesn't matter.'

He pushes me away just far enough to look into my eyes. 'Thanks, by the way,' he says.

'For what?'

'For being here. For coming so soon.'

'You're welcome,' I say, squeezing him in my arms. 'It's where I want to be.' The cold suddenly reaches my bones and I shiver involuntarily.

'You need more clothes,' Victor says.

'I brought a selection of the thickest jumpers I could find,' I say, breaking out of his embrace and returning to my suitcase in the kitchen. 'I think I need one right now.'

'It will be better here soon,' Victor says, following me. 'I promise.'

I crouch down and unzip the front of my wardrobe-like suitcase, then pull a heavy-knit cardigan out.

'It's fine.' I glance up at him. In the dimly lit room, his brown irises are indistinguishable from his pupils.

He smiles at me – a soft, warm, wonderful smile – and I'm suddenly struck by how beautiful he is, surprised by the realisation that he is mine, and how much I'm in love with him.

'What?' he says, grinning.

'Nothing. I'm just happy. And I don't give a damn about the place, as long as I'm here with you.'

Victor's grin slips into a big toothy smile. 'Me too,' he says. 'Come on. Let's get back to the van. It's freezing in here.'

Buying a bed in France turns out to be a surprisingly complex ordeal. The first three furniture stores we visit are full of hideous monstrosities, the like of which I haven't even seen in anyone's house since the early eighties, let alone a store. The showrooms are full of ornately carved sofas with over-stuffed leather cushions and beds that look like they have been designed – if one can use the word – by the same guy who did the Fiat Multipla. A surprising number of them have transistor radios built into the headboard.

When we eventually do manage to find a simple wooden bed, the salesman informs us that it's out of stock, and that, no, we can't buy the display model.

Because healthy eating options appear to be few and far

between, we pause for lunch at Quick, the French equivalent of McDonald's. It's against just about every dietary or moral principle I have and I truly haven't eaten a burger for years. But the burger, a fish finger sandwich with the addition of melted cheese and masses of mayonnaise, is, I'm ashamed to admit, delicious. Surprisingly, doing something as mundane as hunting for a bed and eating burgers with a boyfriend feels lovely.

After our trillion-calorie lunch, we stumble upon an Ikea lookalike store called, rather unfortunately it seems to me, *Fly*. Fly contains a range of simple, apparently cheap, flat-pack beds, which, after some of the space-flight cockpits we have seen, comes as a relief. The pricing turns out to be something of a mirage as, like a Ryanair flight, all of the optional extras – feet, base, headboard, mattress – are really not options at all, but essentials. But they do have it in stock, and so, by 3 p.m., we are happily heading home, excited about being able to use our new bedroom and new bed.

By the time we get back to the house, Clappier has already left. Looking around the house, it's hard to see any signs of progress.

'You see,' Victor sighs, shaking his head. 'Unless you're breathing down his neck . . .'

'It's a good job we bought that blow-heater,' I say, touching the radiator in the bedroom, just in case – it's stone cold.

'So shall we make a start on that bed?'

The instruction sheet looks like it has been drawn – and translated – by a three-year-old and dragged through fifteen different languages, so we end up arguing good-naturedly as we screw random planks together, and then unscrew those same planks, only to decide that we were right in the first place.

By six thirty, the bed is complete and the fan-heater has taken the worst of the chill from the air, so we drag the bedding from the van and I pull my trainers off and throw myself onto the middle of the bed.

'Careful!' Victor admonishes. 'You never know who built that or how capable they were.'

'It's fine!' I declare, bouncing up and down, and then patting the space beside me. 'It's comfy. Come!'

Feigning fear, Victor edges onto the bed, and then slowly crawls all the way up and over me. He nuzzles my neck and then kisses me on the lips before slipping one hand underneath my cardigan and T-shirt.

'Your hands are freezing,' I say, grimacing.

'Then warm them up, woman!' Victor laughs.

I reach down and slide a hand over the front of Victor's jeans, gently massaging the bulge beneath. 'Someone needs to be let out of his denim prison,' I say.

'Yep,' he says, reaching down and undoing the belt, and then the buttons of my own jeans.

'It's very sinky,' I say, fidgeting on the mattress.

'Is it?' Victor laughs, sliding my jeans down and then starting to undo his own belt and fly.

'Can you close the door?' I say, glancing over. 'It's come open and there's a dr—— AGH!'

Distira is standing in the open doorway, holding a plastic bag. She is grinning broadly, showing her grey peg-like teeth and sweeping the room with her crazy eyes.

Victor frantically yanks at the quilt and positions it so that we are both hidden behind the fold.

'*C'est bien ici*,' Distira says quietly, her eyes finally resting on us. *It's nice here.*

She jiggles a plastic bag in her hand. '*Je vous ai amené de la bouffe. Du ragoût.*'

'What's she saying?' I whisper.

'She says she's brought us some stew,' Victor says.

'Please just make her go.'

'*Va à la cuisine, s'il te plaît*,' Victor says, tersely. '*On arrive.*' *Go to the kitchen, please. We'll be through.*

'*Il fait bon ici*,' Distira says, apparently unaware that she is causing any inconvenience. *It's warm here.*

'I know,' Victor tells her in French, sounding almost as annoyed as I feel. 'But go to the kitchen. I'll be right there.'

'OK, OK,' Distira mutters, turning and waddling from the room, but leaving the door wide open.

'She scared the bejeezus out of me,' I complain.

Victor laughs. 'I think I need to get that lock fixed.'

He stands and pulls his shoes on, then checks the crotch of his jeans before heading out.

Before I have finished pulling my shoes back on, Victor is back. 'She's gone,' he says. 'But she left us dinner.'

'I don't want it,' I say.

'You sure? It smells pretty good.'

'I know, but I still don't want it.'

Victor shrugs. 'Ah, you want something else instead,' he says saucily, crawling back onto the bed.

'Maybe later,' I say. 'When you've worked out some way of locking the door.'

Something catches my eye and we both turn to look out the bedroom window, and I jump all over again because there, her nose pressed against the pane, is Distira.

'Oh, for fuck's sake,' I say. 'This is beyond a joke.'

'I'll talk to her,' Victor says, standing. 'I'll sort it.'

'But don't upset her. I need to use her bathroom. I haven't washed properly since England.'

'Come,' Victor says, holding out one hand. 'We'll go back with her now.'

Distira's bathroom turns out to be as grubby and junk-ridden as the rest of her house. But even crouching down due to the lack of a shower curtain – what is it about the French and shower curtains? – getting clean feels wonderful.

After he has showered, Victor joins me back at our house and, with a towel over the window and a chair propped against the door, we do manage to make love. The sensation of our freshly washed bodies together feels ecstatic.

We then eat – Distira's stew for Victor and a Pot Noodle for stubborn me – before drifting into a pleasant slumber.

I'm woken by Victor turning over in an unusually energetic manner.

I start to drift back to sleep, but then he does it again. It's only when I try to roll towards him myself that I realise that something is wrong: my body has sunk so far into the mattress, it's almost impossible to move. I have to edge backwards and then throw myself forwards to lift myself from the body-shaped hole the mattress has created beneath me.

Once I do manage to move from the indent my body has left, I have to put up with lying across the bumps and depressions left in the foam until the mattress starts to mould to my new body shape. It feels a little like being assimilated by the bed.

'There's something wrong with the mattress,' I whisper.

'It's bloody awful,' Victor replies, clearly wide awake. 'I think it's trying to swallow me whole.' He reaches out and switches the light on. 'And when you roll over—'

'You have to trampoline your way out of the hole,' I finish.

'Yeah. And then it's all bumpy from where you were lying before.'

'I know,' I say. 'I think it might be that memory foam stuff.'

'It is,' Victor says. 'But I thought that was meant to be a good thing.'

'It's quite comfortable as long as you don't move.'

'But I *do* move,' Victor says.

'I know. I noticed!'

He rolls towards me and fidgets around a little and then snuggles against my back. 'I wonder if we can take it back?'

'You can be pretty sure that we can't.'

BIOLOGICAL TIME BOMB

The next morning Clappier arrives so early that it's only the chair against the door that prevents him from barging in on us as well. We extract ourselves from the man-eating mattress and watch, blurry-eyed, as he hammers and swears at various bits of piping.

Eventually, despite our terrible night's sleep, Victor and I begin to tidy the kitchen and then scrub the walls. It's hard work to get the layers of food-grime off, and although the stickiness vanishes, the walls look worse than before. But as we can't repaint until we have scrubbed them, there doesn't seem to be any other option.

Just as we have picked up our tools again after a lunch-break in the van, Distira sticks her head through the door on the pretext of retrieving her Tupperware.

She sidles up to the foot of my stepladder. Something about her demeanour makes me nervous, and though I don't imagine for a second that she would *actually* push me off, I do climb down, and it isn't because I want to be closer to her.

'*Qu'est-ce que vous faites?*' she asks. *What are you doing?*

'I'm washing the wall,' I explain in French.

'It doesn't need washing,' she replies, which from someone who never seems to clean her bath is, I guess, unsurprising.

'We want to paint it, Auntie,' Victor explains from across the room, where he is helping Clappier hang a radiator.

'*Pff!*' Distira says. '*Quel intérêt de laver le mur si vous allez le peindre?*'

And then she spins on one foot, grabs her Tupperware from the table, and gives her best shot at flouncing from the room.

I wonder, for the first time ever, if she suffers from some kind of learning difficulty. 'What did she say?' I ask.

Victor half shakes his head in a gesture that says, 'It's not worth it.'

'No, tell me what she said,' I protest. 'It's the only way I'll ever improve.'

'She said that there's no point washing the wall if we're just going to paint over the top.'

I defiantly pick up my bucket. 'So she's a decorating expert now is she?'

'Looks that way.'

Once I have finished one wall, Victor pulls me into a corner. 'Hey,' he says, quietly. 'You know what you were saying about being a good nagger?

'Nagger? Oh, yes!'

'Well, now might be a good time. Clappier said the bathroom won't be ready for another week.'

'Another week!'

'Shh, yes. So, if you fancy a little trial run ...'

'I really can't live for another week without a bathroom

anyway.' I suck the inside of my mouth. 'I'm thinking maybe something drastic.'

'Drastic?'

'Yeah. Women's stuff.'

Victor wrinkles his nose. 'I'm not sure I—'

'What's the word in French for period?' I ask.

'Oh, erm, it's your *règles*,' Victor says. 'You have your *règles*. But you can't say that. You'll give the guy a heart attack.'

'*J'ai mes règles dans deux jours,*' I murmur. 'Will he understand that?'

'Your period is in two days, yes, but you really can't say that to an old French builder, babe.'

'Really?' I pull a face. 'Guys are so weird about girlie stuff. OK, how about, *dans deux jours, je vais avoir une problème feminine?*'

'*Un problème féminin,*' Victor corrects. 'Not *féminine*. A problem is masculine.'

'Even if it's feminine, it's masculine?'

'Yes,' he says, glancing nervously over my shoulder to check that Clappier is still in the other room. 'But I really don't think—'

'And what about, *Donc j'ai besoin d'une salle de bains toute de suite?*'

'Yes, that's fine,' he laughs, 'but I still don't think—'

'It's a girl thing,' I interrupt, arching one eyebrow. 'It's called using your weaknesses as weapons. Watch and learn.'

Victor laughs. 'Jesus!' he says. 'Even if it works, I'm not sure it's one I'm ever going to be able to reuse.'

'No,' I say. 'No, I suppose not.'

Clappier is utterly stunned when I drop my biological time bomb upon him. He stares at me, wide-eyed and speechless, but then drops the blowtorch he is using and immediately starts to do something with the piping to the bath instead, so I can only presume that my words have had the desired effect.

Amazingly, by the time he and his helper – the spotty, moped-riding Jean-Noël – leave, the pristine new bath has been manoeuvred into position, the waste pipe plumbed in, and our electric shower temporarily reinstalled above it. In short, I am spared Distira's sticky bathtub this evening.

Victor heads over to let Distira know that we won't be needing her facilities and returns with another Tupperware container of stew. Judging from the sweet, spicy smell, it's from the same batch as yesterday.

When I turn my nose up at the food, Victor says, 'You are funny about Distira.'

'Funny how?'

'Well, you don't think she likes you, but when she makes an effort and cooks us dinner, you don't want to eat it. I think it's quite sweet that, knowing that we don't have a kitchen, she's gone to the trouble.'

I sigh and nod. 'OK,' I say. 'I'll try it, but if I'm ill again, then it's the last time ever, OK?'

Victor laughs and pulls two paper plates from the plastic bag we use to keep them dust free. 'I was fine last night, wasn't I?' he points out.

The stew tastes good, in fact. It reminds me of something my mother used to reconstitute on camping trips. It came in freeze-dried form and was called 'Hungarian

Goulash'. To her dismay, it was a childhood favourite, and Waiine and I would ask for Hungarian Goulash in preference to her normal cooking once back home. Even Dad once secretly admitted that he liked it better than her own stew.

Once we have eaten and thrown our plates in the bin, Victor says, 'Bed, then?'

'It's eight!' I point out, glancing at my phone.

Victor shrugs. 'I'm knackered,' he says, 'and it's freezing in here.'

And so I laughingly concede.

We cuddle until the bed warms up and then Victor levers himself from our joint impression in the mattress and rolls to his side of the bed, almost immediately starting to snore.

I lie there and think about the feel of the foam closing around my body and wonder if that's how it feels to be eaten by a Venus flytrap. Waiine had one when we were kids and it would snap closed around flies and then open again a week later revealing only a dried carcass.

I am woken at 1 a.m. by one of Victor's gymnastic body-flips and open my eyes to see that the towel has fallen from the window too and moonlight is now flooding the room. My stomach is gurgling alarmingly, so, fearful of a repeat episode of the last time I ate Distira's food, I pull on a dressing gown and quit the warm bedroom for the icy waste-land of our unfinished bathroom.

Sitting on that cold seat, surrounded by pipes and tools and rubble, my breath rising visibly in the frosty air, waiting to see if I'm going to be ill again, is about as depressing at it gets.

Once I have ascertained that I have indigestion, nothing more, I creep back into the bedroom and grab a handful of clothes, which I take through to the kitchen.

Dressed in jeans and a thick sweatshirt, I pull up a chair, and try to imagine the room finished, but only hear instead Distira saying, 'You'll never be happy here', and once again I feel unreasonably desolate about the whole project.

I shiver with the cold. It's impossible to remain here tonight, but I don't want to return to bed. I want to sit in a warm room with a cat and read a book. It would sound silly to some, no doubt, but I miss Guinness. Actually, right now, I miss my entire London life. I acknowledge that I am feeling sorry for myself, but even that self-awareness doesn't seem to help.

The bedroom door creaks and I turn to see Victor appear in the doorway, naked. He hops from one foot to the other and rubs his eye with a balled fist. 'It's freezing in here,' he says. 'Are you OK?'

I shrug miserably. 'I couldn't sleep.'

'Because of the mattress?'

'In part,' I reply. 'And indigestion. And the full moon. It does that to me sometimes. Can I go and sit in the van?'

Victor pulls a face. 'Why?'

I shrug.

'It's freezing out there. Worse than here.'

'Can't I put the heating on?'

'It takes forever to warm up,' he says. 'Just come back to bed. Come and talk to me.'

I return to the warmth of the bedroom to find Victor

stripping the bed. 'I thought we could try the other side of the mattress,' he explains.

'It said to sleep on this side,' I point out. 'It has a label that says specifica—'

'Yeah, well,' Victor says. 'I would if I could, but I can't.'

'You're right,' I say, pitching in. 'It can't be any worse really, can it?'

'No,' Victor says, manhandling the mattress into vertical position and then letting it fall. 'Let's just hope that that shitty memory foam stuff is on one side only.'

Slipping back into the now-cold bed, we snuggle together and wait to see if it will attempt to digest us all over again.

'It's depressing being cold all the time.'

'It's getting me down, too. You're not regretting coming, are you?'

'No!' I say. But I'm not sure if it's a lie.

We lie in silence for a while, and I decide that having Victor's arms around me makes everything seem OK. Just about. But just as I think this he rolls away. He manages this without having to somersault.

'I think the mattress *is* better this way up,' I say, and Victor replies with a snore – which I can only assume means that he agrees.

When Clappier rolls in at eleven the next morning, we decide to put our agreed plan into action. I busy myself tidying the yard while Victor talks to him 'man-to-man'. The agreed script is that his 'wife' is giving him hell, and that Clappier needs to 'help him out here' by getting the heating working.

After about fifteen minutes, Victor comes out to get me. 'Come on,' he says. 'We're on radiator hanging duties.'

'Did he say he can get it working today?' I ask, straightening and leaning the rake against the wall.

'He said he'll try. But he has another job at four. Apparently someone else's wife is even worse than you.'

'Hmm,' I say. 'We'll have to see about that.'

The division of work for the day is that Clappier and Jean-Noël are to cut and braze pipes while Victor and I drill, rawlplug and screw the brackets that hold the radiators to the walls. With all four of us on the job, and Clappier, for once, concentrating on a single task, we make sterling progress. By 3 p.m., the entire heating system has been piped, the range is back in place, and Clappier is ready to open the filler valve.

'*S'il n'y a pas de fuite,*' he says, a Gauloise hanging from his bottom lip, '*c'est bon, on peut chauffer. Sinon ça sera pour demain.*'

As I can't understand anything that the man says when he is smoking, Victor translates this for me. 'If there are no leaks, we can heat. Otherwise it's going to be tomorrow.'

I discreetly beckon Victor through to the bedroom where the radiator is pinging as water fills the system.

'If he tries to leave before it's done, I reckon we should up the ante a bit,' I say.

'How d'you mean?'

'I reckon we should show him I'm worse than whoever the other guy's wife is.'

Victor grins. 'Are you going to become the girlfriend from hell?'

'I could storm off,' I suggest with a smirk. 'If he says he's going to the other job, I could storm out of the house.'

'To where, though? To Distira's?'

'To the van, maybe. I could take the keys. And a bag. I could start the engine, make it look like I'm leaving you or something.'

'It'll never work,' Victor says, but his grin reveals that he thinks that it might.

'And you could say something like, "come on, matey, get the heating working, otherwise I'm gonna lose my bird".'

'*I'm gonna lose my bird?*' Victor says, snorting now.

'Or whatever you menfolk say to each other when you're being patronising, sexist pigs,' I say. 'But—'

I'm interrupted by Jean-Noël asking for a bucket. We have, it transpires, a leak.

We run through to the kitchen and I empty the washing up bowl for the purpose of catching the jet of water squirting from one of the newly soldered joints.

'There's a leak,' Clappier tells Victor, stating the obvious. He then continues with another phrase, but I don't catch its meaning.

'It's gonna be tomorrow,' Victor tells me, raising one eyebrow comically.

'Tomorrow?!' I shriek, and Clappier looks suitably stunned.

'He has to drain the whole system, pumpkin, so that he can—'

'Don't *pumpkin* me!' I spit, rather enjoying myself. 'I don't care *what* he has to do. Either you get that bloody heating working, or ... or I'm out of here!'

179

Victor glances at Clappier, who looks at his watch and shakes his head hopelessly. '*Je ne peux pas,*' he says.

I storm off to the bedroom, smiling to myself as Victor, behind me, pleads with him. I throw some random clothes in a bag, Victor's mainly, and swipe the keys from the windowsill before marching back through the kitchen where the men are now arguing quietly.

Victor grabs my arm. 'CC! Where are you going?' he asks.

'Home!' I shout. 'To England! Where they have HEATING!' And then I storm from the house.

I cross the gravel and open the door to the van, throw my bag inside, climb into the driver's seat and, after a few attempts – I forget the manual choke – start the engine.

Victor appears, jogging across the gravel towards me. 'Are you OK?' he asks.

'Of course,' I say quietly, in case Clappier is listening.

'God, you're good. You had *me* worried. So what now? He still says he can't stay.'

'Go get your wallet, give it a last plea. Tell him you're coming with me to try to talk me out of leaving, or something. We can go and get a pizza in Gréolières and see if we have heating when we get back.'

'Don't get your hopes up,' Victor says, turning to jog back to the house.

'Be convincing!' I tell him.

When he returns, we swap places and bump off down the track. 'So?' I say.

Victor shrugs, glances back to check that we're out of sight, and then leans over and pecks me on the cheek. 'He said he'll see what he can do.'

After our pizza in a near-deserted restaurant in Gréolières, we drive back up to La Forge, counting the wildlife that we pass.

As we round the final corner, Victor says, 'Hare!' and points to the left of the track, and I say, 'Smoke!' and point towards the house.

Victor turns to look, and asks, 'Where?'

'The chimney, silly!'

'God, you had me worried!' he says. 'I thought you meant that the house was on fire.'

We park the van and cross the frosty gravel to the front door. With his hand on the knob, Victor pauses and says, 'Ta-da!' He throws the door open and we are hit by a blast of warm air.

We quickly enter and close the door behind us. Against the far wall, flames are gently flickering through the sooty window of the range. I run, tripping on some pipe as I do so, to the nearest radiator. 'Oh,' I say. 'It's cold!'

'What?!' Victor cries, tearing across the room to feel the radiator. 'Liar!' he says.

I laugh and happily press up against the warmth of the radiator.

Once we have ascertained that all of the rooms are now warm, we return to the kitchen and pull up chairs next to the range.

Victor reaches out to stroke my cheek, and then looks around at the mess within the kitchen and wrinkles his nose. 'We need to spend another day clearing up,' he says.

I jump up to extinguish the lights, before sitting back down close to Victor. 'See,' I say, looking at his face in the flickering orange light. 'Now you can pretend that it's all finished.'

'I don't really care for now,' Victor says. 'I just can't believe that we have heating.'

The arrival of the central heating marks the beginning of a two-week period of bliss. We collect wood from the forest and prepare the walls for kitchen cabinets, while Clappier hammers away in the bathroom, whistling badly.

And every day, it seems, something good happens: a working flush mechanism for the toilet one day; the chance to soak in the bath the next; the delivery of our refrigerator and the first ever meal cooked on the range the day after.

In the evenings, we sit on blankets and drink aperitifs and stare, wide-eyed, at the day's progress and then, sometimes, on those same blankets, in the mixture of moonlight and firelight, we make love. I have never felt happier.

Though the temperatures outside remain around freezing, the sun shines daily and when we drive to the coast for kitchen cabinets, pipes, or screws, we often manage a picnic on the beach, or a beer on a sunlit terrace.

Victor sets something up on his iPhone so that I can surf the web on my computer, and with access to Facebook, reassuring news from home arrives: Mark and Iain are fine, George and Guinness are still in love, and SJ is happier than ever to be living in Primrose Hill.

Even Distira is, in her absence, bearable. Though I see her in the distance, pottering about, or driving past in the Lada with Carole rigid at her side, she doesn't drop by once. When I mention this to Victor, he explains, 'I had a word with her. After the time she pressed her nose against the window. I think she's being more discreet now.'

Naively, I imagine that it will last.

BE CAREFUL WHAT YOU WISH FOR

The spell of unbroken sunshine – both actual and metaphorical – can't, of course, last forever, and the day the sunshine changes to rain is also the day Distira returns to visit us. Because the postman has erroneously delivered my parcel to her house, she appears in the kitchen, water dripping from her mac. As Victor and Clappier have their hands full hanging kitchen cabinets and because I'm bursting with the desire to show the house off to someone, I invite her in for a coffee.

Distira slurps at her drink and watches the men struggling to drill holes in the heavy stone walls, while I rip open the package.

'*Ça ne tiendra pas,*' she tells them when Victor switches the drill off. *That will never hold.*

'*Les murs sont friables,*' she says. The walls are . . . *something.*

'What's "*friables*", Victor?' I ask, lifting first a pot of Marmite from the food-parcel Mark has sent me, and then crumpets and a pack of PG Tips.

'Broken,' Clappier says, the first indication that I have ever had that he speaks any English whatsoever.

'It's more like "fragile",' Victor says. 'Or crumbly.' He then explains to his aunt that the problem isn't that the walls are too fragile, but that the stone is too hard for them to drill into.

Because the men are soon too busy huffing and puffing with the next wall cupboard to talk to Distira, and because conversation between her and myself has never flowed easily, I explain that I need to return to my own DIY task.

When she simply says, 'OK,' and makes a sweeping gesture that I should go do what I have to, that's exactly what I do.

Ten minutes later, I'm completely absorbed in smoothing the holes in the bathroom wall with Polyfilla when she enters the room.

'*Ça change!*' she declares, sounding impressed. She sweeps the room with her bulbous eyes.

'Yes,' I tell her. 'Once it's finished, it'll be lovely.'

'*C'était une chambre avant,*' she tells me. *It was a bedroom before.*

It dawns on me for the first time that she of course knows the history of our house. This is finally a subject that we can talk about.

'Who lived here before?' I ask her.

'*Evelyne et Jacques!*' she says, shrugging as if this is obvious.

'Victor's parents?'

'*Bien sûr . . .*' she replies. *Of course, but they never lived here much.*

Feeling a little proud that my French must be improving, I say, '*Une maison de vacances?*' A holiday home?

185

'*Oui,*' she says. She nods towards the bathtub and tells me, 'The bed was there. That's where Vincent was born.' She smiles at the memory, sounding warm for perhaps the first time since I met her.

'Vincent?'

'*Le frère de Victor.*'

I frown, wondering if she is talking about a different Victor, or if she is just confused. 'But Victor doesn't have a brother,' I tell her.

'He did,' she says. 'For a few minutes.'

I shake my head. '*Je ne comprends pas,*' I say.

'*Il est né là. Il est mort là.*' *He was born there. He died there.*

'Victor's brother *died*?' I ask, horrified.

'He lived for seven minutes,' she tells me.

'God, how terrible. Victor never mentioned him.'

'*Victor ne le sait pas,*' she says. *Victor doesn't know.* She raises one finger to her lips, and adds, '*C'est mieux ainsi.*' *It's better that way.*

'They never came back here,' Distira tells me.

'No, I can understand that.'

And then she spits, '*Pff! Cette maison n'a jamais porté bonheur à personne!*' and leaves. *This house never brought happiness to anyone!*

From next door I hear Victor chirp, 'Goodbye, Auntie,' and then the front door opens and closes.

I look at the bathtub, and think about a baby called Vincent dying in the house that never made anyone happy, and I shiver.

*

That night, snuggled up in bed, it feels safe enough to dip a toe in the subject of Victor's knowledge, or lack of knowledge, about baby Vincent. I haven't decided if I am going to tell Victor of my conversation with Distira yet; I'm just going to see how things pan out.

'Victor? You know you're an only child . . .'

'Yes?'

'Why is that, do you think? I mean, was it a decision not to have any more, or couldn't they, or what?'

'I think they only wanted the one,' Victor says. 'They never said anything about having any more, anyway. But then they never said much about much, to be honest. They weren't the best communicators.'

'And what about you? Did you want a brother or a sister?'

'I would have loved brothers and sisters,' he tells me. 'I was dead jealous of my friends who all had big families. We were pretty much the exception.'

I lie there for a while, the words on the edge of my tongue. But ultimately, I can only agree with Distira that it's probably better that Victor doesn't know how close to having a brother he once came.

'Why d'you ask, anyway?' he says, rolling towards me and laying a heavy, hairy arm across my chest. 'You're not pregnant, are you?'

I laugh. 'No. It would be OK if I was though, wouldn't it? You haven't changed your mind?'

'Not at all,' he says, pulling me tighter. 'Not one bit.'

'Good.'

'Was it nice having a brother?'

I take a deep breath.

'Sorry, I suppose that's not something . . .'

'No, it's fine. It was a long time ago, you know?'

'You don't remember, you mean?'

'No, of course I *remember*. I just mean, it's OK to talk about it.'

'So was it nice? Was Waiine nice?'

'Yes,' I say, smiling at the image my mind conjures up, as fresh as if it were yesterday. 'Yes, it was wonderful having a brother. And horrible losing him. The worst thing ever.'

'It must have been,' Victor says.

'But, well, it was just normal. Him being there, I mean. You take people for granted, don't you? I didn't even visit him much when he was in hospital. I was busy at college, and I never really imagined that he was going to die. Or what that really meant. And I think I hid from it a bit, too. I'm not sure I was old enough to cope. But I wish I had made more of him when he was around.'

'Hmm,' Victor says thoughtfully. 'Was he much like you?'

'Yes,' I say. 'Yes he was exact—' But then suddenly my voice cracks, and I'm unable to continue.

'Sorry,' Victor says.

'It's fine,' I manage, taking a deep breath. 'But it never goes away. And yes. He was exactly like me. Only wilder.'

'I wish I could have met him.'

'Yes,' I say quietly. 'Me too. I was thinking just today that Mark will be able to come and visit us once it's all finished, and SJ and George, and your friends. But not Waiine.'

Without thinking, I almost add, 'And not Vincent.' In

fact, I even open my mouth to do so, but manage to stop myself in time. There are enough ghosts in the room tonight.

It rains all night, and it's still raining in the morning when we get up.

Clappier fails to materialise, but because we're pretty happy with his progress, we decide to leave him be and head down to the coast for some shopping.

As we're driving away from the hypermarket, Victor's mobile rings, so he pulls into a lay-by to take the call. With the rain drumming on the roof, he struggles to hear whoever is on the other end. Eventually he hangs up and says, 'That was Georges. He was phoning to warn us about the weather forecast. Looks like snow.'

I peer out at the water cascading down the windscreen. '*Really?*' I ask. It seems hard to imagine that it could possibly be snowing one hour away. 'We are going to be able to get home, aren't we?'

Victor shrugs and then phones Distira to check on the state of the roads, but there is no answer.

'I'm sure it'll be fine,' I say. 'It was OK last time.'

'That was six centimetres,' Victor points out. 'Not sixty. Georges thinks we should borrow his four wheel drive Panda. It's up to you, but otherwise, we might get stuck up there, that's all.'

'I think it'll be fine,' I say again.

Victor winks at me, checks over his shoulder, and heads back onto the road. 'Well, you were right last time,' he says. 'We'll go with your woman's intuition.'

But by the time we begin the hill on which Georges' farm

sits, the responsibility of this is starting to weigh upon my mind.

'Fine, let's go see what they say,' I concede.

When we arrive, Georges and Muriel usher us into their house, serve us a single beer each, and fill us in on the severe weather warning.

'*C'est une alerte orange!*' Georges says. Which I understand from his raised eyebrows is a serious business.

The men quickly decide that swapping cars is the best thing to do, and Muriel nods at me to say that she thinks they're right, so we swap all of the shopping from our lovely warm van to their frozen red box on wheels, and then we head back, Victor thrashing the Fiat up the hills and taking the first corner at speed.

'Jesus!' he says, belatedly slowing down. 'The brakes are terrible.'

When we do get to La Forge, the sleet has turned back to drumming rain.

'It might be like last time,' Victor says, when I point this out. 'It might happen overnight.'

Stocking up the freezer provides an unexpected sense of security. 'At least if we get snowed in we won't starve,' I say.

'No,' Victor agrees, adding wood to the fire. 'I'm actually quite excited about being holed up with you . . .'

And then I say something stupid. I say words that, forever more, I will suspect were responsible for everything that happened next.

'Yes,' I say, glancing heavenwards. 'We're ready for anything now. Bring it on! Do your worst!'

Does the drumming of the rain double at that precise moment, or had I simply tuned it out while I was stocking the freezer? Whichever it is, Victor hears it too and looks up.

'Be careful what you wish for,' he laughs. 'You might just get it.'

We are awoken at 2 a.m. by a terrifying, ground-shaking rumble. My immediate instinct is to clutch Victor beside me, but because his reaction is to jump from the bed, this leaves us in a confused scrabble of arms and limbs.

Victor flicks on the lights and says, 'What the fuck was that?'

'Maybe the heating exploded?' I offer.

'Nah. Earthquake, maybe?'

We nervously venture out into the hallway and on towards the kitchen, but there are no signs of any damage.

'Maybe the water tank?' I suggest, heading off to open the bathroom door. But the new hot water tank is still attached by its two little bolts, exactly where Clappier fixed it.

When I return to the kitchen, Victor has opened the front door and is peering outside. 'I have never seen so much bloody rain,' he says, closing the door again and crossing the room to throw a log into the range.

'So what was that?' I ask. 'Because it was something big. Do they even get earthquakes here?'

'I think so,' Victor says, grabbing my hand and leading me back through to the bedroom. 'If it was an earthquake, there might be more.'

'Aftershocks. You're supposed to go and stand in the middle of a field,' I say. 'I looked it up when my shelf fell on me.'

Victor frowns at me, indicating confusion.

'Oh, don't ask . . .' I say. 'It's a long story. And a stupid one. But anyway, if a big one happens, you have to stand in a field.'

'If a big shelf falls on you?' Victor asks, grinning.

'No, a big earthquake, *idjit*. You have to stand out in the open where nothing can fall on you.'

As I climb back into bed, Victor crosses the room to peer out of the small bedroom window. He wipes the glass with one hand and presses his nose against the pane.

'What can you see?'

'Nothing,' he says, returning to bed. 'It's pitch black out there.'

I lie listening for aftershocks, and doubt that I will get back to sleep, but I do drift off because the next thing I know, I'm peering blearily at the alarm clock.

'Is this clock right?' I ask with a yawn. 'It says it's gone ten.'

Victor sleepily turns his head and frowns at the clock, then looks the other way towards the darkened window.

'Still raining,' he says.

'It's dark as night.'

'It's the end of the world,' Victor says in a spooky horror-film voice, before rolling towards me, linking his arms around me, and tickling me.

'It's cold in here this morning,' I say when I have stopped laughing.

'Yeah, it's damp. The fire must have gone out. I'll relight it.'

We lie for a moment, but then I hear a drip, and sit bolt upright in bed.

I switch on the bedside lamp and follow the direction of the noise – water dripping onto water.

'Look. The rain's coming under the window,' I say.

Beads of water are hanging along the entire length of the windowsill. Below that, a small puddle is forming.

'Oh fuck!' Victor yells, jumping from the bed and hopping into his trousers. 'I know what's happened. I know what that noise was!' Grabbing a jumper, he runs from the room. 'Don't open the window!' he shouts behind him.

I get up, pull on the nearest clothes available, and peer out the window. But I can't see anything. Puzzled, I head out into the kitchen and grab the umbrella before exiting the front door that Victor has left open.

'Victor?' I shout, and his muffled reply comes from the back of the house, barely audible over the noise of the rain hitting the umbrella and the roof – the rain hitting *everything*.

I scramble over the tarpaulined woodpile and climb down into the narrow alley that separates the back of the house from the higher ground behind. When I turn the corner, I find Victor standing, still barefoot, holding a coat over his head for shelter.

'What is it?' I ask, moving to his side and lifting the umbrella above both of our heads.

Victor says nothing, just nods at the sight before us.

'Oh Jesus!' I say.

Because the noise last night was no earthquake. It was a landslide.

The dry stone wall that used to retain the higher ground behind the house has collapsed and a sea of mud, earth and stones has crumbled against the rear of the house, half filling the depth of the cut-away. The reason that our bedroom window is so dark, I now understand, is because it is underground.

Back indoors over coffee and toast, we debate what to do.

'It'll take days to move all of that earth,' I point out. 'Do you think it's even possible?'

'We might need a digger,' Victor says. 'And we can't do anything until the rain stops. It'll just slide back if we try to move it when it's wet.'

I sigh and rub his shoulder, then lean down to kiss the back of his neck. 'Well, don't fret too much. We've only got a few drops of water seeping in. I'll put a towel down or something.'

I'm not sure even I'm convinced that what I'm saying is true – in fact, I feel an inexplicable sense of rising panic – but I'm somehow aware that I'm doing what I have to do in these circumstances. Calming others down is what women do in the face of adversity. I remember my own mother being unusually calm and reassuring about Waiine's illness. 'It's just a cold,' she would tell me. 'It's just a bad case of flu.' But of course it wasn't. It was Aids.

'I need to board up the window,' Victor says, pulling me out of my reverie. 'Just in case the glass breaks. We don't want to wake up in a mud bath.' He sighs and shrugs sadly at me. 'It's like an episode of *Grand Designs*. Something always has to go wrong.'

'Well,' I say, 'If this is the worst of it, we'll be fine.'

The following morning, leaving Victor in bed, I head to the kitchen to make a cup of tea and lift a box of tea-bags out of one of the new cupboards. The entire box is soaked through.

'Victor,' I call, rushing back to the bedroom. 'We have a problem. There's water seeping into the new cupboards.'

He groans and slips from the bed.

'Look!' I say, pointing inside one of the units at the drips forming.

We check the bedroom and the bathroom, and all the rear walls of the house are the same, covered in tiny pearls of water soaking through from the other side. There's even a small puddle of water forming on the bathroom floor.

'OK,' Victor says, reaching for the phone. 'Looks like we can't wait till it stops raining after all. I'm calling Georges. I just hope he knows someone with a digger.'

Myriam informs us that Georges is out doing farmerly things in the rain, and that he'll call us back, but she says that she thinks someone they know called Stéphane has access to a digger.

When Georges phones back that evening, he confirms this and says that for three hundred euros cash, both digger and driver are ours. As water is now seeping up through the floors as well as the walls, we agree immediately.

That evening, I move all of our food back out of the soaked cupboards and onto the kitchen table, before retiring to the unpleasantly damp bed.

'If we had the van up here, we could have slept in it,' I point out.

'I'll go get it tomorrow,' Victor says.

'Maybe you can buy a dehumidifier as well,' I suggest.

'Sure,' Victor says, clicking out the light and rolling away from me. 'Night.'

When morning arrives, it becomes clear that we will not be fetching the van. Overnight, the heavy rain has turned to heavy snow. In a matter of hours, the entire landscape has been buried beneath twelve inches of whiteness.

'Snow,' I say, simply, when Victor joins me.

'Yes,' he says. 'And lots of it.'

'That won't stop the digger getting up here, will it?'

He shrugs. 'Maybe, actually. I think they move them from one place to another on a trailer. I'm not sure they're even allowed on the road.'

He turns away from the view and crosses the room to start breakfast.

I'm about to follow him when something catches the corner of my eye – a flash of yellow.

'It's here!' I cry, as an enormous yellow bulldozer appears over the horizon and begins to bounce energetically across the fields towards us.

FAST TRACK TO SIBERIA

Stéphane, the digger man, turns out to be a nineteen-year-old municipal employee doing a bit of work 'au noir' so that he can buy himself a new motorbike. He is cute, enthusiastic and instantly likeable, even if his age isn't exactly reassuring.

It transpires that the bulldozer has been 'borrowed' from the regional road authority where Stéphane works, and is visibly too big for our needs – the shovel on the front is twice the width of the alleyway that runs around the back of the house.

I listen to Victor explaining all of this, but Stéphane argues, convincingly, that we'd be better off with a much bigger space around the back of the house anyway, and that we wouldn't even be in this mess had we had more, 'margin for error', as he puts it.

I head indoors and leave them to it, and eventually hear the roar of the engine revving up and the shudder of earth moving as he begins to dig out the back of our house.

Victor returns, ruddy-cheeked from the cold. 'Well, what

he lacks in precision, he certainly makes up for in enthusiasm,' he says. 'And I reckon the place will be less damp with more airspace around the back.'

We try to make progress with our tiling project, but quickly the noise and vibration of the bulldozer just behind the wall becomes too stressful for me to continue.

I'm just about to formulate this thought when Victor switches off the noisy new tile cutter and says, 'You know what? I think I would rather keep an eye on him.'

I down tools. 'Exactly what I was thinking,' I say.

As we pass the bedroom, I see that light is now seeping through the gaps between the planks Victor nailed over the window. Beyond that, the shadow of the huge digger wheel moves back and forth.

'He doesn't hang about, does he?' I laugh, but when we step outside, my smile fades instantly.

In front of the house, just to the left of where we used to park the van, Stéphane is building, out of everything he is removing, a big, muddy, hill.

'Jesus Christ! Your man's not going to dump all of that there, is he?' I ask.

'You sound Irish,' Victor says.

'I am.'

'I know, but your accent isn't usually so strong. Anyway, I'll ask him. I suppose it all has to go somewhere.'

'But not there!'

'No, I'll, erm, talk to him.'

We walk to the edge of the house and see that the alleyway down the side of the house is now three times wider than before, and where it previously comprised a neat stone wall and a gravel path, the wheels of the bulldozer have ground rocks, and snow, and mud and plants into something that looks like an open-cast mine.

'Bloody hell!' Victor says.

We stand for a moment taking in the desolation, both realising that sorting out the mess that Stéphane leaves behind is going to end up being a bigger job than shovelling out the back of the house by hand. And then I walk down the new alley-cum-motorway to the rear of the house.

From this vantage point, we can now see the digger as it revs up and moves back and forth with unnerving rapidity, scraping another road-width channel behind the house.

'How are we *ever* going to sort that out?' I ask.

Victor shrugs and puts an arm around my shoulders. 'We can take our time,' he says. 'At least the house will be dry.'

'He's a bit close to the wall, though, isn't he?'

'Well we need the earth off the wall,' Victor says. 'That's the whole point.'

'I know, but wouldn't it be better to finish off by hand?'

'Maybe. I'll tell him to be careful,' Victor says. 'I think he's going a bit too deep, too.'

'Make sure he doesn't run you over!' I shout, as he climbs up onto what remains of the landslide and waves to catch Stéphane's eye.

They have a shouted conversation and then as the digger begins once again to roar up and down, Victor returns.

'He doesn't do finesse really, does he?' I say, laughing with fake bravado.

We walk back to the front of the house and I open the

front door to step inside, but notice that the new wall-cupboards are trembling.

'Victor!' I say, 'Look! Everything's shaking. Tell him to move away from the rear wall.'

'He needs to slow down too,' Victor says, turning to leave.

'He's going to have the whole house down if he carries on li—' But then my throat constricts and I find myself unable to speak. I grab Victor's arm and he spins back around and, as paralysed as myself, watches as one of our wall cupboards breaks free and falls to the ground. The section of wall where the cupboard used to hang then starts to crumble before our eyes.

'Stéphane!' Victor shouts, now sprinting to the back of the house, but it's too late, because just as he vanishes from view two things happen, seemingly in slow-motion. First, a huge rock falls from the wall onto the counter-top, smashing, like skittles, the two bottles of wine that were standing there. And then the first chink of daylight appears, shining through the rear wall of our house, as it continues to crumble – like the bricks of a toy castle – to the ground.

As the wall disintegrates, and as stones and kitchen cupboards continue to crash onto the counter beneath, I step backwards away from the house, unsure as to how far the chaos might spread.

The crumbling process happens slowly, in little sporadic bursts, and the pause at the end of each of these gives hope that that's the end of the disaster, hope that is dashed, again and again as more of the wall falls in.

During one of these pauses, I hear Victor shouting and

the engine noise from the digger ceasing abruptly. A ghostly snow-muffled silence ensues.

I edge back to the front door and peer in to get a better look. The kitchen is full of rubble and crushed wall cupboards, and I can now see straight through a hole in the rear wall about the size of a door. Beyond this, standing in the mudscape, Victor and Stéphane are staring back at me.

No one moves for a few minutes. Victor is covering his mouth with one hand and Stéphane alternates between looking at the hole, and glancing, warily, at Victor. He looks like a gazelle sniffing the air, alert to danger and ready to run. It seems that everyone is waiting for someone else to say something.

Stéphane is the first person to find his voice. '*Désolé,*' he says. *Sorry.*

Neither Victor nor myself reply to that.

I step across the threshold into the kitchen and glance up at the roof to check that it isn't about to come down upon me. And then I sweep the room, wide-eyed. It crosses my mind that I must look a bit like Distira.

I see a corner of the quiche I made yesterday sticking out from underneath a collapsed cabinet, and, unexpectedly, tears well up. It isn't, I know, brave, but there's nothing I can do about it.

Victor makes to climb through the hole towards me but I shriek with fear and tell him to go around the back way, which, thankfully, he does, vanishing from sight then reappearing moments later, scrambling over the woodpile towards me.

He takes me in his arms and I think, *OK, I have to let this out. I'll pull it together in a moment. But not just yet.*

'I was just starting to like it. I was just starting to like the place,' I sob.

Victor squeezes me in his arms. 'I know,' he says. 'Me too.'

'And then that ... that ... *idiot*!'

Victor sighs. 'I think the wall was fucked,' he says. 'I think Distira was right.'

We hug like this amid the snowy, muddy silence for a few minutes until Stéphane appears around the side of the house, sidling towards us with his hands in the pockets of his fluorescent trousers. He looks like a guilty adolescent who has broken a vase.

'I'm sorry,' he says again when he reaches us. 'But I didn't touch the wall.'

Unable to even look at him, I close my eyes.

'It's ...' Victor says, and the thought that he might be about to say, 'OK,' makes my blood boil. But he doesn't. Thankfully he doesn't say anything at all.

'*Vous voulez que je termine?*' Stéphane asks. *Do you want me to finish?*

I gasp in disbelief, and then have to separate from Victor and get away from both of them before I lose control and scream at Stéphane or, worse, slap him.

'Just ... get rid of him, will you?' I mutter to Victor as I stamp my way through the snow towards the wall at the edge of the property. When I get there, I clear a space just big enough to sit on. In the distance I can see Victor and Stéphane talking calmly, and then Stéphane turns to leave and I hear Victor shout, '*Doucement!*' *Gently!*

The noise of the digger fills the air again and then it comes back into view, moving – for the first time today – slowly and with grace. As if proof were needed, even now that it's too late, that it had been possible all along.

As the digger crosses our land and then swerves and starts to vanish into the distance, I sit and watch Victor staring at the house, and think, *What now?* Eventually he turns and crosses the field to join me. He looks pale. When he reaches the wall, he turns around without a word and leans back so that his back is between my knees. We remain like this for maybe ten minutes, silently surveying the desolation of the front yard.

'I'm sorry,' he says eventually. 'I didn't even imagine that the wall might collapse.'

'It's not your fault,' I say. But I'm aware that I don't sound convincing. In some way this disaster is precisely the fault of the men here, and their gung-ho attitude. That and their inability to listen to the voice of caution. *My* voice of caution.

'Better to find out now rather than later, I suppose,' Victor says.

'Find out what?'

'That the wall was fucked,' he says.

'You reckon?' I say flatly, unable to disguise my sarcasm.

Victor sighs, and I squeeze his shoulder. It's the best I can manage for the moment.

'So what now, eh?' he asks.

I want to say, 'Can we go home?' But of course, home no longer exists. This, for better or worse, *is* home. 'I was going to ask you that,' I say instead.

He shrugs.

'Insurance?' I ask.

Victor shakes his head. 'Stéphane's working on the side. He shouldn't even have borrowed the digger.'

'That's not our fault though, is it?'

'No, but it means that he doesn't have insurance.'

'But what about *our* insurance?'

'I doubt they'll cover us for accidentally knocking down our own wall,' Victor says.

'No, knowing insurance companies, I doubt it too,' I agree. 'I think that this might be beyond Clappier's remit too.'

'Yes,' Victor agrees. 'Yes, I think we might need a proper builder.'

'Do you think we can still live here?' I ask. 'I mean, is it safe? Is the bedroom OK?'

'Let's look,' he says, turning to offer me a hand down. 'Let's go see how bad it is.'

The short answer to my question is no, we can't still live here. The bedroom wall is bowing inwards, looking as if it could collapse any minute onto the bed, while the bathroom wall – the only wall in the entire house to be plastered – is now criss-crossed with fresh cracks.

'I just finished that wall,' I whisper, and Victor slides an arm around my waist and says, 'I know, I know.'

I slump onto the safest edge of the bed and Victor joins me.

'One step forward, one step back,' he says.

'A small step forward and giant leap backwards, more like,' I say. 'What now? I mean, what are we actually going to do?'

'I think I should phone Georges,' Victor says. 'See if he knows a proper builder.'

'Sure, but where do we stay? We're effectively homeless. Maybe we should go and fetch the van,' I say, attempting to head off a different solution that I can sense is hanging in the air.

'How?' Victor says. 'We'd never get it back up here through this snow.'

'Well, we could bring it halfway,' I say hopefully. 'And use the car to drive up and down.'

'CC . . .' Victor says.

'Or we could sleep at Georges'. In the van, I mean.'

'But we're gonna need to be *here*.'

'We can commute. I've done it all my life.'

'Not in six inches of snow you haven't. I'll just go ask—'

'No!' I interrupt. 'I don't want to.'

'You don't even know what I was going to say,' Victor laughs.

'Yes I do. You were going to suggest we stay with Distira.'

'OK. I *was*. But it's the only reasonable option.'

'Well, I'm not being reasonable. None of this is reasonable,' I say, starting to sound a little more frenzied than I intended. 'I'm not staying with Distira. I'm sorry, but I don't want to.'

Victor raises his palms in submission. 'OK. Whatever the lady wants,' he says.

But whatever the lady wants quickly turns out to be an impossibility for the simple reason that the little Panda will not budge from the spot where it is parked. With Victor pushing and me driving, we manage to move it three feet, but as soon as we pause to swap seats, we are stuck all over again.

Victor opens the boot and finds a pair of devilishly complicated snow-chains, which we spend a finger-freezing half-hour attempting to fit. With these finally in place, we try to leave once again, and for ten yards it seems that we could just have the problem licked. But then the car spins out of control and, engine revving, wheels once again slipping in a mixture of mud and snow, it stops dead. When we climb out, the reason becomes apparent. The chains are lying just behind the car.

Victor retrieves them and good-naturedly saying, 'Round two!', crouches down beside one of the wheels to try again.

But with a growing sense that my obstinacy may end up transforming a disaster into a human tragedy, I reluctantly decide to capitulate. 'Leave it,' I say. 'It's too dangerous. We don't know what we're doing.'

'There's only so many ways these fuckers can go on,' Victor says. 'I'll get it in the end.'

'Have you ever driven a car with snow chains before?' I ask.

'Sure,' Victor says.

'When?'

'Just now. For ... erm, twenty feet. It was fine.'

I shake my head. 'You are cute,' I say, 'but I want you alive.' I nod towards Distira's house. 'Go ask her,' I say.

'You sure?' he says, hesitating with the chain.

I grudgingly give a small nod.

He reaches for my hand. 'Come on. We can go together.'

We wade through the fields to Distira's door and Victor explains to her what has happened. In all fairness, the old dear looks genuinely concerned and when she offers immediately and without reservation to prepare the *chambre d'amis* for us, it's such a relief that I feel a fleeting urge to hug her. It fleets, thankfully, before I do so.

We trudge back to our open-shell of a home, where I pack two overnight bags while Victor phones Georges.

Georges insists that Clappier is perfectly able to rebuild a wall, citing their garage, which he built single-handedly, as proof. Victor then phones Clappier, who not only seems unfazed by the task, but also insists that, 'The snow never stopped him doing anything yet', and that he'll be here tomorrow.

I step into the open doorway to leave but then stop dead in my tracks. 'Oh!' I say.

Victor joins me just in time to see Distira's Lada vanishing over the brow of the hill. 'Aw, bless, she probably had to go buy more food,' he says.

'I hope she left the door open.'

'I'm sure she did,' Victor says.

'Well, you know what car to get, now, anyway,' I say.

'They haven't changed the design for forty years or something.'

'You peoples may laugh,' I say in a dodgy accent, 'but Russian technology, best in world!'

Victor smiles. 'You may be right.' He starts to pull our own front door closed, but then laughs sourly. 'Not much point closing it, is there?'

'Close it anyway,' I say, taking a last glance at the devastation.

'Why?'

'I don't know. Because it's bad *feng shui* or something.'

'Or something,' he says, pulling the door shut and reaching for my free hand. 'Come on. Let's go watch Auntie's telly.'

'You know,' I comment, nodding at the mud-hill that Stéphane has created, 'it looks like a Siberian wasteland now anyway. A Lada would be ideal.'

Distira hasn't, by accident or design, left the front door unlocked, so we dump our bags in the porch and for the first time properly explore the grounds behind her house. For the most part these provide a tableau of decay, if not of actual despair: a farm, once rugged and productive, long since beyond the capabilities of its single, ageing owner.

We pass a collapsed shed, the rusty handle of some piece of farm machinery sticking out, a vast pile of car tyres, an almost entirely disintegrated pushbike, and – overgrown with weeds – a tiny three-wheel car, the body of which seems to be made out of plywood.

Beyond this, a path rises up over the hill, so with nothing better to do we crunch through the snow until we reach the summit. We look down on the view of the plateau. From here, Stéphane's mud-pile appears to be even more of a blot on the pristine white landscape.

Beyond the brow of the hill, Distira's land has been carved into wide steps. As we zig zag our way down the far side, each level reveals something of its past life. The first is a flat field, perhaps a vegetable patch, the second has a tool shed and a large, jacuzzi-sized water reservoir; and the third a small, partly collapsed greenhouse next to a criss-cross of wires, perhaps once used for training French beans.

'She has much more land than we do,' Victor comments.

'I'm sure she'll let you use some of it. It looks like it's all getting a bit beyond her. I bet she doesn't even come down here any more.' But just as I say this, we come across proof that she does still come down here, even in winter. Because the next step down contains a vast chicken coop. Standing beneath a sheet of corrugated iron lying on top of the mesh, on the only square of land to be protected from the snow, stand three scrappy-looking chickens. The second they see us they run through the snow to meet us.

I push a finger through the chicken wire and say, 'Hello, chicken.' One of them nips at it.

'Ouch!' I say. 'They look hungry.'

'How does a chicken look hungry?' Victor asks mockingly, crouching beside me.

'I don't know,' I say. 'They're sort of asking for food, aren't they? This one wants to eat *me*.'

'My guess is that chickens *always* want food,' Victor says. 'Anyway, look, there's a feeder thingie over there.'

'Don't they get cold out here in the snow?'

'What, you mean more than all the other birds in the forest?'

'I suppose,' I concede.

'Anyway, they have their little house over there, don't they?'

'It would be nice to have chickens,' I say, straightening up.

'Once everything else is sorted,' Victor says.

'Of course, walls clearly take precedence,' I agree.

We carry on down until we reach the edge of Distira's

land. Beyond this begins a forest, and the silence and lack of life amongst the pine trees is surprising.

'It's beautiful,' I say. 'And so quiet in there.'

A huge pile of snow falls from a branch with a thud and lands on the forest floor below.

'It's kinda spooky too,' Victor says. 'It's a bit *Blair Witch Project.*'

'It is! Shall we go back? My feet are freezing.'

'Mine too,' Victor agrees. 'I think we need those padded snow-boot things.'

'Ooh yes, moon-boots. I want ABBA ones. With shaggy fur around the outside.'

'I always thought they were kinda sexy.'

'You see,' I say. 'We agree!'

'Hmm, sex in shaggy moon-boots,' Victor says. 'There's something to look forward to.'

We climb our way back to the top of the hill and then back down to Distira's house, but because she still hasn't returned, I suggest raiding our fridge to provide a contribution to dinner. I'm also aware that if she attempts to foist vol-au-vents upon us again, whatever we bring may be all that I get to eat.

It's 5 p.m. and the sun has just vanished behind the mountain when Distira's Lada appears, slewing confidently through the snow towards us. Seated beside her is Carole, and it quickly transpires that it was to fetch Carole, not food, that she left.

We spend another surreal evening with Distira, who is visibly trying to be charming, while Carole visibly isn't. In fact, within the first ten minutes, I'm pretty certain that Carole's fiery eyes and near-silence can only make sense if she is furious about something. But Victor takes charge of stoking the fire and just about manages to remove the chill from the room. He also makes a double effort to be jolly and calls Distira *'tatie'* repeatedly, even resorting to tickling her waist at one point, which only serves to make Distira's eyes bulge even more than normal. Carole looks even more furious about this and Victor, I notice, doesn't repeat the gesture. But by the time we have drunk two bottles of wine between us and eaten Distira's reassuringly ordinary macaroni cheese, the atmosphere could almost be described as relaxed.

Once the washing up is done, Distira apologises and says something about 'sleeping' with 'chickens' before vanishing from the room. Carole silently follows her.

'What does *that* mean?' I ask, the second we are alone. *'Elle dors avec les poules?'*

'It means she goes to bed when the sun goes down,' he says. 'The same as chickens do.'

'Right. I was thinking that the chicken coop was going to be a bit of a tight fit!'

I cross the room to the fire and turn so that I can warm my back on it. Victor joins me. 'I'm a bit pissed,' I whisper, leaning into him.

'Me too.'

'Do you even know where we're sleeping?'

Victor shakes his head.

We stand there for another ten minutes until it becomes clear that neither of the women are returning, and then head off on a slightly tipsy exploration of the house.

We ignore the first two bedrooms, the doors of which are closed and I peer into the third. The bed is made up and Distira has carried our bags up and dumped them on the bed. The only problem is that Distira's overweight Rottweiler, thankfully absent during the meal, has also chosen our bed.

'Victor, the dog's in here,' I whisper. 'You have to move him.'

'Why do *I* have to move the dog?'

'Because I'm scared of it,' I say.

'But I'm scared of it too,' he protests.

'Jesus,' I say, heading into the room, and switching on a light. 'OK, we'll do it together.'

Victor follows me into the bedroom and closes the window, which is wide open. 'No wonder the house is cold,' he says.

'It was probably musty,' I say, turning my attention to the dog, who is clearly quite comfortable and has no intention of moving. 'Oswald, come on!' I coax, and bravely attempt to pull on his collar, but he growls and then snaps at me, narrowly missing my hand.

'Well, come on,' I say, jumping well back. 'Do something!'

'*Oswald, viens!*' Victor says, hoping that the dog will respond to French better than English.

'That worked,' I laugh. 'Not!'

Victor shakes his head. 'I'm sorry,' he says, 'but that thing scares the shit out of me. Have you seen his teeth?'

'Yes, I nearly just felt them.' I roll my eyes. 'Men! Useless!'

'Hey, wait here, I have an idea,' Victor says, leaving the room.

I back into a corner and look around the room. The bed

is an ornately carved wooden four-poster. It looks shorter than your average bed and I reckon that Victor will have to scrunch up to get in. With the red satin quilt and bunched mosquito nets, it also looks a bit like a tart's boudoir. Along one wall of the room stands an enormous wooden wardrobe, almost entirely obscured by cardboard boxes, which in turn are hidden by piles of ancient, unattractive women's clothes.

The dog suddenly pricks up its ears, opens its bloodshot eyes wide, and stands. It sniffs the air and, feeling panicky, I start to scan the random contents of the room for a potential weapon. But the dog simply leaps from the bed and scampers off down the corridor. I wouldn't have believed that he was capable of moving so fast.

Victor returns, looking terribly proud. 'See, It's not brawn that counts, it's brains,' he says.

'Dog food?'

'Yep.' Victor looks around the room for the first time. 'God, she doesn't throw much away, does she?'

I shake my head. 'No, I don't think she does. It's freezing in here. I can see my breath.'

Victor shrugs. 'Well the window was open. I expect it'll warm up.'

'OK, you go first,' I say, nodding at the bed.

Victor looks at it, then suspiciously back at me. 'Why? What's wrong with the bed?'

'Nothing,' I laugh. 'But it's gonna be freezing!'

Victor snorts. 'So as well as fighting off wild beasts, I have to warm the bed up now, do I?'

'You do,' I say. 'Those are your manly duties.'

I turn to look out at the moonlit snow and then back to

find Victor now stripped to his boxers and T-shirt, climbing beneath the covers.

'Well, come on then!' he says. 'It's freezing. Get a move on!'

ANGELS VS. DOCTORS

Despite all the wine, I don't sleep well that night. The bed remains freezing and clammy, but when I try to warm myself against Victor, I find that I get hot and sweaty, so the only thing I can do is alternate constantly between the two. At some point during the night, my back starts to ache as well, which I blame on Distira's ancient sprung mattress. It's only when Victor gets up in the morning that it finally dawns on me what all of these symptoms really add up to: influenza.

'Just stay in bed, pumpkin,' Victor says, touching my forehead. 'I'll go see what Clappier says and report back.'

I insist that, no, I *will* get up and join them shortly, but it only takes a trip to the bathroom to convince me otherwise. I can barely stand up, let alone participate in the rebuilding of walls. And so, feeling guilty on top of everything else, I return to bed.

Mid-morning, I'm awoken from a bad dream by Distira. She hands me a cup of warm grog, which I accept gratefully. It tastes of lemon, honey and something bitter – paracetamol perhaps. She stands at the window, her hair glowing around the edges due to the harsh light of the snowscape beyond, and then, once I have finished, she silently takes the cup from my grasp and lumbers from the room.

When I wake up, the daylight has long since fled and the room is bathed in moonlight. The next thing that I'm aware of is someone stroking my forehead, and I turn to see Victor, his face white with brick-dust, perched on the edge of the bed.

'Are you OK, pumpkin?' he asks me.

'No, I'm not. I have flu,' I mumble, realising as I do so that a sore throat has now added itself to my miserable panoply of symptoms.

'You're really hot. But that's a good thing. It's your body fighting the virus. Can I do anything? Can I get you anything?'

I shake my head. 'I just need to sleep,' I say, my eyes already closing.

'Are you sure you want this window open?' Victor asks. 'It's freezing in here.'

I want to tell him that I haven't opened the window, and no, I don't want it open, but sleep is already sucking me under again, so I only manage to stay awake long enough to say, ''s freezing,' and to vaguely hear the sound of it being closed.

From that point on, I fold completely into a world of nightmares and tormented sleep, of achy joints and endless quantities of perspiration that feel sometimes unbearably hot, but almost as often cold and clammy. Victor is next to me in the bed, and then he isn't, and it is sometimes day, and sometimes night. Someone is feeding me soup, or water, or grog, or I am wishing that they were, or wishing that they would go away and leave me be.

One morning, I wake to an empty bed and head to the bathroom. I have to rest to catch my breath both on the way there and back – my limbs feel weak and rubbery, and my lungs don't seem to be working properly. This shocks me quite profoundly, and for the first time I wonder if this really is just flu.

When I get back, Victor is there, and I'm so relieved by this that I rather absurdly start to blub. He resists taking me in his arms for a minute, saying, 'I'm covered in cement,' but when I collapse against him, his arms come up to enfold me.

'You poor thing,' he says. 'Look, I picked up a thermometer. Let's take your temperature.'

He puts the thermometer under my tongue, and sits and strokes my hand for the requisite three minutes, before peering at it and announcing, 'Thirty-nine. You have the flu. It's official.'

'Shouldn't I take something?' I ask.

Victor shrugs. 'It's viral, so there isn't much. You need lots of fluids, and that's about it. The fever's actually a good thing, as long as it doesn't go any higher. I can't prescribe here, anyway. But if you want to see a GP, then you should.'

'I do,' I say.

'I'll tell Distira,' he says. 'She wanted to call one, but you said no.'

I frown, unable to remember this scene – unable even to imagine now that it could be true.

'And you have to stop opening the window,' Victor says. 'It's freezing in here.'

'I didn't,' I tell him.

'No,' he says, laughing gently. 'It must have been the leprechauns, then.'

He guides me back to the bed, tucks me in and lies beside me until I fall asleep again, and then suddenly it's morning again, only I feel even worse, struggling to open my eyes as Victor gets dressed.

'We should finish the bedroom wall this morning,' he tells me brightly, information which, through my fever, barely makes sense.

'I need the doctor,' I say.

'I'll make sure he comes today,' Victor says.

'Good,' I say, attempting to stand and go to the bathroom.

'Here, I'll help you,' Victor says, hiking one of my arms around his shoulders.

He walks me to the bathroom and says, 'A good job he's coming, too. You're all wheezy.'

'I'm dying,' I say, joking, but then suddenly I'm not so sure.

Victor laughs. 'No, you're not,' he says.

'I might be,' I wheeze, beads of perspiration breaking out on my forehead. 'I really might be.'

'Well, I won't let you,' Victor says. And to prove just how much he means this, he promptly vanishes.

As some point that day – at least I think it's the same day – I wake up to find Distira slapping my hand gently. I open my eyes and she holds out two pills, which I swallow along with another cup of her grog.

'Where's the doctor?' I ask.

Distira says something that I don't understand. Understanding French in my current state is pushing my capabilities to the limit. Speaking French seems almost impossible.

'*Médecin?*' is all I can think of. *Doctor?*

'*Je l'ai appelé,*' she says slowly. '*Il dit que ça va aller.*' I *called him. He says you'll be fine.*

'I need to see a doctor,' I say, and Distira just shrugs and shakes her head.

'*J'ai besoin médecin,*' I manage. *I need doctor.*

Distira looks at me and shakes her head slowly. '*T'as un ange gardien qui veille sur toi,*' she says, which I'm pretty sure means that I have a guardian angel watching over me. Which makes so little sense to me that I decide that I am stuck inside one of my feverish dreams again.

When Victor returns that evening he tells me that I *have* seen the doctor. 'Are you feeling better? Are the pills he gave you working?'

'I didn't see a doctor,' I tell him between coughing fits. 'He didn't come. Distira says I have an angel watching me.'

Victor pulls a face and strokes my brow. 'Sure,' he says.

'But she did!' I tell him.

'That's just the fever talking.' And he seems so certain, I assume that he must be right.

'I'm so cold,' I tell him.

'Then stop opening this window! I'll have to put a lock on this if you carry on.'

'I didn't,' I protest. 'And I didn't see a doctor. She says I have an angel instead.'

'The doctor came,' Victor insists. 'He prescribed these, and Distira went all the way into town to get them.'

I pick up the blister pack and check the back, but nothing is written there. 'What is it?'

'I'm not sure, I wasn't here. It's the stuff the doctor prescribed. Antibiotics, I expect. The French are big on antibiotics.'

I feel wretched and, despite Victor's presence, afraid and alone. I don't want to be ill, and I don't want to be ill in France, and I particularly don't want to be ill at Distira's. I start to cry again, aware that I'm ruining any reputation I may have had for ruggedness or suitability to farm life.

'My poor baby,' Victor says, hugging me and rubbing my back. 'You'll feel better soon. I'm sure the antibiotics will start working. Now, you have to let me get you some food. You have to eat. Distira has made you some soup.'

'I don't want it,' I say.

'She says it's the one you like.'

'I don't want it,' I say again, sounding like a spoilt child.

'OK. What do you want?' Victor says, speaking to me like one. 'Something else?'

I have no idea where the reply comes from, but 'Pot Noodle' is what I say.

'Pot Noodle?' Victor asks.

'Pot Noodle,' I groggily repeat.

He helps me back into bed, where I instantly fall asleep and dream of guardian angels who look like witches boiling people in vast cauldrons of foul-smelling soup.

When I wake up again, Distira is leaning over the bed. '*Voilà,*' she says, angrily plonking the pot down on the bedside table. '*C'est vraiment n'importe quoi!*' *Here! This really is madness!*

'*Je veux le medecin, Distira,*' I plead. *I want the doctor.*

'*T'as un ange gardien qui veille sur toi,*' she says again. *You have a guardian angel watching over you.*

This time I'm pretty sure that I'm awake – I glance at the window and see a fly banging against the pane, and conclude that this is too ordinary a detail to be included in a dream.

'*Tu n'as pas besoin d'un médecin,*' she says. *You don't need a doctor.*

'*Si, j'ai besoin,*' I protest. *Yes, I need.*

'*T'as le meilleur de tous les anges gardiens. T'as Jésus lui-même. Ça devrait suffir, non?*' *You have the best of all the guardian angels. You have Jesus himself. That should suffice, no?*

She stands and leaves the room, and I lie and stare at the wall and try to digest my new knowledge that Distira is completely mad. Eventually I attempt to eat the Pot Noodle but, hungry as I am, my illness has ruined my senses and it tastes both bland yet weird, so I quickly abandon it.

For some reason, fearful of Distira's wrath, I stumble to the bathroom and tip it down the toilet to flush away the evidence, but when I come out, she is standing in the hallway, watching me, arms folded.

'*Ha!*' she says angrily. '*C'est ça ton jeu, hein? Me faire travailler pour rien!*' *So that's your game, is it? Have me running around for nothing!*

I open my mouth to protest but, unable in my current state to think of a reasonable excuse, I just stand before her sweating. After a few seconds, she snatches the empty pot from my hand, before lumbering off down the hallway.

*

It's my own coughing that wakes me next – a fit that just won't seem to end. I cough and wheeze and cough some more, and this exhausting episode, combined with a sensation that I just can't get enough oxygen, leaves me feeling terrified.

When it finally subsides, the fear-induced adrenaline rush has left me wide awake and, for the first time in days, thinking clearly.

I lie in bed and wonder what to do. I have a desperate desire to call my mother, which is proof, if any were needed, of just how bad things are.

The only person I trust is Victor, but even he doesn't seem to understand. And looking at the available options, the only thing to be done is to make sure that he does.

I hear the noise of a car outside, and clamber from the bed just in time to see Distira's Lada heading off over the field. Once I have watched it disappear, I realise that the snow has all but vanished, and that there, in front of our house, sits our VW van. And a white Lada – which is confusing. Are my eyes deceiving me? Is Distira at our house, or are there now *two* white Ladas?

I decide to take my chances. It feels like my only hope.

I sweatingly stumble around as I pull on the nearest available clothes: my own jeans, Victor's jumper, but no shoes. Search as I might, I can't find my shoes.

Eventually, with a sense of rising panic, I decide to cross the field shoeless, but thankfully find a pair of oversized wellington boots outside the front door.

The air today is so chilled that it burns my throat and

sets off a fresh coughing fit, but I stumble on across the frozen ridges of the field all the same.

When I enter the farmhouse, Monsieur Clappier is the first person to spot me. He calls out to Victor, who appears from the bedroom wearing blue overalls and carrying a trowel.

'You're up! Are you feeling better?'

'No,' I say, starting to cough afresh.

Clappier looks at me with concern, but then seems embarrassed and turns to continue his plastering.

'You shouldn't be up,' Victor says when he reaches me. 'You look dreadful.'

I try to speak but end up wheezing, and then disintegrating into a fresh bout of coughing.

'Here,' he says, taking my arm in his. 'Let's get you back to bed. You need to rest and wait for the antibiotics to work.'

When I resist, Victor's brow furrows. He leans down so that he can look me in the eye.

'Listen,' I manage to splutter between coughs.

'I am listening,' Victor says, 'and I'm hearing one very sick—'

'Listen to me!' I cough. 'You have to listen to me.'

'OK, let's get you back in the warm and then I'll listen—'

I shake his arm off and shriek, 'Victor!'

His arm drops to his side and his features darken. 'What is it?' he asks.

'I need a doctor. Take me to a doctor,' I say.

'But you saw one,' he says. 'And he agrees that you have the flu and—'

'Not flu,' I say, resorting to the short version in order to get the words out between coughs. 'No doctor. He didn't come.'

Victor laughs. 'But he did, babe. Don't you even remember it?'

'No,' I say.

Victor wrinkles his brow and touches my forehead. His smile fades.

'Doctor, now!' I say. 'Or a hospital. Don't care.'

The H word seems to have some effect. 'Has something else happened?' he asks.

'Just *listen* to me,' I plead, starting to cry now. 'This isn't flu. I can't . . . breathe.'

'OK, I hear you,' Victor says. 'We'll get the doctor back, and I'll sit with you and talk to him, but you have to get back to the house. It's freezing here.'

Overcome by my nightmarish inability to make any progress, beads of sweat form on my forehead. I feel like I'm wading through mud with the grim reaper chasing me close behind. I sink onto a chair behind me and start to cry gently.

Victor crouches down in front of me, and strokes the side of my face. 'I know you feel awful but don't cry.'

I open my mouth to speak but start instead to cough again, deeply and forcefully. The fit this time is entirely debilitating and lasts even longer than the session that woke me in the first place.

Clappier turns to watch this and then downs his tools and shyly sidles across the floor towards us, apparently hesitating about intervening.

'*Tiens,*' he says quietly to Victor, while nodding at me. '*Elle ne va vraiment pas bien, tu sais.*' Look, she really isn't in a good way.

Victor replies that, yes, he can see that I'm not in a good way and explains that I am asking him to take me to a doctor but that I already saw one yesterday, plus he doesn't know where the doctor lives or what his phone number is. That only Distira has that information.

Clappier shrugs and says, '*Amène-la à la clinique. Amène-la à Valderoure.*' Take her to the clinic in Valderoure.

He then reaches into his pocket and produces a bunch of keys which he throws at Victor. '*Vas-y,*' he says. *Go.*

If I had the strength, I would hug him for that.

While Clappier explains to Victor where the clinic is, I sit in his car – the other white Lada – and watch the horizon in case Distira should return, fearful that she might somehow convince him not to take me. Through the mists of my fever, she has become an assailant. But soon enough, we are bumping off over the track.

'Don't worry,' Victor says. 'It's not that far.'

Unable to find the energy to even attempt a reply, I simply nod and turn to listlessly watch the countryside rolling by.

When we reach the clinic in Valderoure, Victor explains to the receptionist that his *femme* is *très malade.* Glancing snootily at my wellington boots, she invites us to sit in the waiting room.

When the doctor comes out for his next patient, he glances at me, performs a double take, and then after a brief mumbled conversation with the receptionist, invites me in first. And I'm pretty sure that it's not because he fancies me.

He's a young, good-looking country doctor with a lovely stripy jumper and a reassuring manner. As he leads me into the surgery, I become embarrassed by the random clothes that I'm wearing and by the fact that I haven't showered. This embarrassment makes me sweat even more, but he shows no sign of noticing any of this.

He takes my temperature – high; checks my blood pressure – low; and checks my glands – swollen. He then looks at my tongue and asks me how long I have been ill. I'm shocked to discover from Victor that it is now six days.

He then admonishes Victor for bringing me into a waiting room full of people and not phoning him before. I have, he explains, got swine flu.

Victor tells him that I have seen a doctor, but unable to say who the doctor is, nor what drugs he prescribed, and faced with my own confusing insistence that I *haven't* seen a doctor, Doctor Charming says that it's best if we just start from scratch.

He injects me with antibiotics and prescribes me with antivirals, more antibiotics, vitamins, and codeine. And then he does something that hadn't crossed either of our minds – he asks Victor to pay him. As neither of us have brought any means of payment, he rather trustingly takes our address and tells us that we can come back and pay when I'm feeling better.

After a short stop at the pharmacy, Victor climbs back into the truck and we start to head home. 'I can't believe it's been almost a week,' I say.

'No,' Victor agrees. 'I've been so busy. I'm sorry. I should have taken better care of you.'

I open my mouth to say that it's OK, but then change my mind. 'The snow has gone, too,' I say instead.

'Yes,' Victor says. 'Sunday was warmer and most of it vanished overnight. I went to get the van back on Monday.'

'I want to sleep in the van,' I tell him.

Victor laughs.

'I do,' I say.

'Don't be silly,' he replies.

I sigh and glance at his profile as he drives, starting to be irritated by this new patronising aspect of his personality. 'I'm sleeping in the van,' I say, in a special tone of voice that people don't usually argue with.

'You're better at Distira's,' he says, equally seriously. 'At least she can look after you. And the van is full of plasterboard. That's why we're in this thing today.'

'Empty it,' I say.

'She'll be offended,' Victor replies.

I cough repeatedly as I try to work out the most succinct series of words that will put across my absolute determination not to return to Distira's. Meanwhile, Victor slides his free hand onto my knee, and, without thinking, I shrug it away.

'OK! I'll empty the fucking van!' he exclaims.

Actions, it seems, speak louder than words.

'We might be back in by Friday anyway,' he eventually adds. 'The wall is almost rebuilt.'

'Friday,' I say. 'What day is it today?'

'It's Tuesday,' Victor says. 'So in three more sleeps. Or in your case, one long sleep. I can't believe you want to go back to living in the van! It's really not—'

I interrupt him. 'Believe it!' I say.

Reaching La Forge, I see that Distira's car has returned.

'You go have a sleep,' Victor says, 'and I'll get the van sorted for you.'

He takes my arm to lead me towards her house, but as we pass a plastic garden chair, I break free and slump into it. 'I'll wait here,' I say.

'Since when were you so stubborn?' he asks gently, looking down at me and shaking his head.

I open my mouth to say, 'Since I got swine flu,' but instead start coughing again.

It takes about fifteen minutes for the two men to move all of the materials from the van and for Victor to convert it back into a bedroom, but because I haven't felt the sunshine on my skin for a week, this is in fact quite blissful.

Once ready, I climb back into bed and instantly start to doze, woken only briefly by Victor when he returns from Distira's with my bag. 'She's a funny old bird,' he says, dumping the bag on the front passenger seat.

'Funny?' I say, dragging myself back to wakefulness. It's not a word I would use to describe her.

'Yeah, I wonder if she doesn't have Alzheimer's. She couldn't find your shoes, and she couldn't find your medicine . . .'

'It doesn't matter,' I say. 'I'm not going to mix those drugs with the new ones, anyway.'

'I found the shoes, though. They were in the back garden.'

'Really? Why?'

'Dunno. One of them had some herbs in it, so maybe she thought they were smelly.'

'My feet are not smelly,' I protest.

Victor shrugs. 'Like I said, Alzheimer's maybe. Anyway, do you need me to stay or . . .?'

'I just want to sleep,' I tell him.

Victor nods. 'You sure you're OK in the van?'

I nod. 'One hundred per cent.'

'If you need anything, toot the horn,' he says, and then blows me a kiss before heading off into the house.

That night I lapse back in and out of fever but as the next three days pass, I feel a little better with each wakening. On day two I prop myself up on pillows to read, and twice I even head into the house to make tea. I rather slovenly reduce my visits to Distira's bathroom to the barest minimum, even going as far as using the toilet of our own open-to-the-elements bathroom, rather than visiting hers.

On Friday morning I wake up feeling as if I merely have a bad hangover, which, compared with the previous week, equates to feeling bloody marvellous.

The bathroom wall now entirely rebuilt, I am able to have a soak in our very own bath, and I arise from the waters feeling like a new woman. Checking myself in the mirror, I realise that I also *look* like a new woman. My face looks as if it has spent seventy years without moisturiser rather than seven days. But the rest of me is as thin as I have been since I was in my twenties – a dose of swine flu is like a free Shrink-Me Waist-Witch. I even have to cut a new hole in my belt.

Victor catches me attempting this operation, badly, using a kitchen knife. He wrestles it from my grasp. 'We need to fatten you up,' he comments, as he makes the hole with a bradawl. 'You're way too skinny.'

'You make me sound like a goose,' I say.

Victor smiles. 'You are my goose,' he says, handing back the belt. 'I tried to get you to eat, but you were so stroppy.'

I start to thread my belt back around my waist. 'I don't trust her food,' I say.

Victor rolls his eyes at this.

'I *don't*,' I say. 'It made me ill every time.'

'Not *every* time,' Victor says. 'And it didn't make me ill, not once.'

'Actua—'

'OK, *once*,' he concedes.

'Maybe you have a stronger constitution than I do. Or maybe she didn't mess with your plate so much.'

At this Victor stops his mixing operation and shakes his head.

'She's a very strange woman, Victor,' I say. 'Even you said so.'

'Strange, yes, but it's a bit of a leap to suggest that she's been poisoning your food,' he says. 'And a bit of an offensive one. You seem to forget that she's my aunt.'

I fill the kettle for tea and wonder whether to continue this discussion. It's clearly veering towards an argument.

'I didn't say *poisoning*,' I tell him. 'Oh, and just out of interest,' I add, thinking that I'm changing the subject, but as I say it realising that I'm really making things worse. 'Did you actually *see* the doctor?'

'The one you say never came?'

'Yes.'

'What about him?'

'I just wondered what he looked like,' I lie.

Victor nods and then shakes his head. 'No, I didn't see him, CC.'

'Right.'

'Your point being?'

'Nothing,' I say.

'I was here holding up stays to stop the roof caving in,' Victor says.

'OK.'

'So am I in trouble for that as well?'

'You're not in trouble for anything,' I say.

'Good,' Victor says. 'Because even *I* can't be in two places at once.'

'I wasn't even complaining,' I protest.

'Good,' he says again.

'I was just . . .' I start, but then I let the sentence dry up mid-way. I had been about to point out that seeing as neither of us saw the doctor except Distira, that maybe . . . well, maybe he *didn't* come. Maybe she *did* tell me that Jesus is all I need. But Victor glances up at me and a shadow crosses his features as if he has subconsciously worked out where I am going with this.

'I can't believe how much work you've done here,' I say, to quickly change the subject. 'Virtually all of the walls are rebuilt now, aren't they?'

As if to confirm that we're walking on eggshells here, Victor replies, 'Yes. I'm knackered. And my back's fucked. And my wrists hurt. Because there have only been the two of us here all week. And half the time Clappier isn't here either. So just, you know . . .'

I lick my teeth and fight the desire to rise to the bait. I wonder what the missing words are. 'Back off', perhaps?

I look around the room and take in the sterling progress they have made, and imagine how much work and strain it must be putting on Victor, and decide to do just that. 'It's amazing,' I say. 'You are amazing. And I'm sorry I was too ill to help.'

Victor blinks at me slowly. 'I didn't mean that,' he says. 'You know that's not what I meant.'

'I know. So is there anything I can do now?'

'You're better off resting.'

'I could do something light,' I volunteer. 'I'm still a bit weedy, but I'd like to do *something*.'

'If you're really up to it, you could tidy up a bit,' he says. 'The mess is getting on my tits.'

'Then that's what I'll do,' I say.

And Victor just about manages a smile.

Though my own contribution is limited by my convalescent state, I manage to get the space tidy and with all of us working on the place, it comes on in leaps and bounds. This process is marked by a series of milestones, many of which, because we have been here before, create a strange feeling of déjà vu. On Saturday evening we light our first fire since the disaster and cook our first meal on the range. On Sunday we remove the temporary supports from the joists and get to sleep in our unfinished bedroom again. And though from the outside the whole place still looks like a tsunami has swept through, the house begins, just about, to feel like home again.

On Monday we have to disconnect the water pipes so that Clappier can replace some tubing, which was bent during the collapse of the wall, but because his blowtorch runs out of gas before he manages to solder the final joint, we are left, temporarily, without water. This is particularly bad timing because having used a roller all afternoon, I'm splattered with white paint. With Victor equally coated with grouting, the obvious choice is to head to Distira's for a shower. Obvious, perhaps, but I fight it all the same.

'I'm fine to stay like this until tomorrow,' I say, causing Victor to raise an eyebrow at me. He wipes a finger across my forehead and points it at me to show that it is now white with emulsion paint. 'You reckon?'

'I'll wash in the van,' I offer.

'Nice solution. Only the tank's empty.'

I roll my eyes, forced once again to capitulate. 'Just in and out then,' I say. 'No dinner invitations shall be entertained.'

'No,' Victor says. 'Although as we don't have any water . . .'

'Then we can take the jerry-can,' I say, 'and come back and cook.'

'Sure,' Victor agrees. 'Now come on, before that paint dries in your hair.'

As we head off to Distira's an uneasy feeling returns – a vague sense of tightness in the pit of my stomach.

TOO MANY GHOSTS

When we get to her house, Distira beckons us in enthusiastically, which makes me suspicious. She leads us into the kitchen, where we find Carole sitting at the table. Oswald, who is on his armchair, begins growling at us the second we walk in. This only stops when Distira shouts at him.

'*Oswald! Ferme-la!*' she shrieks, and the dog responds by grumbling and laying a paw over his nose.

Distira immediately takes her seat at the table and picks up her hand of cards, her apparent enthusiasm clearly not for us after all – she simply wanted to get back to her game.

'*Vous jouez au tarot?*' Victor asks her. *You're playing tarot?*

Distira is holding her hand close to her chest as if I or Victor might gain something by peeping. '*On vient de commencer,*' she says. *We just started.* '*Vous jouez?*' *You play?*

'*Non,*' Victor says.

'Did you say tarot?' I ask Victor. 'As in *actual* tarot?'

Victor shakes his head. 'No, it's just a card game.'

Distira checks her cards and, as I'm standing behind her,

I can now see them. The cards are amazing: each one comprises a water colour – a drunk with an empty bottle, a clown juggling ...

'Gosh, what amazing cards,' I comment, stooping in to look at them better.

'They are special,' Carole says. 'From nineteen seventies. For future reading. She loose the others.'

'*Vous savez lire les cartes, Tatie?*' Victor asks. *You know how to read the cards, Auntie?*

Distira inclines her chin vaguely in Carole's direction. '*C'est elle qui fait ça,*' she says. '*Moi, je ne fais que jouer.*' *She's the one who does that. I just play.*

Carole, apparently seeing this as a request, reaches over and wrenches Distira's cards from her hand, and despite Distira's evident irritation at the interruption of their game, proceeds to shuffle the cards before spreading them expertly across the table.

'*Pensez à votre question, et sélectionnez-en trois,*' Carole says in an abrupt, no-nonsense manner. *Think of a question, and choose three.*

Victor winks at me, and then moves closer to the table. He hangs his towel on a chair-back, and taps three cards, which Carole separates out before folding the rest of the pack away.

'*Et la question?*' she asks.

Victor laughs. 'Oh, I thought it was secret,' he says. 'Sorry, it was, um, can we make money from the farm? Enough to live on.'

She flips the three cards over and nods as if to say that she expected exactly this result. She lays a finger on the first card. 'This one is past,' she says, looking from Victor to me. And who could deny that the image on the card – a castle being hit by lightning – looks a lot like our own 'château' in recent days.

'It means change,' Carole says. 'Not expected.'

'Unexpected changes,' I say quietly. 'Sounds about right.'

'Yes, none-expected change,' she says, apparently mishearing me. 'And this one is what you are obliged to do.'

Victor and I both peer at the card. The image shows a man driving an ox. 'Looks about right,' Victor says.

'It means to travel,' Carole says.

'Travel?' I say, surprised. 'It looks like work. Farm work or something.'

'No, is travel,' she says definitely. 'Perhaps to the south-west.'

'Why the south-west?' Victor asks.

'I feel it,' she says, waving a hand over the cards in a faux-mystic manner.

'And this one?' Victor asks, pointing at the third card – a man standing next to a scarecrow with the setting sun behind him.

'Good,' Carole says.

'Good?'

'Is sunny.'

I run my tongue across my teeth, entirely convinced now that she is making this up as she goes along. When did a tarot card ever just mean 'good'?

'Well, as long as the future is sunny,' Victor says as Carole sweeps up the cards and reshuffles the pack. She nods her head in my direction. 'And you?' she asks, now smiling at me in her unnerving and rather unconvincing way.

'No thanks, Carole,' I say. 'I need to wash this paint off.'

Victor nudges me with his hip. 'Go on,' he urges. 'You saw how long it takes.'

'No, really,' I say, but Carole is already spreading the deck.

'Can I keep the question to myself?' I ask, intrigued to see what meanings she will invent if she isn't told the question first.

'If you want,' she says. 'But it's not so good. Not so *spécifique*.' Which, thinking about the card interpretations she has just done for Victor, seems a laughable idea.

Thinking that this will turn out to be one of those quirky memories that we will look back upon and laugh about, I cave in. 'Go on then,' I say, pointing quickly to three cards in succession.

As before, Carole separates the cards and sweeps away the rest of the pack before flipping over my three cards. The second I see them, I wish that I hadn't got involved in this.

'Not so good,' Carole comments, and even I can see from the sombre colours of the cards that this is so.

'This is past,' she says, caressing with one finger the image of a hanging man. 'Something dead. Life make short.' She stares me in the eye, and I attempt to maintain my poker face.

Victor sighs in a way that communicates that he too is realising that this was a mistake.

'This is what you are obliged to do,' she says, pointing

to the second card, which shows a Dickensian-type character heading off with a knotted parcel on the end of a stick. 'You must go to a new place.'

'I did,' I say. 'This is the new place. So that's good, isn't it?'

'*Non*,' Carole says. 'No, this is the old place. So a different place.'

I nod solemnly and brace myself for the next card: the grim reaper. 'And that one's lovely, I bet,' I say.

'Actually, she is not so bad,' Carole says, staring at me intently.

'She?'

'This card. She is not death.'

'It *says* death on the card,' I point out. '*La mort.*'

'Yes but it is, how you say? A symbol.'

'OK, but a symbol of what?'

Carole shrugs and is already sweeping the cards back into the pack. 'I don't know. I don't know the question because you don't tell. But the end of one thing. Maybe you don't get the thing you want. But after the end is a new different thing. So it's not so bad. Maybe.'

She finally pulls her eyes away from mine and shuffles the cards, before starting to deal their two hands once again. Distira, apparently pleased by the results of my reading, or simply the fact that her game can now resume, starts to smile quite sweetly. Well, as sweetly as one can with those teeth.

'*Bon, nous pouvons aller à la salle de bains?*' Victor asks. *Can we use the bathroom?*

'*Servez vous,*' Distira says, picking up her cards. '*Faites comme chez vous.' Help yourself. Make yourselves at home.*

'What was your question?' Victor asks me once we reach the bathroom.

'I didn't really have one,' I say.

Victor pulls a face and starts to hop out of his overalls. 'I don't believe you,' he says.

He's right. But there's no point spreading the misery. There's no point telling Victor that the answers – a life cut short, the need to leave, and a future of disappointment – were responses to the question, 'When will I get pregnant?' Sharing that would just be cruel.

I will, I decide, push it from my mind. After all, we all know that tarot is rubbish. Don't we?

When we have finished washing and have changed into our fresh clothes, we peep back in on Distira to say goodbye. '*La lettre!*' Carole prompts, and Distira jumps up and crosses the kitchen to retrieve an envelope from a drawer.

'*C'est pour toi,*' she says, handing the envelope to Victor. '*Désolée, mais je l'ai ouverte par accident.*' *It's for you. Sorry, I opened it by accident.*

We both thank her and then start back towards home. As I pull Distira's front door closed behind us, I hiss, 'By *accident*, yeah right!'

Victor ignores me and shakes the letter open, scans the contents, and says, '*Merde!*'

I jog to catch up with him and grab his arm. 'What is it?' I ask.

'It's a tax bill,' he says. 'Inheritance tax.'

'On this place?'

'On both places,' he says. 'Here and Perpignan.'

'Is it bad?'

'Seventy-three thou,' he says.

'No!'

Victor just shakes his head and pulls my arm tighter.

And then I laugh.

'It's not funny,' he says.

'No, I know. I was just thinking about Carole's "trip to the south-west". No prizes for guessing where she got that one from. Carole knew all right, but it wasn't from the cards; it was from reading your post.'

Back at ours, we sit next to the range and discuss our options. Seventy-three thousand euros will wipe out almost all of Victor's remaining savings, which would leave only my meagre four thousand and any future rent from my apartment. Which, if anything else goes wrong – and it seems almost inevitable that it will – clearly isn't enough. This quickly leads to the obvious conclusion that the Perpignan house, worth about one hundred and eighty thousand, needs to be sold.

Victor sits and pores over figures he scribbles on the back of the envelope while I cook pasta and heat up a jar of carbonara sauce, and by the time I serve this, his decision has been made. 'So you fancy a trip to Perpignan?' he asks, pushing the sheet of paper to one side.

'Really?' I ask. 'When?'

Victor shrugs. 'This needs to be paid in June, so I would say as soon as possible.'

'You reckon you can sell the place that quickly?' I ask, winding spaghetti around my fork.

'No way. It takes more like six months in France. I'll have to pay it from my savings, but the sooner the money from the sale comes in after that, the better really, don't you think?'

I nod thoughtfully.

'You OK?' Victor asks, reaching for my hand.

'Sure,' I say. 'I'm just a bit tired. The tail end of the flu still. So when do you want to go?'

'Maybe Wednesday or Thursday? I'll need a couple of days there to empty the contents and get it on the market. But you'll like it. It's a lovely house.'

'Sure,' I say. 'I'd love a break from all of this.'

'And if we give Clappier a hard enough time, the place just might be finished by the time we get back.'

I nod.

Victor forks up a mouthful of spaghetti and when he has swallowed it, says, 'You sure you're OK? You're not thinking about that tarot nonsense, are you?'

I laugh as convincingly as I can. 'Of course not,' I say.

'Did you have a question in mind? I bet you did. I'll bet it was about love or marriage or babies or something,' Victor says.

I close my eyes, smile and shake my head. 'God, you guys think girls are just so predictable, don't you? Nothing's wrong. I'm just tired. I *am* recovering from swine flu.'

'Too tired to go to Perpignan?' Victor asks.

'No, the break will do me good.'

'You'll like some of the furniture,' Victor says. 'And anything you want is yours.'

'Great,' I say.

'I'm glad you're coming. There are lots of memories there for me. Too many, really. But we'll make it a nice trip. We'll make a holiday out of it.'

'Can't wait,' I say. And if I could think about what he is saying instead of Carole's stupid tarot, I would mean it.

The drive to Perpignan is a monotonous succession of mile upon mile of grey French motorway.

But it's a crisp, cold day with a stunning blue sky and very little traffic.

Near Nîmes, Victor suggests that we stop for lunch.

'Oh good,' I say. 'I have never seen Nîmes. It's supposed to be lovely.'

Victor laughs. 'Sorry,' he says. 'But today isn't the day that you get to see Nîmes. I'm just pulling into the services here. I want to get there by nightfall.'

'Never mind,' I say. 'Another time.'

The motorway services are plastered with murals of the many wonderful sights of Nîmes. 'At least we know what we're missing,' I say, pointing.

It's not until we near Perpignan that Victor reveals that his childhood home isn't in Perpignan at all but in a nearby village.

'I'm sorry,' he says. 'I thought you knew.'

'Nope,' I say. 'You always said Perpignan.'

'Yeah,' Victor says. 'Well Dad always said Perpignan, even though it isn't really.'

As we leave the autoroute and begin to plough through the knobbly, out-of-season vineyards that surround the town, the setting sun begins to flame red, casting romantic orangey

242

strips of light across the land. After less than ten minutes drive, the walled town of Baixas, where the house is actually located, comes into view.

'Is that a church?' I ask, pointing at a vast monolithic building dominating the skyline, currently lit red by the setting sun.

'Yep,' Victor says. 'There's no escaping the big guy in Baixas.'

'It's beautiful,' I say.

Victor turns and smiles at me. 'I knew you'd like it here,' he says.

We drive into the centre of the town and park the van in a large empty car park then walk the last thirty yards to the house.

Victor eventually stops in front of a large door and produces a key from his pocket. 'I so know what you're going to say next,' he says, opening the deadlock and pushing the heavy door open.

I shoot him a puzzled expression and step over the threshold then flick a light-switch. 'Oh,' I say. 'There's no electricity.'

'Ah,' Victor says. 'Sorry, hang on.'

'Is that what I was supposed to say?' I ask him as he fiddles with the fuse box behind the door.

'No, not really,' he laughs. He flicks a switch and says, 'Ta-da!'

The entrance is dazzling. The hallway and staircase are entirely built of that rounded, white, organic-looking plasterwork you see everywhere in Greece, while all the doors are painted royal blue. I peer into the first room and turn on the lights to reveal a lounge with a large blue sofa, a big open fireplace, and sandstone walls.

'It's lovely,' I say.

'I know,' Victor says, crossing the room to open the shutters with a clack. 'Dad did it all. Mum inherited the place, but Dad did all the work.'

'Like father, like son,' I say, heading through to the next room, a large, slightly old-fashioned kitchen/dining room. Then I peer out at a beautiful little courtyard. It has a table and chairs covered with plastic sheeting, and in one corner a small fountain, now dry.

'It's beautiful, Victor. It must be lovely in summer.'

'It is,' Victor says quietly. He holds out a hand. 'Come see upstairs.'

Reaching the first floor, I open a closed door onto the front bedroom.

'Mum's room,' Victor says.

'Wow, it's still got all her stuff in it.'

'I know,' Victor says, his voice sounding tense. He slides his arms around me, nuzzles my neck, and sighs. 'I sorted most of it, but I never really had the courage to tackle this room. Maybe you can help me with that tomorrow?'

'Sure. How long ago did ... you know ...?'

'When did she die? Three and a half years ago,' he replies.

'Right,' I say, turning so that I can hug him properly.

'I'm fine,' he says. 'It's just ...'

'Sure. I understand.'

'Here!' he says, visibly forcing himself to sound more optimistic. 'Come see my room.'

He gently closes the door behind him before running

244

upstairs to the next floor and bursting into another bedroom.

'Wow!' I laugh when I catch up. 'Very seventies!' Two of the walls are blood red, and two are lime green. 'How did you ever live with these colours?'

'It's Kawasaki racing colours,' he says. 'I was into motorbikes.'

'I didn't know that,' I say.

Victor points to a poster on the wall, where there is a photo of a biker in green and red racing leathers, cornering so hard that his knee is scraping along the ground.

'I had one until about four years ago.'

'Really? A big, fast one like that?'

He laughs. 'No, just a regular road bike. A Honda Hornet, if that means anything to you.'

'It doesn't.'

'No. Well it was a blue one,' Victor says, mockingly, 'if *that* means anything.'

'Blue's nice,' I say, ignoring the dig.

'Have you ever been on a bike?' he asks.

I shake my head. 'No. I think I'd be scared,' I say, walking to the window and peering outside at the view my man grew up with. I turn to the bookcase and run my finger gently over the spines. 'Your books,' I say.

'Yes.'

'They're all in French.'

Victor laughs. 'Well, yes.'

'Why did you call it your mum's room?' I ask. 'Did they have separate rooms or something?'

'No, they divorced,' he says.

'Oh. I don't think I knew that either. So who lived here? Just you and your mum?'

'No, I was with Dad in England. Surely I told you all this, didn't I?'

I frown. 'No. It's strange, but I don't think you ever said much about your childhood. But you did live here at some point – I mean, if you have a room?'

'Yep. Till I was eleven,' Victor says, switching on an electric heater and bouncing on his old bed. 'After that I was in Lewes, near Brighton.'

'Baixas to Lewes. How did *that* happen?'

'Sorry,' Victor says. 'I'm not explaining this very well, am I?' He pats the bed beside him, and when I join him he lies down, pulling me with him. I fidget until my head is resting on his shoulder. He wraps one arm around me and with the other points at a plastic helicopter suspended from the lampshade. 'That's been there for thirty years,' he says, reverently. Lying here, in his old bed, in the room where he grew up, I suddenly feel the most incredible wave of love for him. It's so powerful that it makes me shudder.

'Cold?' Victor asks.

'A bit. But it's warming up. Go on.'

'You sure you want to know this?'

'Of course I do.'

'OK,' Victor says, with forced laughter in his voice. 'It is long and messy, so you have been warned.'

'Families always are,' I say. After a moment's silence, I prompt him with a, 'So?'

'I'm just trying to work out where to start.'

'This house.'

246

'So this place was Mum's. She inherited it. This place and the farm. Our farm.'

'And Distira got the place next door to the farm? Where she lives now.'

'Exactly. But this place was a wreck. Well, they both were. Dad did this place up. He was a teacher, but he was good at DIY. Better than me. He inherited a fair bit of money from his parents and spent a chunk of it on this place. And they were happily married for about fifteen years before it all went wrong.'

'How old were you when they divorced?'

'Whaw, that electric heater stinks, doesn't it?' Victor says.

'It's dusty. It'll burn off,' I say. 'Carry on.'

'Well when I was about eight or nine, Dad met Angela, my stepmum. They had an affair, I suppose you'd call it.'

'How French.'

'I know it sounds a bit sordid, but I think it was a big love affair, to be honest. Angela used to come here every summer with her husband, and she and Dad just couldn't stay away from each other. I think Dad might even have visited her in England. He used to go away sometimes, purportedly on school trips. Anyway, when I was eleven, Angela's husband somehow found out and threw her out. And she came here and there was the biggest argument ever. Mum, Dad and Angela shrieking at each other in the court-yard.

'Angela went back to England, but the arguing here went on for months. It was civil war really. And Mum started drinking. A lot.'

'And you were only eleven? It must have been awful.'

247

'Yeah. It was pretty bad. I used to have to check her pulse to see if she was dead.'

'I've been there. I dated an alcoholic,' I tell him. 'It's horrible for anyone, but worse for a child.'

'I grew up quickly, I suppose, once Dad moved out.'

'He just left?'

'Well, he had to. This was legally Mum's place, after all.'

'And you stayed here with her, or . . .'

'Initially. But not that long in the end. She was drinking all the time. Distira had to come to stay for a while.'

I must make a face at this, because Victor says, 'I know you don't like her, but she was a very different person thirty years ago. I was glad to have her around, anyway.'

'I'm sure. I didn't say anything. So where was your dad?'

'In England. He sold his share of his parents' vineyard and bought a cottage in Lewes with Angela. And then Mum had to go into hospital. A mental hospital, really. They didn't exactly have detox clinics in those days, so . . . No one told me much. I was too young to live on my own, and Distira couldn't stay forever, so Dad came and got me.'

'He took you to England?'

Victor doesn't reply, but I can tell by the way his shoulder moves that he is nodding his head.

'Did he speak English? Did you?'

'Yeah. He taught it. And mine was OK. Just schoolboy English, but . . .'

'That must have been a wrench, changing countries like that at such a young age?'

Victor shrugs. 'It kinda was and wasn't. It was a culture shock. But it changed my life, really. They put me in school in Lewes. I did really well. I made loads of friends. I went to uni ... I doubt any of that would have happened if I had stayed here with Mum.'

I think about all of this for a moment. Considering his childhood, he's amazingly well-balanced. Comparatively, I have had it easy. 'That's an awful lot to go through,' I tell him. 'I can't believe that I didn't know any of this.'

'I don't know much about your childhood either, other than about Waiine,' Victor points out.

'Did your mum get better?' I ask.

'Not really. It came and went. She was on the wagon for a while but then she met Bruno and fell promptly off again. She met him when she was in hospital. Ironic that they met there, really. They dated for about ten years. Or more like, they drank together for about ten years.'

'But you used to come back?'

'Oh, of course. Summer holidays, Christmas ... Anytime Dad and Angela went off on one of their cruises – Angela was quite high maintenance – they would pack me off here.' Victor pauses and sighs deeply. 'I love this house. It's just ...' He shudders. 'It's just that everyone's dead, aren't they?'

I squeeze him tight for a few minutes, and eventually he continues. 'Dad and Angela split up eventually. I was at college.'

'God, even the big love affair didn't last?'

'No. Dad left her the cottage and moved back to Perpignan. He had blown all his inheritance by then.'

'He moved to Perpignan or here?'

'Perpignan. He rented a little flat. It was a bit sad, really.'

'Did your mum and dad see each other?'

'No! Well, one time Dad drove me out here and dropped me at the end of the road just as Mum was walking home, so they crossed paths. They shook hands and said hello. But that was as close as you could ever get them. Even that was too much. Mum went on a bender the second we got in.'

'I'm sorry,' I say. 'What did they die of?'

'Dad – a heart attack.'

'Like mine.'

'And Mum – liver failure.'

'Of course. I'm so sorry. That all sounds really horrible.'

'It's just life. Shit happens and you get through it.'

'And Angela?'

Victor shrugs. 'I don't know. She found someone else to pay for her cruises, I expect. Dad loved her, but we weren't exactly mates.'

'The house is beautiful, though,' I say. 'Are you sure you want to sell this one and keep the farm, not the other way around?'

Victor snorts. 'Now *that's* what I knew you would say.'

'Well, I hate to say it, but it's much nicer.'

'I know. But there's no land here. And no land means no way to earn a living. And frankly there are too many ghosts for me to be able to live here, anyway.'

'Right. Of course.'

'Look, I'm hungry,' Victor says, suddenly unlinking himself from me and sitting up. 'There's a pasta place at the end of the street. Well, there always used to be. Let's go have a look.'

*

Victor's pasta restaurant has, like two thirds of the world's restaurants, become a pizzeria. But neither of us care much about food tonight.

Victor's mind is clearly stuck in the past and the more he tells me about his childhood, the more I feel that I understand who he is and how he came to be this lovely, gentle man. He recounts amazing stories of hiding his mother's bottles of pastis, of having to call the police because she was so drunk he couldn't summon her to get back into the house, of putting out a fire she had caused by falling asleep while smoking. He tells of how he and his best friend, both sixteen, had to pin his mum's equally drunk boyfriend to the floor to prevent him stabbing her with a kitchen knife.

And then we move, somehow, onto my own family, and I tell him in detail about my father's death, about Waiine, about Mum and Saddam, and though we have told each other snatches of this stuff in the past, by the time we have finished I'm feeling a most unusual sensation of fatigue, emotional rawness, and sadness at the meanness of life, combined with an incredibly strong sense of love for human beings in general – including those no longer with us – and for Victor in particular.

We walk, slightly tipsy, back to the house, and there, in Victor's childhood bed, beneath a plastic helicopter, we start to make love.

'I never did it in this bed before,' Victor whispers, staring into my eyes.

And then, perhaps to scare the ghosts of the past away, we have the most serious, reverent sex that we have ever had before falling asleep entwined in the tiny bed.

I'm awoken twice during the night by Victor's erection pressing against me, and so we have sleepy sex all over again. By the time our regular morning session is over, we have made love four times. Which, being a personal best, makes me like this house even more.

Over breakfast of croissants and coffee in a nearby café, I ask Victor about this. 'So is it the house?' I ask quietly. 'Is it being here that's making you so rampant?'

'Are you complaining?' he asks, grinning wryly.

'Not at all,' I say. 'Not one bit.'

Victor shrugs and sips at his coffee and stares out of the plate glass window where a woman has just knocked over her shopping trolley. She is running around catching onions as they roll away. 'Maybe it's the bed,' he says.

'Maybe we should take it home then,' I say, not entirely joking.

'Maybe it's all the adolescent fantasies that happened in that bed.'

I nod and rip off a chunk of buttery croissant. 'That makes sense.'

'Actually, it might be all the death,' Victor says, seriously. 'Maybe sex is an antidote to death.'

'Which makes even more sense,' I say, speaking through a mouthful of croissant. 'Sex leading to life. Sex *creating* life.'

'Hopefully,' Victor says, with a wink. And the shadow of Carole's tarot reading creeps across my mind.

We spend that first day visiting estate agents and arranging evaluation visits, the second sorting through the possessions in the house, separating out which items Victor wants to keep, those he doesn't care about, and those that he can't bear to see ever again.

What time we have left is spent wandering around the pretty mediaeval town that is Baixas, sipping coffee, sleeping, and, of course, having sex.

Back in the same café, over an identical breakfast, Victor asks, 'So do you still want to go to Perpignan? Because we can, but it's just that I feel kinda ready to get back and get on with things.'

'Me too,' I say, even though it isn't really true. 'With our new sofa and new sideboard and new garden furniture.'

'If it all fits in the van,' Victor says.

HOME ALONE

When we get back to La Forge with our haul – the sofa doesn't fit but the armchairs do – the sense of disappointment at the state of the house overrides any relief at being 'home'. There is no sign whatsoever that Clappier has even visited during our absence.

'Un-fucking-believable,' Victor spits, looking as angry as I have ever seen him and already reaching for his mobile.

As I light the range and warm a carton of soup, Victor leaves Clappier a message that is so acidic it makes *my* ears hurt.

After a bad night's sleep, caused mainly by the cold – it seems that it takes about twelve hours for the house to warm up again – I make coffee and, in an attempt at smoothing the tense atmosphere, pancakes. Funnily enough, it's what my mother used to do when Dad was upset about something.

'I can't believe that he hasn't called back,' Victor says as I place a plate in front of him.

'Well, give him time,' I say, stroking his shoulder. 'It's only half nine. And he does have other clients. He has been incredibl—'

'It's about keeping your word,' Victor interrupts. 'He promised it would all be finished.'

'Well, it doesn't change anything getting all bent out of shape, so just try to enjoy your breakfast.'

He smiles weakly at me. 'Sorry. I didn't sleep well.'

'Me neither. It was cold.'

'I got up and added more wood to the boiler,' he says.

'So did I. I reckon we might need some kind of back-up heating so the place doesn't freeze just because we're out for the day.'

Victor nods. 'Maybe,' he says, fingering his mobile again.

'Does this coffee taste weird to you?' I ask.

He sips his, pulls a face, and stirs in an extra teaspoon of sugar. 'It's just cheap, I think. Robusta instead of Arabica.'

'It's the same coffee we had before,' I say. 'But it tastes like paracetamol.'

Victor shrugs. 'It's just cheap coffee,' he says.

Though I never have sugar in coffee, this morning I follow Victor's lead and sweeten it, but it still doesn't taste right to me.

Victor looks at his mobile and then frowns. 'It says I have a message,' he says. 'How did that happen? The bloody thing didn't even ring.'

He one-handedly forks pancake into his mouth as he listens to the messages.

'Clappier?' I ask when he hangs up.

'No. The estate agent. They phoned yesterday while we were driving home. They have a buyer.'

'No!' I say, realising as I do so that I have a mouth full

of pancake and raising one hand to cover it. 'They're offering the full price?'

'Yep. And they want to rent it until the sale goes through.'

'That is keen. But great news, surely?'

'It is, I guess. I just can't help but think we should have asked for more. I'll have to go back down to Perpignan now. It was hardly worth coming home.'

'How soon?'

He shrugs. 'They're gonna call me back, but it sounds like they want to move in within a week if possible and rent it until the sale completes. I need to get someone in to take away all the furniture.'

'Are you having second thoughts about selling the place?' I ask, hopefully.

Victor shakes his head. 'No. It's just, you know ... the end of one thing. The beginning of something else.'

'You're not going to call Clappier again?' I say as Victor raises the phone to his ear. 'Give the guy time to see he has a message at least.'

'I'm not,' Victor says. 'I'm calling Georges.'

I head through to the bathroom and sit on the cold seat for ten minutes as I wait to see if my feeling of queasiness is going to transform into something more definite. Like projectile vomiting. I might still have, I figure, the remnants of swine flu. But other than a vague sense of icky dis-ease, nothing manifests.

When I get back, Victor is leaning against one of the surviving kitchen cabinets. He looks sheepish. 'What happened?' I ask when he hangs up.

'I wish I could delete that message I left for Clappier.'

'Oh?'

'Georges says he's laid up with swine flu.'

'Oh no! And we all know who he caught *that* from.'

'I wonder if Distira is OK,' Victor says. 'Could be bad for a woman of her age. I better go and check.'

When Victor returns from his aunt's, he has a strange look on his face.

'Is she OK?' I ask, looking up from a pot of paint I'm stirring, the fumes of which are making my head spin.

'Yeah, she's fine. But she asked me if she could come with us!'

'Really?' I say, standing and placing one hand in the small of my back as I stretch. 'Why?'

Victor shrugs. 'I guess she has memories of the place too,' he says.

I nod thoughtfully. 'You said no, right? Tell me that we're not taking Distira to Perpignan?'

Victor laughs. 'Of course not. I knew you wouldn't want to. And I'm not that keen on spending ten hours in the car with her myself, to be honest.'

'So we're leaving tomorrow?' I ask.

Victor nods. 'Now that I know what has to happen, I just want to get it all done. Is that OK?'

I nod and sigh in sympathy. 'There's still so much stuff there,' I say.

'I'm gonna phone them and arrange a meeting at the house tomorrow afternoon. See if I can flog them some of the furniture. And get a local *brocanteur* to come in and take the rest away. Distira asked us to bring that little telephone table back for her, by the way. It's the only thing she asked for. It was their mother's, apparently.'

I nod.

'You look really sexy in that.'

'This?' I say, laughing. I'm wearing an old white shirt of Victor's as a smock. It's splattered with paint.

'Yes,' he says, waggling his eyebrows suggestively. 'It makes me quite ...'

But I don't rise to the bait because I simply don't feel that well. Waves of nausea keep building and then fading, and by mid-afternoon, I give up on painting and announce that I am going back to bed.

'Is that an invitation?' Victor asks me.

'Sorry,' I say. 'But it isn't. I just need to sleep.'

When the alarm clock goes at seven the next morning, it is immediately obvious that I won't be able to go. Not wanting to worry Victor with the state of my health on top of everything else, I tell him that I have slept badly and ask if he would mind terribly if I stay behind. I'm relieved and yet vaguely irritated by how little he seems to care.

By 8 a.m. he has gone, leaving me alone for the first time ever in the farmhouse.

As protection against the supplementary chill left by my guy's departure, I stoke the range to the hilt and return to bed for an extra hour's sleep.

When I do wake up, it is nearly lunchtime, and I have a feeling that I have been summoned from my slumbers by a noise within the house. I lie there holding my breath for a moment as I listen, and eventually decide that it must have been the wind whistling in the eaves that woke me.

I imagine Victor still driving and, thinking guiltily about him sorting through his parent's furniture, I briefly regret not having made the effort to go with him. But then a wave of sickness sweeps through my gut.

I realise that we now have an armchair and that I can spend the day reading next to the range. Though I don't dare use the internet on my phone because of the crazy roaming charges, I can still text my mother and get her to phone me with her Moroccan calling card. I can phone SJ and Mark too, to find out what's happening back home.

Home. I stare at the ceiling for a moment and try to work out what the word means. Where is home? Because the truth is that it still doesn't feel like the answer to that question is 'here'. I wonder how long it might take before that is the case. I wonder if that will ever be the case.

Still vaguely listening to the sounds of the empty house, I get out of bed and pull my dressing gown on. As I open the bedroom door, I hear a noise – a ceramic chink of a cup against a saucer, or a teaspoon against a glass. I freeze and hold my breath.

My skin prickles when through the tiny gap in the open door I see a shadow fly past, followed by the distinct rush of air as our front door opens and closes. I glance around the bedroom for a possible weapon, but there isn't a single heavy object within the room.

My heart now beating double time, I creak the door open and peer out, then slowly edge my way into the kitchen. Seeing that there is no one here, I run to the window and look outside, and then, grabbing a full bottle of Bordeaux for defence purposes, I dash to the front door and run bare-foot outside, determined to see who it was.

The chill of the howling wind takes my breath away. I scan the horizon, half expecting to see Clappier's car, or Jean-Noël's moped, or some other entirely innocent expla-nation as to why someone has been in my kitchen while I was asleep. But other than Distira's distant Lada, no one is present. And then a figure appears from behind the Lada, walking towards Distira's house. It's Carole.

As she crosses the front garden to Distira's porch, she glances towards me. She's a long way away, so it could be my imagination running riot, but it seems to me that the way she moves is somehow fox-like, the way she turns her head is edgy, nervous, guilty, perhaps. And then she raises one hand, and waves and smiles at me. Which, let's face it, is a first.

The front door closed behind me, I stand and survey the kitchen and try to imagine what on earth Carole could have been doing here.

Perhaps she thought that I was out; in fact, that's almost certainly what she would think. They would have assumed that I had gone to Perpignan with Victor, and seeing no car outside would imagine that the house was empty. But that doesn't explain what she was doing here.

I remember the ceramic 'chinking' sound and scan the various pots and pans for a possible source. I cross the kitchen and lift the lids of various jars in an attempt at finding the source, sniffing the contents of the tea, coffee and sugar jars as I do so. But it's no use, because everything smells strange today. Everything smells metallic, like snow.

Maybe they had run out of coffee, I figure. Maybe they came to borrow something. With the nearest shop an hour away, that would be understandable. So maybe she was caught in the act of borrowing something, and suddenly felt like a thief and chose to run away rather than fessing up.

A sinister explanation crosses my mind. Maybe everything smells strange, tastes strange because . . . well, because it *is* strange.

I shake my head and tell myself to think like an adult, rather than a paranoid child. Because what possible explanation could there be for such craziness? Unless they simply don't, as I have always suspected, like having us living next door. But as Victor says, from that to suggesting that Carole is creeping in and *poisoning* the coffee . . . There! I have said it. I only said it in my mind, but I have said it!

Feeling vaguely ashamed, I shake my head and head through to the bathroom. By the time I have showered, the idea seems like nothing more than a silly fantasy I have entertained. I decide to be a grown up and deal with this in an adult, head-on way.

I make coffee from a fresh pack, nibble half a slice of toast and then, because I still have no appetite, bin the rest. Taking a deep breath, I pull my big winter coat from one of the new pegs that Victor put up yesterday and head off to face them.

My knock on Distira's front door goes unanswered, but knowing that if her Lada is present, she is too, I head around the side of the house to see if they are out back. Seeing no sign of either, I weave my way through the junk and head towards the top of the hill, thinking that even if I don't manage to see them from there, it's a beautiful bright day for the walk. As I near the top of the hill I'm rewarded with the sound of Distira's voice carrying on a gust of breeze.

I discover the two women collecting something from the undergrowth. I'm unable to see what this is because the second Distira sees me, she throws a tea-towel over the contents of her basket.

'*Bonjour,*' I say. Thinking that if we're going to live here, it's probably worth knowing what bounty the forest has to offer, I nod at the basket. '*Vous collectionnez quoi?*'

Distira frowns at me as if my question is unintelligible, and well aware that I may have used the wrong verb, I try Carole instead. 'What are you ladies collecting?' I ask her, flashing my warmest grin.

'Is nothing,' Carole says.

'It can't be *nothing*,' I reply.

'*Elle veut savoir ce qu'on est en train de cueillir,*' Carole says to Distira, looking vaguely panicked. *She wants to know what we're picking.*

'*Des herbes,*' Distira says.

'Lovely,' I say. 'Which herbs grow here?'

'Wild herbs,' Carole says. 'Traditional. For medicine.'

'Right,' I say. 'So, did you need something earlier?'

Carole frowns at me, so I try French. '*Vous êtes venue pour quelque chose?*'

'No,' she says, her eyes flicking again at Distira, who looks back at her blankly.

'But you came to the house this morning,' I say, studying her facial expression.

'I'm sorry,' she says. 'I don't understand you.'

'*Vous êtes venue. À la maison. Chez nous. Ce matin,*' I say, thinking, *Oh no, you don't get away that easily.*

'*Non, je ne suis pas venue chez vous.*'

'But I *saw* you, Carole,' I tell her.

Carole shakes her head. 'I don't know what you mean,' she says in a voice that would never pass muster in acting school.

'I don't mind,' I tell her. 'I just wanted to know what you wanted.'

'I did not,' she says again.

There doesn't seem to be anywhere to go from here, so I sigh and turn to leave. But then something possesses me and, disguising it as a joke, I lurch towards Distira's basket and rip away the tea-towel before she has time to react. The basket contains nothing more than some scary-looking wild mushrooms and some sprigs of bracken.

'Sorry,' I say, winking at her and handing the tea-towel back.

The poor dear looks quite outraged, the way she might if I had just pulled her swimming costume off in front of a thousand onlookers.

'*Vous devriez vous occupez de vos oignons,*' she says. *You should mind your own onions.*

A little unnerved by her anger, I decide to beat a hasty retreat. 'OK, well, as long as you don't need anything,' I say. '*Au revoir!*'

I give the women a little wave as I turn to head back over the hill.

Carole replies with her own, 'Au revoir,' but Distira, by now making no pretence to liking me, simply grunts and heads off in the other direction, perhaps to feed her scary mushrooms to her chickens. Or vice versa.

Back at the house, I load some more wood into the range and note that we will have to buy some soon – our stock of scrap wood is fast running out.

I lock the new lock, and turn the key sideways to stop anyone else who might have a key from inserting it. I pull one of the armchairs as close as I can get it to the range, and sit and wait for Victor to call. After an hour, I phone him, but his mobile is off so I leave a message.

At sunset, feeling vaguely freaked out by my morning intruder and the fading light, and particularly alone due to Victor's absence, I lean outside and pull the big wooden shutters closed for the first time since we have been here.

As I swing the final shutter closed, something flutters to the ground outside, so, after checking left and right for potential assailants, I nip out to pick it up.

What I find is a tarot card with some bracken taped to the back. The bracken has been bent into a rounded loop and tied, and the card, I note, is not one of Carole's psychedelic cards, but from a more traditional deck.

A shiver goes down my spine but I pick it up gingerly and carry it inside, then quickly lock the front door again.

I sniff the looped bracken on the back – it has no noticeable smell – and carefully place the card upon the table as if it is a bomb that might go off if jolted.

I get my phone out and thinking, *Hang the roaming*

charges, I Google 'nine of swords tarot meaning' and click on the first response. As I read, all the hairs on the back of my neck stand up: *Suffering, doubt, desolation, illness, injury, death of a loved one, suspicion, cruelty, misery, loss, dishonesty, pitilessness, slander.*

And then I see that there are in fact two cards, back to back, one upside down against the other. I peel off the Sellotape holding the bracken in place to reveal The Empress. I do another Google search and the results are even more upsetting: *Blocked creativity, frustration, miscarriage, abortion, infertility, loveless sex, prostitute, a barren woman.*

I breathe out slowly. Deciding that I will not succumb to random superstition, I grab the card and the bracken, then open the range and throw them inside. I hold my breath until the flames have consumed them.

Superstition aside, the cards reveal something to me that I have long since known in my gut: I am not welcome here. And someone nearby who *is* superstitious does not wish me well.

THE RIGHT SET OF EARS

Victor finally calls me back just after nine.

'Babe!' I exclaim anxiously. 'I've been trying to phone you all day.'

'I switched the phone off to save the battery. What's up?'

'I want you to come back,' I say. 'I need you here.'

Victor laughs. 'I only just got here. And this is going to take a few days. I met the people and they seem nice but—'

'I don't feel well,' I say, still debating how much to tell him. 'I don't want to be on my own.'

'Are you scared?' Victor asks, almost mockingly. 'Are you scared all alone in the big empty house?'

'Yes,' I say sharply. 'Actually, I am. Because I caught Carole in the kitchen this morning.'

'Carole? She's a bit weird, but she's not scary,' Victor says, still apparently amused. 'What did she want?'

'She didn't *want* anything. She was lurking around and before I could speak to her, she ran away. And now she denies that she was ever here at all.'

Victor sighs heavily. His breath rattles against the microphone of his mobile. 'What do you mean she denies being there?'

'Exactly that,' I say. 'I heard a noise, someone fiddling around with the food jars, and by the time I got to the kitchen, they had run away. So I ran outside just in time to see Carole.'

'And what did she say?'

'She didn't say anything. She was going into Distira's by the time I got outside.'

Victor snorts. 'You're not making sense,' he says.

'She was fiddling around with the coffee jar, I think.'

'Well, maybe she ran out of coffee,' Victor says, sounding bored now rather than amused.

'In which case, she'd say, "Oh! You're here, CC. Sorry, I ran out of coffee." Don't you think?'

'You're being ridiculous,' Victor says. 'This is that whole poisoning-the-food thing again, isn't it?'

'Maybe.'

'It's getting out of hand. It's turning into full-blown paranoia.'

'Well, you know what they say – just because you're paranoid doesn't mean that they aren't out to get you,' I say.

'They?'

'Distira and Carole.'

'Oh, for God's sake.'

'What's *your* explanation, then?'

'I don't have one,' Victor says, sounding irritated. 'Because I don't think it happened.'

I pull the phone away from my ear for a moment and glare at it. After a pause, Victor says, 'Hello? CC?'

'I can't believe you just said that,' I say, returning the phone to my ear. 'Not to me.'

'Jesus! Look, I'm sorry. Did you actually see Carole? Did you see her doing something to the coffee?'

'No, she was back over at Distira's by the time I—'

'So you didn't see her in the house *at all*?'

'No, but—'

'I have spent half the day driving, and half the day boxing up the possessions of my dead parents.'

'And now *I* have the neighbours creeping around while I'm asleep and fiddling with the foodstuffs. And it's creeping me out.'

'Right,' Victor says.

'And a boyfriend who doesn't even believe me.'

'I didn't say that,' he says. 'It just sounds, well, a bit unlikely.'

'You think *that* sounds unlikely. Try this! I went over to talk to them. To ask what they needed. And I caught the two of them out the back picking weird herbs and these really ugly mushroom things.'

Victor blows out an angry, exaggerated sigh. 'Oh my *God!* They were *picking mushrooms*!' he says, sarcastically.

'Yes, but they weren't normal mushrooms.'

'Your point being?'

'Victor, don't use that tone of voice with me,' I say.

'Oh, for fuck's sake, CC,' Victor says.

'And *don't* for-fucks-sake me!' I say, starting to tremble. *'Ever.'*

'They were picking mushrooms!' Victor says. 'What do you want me to say?'

'OK. And tonight, when I closed the shutters, a tarot card fell down. Explain that.'

'A tarot card?'

'A bad one. I looked it up.'

'Stop,' Victor says. 'Just stop now. You're scaring me.'

'*I'm* scaring *you*?'

'You sound unhinged.'

'I sound unhinged? Well, I'm not the one creeping around people's kitchens and hiding tarot cards behind their shutters.' I wait for a reply, but when none comes, I say, 'I said . . .'

'I heard you,' Victor says. His voice quivering with anger. 'But you know what? I can't deal with this shit right now.'

'What did you just say to me?'

'I'm not superman. I'm tired, and I'm upset, and I've got lots of stuff going on here that doesn't seem to interest you much. And I'm sorry about that. But I can't be doing with any more of this bullshit about my aunt right now.'

I swallow hard and take a deep breath, resisting the urge to cry.

'CC?'

'I don't know what to say to that,' I answer.

'To what?'

'I don't know what that means. That you can't "be doing with it".'

'You're a big girl. Bin the bloody tarot card, lock the frigging door. Don't drink the coffee if you don't bloody like it. And gimme a fucking break.'

'Give you a break?'

'I have actual *real* stuff to deal with here. So yes. Gimme a break.'

'OK. I will. And thanks for all the support.'

'Same to you, darlin'. I'm gonna hang up now,' Victor says.

'Not if I hang up first.' And then I do exactly that.

I sit watching the flames of the range for ten minutes as I contemplate my first ever major row with Victor. And then I steel myself, and dial his number.

'Yes?' he says, wearily.

'I don't want to row,' I say, in my softest tone.

'Nor do I.'

'I just feel a bit scared,' I tell him. 'Because weird things are going on. And I'm alone here.'

'I know,' Victor says. 'But no one is trying to poison you.'

'. . .'

'You know that, right?'

'I've been feeling sick for days.'

'Well maybe you still have a bit of flu. Or maybe it's something else. Maybe you should see a doctor.'

'I thought I was dating one,' I say.

'Well, if you're pregnant,' Victor says, 'then I might be able to help. In fact, maybe that's it. Maybe it's morning—'

'I'm *not* pregnant.'

'Well then.'

My socked feet are getting cold on the flagstones, so I move a chair closer to the fire so that I can toast the soles of my feet. A bit of grass is stuck to my sock, and as I reach to pick it off, it makes me think of something. 'You know when you found my shoes outside?' I ask.

'Yes?' Victor says, warily.

'You said they were full of herbs or something.'

'One was, yeah.'

'Was it a kind of bracken?'

'Bracken. I don't know what that means.'

'Was it like heather? A bit like lavender? Only not smelly like lavender?'

'I didn't sniff it. It came out of your wet shoe . . .'

'But did it look a bit like lavender?'

'Maybe. Yes. Maybe, a bit. So what?'

I swallow. 'Well that's what was taped to the tarot card,' I say.

'What do you mean it was taped to the tarot card?'

'There were two tarot cards taped together with some bracken. In a loop. And it was wedged behind the window. So maybe it's some kind of traditional spell or something.'

' . . . '

'Victor?'

'Yes, I'm still here . . . but you're off again.'

'I'm not *off* anywhere,' I say. 'I'm telling you what happened.'

'You found a tarot card. Well, it was a tarot card. Now it's a tarot card *mysteriously* taped together with a bit of bracken. Which is *maybe* the same bracken that fell out of your shoe.'

'Yes.'

'Well it's hardly the bloody Twilight Zone, is it, babe?'

'OK,' I say.

'OK?'

'OK. You're right. This isn't working.'

'What isn't working?'

'Let's just talk tomorrow,' I say. 'Goodnight.'

'Goodnight,' Victor says. 'Sleep well.'

I sit fuming for ten minutes, and then mellowing for another ten. A part of me realises that poor Victor *has* got a lot to deal with, and that I must sound a bit mad. But I'm scared. And it's hard to control that. Finally thinking that I'm now calmer, and hopefully more able to explain myself, I decide to have another attempt at finding common ground here. Perhaps if I admit that it all sounds utterly unlikely, but point out that it's quite hurtful to effectively be called a liar ... maybe we can see where things go from there.

Finding Victor's mobile is now switched off, effectively precluding any further discussion, I realise that I haven't calmed down one bit. The inability to continue the discussion leaves me spitting with rage.

I do manage to get to sleep that night, but it's a restless kind of sleep that allows me to keep one ear tuned for potential intruders. As anyone who has ever been truly spooked, or truly angry, knows, a poor night's sleep does nothing to temper either, and I awaken feeling wired for a fight.

I wait until ten before I phone Victor, but his mobile just rings lonely before going onto voicemail. He is clearly either busy or still has the hump with me.

When he still hasn't phoned back two hours later, I try again, and then – a sign of pure desperation – I call my mother in Morocco.

She answers immediately.

'Mum,' I say. 'It's me.'

'Well, fancy that!' she says. 'You phoning me, for a change!'

'I've got a problem, Mum. I need to run it by you.'

'I might have guessed that it wouldn't be to ask how I am!' she says. 'But as it happens, it's perfect timing, darling, because I need to talk to you about dates. I'm thinking April sometime, so I need to know if you'll be free to come and help. I'd need you around for at least a week, maybe two. I know it's short notice but, well, you knew it was coming, didn't you? We—'

'Mum!' I interrupt. 'I'm having problems with Victor. I need to *talk* to you. It's important.'

'Whereas my wedding is hardly worth a mention? Did I really bring you up to be this selfish? Because I'm sure I didn't.'

'I'm sorry, Mum. It's just I'm in a fix. I really am.'

'So answer my question and then we can get back to talking about *you* again. How does that sound?' she says.

I rub my brow and wonder how much this is costing, and wonder if Victor is right now trying to call me back. 'I thought it was all postponed, anyway,' I say. 'Because of his family. Because you're not Muslim.'

'Whatever gave you that idea? No, we want to move forward as soon as we can. Everyone here is being beastly to him now, and frankly I'm not enjoying it like I used to. So we want to get on and get married and get long-stay visas sorted out so that he can just live permanently in England. But I will need your help with the wedding, darling. You're such a good organiser. So, April? Can you?'

273

'I don't know,' I say. 'I'm not sure where I'll be in April. Here, presumably. And Victor might need me.'

My mother laughs sourly. 'Well, thank you, darling,' she says. 'It's so wonderful to be able to count on your only surviving child.'

Realising that she's probably right, and that the only way we are ever going to be able to talk about *my* problems is for me to capitulate anyway, that's exactly what I do. 'You're right,' I say. 'I'm sorry. I'm just . . . distracted. Of course I'll be there.'

'Well, thanks be!' she says. 'I was thinking that we could book a little country house somewhere. Nothing grand, but seeing as there's no church wedding—'

'MUM!' I shriek. 'Please! I know it's important. But not today. I'm in a fix. And I can't be doing with this right now.' I pull a face as I remember Victor saying almost those exact words.

'Go on then,' she says, after a sobering pause. 'What's happened?'

And so I tell her. I tell her about Distira and Carole and her dodgy stew, and the funny-tasting coffee and being sick, and having swine flu, and guardian angels and missing doctors and tarot cards behind the shutters and Victor's dismissive attitude . . . And as I tell her, I can hear my own voice through her ears, and even I would have to admit that it does all sound entirely ridiculous.

'Well?' I prompt, once I have finished.

Mother is remaining unusually silent and I fear that the line may have gone dead.

'I don't know what to say, really,' she says. A first.

274

'Try, Mum,' I plead.

'You'll only get annoyed with me,' she says.

'I won't. I need your advice.'

'Well, it sounds like you're quite hysterical, dear.'

'Hysterical?'

'Yes. I have never heard so much nonsense in my life. Do you remember when you were convinced that the airing cupboard was haunted because the pipes creaked when the heating was on?'

'Mum,' I protest, 'I was about seven.'

'Ten, more like. But that's what this sounds like to me. A load of old codswallop. I'm not surprised poor Victor's lost patience with it all. And his *aunt*, sweetheart. You can't get between a Frenchman and his family. Everyone knows that.'

'So what should I do? Just apologise? Tell him I've been silly?'

'Well, of course you should. It's as simple as that. Now, on to the guest list. Because I can't work out whether to invite—'

'Mum. My battery is just about to run out,' I tell her – a lie. 'Can I find the charger and phone you back?'

'If you must, dear,' she says. 'But I'm pretty sure that we both know that you won't.'

I sit and stare into the middle distance for a while and wish that my father was still alive. Because though I know that the story sounds mad to my mother, it's only because she can countenance the idea that I might be talking rubbish. It's the same with Victor. The problem isn't the story; it's the ears that are listening.

Dad would have taken me seriously. And even if he didn't believe me, he would have at least pretended to and given appropriate advice. But Dad, like Waiine, is gone.

I need to talk to someone else.

I grab my phone and scroll through the contacts list until I get to 'M'.

'*Bonjour!*' Mark says when he answers his mobile. 'How's my little baguette muncher?'

'OK,' I say. 'Well, not really.'

'What's up?'

'I feel terrible, only phoning when something's wrong, but . . .'

'It's fine. That's what friends are for.'

'Are you OK, though?' I ask.

'Sure. I'm good. But what's up with you?'

'Everyone thinks I'm talking rubbish. Mum and Victor both think I'm cracking up. So maybe I am.'

'I'm plumping up my cushions,' Mark says. 'There. Plumped. Fire away!' His voice is so warm, so familiar, that I could almost cry.

'OK. It's a long story,' I say. 'And it'll sound weird. So just suspend judgement till the end, OK?'

'OK.'

'Well . . .'

Mark listens in almost total silence as I tell him my story, making only the occasional 'um' or 'ooh!' sounds as proof that the connection is still working.

When I have finished, I say, 'So, what do you think? Am I losing the plot here? Am I going mad?'

Mark sighs. 'I don't know. I mean, I can see why it might

276

seem that way. It's all pretty outlandish. So I can kind of understand Victor's reaction. And knowing your mum, she probably wasn't even listening.'

I laugh. 'But you think I'm mad, too.'

'Maybe, maybe not. Weird shit does happen. Some people *do* believe in superstitious rubbish: guardian angels and tarot cards and spells and shit.'

'I don't,' I say. 'Well, I don't think I do.'

'But that's not the point, is it?' Mark says. 'If you're finding tarot cards and weird loops of lucky heather – or unlucky heather – around the place, then someone else clearly does believe in it, and that is scary enough.'

I let out a sigh. The fact that there is at least one person who understands what is and isn't happening here – that this isn't about whether *I* believe in tarot cards or not – makes a huge weight slip from my shoulders. 'God, I love you, Mark,' I say.

'But the weird thing is that your boyfriend is assuming that you're the one who's mad rather than the old hag next door. What's her name again?'

'Distira.'

'See, she even *sounds* like a witch. And people do sometimes do weird shit. They do lock people in cellars for thirty years, and they do murder them and bury them in the garden.'

'You're scaring me now,' I say.

'I just mean, well, why would Victor want to side with her?'

'She is his aunt, I suppose.'

'Yes. Blood's thicker than water and all that. But all the

same. I mean she sounds like a pretty random character. You've always been one hundred per cent logical, as long as I've known you. So I think you should listen to your instincts.'

'Thanks. You don't know how much that means,' I say, my voice starting to wobble with emotion. 'So what do you think I should do?'

'I guess bin the coffee. Burn the tarot card. And lock the doors.'

I laugh. 'That's what Victor said. Only he wasn't so nice about it. Anyway, I already did all that.'

'So you see!' Mark says. 'You're not mad at all. Just afraid.'

By the time I hang up, I feel utterly homesick, but also vindicated. I bin the tea in the tea-caddy, the sugar from the bowl, and throw out some flour, herbs and spices. Anything that might have been tampered with. I'm aware, as I do this, that my mother would consider it an absurd waste, and that Victor would be spitting with rage. And it strikes me that the source of much of my tension has been precisely *not* being able to follow my intuition because of Victor's contradictory instincts of his own. Binning the suspect food feels, in some strange way, like liberation.

Once the jars have been emptied and refilled from fresh vacuum-sealed packs, I make myself a fresh pot of coffee. A little of my newfound happiness fades with the realisation that it still tastes disgusting.

Starting to doubt my sanity again, I pour the coffee away and fill the cup with water, but even as I raise this to my lips, the smell of the stuff – mouldy and stagnant – makes me feel sick.

I wrinkle my nose and swap the mug for a glass, which I fill with water. I hold it up to the light. 'God!' I say – a eureka moment. Because tap water should not be milky. It should not have thousands of microscopic bits floating in it, either.

'I knew it!' I mutter out loud, thinking back to my insistence – much mocked – that we buy bottled water. 'Right from the start!'

I check the cupboards and find a single, sealed bottle of Volvic and swig some straight from the bottle. It tastes fine, if vaguely plasticky. As an experiment more than anything else, I make yet another cup of coffee with water from the bottle. It tastes fine.

And then I restoke the range and settle down to phone Victor with my good news.

'Hello,' he says warily.

'Hi, babe,' I say.

'Before you tell me off, I wasn't ignoring your messages. I've been run off my feet. The *brocanteur* guy turned up before nine. He's still here. And I haven't even had breakfast yet.'

'I wasn't going to tell you off,' I say defensively. 'Anyway, I was just phoning to share some good news. I found the reason why everything tastes funny.'

Silence.

'It's the tap water. I knew it from the start, and I was right. There's something wrong with the water.'

More silence.

'Victor?'

'Please don't start all that again,' he pleads.

'Start what? Jesus, Victor! What's wrong with you? I'm telling you that I have found the cause.'

'Only there is nothing wrong with the tap water. I've been drinking it for weeks.'

'Only there *is*. It's all milky. It looks like wallpaper paste.'

'It's bubbles, CC,' Victor says. 'It's just tiny bubbles of air. If you leave it to stand ...'

'I'm not liking this new attitude of yours much,' I say.

'And which attitude would that be?'

'The one that assumes that everything I say is rubbish, even before I say it.'

'Only it is rubbish. I don't know what's got into—'

'It's not fecking air bubbles!' I shout. 'It smells like dog-shite and—'

'So now you've gone all Irish on me.'

'Well that would be because you're making me angry. I mean, you can't even believe me about the state of the water.'

'You know what, CC, I don't *need* to believe you. Because if you don't like the tap water, if you think my aunt has put a spell on the well or something, then just drink bottled water. And leave me out of it.'

I open my mouth to speak, but words fail me.

'I have to go. They need a hand moving the wardrobe.' And with that, he hangs up.

As the day passes, and as Victor fails to phone me back, my mood swings wildly between anger and concern. Because who could have imagined, even three days ago, that we could end up here?

After a few cups of tea, and a bowl of rehydrated soup,

I realise that my bottle of Volvic isn't going to last, so I set all the cold taps running in the hope that I can clear whatever is causing the problem from the system, and when I check a glass of the stuff a bit later, it does look, and smell, better. I even boil a batch, just in case, and leave it to cool. But with the thought that if the well or spring or wherever our water comes from has been poisoned, boiling might not suffice, I'm unable to drink the stuff. Instinct simply won't let me do it.

So I open a bottle of wine instead. And when that one's empty, I open another.

At 6 p.m., once the sun has set, I close the shutters while watching carefully for fluttering tarot cards or voodoo dolls. I see neither.

Safely barricaded against the world, I attempt to phone Victor, but his mobile is still switched off, so I briefly fantasise that he has realised the error of his ways and is driving home right now to apologise and somehow make everything right. But as evening continues, and I drink more and more wine, I'm finding it harder and harder to work out how things can ever truly be right again.

By the time my phone does finally vibrate, it's 10 p.m. and I'm indisputably drunk. I peer at the screen of my mobile and am only just able to read that it is Mark who is calling rather than Victor.

'Hello, chicken,' Mark says. 'I thought I should check up on you. Make sure you haven't been turned into a black cat or something.'

'It'sh not funny,' I slur.

'No. I know.'

'I'm drunk.'

'You sound it. Drinking on your own! You always say that's the sign of a true alcoholic.'

'Do I? Well, I can't drink water, sho I switched to wine. Some very expensive Bordeaux. Victor will be furious.' I frown at the effort it is taking to get my tongue around complex words like *expensive* and *furious*.

'Why can't you drink water?'

'It's murky. She's done something to it.'

'Maybe you should drink Perrier or something,' Mark says. 'You sound like you've had enough to me.'

'I haven't *got* any bottled water! I drunk it.'

'Then tomorrow you should go and stock up,' Mark says, using a parent-talking-to-recalcitrant-child voice that I find strangely reassuring.

'I can't. Victor's got the van,' I explain, doing a baby voice to better fit the role. 'And it's too far to walk.'

'When will he be back, sweetie?'

'I don't know. He won't say. And now he's not even talking to me.' I swipe at my cheek and realise that it's wet, and that my fake childish misery is morphing into real adult tears.

'Can you walk to a shop?'

'No. It's too far. It's forty minutes away.'

'You're fit. You can walk for forty—'

'In a car! Doh! It's forty minutes *in a car*.'

'Are you crying?' Mark asks.

'A bit,' I say stubbornly. 'Not much. I feel really miserable, Mark.'

'Why do you feel miserable, chicken?'

'Because I'm in the middle of nowhere, and the shops are miles away, and the only person here is Distira and she's a witch, and it's freezing cold and we're running out of wood and the land looks like a tsunami's swept through it, and the house isn't finished, and the water's poisoned, and the walls fell down, and my boyfriend won't talk to me, and when he does he's horrible, and the neighbours are creeping around while I'm asleep, scaring the fecking bejeezus out of me, and I bloody hate it here and I miss London and my friends and my cat, and clean water. And you. I miss you.' My lungs spasm as a wave of drunken angst rolls over me.

'That Victor's a bit of a prick to fuck off and leave you on your own with all this going on, isn't he?'

And even though I know that it's untrue, that this isn't quite how it happened, I agree. 'He is. I hate him.'

'But you still love him, right?'

I swallow. I know that I do, but I really can't bring myself to say it right now.

'Oh dear,' Mark says.

'What am I going to do?' I say, starting to cry again.

'Can you rent a car?'

'How? I'm in the middle of fecking nowhere here.'

'Aw. You are in a mess, aren't you?'

'He won't even answer the phone,' I say again. 'And when he does, he just shouts at me. I don't know what to do, Mark.'

'Shall *I* call him?'

'He's switched his mobile off. Honestly, I wish I never came here. I hate bloody France.'

'You don't mean that.'

'I do.'

'OK. Here's what you do,' Mark says. 'You need to stop drinking now. You're slaughtered.'

'I know. I'm so thirsty, too.'

'So will you do that for me?'

'Will I shtop drinking wine?'

'Yes.'

'OK.'

'Have you got any water?' he asks.

'No. Only poison water.'

'Fruit juice? Coke?'

'There's some tonic, I think.'

'OK. Drink some tonic. No gin though, OK? And go to bed. And in the morning, it'll seem better. I promise.'

'How will it seem better in the morning, Mark? How?'

'It will. You'll see. Things always seem better in the morning.'

'It better,' I say.

'It will. Goodnight, sweetie! I love you lots.'

'Thanks, Mark. You're my best friend.'

I attempt to place the phone on the arm of the chair but miss and it falls to the floor. I don't care. It can stay there.

I sit and stare at the fading flicker of the range and think about everything that I have left behind, as tears silently slide down my cheeks.

FIVE LITTLE DEATHS

I wake up with a hangover, dehydrated and gasping for water. I drink half a litre of the water I boiled yesterday. And then I promptly throw it all back up. Whether this is the result of the hangover, the water itself, or simply the *idea* that something is wrong with it is anyone's guess.

For a while I can't find my mobile, and hunting for it produces a vague sensation of panic. When I eventually do find it beneath a blanket on the floor, the battery is flat, so I plug it in to charge. While I wait the requisite five minutes required for it to become functional, I relight the range and open the shutters onto a cold, sunny day. I stare at the moon-like landscape and wish that I was anywhere but here.

I check my voicemail and phone Victor, only to find that his phone is still switched off.

'Call me,' I say into his answerphone, 'and at least tell me when you're coming back. I love you.'

I wrinkle my nose as I force out those last three words, and then wonder for a moment what the fact that I can no longer say them without pulling a face might mean.

Thinking about the conversation with Mark last night, I pull on my coat and shoes then head outside with the jerry-can, wondering if I can find a pool of clean water somewhere. Seeing that Distira's Lada is missing, I have a better idea. I cross the garden and, nervously glancing around, fill the can from her garden tap. Her water may come from the same spring as mine, but it smells, and tastes, fine.

I attempt to call Victor's phone three more times that morning, and become a little more angry with each attempt. And beyond the immediate anger, I begin to have a nagging sense of doubt about our relationship. We have survived so many things together, I was beginning to think that we were invincible. But maybe, just maybe, this episode is going to prove otherwise. You really never know where the fatal fault-line of a relationship will appear. Lack of belief in what your partner is saying might just turn out to be ours.

At two, my mobile rings and I run to check the display. It's Mark.

'Hello, you,' I say. 'Are you checking up on me?'

'Yes!' he says. 'How are you this fine day?'

'Fine,' I say. 'Well, hung-over.'

'Look out the window,' Mark says.

'Why?'

'Just look out the window and tell me what you see.'

I sigh and cross the room. 'Mud. Mountains. Mayhem. Things beginning with "M".'

'Oh,' Mark says. 'Can't you see me? I begin with M.'

'No, Mark. I can't see you. Even my eyesight's not that good.'

'Really? Are you looking now?'

'Yes.'

'Are you sure?'

'Of course I'm sure.'

'Are you looking out of the front or the back?'

'The front.'

'Oh. Shit! I must be in the wrong place, then.'

'You're not making any sense, Mark,' I tell him.

'But I'm here,' he says. 'Well, I'm supposed to be. Is your place the big one or the little one in all the mud?'

'No!' I gasp, rushing to the front door, fumbling with the key, and then running outside.

There, in front of Distira's house, I see a little blue Renault Kangoo. Mark is standing in front of it, holding a big bottle of water.

'You're in the witch's garden, you twit!' I laugh, and he turns to face me and waves at me with his bottle of water. 'Water, water, everywhere!' he laughs, and I can now hear him both through the phone and across the field.

I start to run towards him. For the first time in days, I begin to smile. 'You crazy man!' I shout. 'I can't believe you're here,' I splutter as I reach him and we embrace.

Mark pulls away just far enough to see my face and smiles lopsidedly. 'Looks like it's a good thing I came,' he says.

'Oh these?' I say, swiping at a tear. 'It's just the cold wind. You had better move your car over here. You don't want to upset the witch.'

Once he has moved his car, Mark stands and appraises the house. 'Well,' he says, wrinkling his nose.

'I know,' I say. 'It's not looking its best.'

As we enter the house, he points at the bowl of food I have put out. 'New cat?' he asks.

'No,' I say. 'There's a wild tabby. She was pregnant. I only saw her once, to be honest, but every time I put food out it vanishes pretty quickly. She's feeding her kittens, I expect.'

'Guinness will be jealous,' Mark says.

'Well, just don't tell him.'

I offer him lunch which he declines, so I make tea instead, using his bottled water.

While I do this he crosses to the sink and declares, 'You're right. It's rank.'

'The house?' I ask.

'No, the water,' he says. 'But the house is in a bit of a state too, isn't it?'

'I know. It actually looked better three weeks ago before the digger guy wrecked the yard and knocked down half the walls.' I drop two teabags in mugs and pull out the two chairs nearest the range. 'So what the hell are you doing here, Mark?'

He slides into a seat. 'Nice range,' he says.

'Isn't it.'

'What am I doing here? Well, I had a barney with Iain. We were going to Wales to his sister's place, but he left on his own. So I thought, *What to do with a long weekend? I'll go see my friend CC.*'

'You are brilliant, you know,' I say.

'Plus you sounded like you could do with the company.'

'You have no idea.'

'And water.'

288

'Well quite,' I say, jumping back up to pour the boiling water into the cups. 'The flight must have cost a fortune though, didn't it?'

'It was OK. A hundred and twenty quid. The car rental cost more. But I don't care at the moment. Since I left Spot On, I'm earning loads. And I don't even have any housing costs – Iain won't let me contribute anything, so . . . Anyway, when's Victor back?'

I return to the table and plonk down the two steaming mugs of tea. 'I have no idea. He's got the hump with me. Big time. He's not even taking my calls. He thinks I'm turning into a hysterical nightmare.'

'*Turning* into . . .?' Mark says. When I frown at this he adds, '*Joke*, sweetie!'

'Sorry. I think I lost my sense of humour lately.'

'Well, swine flu and collapsing houses will do that to you,' Mark says. 'So Victor's still not answering then.'

I shake my head. 'I tried again just before you arrived. I hope he's OK. I'm quite worried, to be honest. God, I still can't believe that you're here!'

'Maybe we should go see him. I have a car, after all.'

'To Perpignan? It's six hours each way.'

'Oh. I didn't realise. That would probably take me over my one hundred kilometres a day then.'

'Yes. I think it would a bit. How long are you here for?'

'Just two nights. If that's OK. Otherwise I can find a hotel.'

'God, no! I need the company sooo much. I don't know how to tell you how grateful I am.'

'Don't start blubbing again,' Mark says, placing his hand over mine on the table.

'I'm fine,' I say. 'It's just so ... so ...'

'Grim?'

'It is, isn't it?'

Mark nods solemnly.

'But isolated is what I meant,' I say, looking around the house now and seeing through fresh eyes what Mark is seeing – the sordid reality of it all.

'I can't believe that he has left you here like this,' Mark says.

I sigh. 'I know. But he had to go. And I was ill. Anyway ...' I shrug.

'It's nice and sunny, though,' Mark says. 'It's pissing it down in London.'

'It is actually sunny most days,' I say. 'Just incredibly cold at night.'

'D'you want to go for a walk or something? I've been sitting down all day. Trains and planes and cars.'

'Sure,' I say. 'Let's drink this and go. It will do me good.'

It is a stunningly crisp day, and it is in some way proof of how miserable I have been feeling that I hadn't really noticed that until now.

Not wanting to approach Distira's place, we clamber up the hill behind our own farm and discover a similar track to hers winding its way into our land. We follow the track up a hillock, across a barren plateau, and on up another climb beyond that.

'So is this still your land?' Mark asks.

'I don't even know,' I tell him. 'We never even walked

this far before. Victor knows where our land ends from the deeds, but I'm not sure, to be honest.'

Coming across a little ledge, we pause to look out at the view, which stretches from the distant rocky outcrops on the other side of the valley to the plateau on which the two houses are built.

'Now, that's a view!' Mark says.

'It's beautiful, isn't it?'

'I couldn't live here, though.'

'Hmm,' I murmur.

Mark laughs. 'You're not regretting this, are you?'

'A bit,' I admit.

'Oh dear.'

'Oh, I don't know, to be honest. What with being ill and Victor being a dick, it gets hard to separate it all out.'

'You'd think what with him being a doctor and everything, he'd be a bit more sympathetic,' Mark says.

'I know,' I agree, taking his hand so that he can help me up a steep section of the track. 'He didn't even look after me much when I was ill, really. He was having a terrible time rebuilding the walls and he just thought I had the flu. And he kind of thought Distira was looking after me, I think. He's just a bit of a low-maintenance kind of a doctor, I guess.'

'Whereas you're a high-maintenance kind of patient?'

'Maybe. I mean, he's not even a doctor really, is he? He's a gynaecologist. But all the same . . .'

'Maybe that's the problem,' Mark says. 'Maybe it's like garage owners having rubbish cars. Or cobblers having holes in their shoes.'

'Or gynaecologists having badly-maintained girlfriends?'

'Exactly. Anyway, they're all dickheads at some point.' He pauses and points up at the ridge above us. 'Shall we go up there?'

'Sure,' I say. 'Slowly, though. I'm a bit out of breath. So what's going on with Iain, anyway?'

'Oh, it's complicated,' Mark says.

'What isn't?'

'He's shagging around.'

'God, he's cheating on you? Already?'

Mark glances back at me and smiles glumly. 'Not really. Not cheating per se.'

'What does *that* mean?'

'Well, we agreed that it was OK. So it's not really cheating.'

'Oh,' I say. 'And is that OK? For you, I mean.'

'No, that's the problem. I agreed to it, but I hate it. I get so jealous that even when he *isn't* out shagging someone else, I still behave like he is. It's awful.'

'God, that's terrible, Mark. You can't put up with that. Have you spoken to him about it?'

'I ... I'll tell you later,' he says. 'I can't climb this hill and talk at the same time. Well, not without dying, anyway.'

Just before the final rocky outcrop we come upon a tiny brook. Though only a foot wide, the gargling water has carved a deep channel into the ground as it winds its way down the hillside, and running alongside is a thick black plastic tube, tied, at various points, to trees.

'D'you reckon this is where your stinky water comes from?' Mark asks.

'Maybe,' I say, starting to follow the little stream upwards by walking with one foot either side.

When we reach the final crop-face, the stream and pipe vanish into a tiny cave that appears to be the source. I peer inside. The water – fresh and sparking – is bubbling from amid the broken rock on the floor of the cave.

'How does that work?' I ask, pointing.

Mark laughs. 'What do you mean, "How does it work?" It's a natural spring.'

'I know *that*,' I say. 'I'm just not that good on how natural springs work. I mean, we're at the top of the hill here. How can water flow out of the top of the hill?'

I turn to look back at Mark and he pulls a face. 'Sorry, but I don't know either,' he says, sheepishly.

'Anyway, this can't be our water,' I say, scooping a handful and sniffing it. 'This stuff's lovely and clean.'

'Shall we go back?' Mark asks, suddenly sounding bored. 'I'm starving.'

I stand up. 'I did offer you lunch,' I say.

'I know. I wasn't hungry then. But I am now. Must be all this fresh air.'

Walking down the track is for some reason much harder than walking up. The shattered rock strewn across the track slithers and slides beneath our feet in a completely unnerving way, so we end up holding hands for much of the descent.

Halfway down, something to our immediate left rustles the branches. We both freeze and stare in the direction the sound came from. After a few seconds I say, 'Probably a deer. We see lots of those around here.'

'Wow,' Mark says. 'I would love to see a deer. Are they dangerous?'

'No. But the wild boar can be, apparently. Especially when they have their young.'

'You sound like a proper country girl,' Mark says.

'Do I?' I laugh, feeling strangely flattered by the comment. 'What's that grey thing over there?'

I follow the direction of his gaze and spot a grey rectangle in the undergrowth. 'I don't know. An old water tank, maybe?'

'Maybe,' Mark agrees. 'I guess that needs investigating then.'

He clambers up onto the ledge and holds out one hand to pull me up. 'It's really overgrown,' he says. 'Stay here and I'll try to see what it is. It might just be something someone dumped.'

He fights his way through the brush and shouts back, 'There's definitely water pipes going into it, so it might be something to do with yours.'

He lifts the lid and shouts, 'Phaww!' and drops it with a metallic clang. 'God, it stinks.'

I push through the undergrowth to his side and pull my phone from my pocket and press the torch button on it.

'Can you lift that lid up again?'

'Do I have to?'

'Stop being such a poof, will you?'

'Says big, butch CC,' he says in an over-the-top camp voice. 'Ugh! Fuck it's heavy. Quick.'

I crouch down and point my phone through the gap. 'It's the same smell. Can you lift that lid right off?'

Mark pulls a face. 'The smell's making me retch,' he says. 'And it's really heavy.'

I drop the phone into my pocket and take the other side of the lid. 'One, two, three . . .' I say, and the heavy lid lifts and slides uncontrollably into the undergrowth.

I recover my phone and point the torch into the water. 'There's something in there,' I say, glancing at Mark who is covering his nose with his jacket sleeve.

I look around and find a broken branch with which I manage to hook one corner of the object – a hessian sack – from the depths.

'D'you want it out?' Mark says.

'Yes. If you're man enough.'

'God, the things I do for you!' he laughs, pushing up one sleeve and grabbing the other corner of the bag. 'Stand back,' he says, lifting the bag from the tank and slopping it onto the grass.

I crouch down and undo the knotted string fastening the neck.

'You're not going to open it?' he says. 'You don't know what's inside.'

'I know. But I want to know what's inside,' I say. 'That's the exact smell coming out of the tap. I've been living with that smell for days. Every shower. Every drink . . .'

The slippery string comes away, and so I open the neck of the bag and point my torch inside, and what I see makes me jump back so fast that I fall onto Mark's feet behind me. 'Jesus!' I exclaim.

'What is it?' he asks, touching my shoulder lightly.

'It's . . .' But then I decide that I need a witness for this.

'Have a look, will you? But hold your breath!'

'I'd rather not,' Mark says. 'You're scaring me.'

I gingerly grab the base of the bag and, standing as far back as possible, I tip the contents onto the grass.

'Oh, fucking hell,' Mark says, turning away. 'Oh, God, that's the worst thing I have ever seen.'

'I know,' I say. 'I think I might throw up.'

'They're ... aren't they?'

'Yes,' I say, raising my phone. 'They are. Five of them.'

'You're not going to photograph the poor fuckers.'

'I have a boyfriend who doesn't believe anything I say,' I tell him. 'So yes, I'm photographing them.'

I point the camera at the tiny rotting animals with their ten swollen eyes, lying next to the bag in which they were drowned, and then retreat.

'God, that's horrible,' Mark says, looking green. He jumps back onto the track and offers me a hand. 'That's really sick. Who the fuck would do something like that?'

'Well, there are only three people living up here, and it wasn't me, and it wasn't Victor.'

'The witch?' Mark asks.

But I don't answer, because I'm thinking about washing this slime off my hands when I get home and realising that I can't because our water comes from here, and so every shower I have taken, every glass of water that I have drunk, every bowl of pasta that I have eaten, has contained particles of rotten, dead kitten.

'I'm sorry,' I say. 'But I ...' And then I turn and vomit into the bushes.

*

Back inside the house, I open all the taps in the hope of flushing the pipes clean.

'I reckon it'll take more than that,' Mark says. 'I think you need a new tank.'

'I know,' I agree. 'But in the meantime, if I can just flush out the gunk that's in the system, at least I can shower in vaguely clean water.'

'Gunk,' Mark repeats, and we stare into each other's eyes for a moment as we think about what that gunk is comprised of.

'I could go back up there and pour some bleach in, I guess,' I say.

'It's an idea.'

Despite the fact that we have lost our appetites again, I make a simple lunch of cheese on toast and, this served, I reach for my phone.

Then I call Victor. Once again, his mobile rings into the void before switching to voicemail. 'Damn you!' I say, putting the phone down and reaching for a slice of toast.

'Still not answering?' Mark says.

'Nope. His phone's on but he's filtering me. Unbelievable.'

'I doubt he's filtering you,' Mark says. 'Maybe he's busy. Give me the number. Let me try.'

I jab at my phone until the number comes up on the screen and then slide it across the table to Mark, who types it into his iPhone.

'If he answers to you but not me, I'll be furious,' I say.

Mark lifts the phone to his ear. 'Victor?' he says. 'Yes, it's Mark. Guess where I am.'

I cover my mouth with one hand and shake my head slowly.

'No, I'm sitting opposite your lovely girlfriend . . . Yes, I know. But she wants to talk to you . . . Yes, I'm in France. At your place, that's right. Anyway, I think you two need to talk. I'll hand you over.'

Mark hands me the phone and makes meditational circles with his fingers and thumbs to indicate that I should be Zen.

'Hello?' I say, trying to keep the angry tremble out of my voice.

'Hi.'

'You've not been taking my calls. I've been worried,' I say.

'I'm sorry. I'm just so stressed out at this end. It's horrible having to do all this.'

'I know that,' I say, 'but it's not fair. I haven't done anything wrong.'

'I guess I thought we needed some time to calm down.'

'I'm perfectly calm,' I say – a lie, of course.

'Well, *I* needed time to calm down then.'

'So how's it all going?' I ask – an attempt at normalising the conversation before I bring up the challenging subject of the water supply.

'Oh, it's slow. You know how these things are. I'm waiting for the *advocat*, the lawyer or whatever, to draw up a contract. The *brocanteurs* didn't want much of the stuff, so I'm organising shifting it into storage for now.'

'So when will you be home?'

'Hopefully the day after tomorrow. If everything goes to plan. But you have Mark staying now, so that's good.'

'Yes,' I say. 'He just got here.'

'Does he like the place?'

'Erm, yes, I think so. We, um, went for a walk. On the hill above our house, this time.'

'That's our land. Nice, isn't it? Is the weather good?'

'Yes, it's sunny but cold. Guess what we found, though?'

'I don't know. Gold?'

'No, I wish. No, we found the water tank that feeds our place.'

'Right. And?'

'Someone had dumped some kittens in it.'

'I'm sorry?'

'There was a bag floating in the tank. We fished it out. It had five dead kittens in it.'

'Yuck, that's gross.'

'I know. I think they might have been the babies from that poor cat we saw, the one I've been feeding. Do you remember?'

'Sure. Are you sure it's our tank?'

'Yes. The smell was the same as the tap water.'

'Well, I never smelt anything wrong with the tap water.'

'Well, I did.'

'Right. So did you take them out?'

'No. I left them in. Of course I took them out!'

'Right. There's no need to be ... Anyway. Good.'

'But I think we need a new tank.'

'Yep. Well, I'll look into it when I get back.'

'And some different neighbours.'

Silence.

'Victor?'

'Yep, still here.'

'Well, you understand what this means?'

'What *what* means?'

'Finding dead kittens in the tank.'

'No. What does it mean?' he says.

'Well, someone put them in there.'

'Yes. I would suppose so.'

'Well, who do *you* think it might have been?'

'And here we go again! I suppose my auntie put them in there to kill you?'

'Well, I can't see who el—'

'Were they black kittens, by any chance?'

'No, they were tortoiseshell, why?'

'Dunno. Thought it might be more *witchcrafty* or something if they were black.'

'Oh, come on, stop that! Mark was with me. We both saw them. You can ask him if you don't believe me.'

'I'm not disputing you found some dead kittens.'

'So who else could it be? There's no one else around here.'

'Maybe it was an accident.'

'An accident?' I look at Mark and shake my head. He pulls a face.

'Yeah, maybe Distira doesn't know what the tank is for. I mean, I don't like it either, but people do drown kittens. Especially country folk.'

'Oh, come on!'

'She's my auntie, CC. The same auntie who looked after me when I was little. When my own mother was too paralytic to do so. And she isn't dropping bags of dead kittens in our water supply.'

'Only she is. But you refuse to accept it.'

'Jesus, CC. This is exactly why I haven't called. You have an obsession with Distira. It's all you talk about. Since the first day you met her.'

'It's not an obsession,' I say, my voice quivering. 'She's a horrible old witch and she hates me, and—'

'She's my *aunt*. And you're going on about it so much that I don't even want to ... She's my only living relative. Why can't you grasp that?'

'You don't even want to what?'

'Nothing.'

'And I *do* grasp that. But I *also* grasp that she has dumped a bag of dead kittens in our water tank.'

'I can't do this any more,' Victor says.

'So what, you're hanging up on me again?'

'Yes,' he says. 'That's exactly what I'm doing.'

Once the line goes dead, I sit and stare at Mark's phone for a while before I hand it back. The aggregate of everything that has happened these last few weeks washes over me, and I feel myself becoming outraged by Victor's behaviour towards me, the anger rising in waves. I have no idea why this is happening only now. Perhaps I was simply too ill before. Perhaps I have been intentionally suppressing thinking about it, the alternative too hard to face. But now that I'm letting myself feel those emotions, something big is snapping. Something fundamental.

I shake my head slowly, as much in amazement at my own passivity as at Victor's behaviour.

'That didn't go well then,' Mark says.

'No,' I reply – an understatement.

Mark arches his fingers around his nose and rests his elbows on the table. 'So what now?'

'Can you take me to the bar?' I ask, a shock decision taken. 'It's about fifteen minutes away.'

'The bar? Are we going to get slaughtered?'

'Nope. They have internet. I'm going to book a flight.'

'To where?'

'I need to get away from here. Can I stay with you?'

Mark stares at me. He looks worried. 'Of course,' he says, 'but I'm not sure that—'

'I am,' I interrupt. 'I'm *totally* sure. I'm sick to death of Victor, and sick to death of this place. And if I don't get away soon, I'll be the one killing someone.'

'Well in *that* case,' Mark says.

After a few minutes' discussion, we decide not to head for the bar after all. Mark, claiming that he wants to make the most of his mini-break, suggests a couple of nights in a cheap hotel he knows in Nice. I suspect that this is partly true, but that he is also hoping to use the delay to change my mind about leaving as well.

I leave a note for Victor saying that I'm sorry, but that I'm sick to death with the way he has been treating me, that I've had enough of not being taken seriously, and that I'm fed up with being stranded alone in an icy building site. I finish by telling him that I am off to England.

When I reread this, it sounds harsh, which I intended, but also a little too final. Some part of me that can see beyond the fury wants to leave the door ajar – so I add a second page saying that I still love him but that I need time to think.

I then throw a week's worth of clothes into a bag, switch everything off, close the vents on the range, and declaring, 'OK, get me outta here,' I pull the front door closed behind us.

The sun is setting behind the mountain ridge as we pull away and my relief at leaving is such that it crosses my mind that I may never want to come back again.

We book into a twin room at the hotel – La Petite Sirène. It's a small independent hotel run by a Swedish family – nothing fancy, and certainly not a patch on the Negresco, which we drive past to get there. But it's reasonably priced and clean. And after La Forge, cleanliness feels like heaven.

The first thing I do is take a long, hot shower.

While Mark takes his turn in the bathroom, I open the laptop and use the hotel's wifi to book myself onto the same Sunday night flight home. Faced with the option of booking a single or a return ticket, I'm suddenly overwhelmed by a sense that I'm making a mistake – that buying a one-way ticket is, in some way, a one-way choice. But I tell myself that I'm just being dramatic, and that as soon as things calm down, I can just book another single to come back. And again, I try not to think about the fact that I simply can't imagine ever wanting to do that – the fact that this feels like escape.

I have just clicked on the confirmation button when Mark appears from the shower. 'You haven't!' he says, peering at the screen.

I nod. 'Same flight as you.'

'God,' he says. 'Victor's gonna hate me.'

'It's just a break,' I say, even though I'm not sure this is true. 'So what are we doing tonight?' I ask, feigning normality.

'A spot of dinner somewhere. And then I think we should get trashed.'

'Trashed?' I say, pulling a face. Because the truth is that getting trashed is the last thing on my mind.

'There was a time, not so long ago, when you and I did that *every* weekend,' Mark points out. 'And it was fun. Remember that?'

I think back to those days. They feel like they were years ago – almost like a different life. And I remember the fun we had together, and struggle to remember what it was that I didn't like about it. It was the loneliness, I suppose. It was having a great time with Mark and everyone else and then finding myself alone at home, with my cat, in London. Strangely, the simplicity of a clean flat with running water and a purring cat seems quite appealing nowadays. How quickly things change.

I glance up at Mark, who is frowning at me as he hops into a tight pair of combat trousers. 'Look,' he says. 'I've fallen out with Iain. You've fallen out with Victor. Getting splendidly drunk is the only logical thing to be done here.'

I nod thoughtfully. 'OK. Getting trollied sounds like a great idea.'

SOMEONE JUST NEEDS
TO STOP ME

I open my eyes and stare blearily at the ceiling. I think, *That's not my ceiling.*

I attempt to swallow but my mouth is so dry that it's a physical impossibility. I chew my tongue in an attempt at making some saliva but nothing happens – I'm too dehydrated.

I fidget in an attempt at getting comfortable and think, *This isn't my bed.*

I roll to the left and am faced with a muscular, naked back and a crew-cut head.

I think, *Shit! That's not my boyfriend!*

Shocked into wakefulness, I roll away, climb from the bed and pull a blanket around my naked body. The man groans and rolls onto his back.

'Mark!' I exclaim. 'You're in my bed. Why are you in my bed?'

'Hmm?' he grunts.

'I . . . I need water,' I say.

I fill a glass in the bathroom and return to the relative safety of the armchair, where I sit and struggle to remember.

After a few minutes, Mark rolls onto his side and blinks at me. He makes a clicking noise with his tongue and says, 'Water, please,' and holds out an empty hand, so I fill a second glass for him and once he has sat up in bed, I hand it to him.

'You're hairy,' I say.

'Huh?' he says, rubbing his chest with his free hand.

'I don't think I knew that,' I say. 'How can I not know that?'

'I used to wax it,' he says. 'But Iain likes it this way, so . . .'

'Anyway, you're naked, in my bed,' I say. 'Why are you naked in my bed?'

Mark lifts the covers, peers underneath, and says, 'I'm not *quite* naked.'

'Why aren't you in *your* bed?'

Mark sighs, sips his water, then says, 'You wanted a cuddle. Don't you remember?'

'No,' I say. 'No, I don't remember. We didn't . . . you know . . . do anything, did we?'

Mark laughs.

'Don't laugh at me!'

'I'm gay, sweetie. And you have a vagina and huge breasts. What do you think happened?'

'I don't have huge breasts,' I say, pulling a face.

'Well, they're too big for me,' Mark comments.

'Anyway,' I say. 'Good. I'm glad you're gay and you don't like breasts.'

'You sound disappointed,' he murmurs cheekily. 'If you want, I could make an effort.'

'Don't flatter yourself,' I say. 'God, I don't remember anything from last night. Except that first pub. The Irish place.'

'Ma Nolan's?'

'Maybe. Jesus, that Irish crowd knew how to drink, didn't they?'

'They did.'

'At one point I had a pint in my hand and two more lined up on the bar. It was like a bloody drinking competition. Did we go to a restaurant after that?'

'No, that was later. Remember the Russian bar? And vodka shots. Do you remember those?'

'Oh God, yes,' I groan. 'All different colours, weren't they?'

'And do you remember cuddling Vlaster? The Ukrainian guy. With the weedy little beard.'

'Cuddling?'

'Calm down. It was all very innocent. Well, fairly.' Mark winks at me and scratches his chin, to mime the beard.

'Oh God, I do. He was sweet. About twelve, but sweet.'

'He was twenty, actually. He was hot on you, baby.'

I wrinkle my nose. 'Really?'

'Said he was into older chicks.'

'Not sure how to take that,' I say. 'Was I bad?'

Mark shakes his head. 'You were too pissed to be bad. We went to that Indian, do you remember?'

I shake my head.

'The Delhi Belly,' Mark says. 'You must remember. We couldn't stop laughing about the name. And Vlaster sat opposite you staring into your eyes, hanging on your every word.'

'Stop it!'

'Until you vommed on him.'

'I didn't!'

'Well, not on him, as such. In the street outside. It was a lucky escape, though. I think he was about to kiss you. A few seconds later and it could have been a disaster.'

'I can't believe I did that,' I groan.

'Believe it.'

'What happened next?'

'I brought you back here in a taxi.'

'And I cried?'

'That was later. When I got back.'

'Jesus, Mark. Where did *you* go?'

'D'you remember the Jewish guy? Dan?'

I shake my head.

'Nah. You were too busy wooing Vlaster.'

'I was *not* wooing anyone.'

'Anyway, I went back to Dan's.'

'For a bit of how's-your-father?'

'For sex, yeah. Supposedly,' Mark says. He yawns and stretches.

'Was it no good, then?' I ask.

Mark shakes his head. 'Totally frigid. A religious thing, I think.'

'Religious?'

'As in, if I don't move, then it isn't a sin. I got bored after ten minutes and came back. But to be honest, I wasn't that into it. I was just trying to do this whole open-relationship thing.'

'God.'

'I know. I'm a tramp.'

'No, I mean, God I feel dreadful.'

'I bet you do.'

'Don't you?' I ask. 'You look OK.'

'You drank me under the table.'

'I was stupidly trying to keep up with the Cork guys.'

'And I was trying to stay sober enough to shag Dan sense-less. Waste of a good drinking opportunity.'

'Ugh.'

'Oh, and you had better check your phone,' Mark says, grimacing. 'You kept texting Victor.'

'Oh Jesus! I didn't.'

Mark nods solemnly, so I shakily manage to stand, cross the room, and pull my phone from my jacket pocket. I sink back into the armchair and poke at the screen until the list of sent messages appears.

Victor. I live you but you're mean to me. Why baby?

'Oh hell,' I mutter. 'Why didn't you stop me?'

Your ant is a which and you need to believe me. She is dangerous.

'Shameful *and* illiterate,' I mutter.

'I tried to stop you,' Mark says. 'In fact, every time I saw you doing it, I stopped you. But you were surprisingly tena-cious.'

I'm sorry but in leaving. I need a brake.

'God,' I say. 'They need to build an alcohol test or something into these to stop this kind of thing.'

So hurt that you can bee this way. You dent love me. You can't.

'At least I got "can't" right,' I mutter. 'That could have been awful.'

I never sine up for this bowl locks anyway.

Goodbye baby. Love you but hat farm.

'Love you but *hat* farm?' I say out loud. 'What the fuck is that supposed to mean?'
'Show me,' Mark says.
'No! Oh! *Hate farm.*'

Ts Rubbish. Am very drink. Don't listen. Am going sick now.

I gingerly place the phone on the arm of the chair and cup my hands over my face. 'God, what's he going to think?'
'If you don't show me, I can't help,' Mark says.
I shake my head and toss him the phone.
Mark starts to read the messages 'Classic,' he says, grinning.
'It's not funny, Mark. Is there any way to . . .'
'Delete them? No. Not once they're sent.'
'Fuck. Someone just needs to stop me sometimes.'

'It's easier said than done,' Mark says.

In response, I simply groan. And then my mouth fills with saliva, and I run to the bathroom.

Our hangovers, well, *my* hangover, preclude any notion of an enjoyable weekend of tourism. But Mark, feeling somewhat responsible for my sorry state, is suitably sympathetic and undemanding. In the end we do little more than wander to the nearest restaurant for large bowls of stomach-lining pasta, and then on to a sea-view café for afternoon tea. Here, Mark tells me in detail about his dispute with Iain, and I give him a detailed account of the build-up to my own predicament. But neither of us attempts to come up with answers.

In the evening, I finally pluck up the courage to talk to Victor, but his phone is yet again switched off, so I resort to sending a text, which hopefully he will see before he reads the others.

Please delete my drunken texts, or just ignore their contents. I was pissed off my head, and it's meaningless babble. Personally, I blame Mark. Love you. xxx

Whether Victor sees any of the messages, I don't know. The only thing that is certain is that he never replies.

The hangover exacerbates my natural propensity for drama, leaving me feeling utterly depressed about my prospects of ever fixing things up with Victor again. Both Mark and I attempt to talk down our respective relationship crises, but just as Mark can't see how his own situation – a boyfriend who refuses to be faithful – can ever be resolved, a part of me that I'm trying desperately to ignore is acknowledging that the ground has shifted unexpectedly beneath my own feet and the dream of nest-building in La Forge and living off the land has turned into a nightmare from which my only true desire is to escape. And unless something happens to shift that – something my mind can't even begin to imagine right now – then we are, basically, doomed.

FOR EACH THOUGHT,
AN EMOTION

When we get back to London, it's a cold sunny day, not dissimilar to the weather we left behind us in Nice.

Once we're seated side-by-side on the Gatwick Express, I ask, 'It's not going to be a war-zone, is it?'

Mark shakes his head. 'Of course not. Iain's nothing if not polite.'

I pull a face.

'What?' Mark asks.

'What you're saying is that even if he doesn't want me there, he won't say so.'

Mark shrugs. 'Who gives a fuck? I want you there. It's where I live too.'

The woman opposite, a severely overweight twenty-something, who is munching her way through a packet of Jaffa Cakes, is staring at me as she listens intently to our conversation. There is something aggressive about her regard that annoys me, so I give her a good stare back, and after a few nauseating seconds where I have to look at the half-eaten mush in her open mouth, she pops another Jaffa Cake in and turns to look at the view instead.

'I can still phone SJ and go stay at my place, that's all I'm saying,' I say, returning my attention to Mark.

He shakes his head dismissively. 'We have a spare room; it makes sense. And Iain won't mind, I know he won't. And I *want* you to come and stay. I've missed you like crazy.'

'OK,' I say. 'We'll see how it goes.'

'Just don't mention his tricks.'

'He doesn't bring them back, does he? I mean, we aren't going to surprise him in bed with—'

'No,' Mark interrupts. 'But if he goes out or something, don't ask where he's been. That's the minefield in our relationship.'

I shake my head. 'I don't know how you cope, I mean, trust – it's fundamental.'

'It is,' Mark agrees. 'Whether it's about sex or crazy witches next door. And what makes you think that I *am* coping?'

As we sit in silence watching the countryside spin past, I think about those words, and realise that ultimately trust is what all of this is about. And almost from day one, Victor hasn't trusted my instincts, or my words, preferring time after time to side with his aunt. And it *is* fundamental, because those aren't foundations you can build a future on.

Eventually Mark says, in a dreamy voice, 'I miss the old days, when we were neighbours. Does that sound crazy?'

'Me downstairs, you upstairs . . .'

'A bottle of wine together. Some crap TV.'

'We had some fun, didn't we? I'm not sure we appreciated it properly at the time, though.'

'No, we definitely didn't.'

'Not having boyfriends kind of undermined everything, didn't it? But yet having a boyfriend isn't the answer to everything either.'

Mark shakes his head. 'Against all expectation, it isn't. Crazy but true.'

On arrival, Iain is the epitome of charming. He welcomes us both with a broad grin, and looks genuinely thrilled to have me staying. He makes up the spare room beautifully for me, even stealing a few flowers from a vase in the kitchen and placing them in my room. He doesn't even ask me how long I'll be staying, which is just as well as I think the question would make me cry.

We eat Chinese from a local takeaway and then, by the flickering light of their entirely convincing gas-powered 'coal' fire, we settle on the sofa to watch a film.

With Mark snuggled against Iain, and Iain's arms enveloping him, they look like an image of domestic bliss. No one could imagine the cracks in the foundations of their relationship.

I try to watch the film, but my mind won't settle. I can only concentrate upon a single set of thoughts: Is Victor home yet? Has he seen my texts? Is he replying to me right now?

But no matter how often I check my phone, there are no calls, no texts, and no emails.

Later, I sleep as if I have been drugged. But despite my ten-hour marathon, I wake up feeling tired and queasy, and vow to make a doctor's appointment to get myself checked out.

Both Mark and Iain are out at work by the time I surface, so I wander around Iain's beautiful flat, now somewhat crammed with Mark's junk, and then sit in their tiny garden and drink tea. I toy with the idea of breakfast, but in the end I simply can't convince myself that it would stay down.

My phone starts to beep its 'battery low' warning, so I fish the charger from my bag and sit and think about whether to make one final attempt at calling Victor. In the end, I can't resist.

The fact that his phone is still switched off makes me so angry that despite my best intentions, the message I leave is nothing more than: 'It's me. I'm in England. Call me.' I can't even manage an, 'I love you'.

Next, I phone my old flat, where I'm greeted by a heartening shriek of joy from SJ. 'Get your arse over 'ere!' she says.

Ringing my own doorbell feels strange, but being led by a grinning SJ into what was once my home feels even stranger. Just as Mark's junk has transformed Iain's minimalist interior, SJ and George's piles of ethnic tat sit uncomfortably next to, on top of, and underneath my own furniture. The place looks like a boot sale.

'Where's Guinness?' I ask, scanning his usual sleeping places and seeing that they are all occupied by embroidered cushions embellished with tiny, uncomfortable-looking mirrors.

'He'll be in the kitchen,' SJ says.

'Really?'

'Yes. He always sleeps in the kitchen. On the chair in the corner.'

'News to me,' I say, leaving the room and following SJ down the hallway.

'Shit it's good to see you,' SJ says. 'And totally unexpected.'

'I know. It was a bit of a snap decision.'

'Any particular reason?'

'Yes, I'll tell you all about it.' I crouch down next to the table so that I can see Guinness underneath. He is snuggled up on a thick grey fleece. 'Hello,' I say. 'Have you found a new nest?'

Guinness looks at me with the catty equivalent of sleepy disdain, sniffs my fingers, and closes his eyes again. The message is clear. Do not disturb.

'Nice to see he missed me,' I say, straightening up.

'You know cats,' SJ says. 'He only has eyes for George now. Anyway, *I've* missed you.'

I scan the kitchen. It too looks quite different now that every surface is cluttered with spice jars. 'You don't need the flat back, do you?' SJ asks.

'No,' I laugh. 'Of course not.'

'God, that's a relief,' she says. 'Tea or coffee?'

'Tea,' I say. 'I've gone off coffee at the moment.'

'Hey! You haven't commented on my bump!' SJ says as she fills the kettle.

'It's huge,' I say.

'There's a reason for that,' she says, a twinkle in her eye. 'Twins!'

'No!'

SJ nods and grins.

'That's brilliant news. Isn't it?'

'Bloody right, it is! We weren't sure if we'd be able to have another one. I mean, you know how hard this one was. So twins is pretty much the jackpot.'

'And everything's OK?'

SJ nods. 'Seems it.'

'Sex?'

SJ switches the kettle on and leans back against the counter. 'A bit. Less than before, of course. And we have to do it from behind more because of the——'

'The sex of the twins!' I interrupt.

SJ winks at me. 'I know. I was winding you up. I told them not to tell me. I don't wanna know.'

'I don't think I could resist.'

'So how long are you here for? I'm so chuffed to see you.'

'I don't know yet. I haven't decided.'

'Where are you staying? Do you need to . . .'

'At Mark and Iain's. It's fine. They have a spare room.'

'Because you know the door's always open. Well, it's your door anyway! But you don't know for how long?'

'No.'

'That sounds omnious.'

'*Omnious?*'

'Yeah.'

'It's om-i-nous. But you're right. It is a bit.'

SJ fills the cups and then nods at the table. 'So sit down and tell me all about it.'

'Unbelievable,' SJ says once I've finished.

'I know. That's half the problem. No one believes me.'

'And why is Victor behaving like such a wanker, anyway?'

'It's his aunt,' I say. 'Like he said, she's his only remaining family, so . . .'

'I suppose,' SJ says. 'But you're supposed to be his only girlfriend. And if the bitch really was trying to poison you, well, that's serious shit.'

'I still feel pukey,' I say. 'Even this morning.'

'You should go see the doc.'

'I intend to. I was going to phone and make an appointment, but it's only when I get up, really, so I forgot. I'm OK now.'

'Hum, let me see,' SJ says. 'Sickness in the morning . . .'

I laugh. 'I'm not pregnant.'

'You did a test?'

'I don't need to. I had my period. It was light. And late. But it was a period all the same.'

'How light?' SJ asks.

I shrug. 'Very. But it still happened. I put it down to being ill. I hardly ate anything for weeks.'

'Your boobs look bigger too,' SJ says, staring at my chest in a way that makes me uncomfortable.

'They do not!'

'They do!'

'It's because the rest of me has shrunk, I think. I lost about six pounds when I had swine flu.'

'You *are* skinny. But they still look bigger to me. Any sensitivity? Around the nipples?'

'SJ!' I say. 'I'm *not* pregnant. I had my period.'

'Your half-a-period.'

'But it still means I'm not pregnant.'

319

SJ crosses the room and returns with a thick hardbound volume: *The Big Fat Baby Book*. She places it in front of me and leans past me as she flicks through the index and then opens it to a page entitled 'Signs and Symptoms'. Something about her proximity, the feel of her bump against my back, the smell of her familiar Euphoria perfume, makes me feel quite emotional, like this is home. There really is something wonderful about having friends you have known for this long.

'There,' she says, running a fingernail across the page. 'Sickness, nausea, vomiting.'

'Which are also symptoms of swine flu, and/or being poisoned,' I point out.

'Absence of period, or an unusually light period with little blood,' she reads.

'Oh,' I say. 'I didn't know you could have a period and still be pregnant.'

'If it's a small one.'

'It was,' I say, pointing to the next line. 'A strange taste in the mouth which many describe as "metallic".'

'You have that?'

'Yes, but, well, as I say. The water was funny.'

'Feeling tired?'

'Well, of course, but . . .'

'Loss of interest in certain foods or products that you previously enjoyed?'

'Nope.'

'You said you've gone off coffee.'

'OK,' I say. 'Yes, that's true. It tastes funny.'

'Constipation?' SJ says.

I push my chair back and stand.

'Where are you going?' SJ asks.

'Where do you think?' I ask. 'To buy a bloody pregnancy test.'

'No need,' SJ says, raising one hand. 'I've got a whole box of the buggers. When we were trying, I got a load off the internet. They were cheaper that way.'

She scuttles from the room, so I sit back down and stare out at the dead Leylandii and wonder if it's OK to do a pregnancy test without Victor being aware. It feels inexplicably like a kind of infidelity.

'How exciting!' SJ says, when she returns. She drops the package on the table in front of me and says, 'Pee on that, dear.'

'Can we have another cuppa first?' I ask, looking up at her grinning face.

'You don't need to pee much! You only need a drop!'

'It's not that. I just need a moment. To pull myself together.'

SJ squeezes my shoulder. 'Of course,' she says. 'If anyone knows what a big deal this is, it's me.'

When I open the bathroom door, SJ is standing right outside, a broad grin on her face and her arms crossed. 'So?' she says.

I raise the strip so that she can see it. 'Does that mean what I think it means?' I ask, my voice flat. I am so emotionally numb that I feel like I have had whatever organ produces thoughts surgically removed.

'Yes!' SJ shrieks. She wiggles on the spot with excitement and then throws her arms around my rigid body. 'I can't believe it,' she says so loudly that her voice hurts my ear. 'We're going to be mums together!'

I do my best to enjoy the hug, but I still feel like the Google search, *How to feel when you find out that you're pregnant*, has yielded the blankest of pages. I can't even seem to think properly about the meaning of the word 'pregnant' for the moment.

'Come!' SJ says, stepping away and reaching for my free hand. 'You're shaking. Come and sit down.'

We return to the kitchen and I lay the test on the table and sit and stare at the two coloured lines – two lines of semaphore which mean 'everything changes'. SJ watches me staring at the strip and waits.

'Is it certain?' I ask eventually. 'Or can these be wrong?'

'In theory they aren't one hundred per cent. But I have never seen a false positive,' she says. 'And I've done hundreds of the buggers.'

I nod and finger the strip. 'God,' I say. 'Pregnant! I thought this might never happen again.' I think about the abortion and an almost spiritual sense of relief for this second chance washes over me. My vision goes cloudy as tears well up.

'Hey, hey,' SJ says, squeezing my hand. 'It's different this time. Everything's going to be fine.'

I nod and wipe my eyes on my sleeve. I start to smile, and another feeling, joy this time, starts to build like a wave rushing up the beach. Right at its peak, it reaches me and crashes over my head.

'I'm pregnant, SJ,' I say, suddenly astonished.

She touches my chin and forces me to look her in the eye. 'It's all gonna be OK,' she says.

Obtusely that statement makes me realise that it all might *not* be OK – that the pregnancy might fail, or the baby might have something wrong with it, or . . . Or my partner might change his mind about having a child and leave me. Again.

'I need to phone Victor,' I say, fumbling in my bag for my phone.

'Of course you do,' SJ says, touching my shoulder and discreetly exiting the room.

As I hunt for my mobile, I am simply assuming that he will answer. My brain has decided that if there is any reason, any logic to the universe – if there is any sense of fairness in our lives, any connection between Victor and me – then it must be this profound miracle of life itself. So not only will Victor know to answer the phone, but what I tell him will ultimately fix everything between us.

I raise the phone to my ear: voicemail. The wave of optimism vanishes into the beach, leaving only a wet stain to show that it was ever there.

'Victor,' I say quietly. 'It's me. I have to talk to you. It's urgent. It's *really* urgent.'

I lay the phone on the table and, feeling suddenly panicky, I turn to scan the room. 'SJ?' I call out. 'SJ!'

'I'm here,' she says, reappearing in the doorway.

'He's not answering,' I say. 'He's still not bloody answering.'

She crosses the kitchen, pulls a chair next to mine and wraps me in her arms as tightly as her unborn twins will allow. 'He'll phone back,' she says. 'And it'll all be fine. You'll see.'

'Will it?' I say, my voice trembling as a surge of something different – fear – rises within me. 'Because . . .'

The thought provoking that fear is this: that getting pregnant didn't fix my relationship with Brian; getting pregnant was the moment that everything went horribly wrong.

'Of course it bloody will,' SJ says. 'Think. We'll be mums together. Our kids will be the same age. They can play together. Go to school together. It's brilliant.'

I nod and smile as the image she has described takes form and begins to warm my heart.

SJ reaches behind her for the kitchen roll and rips off two sheets and hands them to me. 'You see?' she says. I nod and wipe my face and blow my nose.

'You wait till Victor finds out,' she says. 'He'll be home on the next flight.'

The word 'home' triggers yet another train of thought. Because, of course, this isn't home any more. France is supposedly home now. And if France isn't home, then I'm home*less*.

'Will it be French?' I ask, suddenly.

'I'm sorry?'

'Victor's French. If we get back together—'

'Of course you'll get back together.'

'Maybe. But if we do, and I have the baby in France, will it be French? Or Irish?'

'I don't know,' SJ says. 'You'll have to check. Doesn't it depend if you get married and that?'

I shake my head. 'I don't know. I think it might depend where I have the baby.'

SJ frowns. 'Actually, they aren't gonna go to school together, are they? If you're in France. Your kids will grow up to be Frenchies. You'll have to give 'em names like Jean-

Pierre or something. "Here comes CC and little Jean-Pierre." It's got a certain ring to it. A certain *je ne sais quoi* . . .'

She seems to find this funny, but I must be frowning, because her smile drops. 'What is it? What's up?' she asks.

I shake my head, robot-like. 'Even if we do end up back together, I don't *want* a French kid,' I say.

SJ laughs.

'I'm serious. It would be like it wasn't my child.'

'It's really not a big deal,' SJ says. 'Victor's French, isn't he? And you love *him*.'

But I have just understood something important, which incredibly has never crossed my mind up till now: if I bring my child up in France, it will end up learning French as its first language. It will go to French school, have French friends, watch French TV, and – heaven forbid – listen to French music. In short, my child will be French.

And that *is* a big deal. Because though I have never even suspected that I might have the vaguest hint of xenophobia in my reasoning, I am absolutely certain of one thing. That's not going to happen.

'God,' I say. 'How could I not have thought of that? I mean—' I'm interrupted by the sound of the front door opening.

'George?' I ask, grabbing the pregnancy test and the packaging, and stuffing it under my jumper.

'Could be any of my lovers,' SJ says, mockingly.

'Don't say anything!' I tell her.

George appears in the kitchen doorway, wrestling his way out of a huge overcoat. 'Evening, ladies,' he says. 'I didn't know we were due for a visit from our landlord.'

We both turn to smile at him, apparently unconvincingly, because the next thing he says is, 'And what are you two plotting?'

'Nothing,' we both say simultaneously.

George raises an eyebrow. He looks amused and entirely unconvinced. He hangs up his coat and takes a seat at the table where he looks intently from SJ to me, and then back again.

'Nice suit,' I say. It's initially just an attempt at creating a decoy conversation, but the second I say it, I realise that it's true. In fact, I have never seen George look so good.

'They gave him a suit allowance,' SJ says, latching onto the subject with a little too much enthusiasm. 'Imagine!'

'My new boss told me off for dressing like a tramp,' George says. 'It's the carrot and stick approach.'

'That really is lovely, though,' I say, reaching out to stroke the lapel between finger and thumb. 'Is that Paul Smith?'

George laughs. 'It is. How did you know?'

'I have no idea. I must have seen that check pattern somewhere.'

'Anyway,' George says, rather proudly fiddling with his tie, and then, becoming aware of his own gesture, loosening it instead. 'What's been going on here?'

'Nothin',' SJ says a little too quickly. 'Nothing at all, right, CC?' Her tone of voice is so unconvincing, it makes me cringe.

'Nothing at all,' I agree.

George fixes me with his blue eyes, so I shrug and gently shake my head. He snorts and stands and crosses to the refrigerator. 'Drink, anyone?' he asks.

We both decline.

While he fishes in the fridge for a beer, SJ mouths at me, *Tell him!* then, *You know I can't lie!*

When George sits back down, he grins at us both falsely, then sips his beer. 'I don't believe you at all, of course,' he says. 'You ...' he looks at me, 'have eyes like a panda, and you ...' he turns to SJ, 'look as smug as I have seen you since you found out you were pregnant.'

I dab at the corner of my eye, and seeing that my finger indeed comes back covered with smudged mascara, I realise that this isn't going to work at all. I nod at SJ, indicating that she can tell George after all.

'CC has some news,' she says. 'Don't you?'

'I do,' I say.

George smirks at me and takes another sip of beer.

'I'm pregnant,' I say.

'Ha!' George says. 'I knew it.'

'Really?'

'Oh yes.'

'How?'

'Your—' he says, glancing briefly at my chest. 'Never mind.'

I cross my arms protectively across my boobs.

'Anyway,' George says hurriedly. 'That's brilliant news, isn't it? I bet Victor's ...' His voice fades away, and I turn to catch SJ shaking her head vigorously.

'Oh, sorry, I just assumed,' George says, getting entirely the wrong end of the stick. 'So who is the fa——' He pulls a face, then turns to his wife. 'Can I ask *that*?' he says. 'I can't, can I? Help me out here.'

'Of *course* Victor's the father,' I say.

'They've had a barney,' Sarah-Jane explains.

'Oh!' George says. 'Well, I wouldn't worry about that. I'm sure there'll be plenty more of those!'

'I'm going to make tea!' SJ says brightly, clearly keen to have something to do.

When she brings the two steaming mugs over, we chink them against George's can of Kronenbourg and pretend for a while that we're celebrating.

'To CC,' George says, 'and all who sail in her.'

'George!' SJ protests. 'You make her sound like she's full of seamen.'

This produces a brief moment of hilarity, and George spits some beer out through his nose. But though I make my best effort to look celebratory, my emotions are still so mixed up that the truth is that I can't work out how I feel. It seems as if I won't be able to work that one out until I have spoken to Victor, and there is, it strikes me, a certain logic to that. This news, this event, this miracle, is, after all, half his, half mine. So perhaps it needs both of us present in order to form any kind of cohesive emotional response. But after another fruitless phone call, it seems Victor still isn't playing ball.

OTHER PEOPLE'S BUSINESS

When I get back to Iain's house, Mark is so down that even my smudged make-up fails to break through his personal bubble of misery.

He's drinking gin and tonic, and offers to make me one too.

'Not tonight, thanks,' I say, thinking, *And not for another eight months, either.*

When even this refusal fails to intrigue him, I become concerned enough about him to put on hold my own drama.

'Mark?' I ask. 'What's up, babe?'

He shakes his head sullenly.

'Come on,' I say. 'Out with it.'

'He's out,' he says. 'For the evening.' He pushes his phone towards me, so I pull up a chair and take a look. The screen is showing an SMS from Iain.

Sorry babe. Someone made me an offer I couldn't refuse. Have a nice evening. Laters. x

'Oh, darlin'.' I tut. I lay one hand over his. 'That's no

good. You can't be putting up with that. You'll have to talk to him.'

'I've tried,' Mark says quietly. He clears his throat before continuing. 'It doesn't do any good, though. He just says that I knew what he was like when I met him, and that if I'm not happy, then maybe I need to find a different kind of guy.'

I cover my mouth with one hand to stop anything unhelpful escaping. Because what I *want* to say is that Iain is behaving like a callous, greedy slut.

After a moment, I do decide to allow the words, 'You deserve better than this,' to escape my lips. 'Have you thought that maybe he's right?'

'Right?' Mark says, shooting me a glare.

'In that, yes, maybe you do need a different guy,' I say softly. 'Someone who can be faithful.'

Mark sighs, then lays his head against my shoulder. 'It's not like cars,' he says. 'You can't just pop in somewhere and change for a better model.'

'I know that,' I say. 'But surely . . .'

'You know how long I was single for before Iain.'

'I do.'

'And I didn't meet anyone better, did I? Not in ten years.'

'No,' I say, wondering momentarily if I have already lost Victor. Because despite his faults, neither did I.

'But I can't stand all this,' Mark says, his voice trembling. He starts to push his phone around the table with one finger like a toy car. 'And I love the fucker,' he adds, starting to cry properly now.

'Oh, babe,' I say, pulling him closer as a set of tears,

primed by my own predicament, but released by his, plop from the corners of my eyes.

Though I don't have any answers for Mark, we both eventually stop crying. We wash our faces and reheat a meal before snuggling together in front of the TV.

Iain returns at 10.45 p.m.

'Aw, how sweet,' he says, when he sees us together on the sofa.

I smile weakly.

'Shh!' Mark admonishes. 'It's almost the end.'

'Sorry, I'm sure!' Iain says, pulling a face and retreating to the kitchen.

I give Mark another squeeze, and we continue to watch the film until the final ad-break, when he drags himself from the sofa and follows Iain through to the kitchen.

'So, you have a nice time?' I hear him ask.

'Yeah,' Iain replies. 'He was hot.'

Despite a nauseating advert, I turn the TV up, but even the singing idiot from Go Compare can't quite drown them out.

'Hot?'

'Yeah. Sexy. Hung. Built. Dirty. Busy in bed. *Hot*.'

'Hotter than me, you mean?' Mark asks.

At this point, I realise that I can't sit here and pretend not to hear their conversation – it's just too personal.

'Hey, guys, I'm off to bed,' I call out. Neither of them reply.

'No, *not* hotter than you,' Iain is saying, his Scottish accent suddenly stronger now that he is angry.

'So why go?' Mark asks, just before I close the bedroom door. 'Why do that to me?'

The closed door muffles their voices enough that I can't understand the content of their argument. But the gist, communicated by raised voices and slamming doors, is clear enough, and I start to feel so angry on Mark's behalf that a few times I consider getting up and going out there to help him out. But it never was a good idea to get involved in other people's business. No couple ever welcomed outside interference in this kind of thing, so I restrain myself. Just about.

At 4 a.m. I have to get up to go to the bathroom, and as I cross the darkened lounge, I see that Mark is camped out on the sofa. 'Do you want my bed?' I ask in a whisper.

'Nope,' he says angrily, clearly awake.

'OK,' I whisper back.

The next morning, I wait until I think that both Mark and Iain have gone to work before leaving the sanctuary of the guest room. But no sooner do I switch on the kettle than Iain appears from the bathroom.

'Hi, CC,' he says, leaning in the doorway. 'Make me one of those, would yee?'

'Sure,' I say, surprised at his chirpy tone. 'Tea or coffee?'

'Coffee, please. White, no sugar.'

I make the drinks and carry them through to the living area.

'Sunshine!' Iain says, nodding at the window as I hand him his cup. 'About time too.'

'You not working today?' I ask.

'I worked Saturday, so I get the day off,' Iain says. 'I'm gonna go see the Seager exhibition at the Tate.'

'Cool,' I say. 'And Mark, he's at work?'

'I expect so,' Iain says. 'Who knows. He's being a dick at the moment. As you no doubt heard last night.'

I attempt to freeze my features into a neutral state, because I understand how very dangerous it would be, as a guest, to get involved in this. I must somehow fail, though, because Iain says, 'What?'

'Nothing,' I say. 'I didn't say a word.'

Iain laughs. 'I can just imagine what Mark told you.'

I nod and sip my tea, praying that the subject will go away of its own accord.

'I don't suppose for a minute that he told you the whole story,' Iain says.

'Iain,' I protest. 'It's really none of my business.'

'No, it isn't.'

'But you will lose him,' I say, wincing internally that I have lost control of my tongue for a few crucial seconds.

'You reckon?' Iain asks, sounding both interested and relaxed about the prospect.

'He's a lovely guy. I have known him for years, and if I were you, I would want to hang onto him. That's all I can really say on the subject.'

'Sure,' Iain says, sifting through a pile of letters on the chair-arm, and then ripping one open. 'But he needs to grow up.'

I nod slowly and lick my lips as I deliberate whether to say more. Because though I clearly *shouldn't* get involved, I'm not sure I can sit here and let him trash my friend either.

'Does he?' I ask, the decision apparently taken. 'Or do you?'

Iain frowns at what looks like a bank statement and then turns the frown upon me. 'Beg pardon?' he says.

'Well, you're the one who wants to have his cake and eat it,' I point out. 'Mark's in love with you. All he wants is a bit of commitment. So I'm not so sure that he's the one who needs to grow up.'

Iain looks at me coldly. 'As you said, it's really none of your business.'

'Fine!' I say, standing and heading through to the kitchen for some breakfast.

As soon as I return with my bowl of cereal, Iain says, 'What Mark hasn't told you is that we agreed all of this before he moved in. We agreed to have an open relationship.'

'You said it was none of my business, so . . .' I say.

'So whinging on now about what we already agreed is just childish,' he continues.

I clench my teeth, but it's no use, I can't help myself. 'God, you're a hard man,' I say. 'I thought you were supposed to be Buddhist.'

'I am.'

'So where's the love and respect in that?'

'I'm sorry?'

'He *loves* you, stupid. And your actions are hurting him. So why do it?'

'Stupid, am I?' Iain says with a caustic laugh.

'I think you're being stupid in this situation,' I say.

'As a Buddhist, I get that the search for constancy is the

source of all suffering,' Iain says. 'But I wouldn't expect you to understand.'

I wrinkle my nose. 'What?'

'The Dalai Lama said . . . Have ya even heard of him?' he asks, rolling the 'r' in heard.

'There's no need to be rude, Iain.'

'Well, he said . . . oh, never mind. Anyway, the point is, Mark wants everything to stay the same. He just needs to wise up. No one else can cause our suffering, and the only thing causing Mark's is his own wee mind.'

I laugh sourly.

'And don't laugh at it. I will nee have you in *my* house laughing at my beliefs,' Iain says.

I think, *Ah, here we go. Who would have thought that we would get to whose house I'm staying in so quickly?*

'Well, I won't let you pretend that your medieval belief system is the reason you have to hurt my friend,' I say.

'Medieval, eh?' Iain says. 'And that, coming from a Catholic.'

'Only I'm not Catholic,' I retort. 'Sorry to disappoint.'

'Whatever,' Iain says. 'You don't get it. That's all that counts.'

'Get what? That Mark—'

'That we *agreed* on an open relationship. We agreed not to emulate hetero norms of binary coupledom. So if Mark gets a wee bit upset, it's something he has to deal with on his own.'

'Sounds like a cop-out to me,' I say.

'You Christians bang on about treating others the way

you want to be treated yourselves, but we're all different. In fact, you have to treat people the way *they* want to be treated. And Mark needs to treat me the way *I* want to be treated. And I need freedom.'

'That's fine,' I say. 'But where do your actions come into all of that? Where's your responsibility to treat Mark the way *he* wants to be treated?'

'But I do. Totally. What I do with other people has nothin' to do with Mark.'

'You can't possibly believe that. He loves you and your cheating hurts him. So it's your responsibility as a loving human being not to do it any more.'

'Except that we *agreed* to this,' Iain says. 'If he now can't cope with it, that's his problem, not mine.'

'Only it *is* your problem,' I point out. 'Because he'll leave you.'

'Well, if that's what he says he wants, then good for him. He has his own destiny to live out.'

'He didn't say that.'

'But that's his option,' Iain says. 'Now I'd love to hear more of your wisdom, but I need to get dressed.'

I sit and stare at the sunlit courtyard and think about Mark and Iain. It feels like a kind of respite to be thinking about someone else's problems. It's certainly easier to see things clearly.

When Iain eventually reappears – clearly dressed to kill – he says, 'Still here, then?'

'Yep,' I reply evenly, thinking, *You want war then, huh?*

'Actually, how long *are* you staying?' he asks.

'I don't know. Why, do you want me out?'

336

'Not this second,' Iain says. 'But . . .'

'I'll be gone today. Don't worry,' I tell him.

'You don't have to go *today*,' he says. 'It's just . . .'

I think, *So that's what passive aggressive means.* I force a smile, wink, and nod my head sideways, in a *way-to-go* kind of gesture.

'What?' Iain asks.

'I just love it when people don't say what they mean,' I tell him.

'Oh, sorry. I'll take a few more minutes out of my busy schedule to be more explicit for you, if you like. I don't think I want you siding with my partner and turning him against me and, if that's the path you have chosen, then I would rather you leave.'

I laugh. 'I thought you people believed in karma,' I say.

'We people, as you put it, do. Your point being?'

'Well hadn't you better start being nice to people at some point? If you don't want to be reincarnated as a worm or something?'

'Nice? Like you, you mean?' Iain asks.

'No. I don't have to,' I say. 'Because I don't believe in karma, or reincarnation. And I don't have to live with you.'

'I thought you *were* living with me,' Iain says, gesturing at the room.

'Not for long, believe me,' I say flatly. 'But I wish you'd be nicer to my friend. To the man you claim to love.'

'As I said, CC, if Mark chooses to get all bent out of shape over where I stick my dick, that's his own responsibility.'

'Nice,' I say. 'So presumably you'd rather he didn't give a damn?'

Iain shrugs.

'Think about it,' I say. 'Would you *really* rather he didn't care what you do or who you see?'

'I don't want to discuss this with you any more,' Iain says.

'Right.'

'But the answer is yes,' Iain says. 'I would rather he didn't care and left me to follow my own path without judgement.'

'Then you know what? Find someone who *doesn't* love you,' I tell him. 'Because that's the way it works. Caring goes hand in hand with loving.'

'I'm going out now,' Iain says, pulling his jacket from the chair-back. 'Will you be gone by the time I get back, or . . .?'

'I will, Iain,' I say. 'But I have one last gem of wisdom for you.'

He rolls his eyes and starts to pull the jacket on. 'Go on.'

'Think about what I've said. If you carry on like this then Mark will leave you. I know him. And he loves you. But he can't cope with this. If you ever find someone who *can* cope with this kind of relationship, it will be with someone who doesn't give a damn. And if that's what you prefer then my guess is that you're too scared to let yourself be loved.'

'Thanks, Doctor Freud,' Iain says. 'Got it.'

'I haven't finished.'

'I feared as much.'

'If you *don't* want to be with someone who is indifferent . . . I mean, if you do like the fact that Mark loves you and still you carry on doing what you're doing, then what *that* means is that you like hurting him more than you like loving him back. And either way, as far as I can see, you're the one who needs to grow up.'

Iain reddens slightly, then says, 'Thanks, CC. You can just drop the keys in the letterbox. I'll pick them up when I get back.' And then he turns, opens the door and leaves. When the door closes, it slams so hard that the entire house shakes.

'Fuck!' I say to no one in particular.

I sit and stare at the wall for a few minutes, and then realising that I can't even *think* clearly until I get out of Iain's stress-filled space, I shower, dress, pack my things into the smallest corner of the spare room, and step outside. It's icy cold, but the sky is blue and the sun is shining.

I only have to walk two hundred yards before I come to a Starbucks, and lured by a comfy sofa in the sunny window, I enter.

Armed with a mug of tea, I attempt to call Victor's mobile, but yet again it is switched off.

I sip my tea and run a hand over my belly. I think about the fact that I need to see a gynaecologist to check that everything is OK, and think about the fact that the man I'm supposedly dating, the father of this child, is, or at least *was*, a gynaecologist. He was *my* gynaecologist. The fact that he isn't even aware that he has probably fathered a child seems really quite obscene.

Clutching at straws, I desperately try his number one 'last' time. Uttering, 'Well be damned with you then!' I cast the phone back into my bag.

I take another sip of tea and stare out of the window. At the end of the street I can see a vast billboard carrying an orange advertisement for easyJet. Which is pretty much the only answer here.

I sigh deeply, retrieve my phone from my bag and call SJ.

'Are you at home?' I ask. 'Because I think I need to book a—'

'I was just this second going to call you,' she interrupts.

'Right. So can I come over?'

'You've got a visitor,' she says. 'Someone's here to see you.'

'Really?'

'Yes. A very angry someone.'

'Iain?'

'No! Not Iain! Victor's here. Can you come over? Because he's doing my head in.'

'Victor? He's *there*?'

'Yep.'

'What's he doing there?'

'Just come over, will you?'

'And he's angry?'

'Oh yes!'

'You haven't told him about the baby?'

'No,' SJ says. 'I thought I'd leave that to you.'

'I'll be there as soon as I can,' I tell her. 'About half an hour, I expect.'

'Take a Valium,' she says.

'I'm sorry?'

'If you've got any Valium, take one now.'

'I don't do Valium,' I say.

'Shame,' she says. 'I think you're gonna need it. Maybe bring a crash helmet instead.'

'Don't let him go till I get there, OK?'

'I don't think he's going anywhere,' she says. 'Not until he's given you a right bollocking, anyway.'

ROUND ONE

By the time I get to my old flat, my stomach is knotted with stress. I ring the doorbell, and it is Victor who opens the door. His expression alone is enough to communicate that he hasn't calmed down in the intervening half an hour.

'She's out,' he says. 'We have the whole place to fight in.' He gestures inwards, indicating that I may enter, which, seeing as it is my flat, rather annoys me.

Feeling more nauseous than ever, I walk past his rigid body without making contact. 'I already spent all morning fighting with Mark's boyfriend,' I tell him softly. 'I don't want to fight with you at all.'

'Well, I do,' he says menacingly, as he closes the door behind me.

Because the hard surfaces of the kitchen seem somehow better suited to the tense atmosphere of this reunion, that's where I head for. I'm hoping to end up in the soft furnishings of the lounge later on, but we're clearly not there yet.

When I reach the kitchen, I pause just inside the doorway in the hope that I can force a hug to soften things up, but as Victor squeezes past me he raises one hand to hold me at a distance – a shocking first.

'Victor?' I ask, my fake smile fading. 'What is the matter?'

'The matter?' he asks, crossing to the farthest corner of the room and folding his arms defensively. 'I'm so fucking angry, I can barely speak,' he says.

I stare at him warily. His eyes are cold and glassy. He looks like he has lost weight. In fact, with his new beard, he looks so different that he looks like someone I barely know at all.

It crosses my mind that if anyone should be angry here, it's me. But expressing that isn't going to help, so I say, 'OK. Why are you angry? Let's start there.'

'Why?' he spits. '*Why?!*'

I swallow hard. 'Yes,' I say in a pleading tone. 'Why?'

'You fucked off.'

'I didn't *fuck off*,' I say, starting to feel annoyed myself now. 'I needed a break.'

'A *break* . . .' Victor repeats angrily.

'Yes. I wasn't feeling well, and my boyfriend was being horrible, and there were dead cats in the water supply, and I was cold and lonely, and I needed a break from that hell-hole.'

Victor fumbles in his pocket and produces a folded slip of paper. 'And this?' he says.

I peer at the paper, but don't cross the kitchen to take it from him. I'm feeling a little scared of him, no doubt because he's reminding me of Ronan when he was on one of his drunken benders.

'I don't know what that is,' I say. 'Have you been drinking?'

'No, I haven't,' Victor says. 'Unless you count tea. This is the note you left.'

'I tried to phone you,' I explain. 'You were ignoring my calls, so—'

'I wasn't *ignoring* them,' Victor says. 'You see, that's what you're like about everything. I dropped my phone in the fucking toilet. So it's fucked. Sorry 'bout that. But shit happens, you know?'

'Right,' I say. 'Well, I couldn't get through, that's all I was saying, so I left you a note to explain where I was. But I still don't see why you're so angry.'

'Did you even read it?' Victor says.

'I don't need to *read* it,' I say, my irritation now creeping into my voice. 'I *wrote* it.'

'Here,' he says, proffering the letter.

I sigh angrily and cross the room to take it – at arm's length – from his grasp. I rescan the letter.

'I know what's in the note. I wrote it. And?'

'Well, that's not a note that describes a weekend break, is it?' Victor says. 'It says you're sick of everything and sick of me, and you're leaving.'

'No, it doesn't,' I protest. 'It says ...' I reread the letter, but as far as this page is concerned, he's actually pretty close. 'OK. Well I felt really let down, Victor.'

'*You* felt let down?'

'It's maybe a *bit* harsh,' I say, unnerved by his rage. 'But the second page—'

'A bit *harsh*?'

'Yes. But the other page ...'

'There *was* no other page.'

344

'Yes there is. I wrote two pages.'

'No there wasn't,' he says. 'That's it.'

'But you *saw* the second page. You must have.'

'Nope.'

'You must have, Victor. It said that I love you and I need a break, and ...'

'CC,' Victor says. 'There. Was. No. Second. Page.' He crosses the room and snatches the letter back from me before retreating again to the other side of the room. 'Look,' he says, waving the sheet at me. 'You even signed it at the bottom. At the end.'

'I know I did. But then I felt bad, and I added a second page.'

'Well, I didn't find it.'

'How could you not find it?' I ask. 'The two sheets were folded together.'

'Only they weren't,' he says. 'Cut the crap, CC. You walked out on me, and now you're feeling bad, and—'

'So you don't believe me? Again?'

He shrugs.

'Jesus, well doesn't that make a *fecking* change,' I say, unable to contain my own anger any longer. 'You don't believe me when I tell you the food's making me ill, or when your crazy aunt is putting tarot cards under the shutters, or when I tell you she has been putting dead kittens in the water supply. There's a real theme there, Victor. Can you spot it? Go on. Have a go. Try. Win yourself a fecking prize.'

'It wasn't her,' Victor says flatly.

'What?' I say, so angry that the 'wh' of what whistles past my lips.

345

'It wasn't Distira,' Victor says. 'It was Carole.'

'What do you mean?'

'It was Carole. OK? I know that. So I *do* believe you.'

I shake my head. 'I don't understand.'

'I saw the cats. In the bag. I took them over there and dumped them on the kitchen table, OK? And Distira didn't even know. It was Carole.'

'But why? Why would she do that?'

'I don't know,' Victor says. 'Maybe she was jealous? Maybe she's fucking crazy. Maybe all women are. How should I know?'

'Well now you know,' I say. 'I *wasn't* making things up.'

'Yes. I know. I believe you.'

'*Now* you believe me,' I say. 'But not before. It took Carole to tell you, didn't it? My word alone wasn't enough!'

'CC! The whole thing sounded crazy. Even you can see that.'

'Even me? Even I can see that?'

'I mean . . .'

'I know what you *mean*. And yes. The whole thing sounded crazy because it is crazy. Only I'm not the crazy one, am I?'

'Maybe not, but—'

'Maybe? *Maybe?!* Victor, you just said yourself that it was Carole. So now you know that I wasn't making anything up. And what I can't quite get, what I'm finding absolutely unbelievable, is that you're not even here to apologise. You're here to have a go at me. How do you manage that little acrobatic feat, eh?'

'I never actually said that you were making it up.'

346

'That's *exactly* what you said,' I spit.

'I didn't. I just said that Distira wouldn't do that, and I was right.'

'Well, that must feel so good,' I say, aware that I'm starting to sound like a bitch, but unable to control it.

'It feels better than being told that my aunt is trying to poison me!' Victor says, shouting now.

'Really?' I say, shouting back. 'So no regrets, then? No apologies? Nothing?'

'Why should I?' Victor says, turning bright red now. 'Why make this about me? What about you? Running off with your little gay friend at the first sign of trouble.'

'My little gay friend?' I shake my head and glare at Victor. 'How fucking dare you! Mark's one of my closest friends. And you know it. And if I called him, it's because he, at least, trusts my judgement.'

'Right, but—'

'When you, you didn't believe a word I was saying.'

'That's not fair, CC. You've known Mark for years,' Victor says.

'What, so now you'd need to know me for fifteen years before you can take my word that someone's putting dead cats in the water tank?'

Victor's nostrils flare. 'If you're gonna bang on about the same stuff over and over, then this is pointless,' he says. 'We're just going round and round here.'

He sounds like he's losing, which gives me a fresh burst of energy. 'You're right,' I say. 'It is pointless, because if you can't even take my word for—'

'I suppose you're staying with him as well? At Mark's?' Victor asks, interrupting me.

'I'm sorry?'

'I suppose that's where you're staying? Mark's?'

I shake my head. 'No, Victor,' I say. 'I'm not. I'm staying *here* tonight.'

'But SJ said I— Never mind.'

'Sorry. This is *my* place, remember?' I say meanly. 'And SJ is *my* friend.'

Victor stares at me in silence for a moment, his mouth slightly ajar, then says, 'Fine, if that's the way you want it.' He turns and heads down the hallway, then reappears from the lounge with a hefty backpack. 'I'll find somewhere else to stay,' he says.

'You could try my little gay friend,' I shout after him. 'Maybe he'll put you up.'

'I have friends,' Victor says. 'Don't worry about me.'

As he heaves his backpack on and turns to leave, I open my mouth to call him back. But then the door slams, and it's too late. He has gone.

I suddenly realise that because I don't know where he is going, I have no way of contacting him, and lurch towards the front door. But as I reach for the door handle, and as his silhouette behind the patterned glass shrinks, pride holds me back, and my hand drops to my side.

After Victor's departure, I pace angrily up and down the kitchen for ten minutes, unable to find a way to release the energy trapped in my body from so much anger. Tears would help, and I'm kind of expecting them to burst forth at any minute, but for the moment there is nothing but a trembling rage. I pace up and down a few more times, and then, feeling like a caged animal, I pull on my jacket and rush out of the front door before beginning to stomp my way up Primrose Hill, and then on into Regent's Park.

The air is so cold that it hurts my lungs. The view down to central London is stunningly crisp and clear, but my vision is too red-tinged right now for me to be able to appreciate it.

By the time I have lapped the park twice, I'm starting to feel calmer and when a glance at my phone reveals that over an hour has passed, I realise that I am also incredibly hungry. I decide to head back.

SJ opens the door wearing an apron. The flat reeks of vegetable soup.

'I wasn't sure if you were coming back,' she says, heading back through to the kitchen. 'But I've made masses of soup, so if you're hungry ...?'

'Sorry,' I say. 'I needed a stomp. And yes, I'm starving. I'd love some.'

'Things didn't go well with Vicky-Vick then?' she asks, returning to stirring the soup.

'No, they really didn't.'

'Oh dear,' she says, in a tone that so understates the seriousness of the situation that it almost makes me laugh.

Over soup and bread, I give her a blow-by-blow account of the argument. Being my best friend, she of course agrees that Victor is being a bastard *and* a dickhead. In fact, she agrees entirely with everything I say. And with the mood that I'm in, that's probably just as well.

'And then he grabbed his bag from the lounge and stormed out,' I say, finishing my story and omitting the bit where I reminded him that this was my flat and that SJ *my* friend.

'Well, like you say, dickhead covers it,' she says. 'But what about the baby? What did he say about you being pregnant and that?'

'I didn't tell him,' I say.

She raises both eyebrows and stares at me over her soup. 'You didn't tell him? Why the fuck not?'

'I don't know, SJ. He was too angry. And I didn't want to use the pregnancy to fix all of this other stuff. Because it can't fix it. And I don't want to use the baby to trap him. I want us to be together in spite of this, not because of it. I want to be sure I *want* to be with him before I tell him ...' My voice peters out, because suddenly I'm not sure *why* I didn't tell him.

SJ nods.

'I'm not making much sense, am I?'

'Actually yes,' she says. 'I understand, but I still think you should have told him. If you love him, that is.'

I lift a spoonful of soup to my mouth and think about that phrase.

'So? Do you?' SJ prompts, tearing into a chunk of bread.

'I'm not sure,' I say. 'I'm really not sure any more. I guess that's the real problem. I mean, can you love someone who doesn't believe a word you say? Someone you can't trust to look after you when you're ill? I don't know.'

'I know what you mean, but he's only human. We're all dickheads from time to time. Even you. Even me. Even George.'

'George is *never* a dickhead,' I say.

SJ wrinkles her nose. 'OK, maybe George isn't that much. But *I* am. I'm totally out of control at times. And he puts up with it. Because that's what you do if you want to make things last.'

I nod thoughtfully.

'So you'll get over this. Vic will calm down and he'll come back, and you'll forgive him for being a dickhead, and this will all be a funny story you'll look back on when you're old and your kids are all grown up.'

These, finally, are the words that bring forth tears. Because they remind me, beyond being right or wrong, or Victor being fair or unfair, what is really at stake here. On the one hand, being a single mother and remembering the fateful argument that split us apart. Or on the other hand, growing old together and looking back on all of this as a funny episode we got over. And being visited, together, by our child.

ROUND TWO

Victor returns before SJ or myself are even out of bed the next morning. George lets him in, has a brief, blokey-sounding conversation with him – all action verbs and no feelings, you know the kind of thing – and then heads off to work.

I pull on some clothes and, unsure if I feel sick due to morning sickness, nerves, or both, I head through to the kitchen, where I find Victor making himself a cup of tea.

'Hi,' he says, looking up from his mug, his face giving nothing away. 'I thought we needed to talk, so . . .'

'We do,' I say, hesitating about crossing the room to be nearer him until the moment has passed and it's too late to do so without it assuming more meaning than I would have intended.

I hear SJ moving around in the bedroom next door and realise that we can't really have this discussion right here, right now.

'The thing is—' Victor starts.

'You know what?' I interrupt. 'I'm not even awake yet.

Can I have a shower and meet you somewhere?' My voice is trembling.

'Oh, OK. Sure,' Victor says, sounding almost as nervous as I do.

'You look awful,' I say. 'You didn't sleep rough, did you?'

'No. I stayed with Jeremy,' Victor says. 'Though that amounts to pretty much the same thing.'

'Right,' I say.

'So where shall I meet you?' Victor asks.

I glance at the window. 'It's sunny. So how about the park?'

'Regent's?'

'Yeah. I'll, um, meet you at the top of the hill. Where Primrose Hill Road meets the green.'

Victor nods slowly. 'Right, sure. In an hour, then?'

I nod.

Victor smiles weakly, turns to leave, but then hesitates. 'You will come, won't you?' he asks.

I look at his face and see raw emotion, and all I want to do is run across the room and hug him close. Instead I simply say, 'I'll be there.'

Once Victor has left the house, I add milk to the cup of tea that he started and sit and stare out at the back garden. The Leylandii, once the bane of my life, is now a withered brown pole with not a trace of green left.

Where once its shadow had turned my lawn into a patch of mud, now grass is starting to sprout again. For a while, I superstitiously saw that tree as some kind of inverse barometer of the happiness in my life. The bigger it got, the worse everything else seemed to get until I thought the darkness it produced was going to swallow me whole. But now despite the fact that it's all but gone, everything is still a big complicated mess: I'm pregnant by a man who doesn't trust a word I say, and who wants to live in a place that despite my most determined efforts, I hate.

A hand touches my shoulder, making me start. I turn to see SJ standing beside me. She's wearing a pair of men's pyjamas.

'You OK?' she asks.

'Sure,' I say. 'I was just looking at that tree.'

'Oh God,' she says. 'I just remembered. They're supposed to be coming to cut it down today.'

'Really?'

'Yeah. The old lady over there asked if we'd chip in.'

'Mrs Pilchard?'

'Yeah. I know you don't like her, but she's really nice with me.'

'Words fail me,' I say.

'Anyway, George was worried it would fall on the house, so we gave her fifty quid towards the cost of the tree-feller fella. Is that OK?'

'Oh, absolutely,' I tell her. 'Gosh, is it really going today?'

'That's what they said,' SJ says. 'She asked if we wanted the wood, but we said no.'

'No, there's no fire to burn it in, so . . .'

'Exactly,' SJ says, then, 'Was that Victor's voice I heard?'

I glance at the kitchen clock and then stand and swig down the last of my tea. 'It was,' I say. 'And I need to get a move on. We're meeting in the park. To talk.'

SJ rubs my shoulder and smiles at me. 'Be nice to him,' she says, 'and he'll be nice back.'

I snort. 'I'll try,' I tell her.

'No,' she says. 'Don't *try*. Be *nice* to him.'

When I get to the green an hour later, I can see Victor, his back to me, hunched against the cold and sitting on a park bench. His breath is rising in little white bursts.

'Hi,' I say, when I reach him. 'You're not too cold, are you?'

'Huh?' Victor says, looking startled, his mind apparently elsewhere. 'Oh, a bit, maybe. Let's walk.'

We start to cross the green in silence then Victor says, 'Look. All that stuff about Distira and Carole—'

'It doesn't matter,' I say, it seems to me, rather generously.

'Exactly,' Victor says. 'That's what I was thinking.'

I raise an eyebrow and glance at him from the corner of one eye. Despite my downgrade of their status as relationship-wreckers and attempted-murderers to 'unimportant', I had still been hoping for an apology.

'What?' Victor asks, apparently picking up on my glare.

'Nothing,' I say defensively. 'Nothing. It's fine.'

'So if we both agree that all that shit that happened was just a hiccup . . .' Victor says.

'Yes.'

'Well, we're OK then, aren't we?' he asks earnestly.

I turn to look over at the horizon, thinking, *Men!*

A group of school children are jogging across a different track towards the park, and I remember briefly the hell of being forced to do cross-country running on a cold morning.

'Aren't we?' Victor asks again.

I turn my head and look back at him. 'I don't know,' I say. 'That's the truth.'

We reach the main road and have to pause with some other pedestrians before we can cross. When we get to the other side and the space between us and our fellow park-goers has increased again, Victor asks, 'You do want to, don't you?'

I frown. 'Want to what?'

'Carry on,' he says. 'You do want us to carry on together?'

'My main problem is that I don't want to live there any more,' I say, avoiding his question.

'In France?'

'Yes. In La Forge.'

'Oh,' Victor says. 'I had no idea. Is this because of Distira and Carole?'

I shrug. 'A bit,' I say. 'They aren't the house's strongest selling point, I'll give you that. But it's not just that. The truth is that it's also cold and it's miserable, and frozen and muddy and—'

'It *is* cold,' Victor concedes. 'But I'm not sure that calling it miserable is being objective.'

'I am,' I say.

'I'm not sure that a place *can* be miserable. Isn't that more how *you* feel than the place itself? Isn't whether you feel miserable about it up to you?'

This comment reminds me of Iain's justification of his behaviour with Mark, which of course unintentionally annoys me. 'So it's *my* fault?' I say. 'Is that what you're saying?'

'No, I wasn't saying anything is your fault.'

We pause to cross the Outer Circle, then once over, we walk for a few minutes in thoughtful silence before either of us speaks.

Finally I break the silence by saying, 'What are you thinking?'

Victor snorts lightly.

'What's funny?' I ask.

'Oh, it's just … Jeremy was saying last night … the way women always ask what you're thinking. And most of the time we're thinking about football or motorbikes or sex, and we have to pretend to be thinking about relationships, or love, or whatever.'

I nod, not quite sure how to take this. 'So are you thinking about football or cars right now?' I ask.

'Of course not,' Victor says. 'No, it was just a funny thing Jeremy said.'

'Right,' I say. 'Anyway. It's just not how I expected the South of France to be. That's the point.'

Victor exhales sharply through his nose. 'I had a feeling this would happen.'

'What?'

'You not wanting to live there. And it not living up to your glitzy expectations. And me having to choose,' Victor says.

'I didn't have glitzy expectations.'

'But you don't want to live on a farm any more.'

'No, not on that farm. I'm sorry.'

'It isn't fair, you know. I mean, you knew when you met me. This was all already planned. I warned you. And you said you wouldn't ask me to stay.'

'I know.'

'So was that, like, part of the plan?' he asks.

'The plan?'

'Yes,' he says, sounding almost snide now. 'Did you plan to get your claws into me nice and deep before you dropped your little bombshell?'

I stop walking, and turn to face him so that he can appreciate the full anger I'm working into my expression here. 'I don't have *claws*, Victor,' I say, raising my hands to show him. 'Just fingernails. Fingernails damaged by lots of DIY.'

'It's a figure of speech,' he says.

'It's a figure of speech that I don't appreciate the tiniest bit.'

'No,' he says. 'I'm sorry. It's something Jeremy said.'

I think, *Jesus, I hate that creep.*

'Wipe that,' Victor says.

And I think, *I wish I could.*

'And no,' I say, 'I didn't *plan* anything. I didn't *plan* for the South of France to be like Siberia. And I didn't *plan* to have a digger knock the walls down and turn our garden into a mud-field. And I didn't *plan* to have our drinking water contaminated by dead kittens.'

'But that will all get sorted. You know that.'

'How?' I say. 'What are we going to do? Wait for global warming to turn La Forge into St Tropez?'

'Summer will come,' Victor says. 'It's already warming

up down there. And everything's sorted with Distira and Carole. And we'll sort the garden out again.'

'But I don't want to live there,' I tell him. 'It's too isolated. It's too far from everything and everyone. And above all, I don't ... I'm just not sure I ...' My little speech peters out because what I was just about to say – that I don't want to bring a child up there – would change everything. And dropping it on poor Victor at this point still doesn't seem fair.

'You don't love me any more?' Victor says, misinterpreting my hesitation. 'Is that it?'

'I ... I do,' I say. 'I think I still do.'

'You *think* you still do,' he repeats, and I hear how hollow – how devastating – that sounds.

'I'm pretty sure I do,' I say, realising as I say it that this doesn't sound much better. 'It's just that there's been so much ... so much *bad blood*. With Distira and the water and everything ...'

'That still?' Victor says.

'Yes, that, *still*,' I say.

'But you just said that it didn't matter.'

'It doesn't. But the fact that you didn't believe me *does* matter. It matters a lot.'

Victor nods. 'I see,' he says, and of some unspoken common accord we start to walk again.

'You're right,' he says, eventually. 'It was wrong of me. I'm sorry.'

'You weren't there for me when I was ill. I was counting on you, Victor, and you let me down.'

'I thought it was flu,' Victor says. 'The symptoms were flu symptoms. I couldn't have known.'

359

'I thought you were a doctor.'

'Look. I know you won't believe this, but actually there's no way to know. The symptoms are the same. I mean, there are blood tests you can do, but mainly doctors diagnose swine flu by knowing that it's going around. That's why they do it by phone. And they know that it's going around because they get bulletins to tell them so, and they see other patients who have it. And I didn't know. Because I'm *not* a GP.'

'But you could see how ill I was.'

'True. So I fucked up. And I'm sorry. But so did the other doctor, he didn't spot it either.'

'Which doctor?'

'The one who came to the house.'

'Only he didn't. He never came.'

'No,' Victor says. 'OK then. Well if he didn't, I *thought* he had. But I'm sorry.'

I reach briefly across the icy divide between us to touch his back, but he doesn't react. In fact, I'm not sure he even notices, so I let my hand fall back, and then stuff it back in my pocket.

'So what can I do to fix all of that?' he asks. 'What can I say to make that OK?'

'I don't know. I'm not sure there's much you *can* say.'

'If I promise never to doubt you again? Would that do it?'

I glance at him and see that he's being entirely genuine. He looks like a twelve-year-old pleading for a train set.

'If I promise to always believe you . . .' he says.

'That's sweet,' I say softly.

'But it doesn't help?'

360

'No, it *does*,' I tell him.

We cross paths with an old woman walking her dog. I notice that she has the same handbag as mine, and wonder if she is a vision of my lonely future.

'So will you come back?' Victor asks, once she is past.

'To you, or to La Forge?'

'Well, both,' Victor says. 'Seeing as that's where I live. Where I thought *we* lived.'

We must walk almost half a mile in silence as I struggle to reply to that question. Because the wise part of me – the loving part – is screaming for me to reply, 'Yes, yes! Of course!' But the truth is that La Forge has come to symbolise a nightmare in my mind, a nightmare of cold and loneliness and illness, and even fear. And it's beyond my powers to say 'yes' to going back there.

'Well, that's my answer then, isn't it?' Victor says finally. 'It's hopeless.' And indeed, every ounce of hope has vanished from his voice.

He has stopped walking, so I pause and turn back to face him.

'Basically I give up my dream, or it's over for us,' he says. 'That's what you're saying.'

I shake my head. 'No. Look, I'm so sorry. But I hate it there. I want to say "yes", really I do, but . . .'

'Then say it,' he says. 'It's just a word. Say it.'

'I can't. I'm sorry. I'd go with you anywhere else. Honestly I would. But not there. I've tried it. I put everything I had into it. But I don't want to go back there.'

'Right,' Victor says, then, 'God, I had no idea you could be so hard.'

I shake my head. 'I'm sorry,' I say. 'I had no idea it would be so horrible.'

Victor's eyes flit across my face for a second, and then he sighs and says, 'Any chance of a hug?'

I stare at him for a moment then step towards him, wondering if somehow physical proximity can heal all of this.

As he wraps his big arms around me, he sniffs my neck and says, 'I just want to remember the smell of you,' and suddenly I realise that this is not a healing hug, but a *final* hug. I gasp and feel tears forming.

'I really thought that this was going to work,' Victor says into my ear, his voice cracking. 'Bummer, huh?'

I move my own lips to repeat the word, 'Bummer,' somehow so incongruous and yet so descriptive. He pulls away and grips my shoulders so hard that it hurts a little.

'You take care, OK?' he says, and I see that his own eyes are watering.

'Victor,' I say. 'Don't . . . Please don't . . .'

He shakes his head, swallows hard, rubs one hand across his beard, and then turns and starts to walk away.

'Victor!' I cry.

But he simply raises one hand over his shoulder as if to say 'stop', or perhaps 'bye', and then hunches down and starts to walk even faster away, leaving me standing, alone in the icy wind, tears rolling down my cheeks.

By the time I leave the park, I have managed to pull myself together just enough to stop crying, though I'm still shivering. Whether this is from cold or shock, I'm not quite sure. It only takes one look at the concern on SJ's face to set me off all over again, though.

'Oh darlin'!' she exclaims as I collapse into her arms. 'Whatever's happened now?'

We hug in the hallway for a moment then move inside the flat and close the door.

I shake my head and sink into the armchair. 'It basically came down to would I go back and live there or not. I think I fucked up.'

'You said no?' SJ asks, apparently astonished.

'I hate it there, SJ,' I say. 'I hate it so much.'

'More than being single?' she asks. 'More than bringing up a baby on your own? Are you sure you're not being a bit dramatic about it all? I mean, how bad can a place be?'

'You have no idea,' I say. But I suspect that she may be right.

For the next hour, as on TV, a snide chat show host coaxes a bunch of other couples to argue for the cameras, I continue to ponder this.

SJ sits and knits her tiny baby jumper. She claims that knitting relaxes her, and even suggests that I should give it a try, but because she spends most of her time swearing about dropped stitches, I'm not entirely convinced.

Around four, I head through to the kitchen to make tea and notice that the dead tree is still standing. 'What happened to the tree feller?' I shout down the hall.

'Dunno,' SJ calls back. 'He didn't come.'

'That old bag Pilchard has probably run off with your fifty quid,' I tell her.

'Probably!' she agrees.

Just as the kettle starts to boil, the landline rings, but it's a short call because by the time I get back to the lounge, SJ is hanging up. She looks up at me and licks her lips. She looks grim.

'What?' I ask.

She sighs.

'*What?!*'

'That was Victor,' she says, her mouth turning downwards.

My heart misses a beat. 'Victor?'

'Sorry, I tried to get him to talk to you, but . . .'

'What did he say?' I ask.

'He just asked me to tell you that he's leaving.'

'He's leaving,' I repeat, flatly.

'Tonight. He's just bought a flight back.'

I nod numbly. 'OK.'

'He said he'll be in touch.'

I nod again and try to work out whether the fact that he'll be in touch is a positive or a negative. I sink onto the edge of the armchair.

'Is that all? What did he say *exactly*, SJ?'

'That's pretty much it,' she says. 'I'm sorry.'

'I need to know the exact words he used.'

'Of course. Um . . .' she rolls her eyes to the ceiling and then looks back at me and continues. 'He said, you know, "Hi, Sarah-Jane. It's Victor. Can you give a message to CC?"'

'Right,' I say, annoyed that she's now giving me a little too *much* detail.

'I said I would rather he spoke to you himself.'

'OK.'

'And he said, no, would I just give you the message that he's found a flight and is off back tonight.'

'And that's it?'

'He said to tell you he'll be in touch.'

I sigh deeply. 'Well that's something, right?' I say.

'He said he'll be in touch,' SJ says, pulling her unhappy face again, 'about your stuff.'

'Mary mother of Jesus! So that's it then?'

'I . . . I'm sorry, CC.'

I stare at the floor. From the edge of my vision, I see SJ standing to come and comfort me, but I raise one hand to stop her. 'Don't,' I say. 'You'll just start me off again.'

She nods and obediently sinks back onto the sofa. A few minutes later, her knitting needles start to click again briefly, but then pause, so I look up at her.

'You should have told him,' she says. 'That's all I'm going to say on the whole thing.'

'I know.'

'It's his kid too. He has a right to know.'

'I *know*,' I say again.

I stare out the window and attempt to analyse how Victor and I got to this point. Because although I remember everything that has happened, although I know every word that was said, and, of course, every word that *wasn't* said, none of it adds up to this finality. None of it makes sense.

'Did Victor's number show up when he called?' I ask her, the sharp urgency of my voice surprising even me.

SJ reaches for the phone and then hands it to me.

'Shite,' I say, pressing buttons on the handset. 'Hidden number.'

'Surely you have his number though?' SJ says.

I shake my head. 'He dropped his phone in the toilet back in France. He said he was getting a new phone and a new number.'

'And you don't have it?'

'I don't think *he* has it yet,' I explain.

'And Jeremy? You said he was staying with Jeremy.'

I shake my head. 'I don't know his number. I don't even know his surname.'

SJ shakes her head. 'Then I think you're gonna have to be patient, sweetie. Or get a flight yourself.'

My mobile rings. I frantically search for it in my handbag, but when I do manage to fish it out, the name on the display is Mark.

'Hey, chicken,' Mark says, his chirpy tone revealing that he is blissfully unaware of any of the drama. 'I was wondering if you were gracing us with your royal presence *ce soir.*'

'Have you got a number for Victor?' I ask.

'Victor?' Mark says, his tone changing. 'Sure. Why? Have you lost it?'

'Not his French mobile. It doesn't work any more. Have you another number for him? Or for his friend Jeremy?'

'Jeremy? No,' Mark says. 'I can't stand the guy. What's happened? You sound funny.'

I give Mark the shortest version possible of the story.

'Are you staying put?' he asks, once I have finished my brief synopsis. 'Because I can call over on my way home if you want.'

'There's no need, SJ's here.'

'I think there is,' he says. 'Three brains are better than two. I'll bring a bottle of wine, shall I?'

'I can't drink, Mark,' I say.

'You? Since when?'

'I'm pregnant, OK?'

'Jesus! OK, I'll bring chocolate instead,' he says. 'Unless you have some other special request for fennel or something.'

'Fennel?'

'I don't know. You're supposed to crave weird shit, aren't you?'

'Chocolate's fine,' I say.

'Right.'

'Actually, dark chocolate Bounty. OK?'

'Sure.'

'And bring lots of them.'

'Sure thing.'

An hour later, the doorbell rings. I turn from the television to SJ and say, 'Mark, or George?'

'Mark,' SJ says, glancing at the clock. 'George has a key.'

I stand, steel myself to hopefully avoid crying again, and head out into the hallway.

When I reach the front door, I place one hand on the doorknob, take a deep gasp of oxygen and wrench the door open. But the sight before me knocks all of the air back out of my lungs. Because there, on the doorstep, I find not Mark but a haggard Victor

'You!' I say, rather stupidly.

'Yes,' Victor replies quietly.

SJ comes out, already pulling on her coat. 'I have to, um, nip out for something,' she says.

When she reaches the end of the path, she pauses and adds, 'And get it sorted, eh? Tell him, OK?'

I nod at her, and she winks, and, still buttoning her coat, she strides away.

ROUND THREE

'You had better come in,' I say to Victor. 'It's freezing out here.'

He pushes past me, unintentionally barging me with his backpack and then apologising as he does so. I close the door behind me and follow him into the kitchen.

'I thought you were leaving,' I say. 'I thought you had already gone.'

Victor lifts off his backpack, leans it against a wall, and turns to face me. 'I went to the station, but I couldn't do it. I couldn't get on the train. Not with things the way they are.'

'No?'

He shakes his head. 'I keep thinking about what George Harrison's wife said.'

I frown as I struggle to remember what George Harrison's wife might have said but my mind draws a blank.

'It's just a documentary I watched with Jeremy,' Victor explains.

We are interrupted by the almighty buzz of a chainsaw being started up outside. We turn to look out at the garden, and as we do, a floodlight comes on illuminating the dead tree. A guy in an orange safety helmet starts to climb a ladder.

'They're cutting the tree down,' I tell him, speaking loudly to be heard over the scream of the chainsaw.

'Finally!' Victor says.

'We had better go through to the lounge.'

I lead the way through, and then close the lounge door against the noise. Victor crosses the room and stands with his back to the gas fire, so I take a seat on the sofa and look up at him.

'You were saying something about George Harrison's wife. He's the guy from the Beatles, right?'

'Yes, that's him. They had this really stormy relationship. And she said people were always asking her what the secret of a long marriage was.'

'OK . . .'

'And she said she always replied that the secret of a long marriage is to never get divorced.'

I give a small smile in spite of myself.

'I know it's silly,' Victor says uncertainly.

'No, it's not silly at all. It's quite profound.'

'Yes, that's what I thought. She said they had loads of difficult times, but they stayed together, and in the end she was glad they did, because they just always had more and more shared memories to look back on.'

I see Victor's Adam's apple bob as he swallows and struggles for words.

'This isn't what I want,' I tell him. 'You know that.'

A shadow crosses his features, and I realise that he has

misunderstood me. 'Splitting up, I mean. *Splitting up* isn't what I want.'

Victor exhales with visible relief. 'Oh,' he says. 'Well, me neither.'

'I don't ...' we both say simultaneously.

'You go first,' Victor says, smiling weakly.

'No, you ...'

'I was just going to say that, well, I don't think I give a fuck where we live,' he says. 'Not really. And you? What were you going to say?'

I smile but also feel a tear slide down my cheek. 'The same thing, really,' I manage.

'Really?'

'Yes.'

Another batch of tears are now clouding my vision. I reach for a tissue and blow my nose. 'I don't know where all these tears keep coming from,' I say. 'I should have run out of supplies by now.'

Victor dabs the corner of his eye and points the finger at me. 'The same place as these, I expect,' he says.

'Yes.'

'So,' Victor says. 'If neither of us really care where we live, then wouldn't you think that two clever people like us should be able to get this sorted?'

'You would think so,' I say. 'But we don't seem to be that clever, do we?'

'I've been an arsehole. I had a lot on my plate, but it's no excuse. I know that. I didn't know I could get it so wrong. But I've learnt from this. Let me prove it to you.'

'I needed you, Victor,' I say. 'I was away from home, and I was ill, and I needed you.'

'I fucked up. But I'll make up for it,' Victor croaks. 'People fuck up, and you either stay together and learn from it, or you give up and start all over again with someone new. But at some point, you have to stop doing that. At some point you have to say, "Let's stay together and fix this".'

Tears are streaming down my face now and I'm too choked up to reply.

'But it was a really hard time for me too. I had so much emotional stuff going on down in Perpignan.'

'I know that,' I tell him. 'I am sorry about that. I was scared. I really was. But it's no excuse either.'

Victor sighs and shakes his head. 'Come here,' he says, standing and opening his arms.

I look up at him but my eyesight is so blurry that I can't make out his features. 'There's something else,' I tell him, dabbing at my eyes with a tissue. 'There's something I have to tell you. Something I should have told you before.'

'Oh?' Victor says. He looks worried.

'It's . . . Well, the thing is . . . I . . . I don't want to have a kid in France.'

Victor frowns. 'A kid?'

'Yes. If I'm going to have a child, I want to bring it up here.'

'Why?' he says. 'What's wrong with France?'

I shrug. 'I don't know. It's sort of an instinct thing. I want to have my friends around me. I want my mother nearby. I want to understand what the doctors are saying. I want the kid to learn English and watch *The Apprentice*, and like Irish stew and Marmite.'

Victor nods. 'OK. But we can cross that bridge when we get to it, can't we?'

'I'm pregnant,' I blurt out. I lower my gaze and stare at my hands for a moment, because I'm almost too scared to see his reaction. But then I hear him sigh deeply, and have to look back to check out what's happening. He is staring at me like a madman, both hands cupped over his mouth.

'I'm pregnant,' I say again, this time staring him in the eye.

Victor's brow wrinkles and then he shakes his head, revealing the beginning of a smile. 'Really?' he says, his features such a mix of emotions that he looks confused as much as anything else.

I nod and bite my lip as I struggle to hold back more tears.

Victor steps towards me, beaming now. 'Come here!'

When SJ returns home an hour later, she finds Victor and me sitting at the dining room table holding hands.

'Mission accomplished?' she asks.

I nod and smile.

'Good,' she says. 'I'm going to phone George and get him to take me to that new Thai place in Camden so you two will have the place to yourselves.'

'You don't have to do that, SJ,' I say.

'No, you don't,' Victor agrees.

'Mark's coming anyway,' I remind her.

'He isn't now. I phoned him and told him it was best if he gave you two some space. Is that OK?'

'Sure. But all the same, you don't have to . . .'

But SJ shakes her head. 'I'm not good around lovey-dovey couples. It makes me feel icky. I prefer it when everyone's shouting, to be honest.'

So for an hour, out of general respect to SJ's ickiness, we resist the magnetic attraction between our two bodies and pretend to make bland chit-chat over cups of tea.

But the second SJ leaves the house to join George, Victor grabs my hand, swings me around, and pushes me against the wall to kiss me.

For a second, my stomach somersaults – a reaction to the sensation of his prickly beard, but tonight, my desire to be close to him is more powerful than my phobia.

Images of my bearded father spring to mind, images specifically of his death, of my desperate attempts to resuscitate him. And then I think of Waiine, ill in hospital, stubbly and unshaven too, and I think, *What strange images to come up in the throes of a passionate kiss*, but then these images also fade, squeezed from my mind by the sudden realisation that we are three, here, together. Victor, myself, and our unborn child. I start, unexpectedly, to weep.

'Hey,' Victor says, looking into my eyes with concern.

'No,' I say, putting a hand behind his head, and pulling his mouth back against mine. 'No, don't stop.'

Between kissing and crying, breathing becomes a little difficult, but there's nothing I can do to resist either, so kiss and cry and gasp for air is what I do. And then slowly the tears fade and the kiss becomes more passionate, more urgent.

I feel Victor's bulge beneath his jeans, pressing against me, and then feel his hands beneath my clothes, touching my breasts. And then suddenly we're both lost in a frantic mix of sadness and joy, regret and relief, and the animalistic desire to mate.

'Here?' Victor asks in surprise, making me realise that I am in the process of unbuttoning his jeans.

In reply, I yank them down to his thighs, and there, against the wall of the hallway, we urgently, frantically, make love.

Victor comes quickly, and apologises for his lack of willpower, which just makes me laugh.

'What?' he asks, nuzzling my neck. 'Why are you laughing?'

'I don't know. Just us. Human beings. We're so ridiculous. We're such an absurd mix of animal desire and pride and jealousy and general fucked-up-ness, aren't we?'

Victor starts to laugh as well, and tries to pull away, but I clutch him close. 'No, stay,' I whisper. I love the feeling of him slowly shrinking inside me.

'I just mean . . . well, it should all be so simple, shouldn't it? It's just . . . *this*.'

Victor kisses my neck. 'I love the smell of you. That's what I miss the most when you're not there. Your neck.'

'Vampire,' I say.

'Maybe.'

'Ah, that tickles,' I say.

'Sorry, I forgot to shave.'

I lean away just far enough to look properly at his beard, and then raise one hand and caress it gently.

'It's fine,' I say.

'Really?'

'Yeah, something happened just now. I think I got over it. I think I got over my beard thing.'

'Really? Because I can shave. I can shave it now.'

'No. It's you. It's part of you. And I love you. All of you.'

'Me too,' Victor says. 'I love you so much.'

'God, I'm pregnant,' I suddenly say, surprising myself at the utterance.

'I know,' Victor says, squeezing me tight. 'It's amazing, isn't it?'

WHAT YOU DID TO ME

The next morning, aware that it's our turn to give SJ some space, Victor and I head out for breakfast. It's a grey drizzly day, so we end up going no farther than the first coffee shop.

Comfortably installed with our drinks, Victor says, 'So, at risk of spoiling the love-in . . .'

'We need to talk about what happens next?' I offer, completing his phrase.

'Exactly.'

'I was thinking about it this morning while you were asleep. I think I'll need to stay here a while. I want to get a check-up. And I need to see my mother.'

'Right. Well, you know that I need to get back to France, right?'

I nod. 'I know,' I say glumly.

'I have to finish the place, whether it's to sell or to live in.'

'And I *can* come back there and try again for a bit if it's what you really want,' I say, in a voice that I hope will lead to refusal of my generous offer.

'But it isn't what you really want?'

I shake my head. 'No, I can't pretend that it is. And I want to have my baby here in England, whatever happens. Somewhere where my mum, SJ and Mark are within striking distance. Being pregnant has suddenly made all of that seem incredibly important.'

Victor nods. 'I understand that. So where will you stay? Surely you can't carry on camping on SJ's sofa?'

'No. But I can't just kick them out. And I can't stay with Mark and Iain either.'

'Why?' Victor asks. And so I fill him in on what happened.

'You don't hold back, do you?' he comments, once I have finished.

'Do you think I was wrong, then? Did I overstep the mark?'

Victor shrugs. 'Not in *principle*. But I'm not sure I would get that involved in someone else's personal stuff. But then, what do I know?'

'Anyway,' I say, 'the point is that I can't stay with SJ forever, and I don't want to go back to Mark's. And I do need to spend some time with my mother, mainly to see if I can talk her out of this wedding nonsense.'

A shadow crosses Victor's face.

'What?' I ask.

'I just think that you should maybe let other people live their lives more,' Victor says. 'Don't get so involved.'

'She is my mother.'

'I know. But if she's happy with Saddam, surely that's all that matters.'

'He's *twenty-three*, Victor. Well, twenty-four now.'

Victor raises his hands in submission. 'OK, it's none of my business.'

I reach out and take his hand. 'No, it is. And maybe you're right. I think she's wrong, but I may not have much say in the matter.'

'No. She sounds pretty determined, from what you've said.'

'I think it runs in the family,' I laugh.

'OK. So how about you go try to cancel your mother's wedding while I go back and finish the place off. It should only take a couple more weeks to get everything ship-shape. And then when everything's OK, and the water's safe, and the cherry tree is in blossom, maybe you can come back and just see the finished thing. Just in case you change your mind.'

'That sounds like a plan. But if I agree to come back and have another look, how will you feel if I don't change my mind? If, after all that work, I say that I still don't want to live there? Because that's what I honestly think is likely to happen.'

Victor squeezes my fingers tightly. 'Then we'll just have to come up with another plan. I won't mind. I promise I won't mind anything ever again.'

I laugh. 'If only that were true.'

Victor smiles at me. 'You're right, of course,' he says. 'I suppose when these things come up, we just have to try to remember what's important and what isn't.'

'You and me,' I say.

'And . . .' he says, nodding in the direction of my tummy.

'Yes,' I say, my vision suddenly becoming watery again.

'You're crying,' Victor says.

'I know.'

'When I met you, you said you wanted to live on a farm, that you hated beards, and you never ever cried.'

'I know,' I say. 'See what you did to me?'

LIKE MOTHER, LIKE DAUGHTER

I see Mum's battered Volvo the second I step out of the train station. I wave, but she toots me anyway.

'Hello, dear,' she says as I climb in. 'How was the trip? I suppose you're all annoyed because the train was late? Still, never mind, it's nothing a slice of cake and a cup of tea won't fix.'

'Actually, I'm fine, Mum,' I say as I fasten my seatbelt.

'Well, you'll feel better once you've had a cuppa,' she says, characteristically discounting what I just said. 'Anyway, I'm so glad you could come at short notice,' she continues, pulling away from the pick-up point. 'Because I need to talk to you about the wedding arrangements. The thing is . . .'

She lurches out onto the main road, right in front of a Smart car, which blares its horn at us angrily.

'Beep away!' she mutters. 'Honestly, everyone's in such a hurry these days. What is it they call it? Road rage?'

'It *was* his right of way,' I point out.

'Well, there's still no reason he couldn't let me out,' she says, now waving in her rear-view mirror at the poor guy. 'It's not like he's going anywhere fast; he's only heading for another traffic jam farther up. Anyway, the thing is that poor Adam has been having a horrible time with his family.'

'Ever since that bust up you had with them all?' I ask.

'Yes,' she says. 'Yes, ever since the "bust up", as you call it.' She lets go of the steering wheel in order to do the speech marks for 'bust up', so I make a grab for it myself.

'You always were a nervous passenger,' she says as she seizes the wheel and brushes my hand away. 'It started when you did your driving test.'

'I'd just rather you held the wheel, Mum,' I say. 'I'm old-fashioned that way.'

'So he has a trip booked for the twentieth, and I found a registry office in Weybridge that can fit us in on the twenty-fourth.'

'The twenty-fourth of *April*?!'

'Yes, dear.'

'Isn't that a bit soon, Mum? That's in two weeks!'

'Well, that's what I need to talk to you about. Because I don't even know where to start, and you've always been so good at organising things, haven't you?'

'But why so soon, Mum? Why rush it?'

'I told you, dear. Adam's family are being horrid, and he's lost his job at the hotel. I think it's all linked, but he insists that it isn't. But anyway, the best thing is if we can just get everything sorted out so that the poor little soldier doesn't have to go back to it all unless he wants to.'

'God, Mum, the twenty-fourth of April?'

'Even though it's only going to be a small affair, I'm worried there won't be time. Which is where your famed organisational skills come into play. Your father was good at that planning lark, too. Not that I could have asked him to help with this one, but anyway, if we could sit down together and work it all out on one of your computer-sheet thingies . . .'

As we negotiate the route home, she continues to blather on in a random manner about Saddam and Morocco, and the wedding, and her friend Poppy who she had hoped would help, but who seems to have gone unexpectedly cold on her, which may or may not be because she's having an affair, but more likely is because she doesn't approve.

When I'm on my way to meet someone, I often imagine the conversation that we will have, and today I had imagined that we would be celebrating my pregnancy by now. But as Mum waffles on and on, and as it all washes over me, I come to realise that getting this wedding even postponed is going to be challenge enough, let alone getting her to reconsider the whole thing.

Still talking nine to the dozen, she parks the car and leads me into the house, where she hangs up her coat and puts the kettle on.

'So my feeling is, that if Poppy doesn't want to get involved, well, she can go hang herself. I don't think that I even want to invite her any more, though I probably will, because, well, you just don't undo thirty years of friendship.' She turns from the kettle to face me, and pauses. 'What's wrong?' she asks.

'Nothing, Mum. I'm just listening.'

'Your arms are folded,' she says.

'And?' I ask, uncrossing them self-consciously.

'You never cross your arms unless you're angry. You used

to stamp your little feet, too, but that stopped when you were about thirteen. But you look just the same right now.'

'I'm not angry, Mum,' I insist. 'I'm just listening.'

'Hum,' she says. 'Am I going on too much? Is that it?'

I shrug.

'So that is it. OK, what's been going on with you, then? Anything much?'

I snort and raise one eyebrow. 'Oh, this and that,' I say.

She squints at me, staring right into my eyes and furrows her brow.

'Come here,' she says. 'You look like you need a hug.'

Feigning reluctance, I cross the kitchen and she wraps her arms around me. But the truth is that it feels nice. We never were a tactile family, and this kind of physical contact has always felt like stolen treasure.

'So what's been happening?' she asks again.

'As I say, nothing much. Victor's aunt tried to kill me. We split up. I was homeless. We got back together. I'm pregnant.'

'You're pregnant?' she says.

'Yes, Mum.'

'And are you happy about that?'

'Very.'

'Then that's a good thing,' she says, squeezing me, and then pulling back. 'Let me finish the tea and you can have a slice of Battenberg and tell me all about it.'

'OK,' I say.

'And I don't want to sound like a one track record here, but that's another reason to get this wedding sorted out as soon as possible.'

'Why's that?'

'Well, people are being difficult enough about our age difference, without waiting until I'm a grandmother to boot!'

Over tea and multicoloured slices of cake – Battenberg was my favourite when I was about five, a preference lodged, in stasis, in my mother's mind ever since – I recount the last two months, and amazingly, for once, she listens.

At one point, she even interjects, 'And that's when you phoned me and I didn't believe you. Gosh, I'm terrible, aren't I? Am I a terrible mother, do you think?'

When I have finished my tale of woe and reached the happy ending, she says, 'Well, you have had a rough time of it, haven't you?'

I shrug. 'It's not been fabulous, frankly. It's certainly not how I imagined being in love was going to be.'

'Is it ever?'

'No, I suppose not. But we're OK now, and that's the main thing.'

'And Victor's already back in France, you say?'

'He's travelling back today. He stayed to come to the doctor's with me. I wanted to check everything was OK. With the pregnancy and stuff.'

'I would have thought he could have done that himself,' Mum says.

'Yes, I know. But he thought it was better this way.'

'It's a shame he's gone. I was so looking forward to meeting him.'

'I know, but there's plenty of time for all that, Mum. Thirty or forty years, hopefully.'

'You always were ambitious.'

'Well, I waited a long time for Victor to come along.'

'I know,' Mum says. 'And I know how that feels.'

'Yes,' I say vaguely.

'Anyway, everything's OK with Victor and everything's OK with the baby?'

'It is,' I tell her. 'I'm about seven weeks gone, apparently. They did some blood tests and stuff, so I'll have to wait for those, but everything seems OK.'

'Did they tell you if it's a boy or a girl?'

'It's too early to tell.'

'Of course. And names?'

'We're nowhere near that yet,' I tell her.

'Gosh, I'm so excited,' Mum says.

'Me too.'

'I'm dreading being called Granny, but it is exciting. It's the best wedding present you could give me, really. And Saddam loves kids too. I saw him with his nieces and nephews.'

I must sigh or something, because Mum says, 'What? I'm happy for you and Victor. Why can't you be happy for me?'

'I'm trying, Mum,' I say. 'I'm doing my best. But you have to admit, it's unconventional to say the least.'

'And since when did you give a damn about being unconventional?'

'You're right. Really, I'm trying, Mum. And if you're still sure about this, then I promise I'll try harder, OK?'

'Of course I'm sure. It's not complicated. He makes me happy.'

'But you don't have to marry him in a rush in two weeks, do you?

'I don't *have* to do anything. I want to. And I know you don't approve. Giles told me that you think he's a gold digger.'

Giles is Dad's old colleague from the legal practice. I had a *supposedly* secret conversation with Giles about Mum's new boyfriend.

'I didn't exactly say that, Mum.'

'Anyway, he's drawn up a pre-nup agreement. So can you just relax about it all and help me make it happen?'

'Even if I do stay, Mum, two weeks is pushing it.'

'You always said you liked deadlines.'

'That was in advertising. This is different.'

'You said you worked best under pressure.'

It's undeniable that I have said this many times, so I don't argue.

'So there's your challenge. Organise a wedding, a reception, and your dotty old mother's outfit in two weeks.'

I smile weakly at her and shake my head. 'You're barking mad, you know that?'

Mum winks at me. 'Like mother, like daughter. Humour me.'

I nod.

'Now have another piece of this cake. I bought it specially for you because it's your favourite.'

JE L'AIME

Mark dashes across the car park and hurls himself into the car. 'Jesus Christ!' he exclaims.

'It's dreadful, isn't it?' I laugh. 'The only thing I forgot to book was decent weather! Anyway, hello you!'

'Hello, sweetie!' Mark says, holding his wet coat away from me as he leans over to give me a peck on the cheek.

'Thanks for coming. I honestly don't think I could have faced it on my own.'

'No worries,' Mark says. 'So, time for a pint, or not time for a pint? That is the question.'

'I can't. Mum's on the verge of a nervous breakdown. Saddam hasn't said a word for twenty-four hours. I'm not even sure if he'll manage "I do". I need to get back there.' Peering out through the rain, I pull out of the station car park and onto the main road.

'So how are you?' Mark asks.

'Knackered. I've been managing a very demanding princess and organising her wedding for two weeks.'

'Has it been bad?'

'Well, Mum's never been the easiest person, you know

388

'... But it's been OK, I guess. She just changes her mind all the time about every detail. It's exhausting.'

'Is it a big do?'

'No. Mum doesn't know that many people, really. At her age, quite a few of them have already moved on, if the truth be told. There's eight of us for the service and twelve back at the house.'

'Twelve can't be *that* hard to organise, can it?' Mark says.

I shrug. 'Well, Mum wanted it to look like four weddings and a funeral, even if it is tiny.'

'Without the funeral hopefully,' Mark laughs.

'Well yes. So we have a gazebo – not that we'll be able to use it in this rain – and a DJ ...'

'Ooh, do I get to dance?'

'If you like waltzes. Mum specified the music, and found this really decrepit DJ. I feel a bit sorry for Saddam, really, but I guess that's what you get if you marry an oldie.'

'And Victor's stuck in France, huh?' Mark asks, fiddling in his satchel and pulling out a pack of cigarettes. 'Can I smoke in here?'

'If you open the window a bit,' I say, 'and yes, Victor's stuck in Nice because of all the fog.'

'I saw on the news. Three hundred flights cancelled at Heathrow or something.'

'Victor was flying to Gatwick, but his flight was still cancelled. He's been on standby since yesterday, but so far zilch. I'm really quite heartbroken about it all, but ...'

'So how is everything now? Did you get all your issues sorted? You look fabulous, by the way.'

'Thanks,' I say. I'm wearing a rather expensive Whistles dress that my mother treated me to. It disguises my swelling boobs wonderfully. 'You're looking jolly dashing, too. Shiny, but dashing.'

'Shiny suits are in,' Mark tells me, fiddling with his tie. 'It's the whole fifties thing.'

'I'm just not used to seeing you look so suave.'

'That's Iain's influence. He keeps buying me cufflinks and ties. In the end, you have to take the hint. Anyway, you didn't answer my question. How's stuff between you and Victor?'

'It's all fine ... Jesus! This rain!' I turn the wipers onto full speed and slow down. 'I haven't seen him for two weeks, of course, but he phones every day, and the house is just about finished.'

'Does this mean you'll be going back there?'

'I'm not quite sure. We need to have another talk about all that.'

'So you're not keen.'

'No ... No, not keen would be an understatement. And what about you? How are things with Iain?'

'Fine. Perfect, actually.'

'And all that open relationship stuff?'

Mark shrugs. 'It's all sorted. He had a revelation one morning and stopped shagging around.'

'Really!'

'Yep.'

'What caused *that*?' I ask.

'I don't know,' Mark says. 'I think he just thought about it all and decided that I was right. His sexuality is based

390

on a lot of fantasy stuff, so we're being a bit more experimental. That seems to be enough for him for now.'

'Hmm. Not sure I need to know about that.'

'Oh, it's nothing that freaky,' Mark says. 'But he likes guys in suits, bikers in leather, and that kind of stuff . . .'

'It sounds like the Village People,' I say.

'It is a bit. But anyway, we've been experimenting more. I'm managing to keep him satisfied better now. I'm sure we'll have rampant sex when I get home in this little number.'

'Well that's good.'

'It is. It's been fun. But yes, since we had our big talk, we've been totally in love, really.'

Just for a second, I consider telling Mark of the conversation I had with Iain. Ultimately, though, I decide that I may never know what influence my harsh words had, and that even if I did somehow contribute to saving their relationship, it's probably better if Mark never knows this.

'You must come round for dinner again, next time you're in London. Iain seems to really like you.'

It's as much as I can manage to keep the shock off my face.

'What about you?' Mark asks. 'Did Vic believe you about the witch woman in the end?'

'Yes. Well, it turned out that it wasn't his aunt who was doing it. It was her girlfriend, Carole.'

'So she's a lezzer?'

'Apparently so. And a jealous one, at that. She thought I was going to steal Victor's aunt away or something.'

'Erhhh,' Mark says. 'You said she was rancid.'

'Well, not *rancid*, maybe, but I wouldn't say she was a

looker. But Carole loves her, apparently. She was prepared to fight to the death for her, it would seem.' I put the indicators on and swing onto the drive of Rylston Manor.

'Wow,' Mark says. 'I thought we were going to a registry office.'

'This *is* the registry office. Nice, huh?'

'Very! And are they all here already?'

'I brought Mum and Saddam before I came to get you. The others hadn't arrived yet. There's only eight of us at this bit anyway.'

'What's he like then, Saddam? Do you like him now?'

I park the car and switch off the engine. Rain drums against the roof.

'He's shy. Quiet. Overawed by everything. You'll see.'

'And do you *like* him?'

I shrug.

'OK,' Mark says, nodding at the door. 'Let's do this thing!'

We jump from the car and run towards the manor as fast as my heels will allow. The main hall is chock-a-block with the previous wedding group, so we struggle to even get in out of the rain.

'We're in the little room,' I tell him, grabbing his hand and pulling him through the crowd and along the hall-way.

When we enter, the only person present is my mother. She is standing in the bay window, looking out at the rain.

'Where is everyone?' I ask.

She turns and smiles at me weakly. 'Bloody weather! Still . . .'

We pull off our wet coats and hang them on the coat stand and I now see Mark's fifties suit in all its glory. It is made of a rough silky weave, and is beautifully tailored. He is wearing a white shirt with a pinned collar and a thin grey silk tie. 'You do look amazing today,' I say.

Mum crosses the floor to join us. 'Hello. Mark, isn't it?'

'Yes,' he says. 'You look *faaabulous*.'

Mum breaks into a smile. She is wearing a Max Mara cropped bouclé jacket and skirt combo. On my advice, she's had her hair bobbed, and we have both had our make-up fixed this morning by Vanessa Chan who we used at Spot On to fix up our sickly supermodels before photo shoots. Vanessa is as good as make-up artists come, and Mark's right – Mum is looking fabulous.

'You're very brave coming to such an old fogey do,' Mum says.

'Well, you know what they say: you're only as old as the man you feel,' Mark says cheekily.

Mum flashes the whites of her eyes at him and blushes. 'Yes. Well . . . I'm sure Adam will be glad you're here too. It'll be nice for him to have some youngsters to talk to.'

I think about pointing out that Saddam probably considers Mark and me to be too *old* to talk to, but decide against it. 'So where are the others?' I ask.

'Penny's here. And Giles. They went off together to smoke cigarettes. Saddam's lurking somewhere looking moody, and I've not had a peep from Lindsay and Jack since last week, so I'm not even sure they're coming.'

She turns to Mark. 'I don't think they approve, to be honest,' she says.

'Are you bovvered?' Mark asks, and Mum surprises me by getting the reference.

393

She points to her face in a very Catherine Tate fashion and says, 'Does my face look bovvered?'

'Not one bit,' Mark laughs.

'I'm sure they'll be here,' I say.

'They had better be. Otherwise they'll be off the Christmas card list faster than you can say it.'

I wink at Mark. 'Beware,' I say. 'One false move and it's the end of Christmas cards forever. Devastating!'

'Are you doing the whole walk up the aisle thing?' Mark asks her.

'Yes. CC and I are vanishing next door just before the service and then coming back in,' Mum tells him.

Suddenly aware that without Saddam, there won't be anyone to come in *to*, I say, 'I'll go check on Saddam.'

'I'll stay here with you, if that's OK,' Mark says to Mum.

As I leave the room, I hear her say, 'Thanks so much for coming. I've been telling everyone about CC's boyfriend, but I'm not sure anyone believes me. And as I say, it's so much nicer for Saddam to have some young—'

'I'm not her boyfriend,' Mark interrupts.

'I know *that*, dear,' Mum replies. 'I'm not completely gaga. But Poppy will assume that you are, and that's fine with me.'

Due to the rain, the corridors are still packed with the departing wedding party, who are waiting for cars, so I have to fight my way through them as I hunt high and low for Saddam. They are a surprisingly rowdy bunch; in fact I would hazard a guess that they have had some kind of boozy reception *before* the wedding.

Eventually, at the rear of the building, I find Poppy Meyer – one of Mum's oldest and stuffiest friends – smoking beneath the overhang of the back porch.

'Oh, hello, CC,' she says. 'You can't bloody smoke anywhere these days. It's like being a social outcast. Lovely outfit, by the way.'

'Thanks,' I say.

Poppy is wearing a dreadful orange smock with a matching jacket and a netted hat, which looks like something the Queen Mum might have worn. But one has to lie in these circumstances.

'Yours too. So lovely to have a bit of colour on a day like this.'

'It's awful, isn't it?' she says, and for a moment I think that she means her dress, not the weather.

'It's such a load of old nonsense,' she continues, and I realise that she isn't, in fact, referring to either. 'Ciggy?' she asks, pulling a packet of Consulate Menthol from her bag.

'I don't usually,' I say, taking one, 'but what the hell.' I know I shouldn't be smoking, but this is, after all, an unusually stressful day.

'Yes, utter nonsense,' she says again, as she gives me a light.

'What is?' I ask, dragging on the cigarette, which tastes surprisingly good.

'Well, all of this. I mean, I've known Angela for forty years, and she's perfectly lovely, but let's face it, Saddam's not in love with her. How could he be? He's in love with the idea of a nice red English passport.'

'Well, that's what I thought too,' I say, 'but Mum doesn't see it that way, and ultimately ...'

The guilt about smoking while pregnant is too much for me, so I fake a coughing fit and stub it out. 'Sorry, Poppy,' I say. 'I'm out of practice.'

'Once he gets his green card or whatever,' Poppy continues, dragging deeply on her own cigarette, 'he'll be off, you mark my words.'

'That's America,' I tell her.

'Well, whatever it is he wants out of the deal – money, or passport, or what-have-you – he'll be off like a shot. And then Angela will be devastated and guess who will have to pick up the pieces.'

I think that if anyone is likely to be picking up the pieces, it's me, not Poppy, but I'm not going to make waves now. 'Well, I'm just trying to be positive about it all,' I tell her. 'It's what Mum wants, and once she has made up her mind about something . . .'

'Well, I'm glad you agree it's a mistake,' Poppy says. 'I'm glad that at least you can see that it's not right for a woman of her age to be waltzing around with an immigrant lad who's barely out of school.'

I'm just formulating the best way to express – without causing a ruck – that I don't entirely agree with her point of view, and I definitely don't agree with her terminology, when something at the corner of my vision catches my eye, and I turn to see Saddam turn and walk away from us.

'Sorry, Poppy. I have to . . . I won't be a minute.'

I leave her blowing smoke out into the rain and start to trot along the hallway in pursuit. 'Saddam!' I shout. 'Saddam?' But he is already vanishing into the huddle of the diminishing wedding group.

By the time I have fought my way through the remaining ten people – who, because they are pulling on their coats, form an impenetrable wall of arms – there is no sign of him. I stick my head into our reception room, where I find Mark holding forth to Mum and Giles about electronic music. He's explaining that techno is our generation's opera. Which is pretty much preaching to the unconvertible.

'It's little Chelsii!' Giles exclaims when he sees me, opening his arms in anticipation of an embrace.

'Hi, Giles,' I say. 'Sorry, but I'll be right back.'

I start to stride from room to room, then break into a high-heeled trot as panic about what exactly Saddam might have overheard sweeps over me. Running out of options, I check the men's toilets, where an overweight guy in a white shirt and Donald Duck tie says, 'All right, darlin'! What can I do you for?'

I finally run to the front door and peer out into the downpour just in time to see Saddam's hunched form round the corner onto the main road and vanish from sight.

I steal an umbrella from the stand by the door and start to run after him, instantly wishing that I had chosen the larger multicoloured golf umbrella. The downpour is lashing against my stockinged legs.

Saddam has his suit jacket pulled over his head, and is striding into the distance almost as fast as I can run, so I pause and pull off my shoes so that I can run barefoot instead. After about a hundred yards he pauses beneath a bus shelter and I finally start to catch up with him.

Just before I reach the shelter, I see him sink onto the bench seat and put his head in his hands.

'Saddam!' I say breathlessly as I reach him.

He looks tearily up at me. His expression instantly shifts to anger. '*Va-t'en!*' he says. *Go away.*

'Saddam,' I say again. 'What's wrong? Where are you going?'

'Away!' he says. 'You not my friend.'

'Yes I am!' I say, folding the umbrella and sinking onto the seat beside him, 'God, you're soaked.' I start to brush as much water from the shoulders of his new suit as I can.

'*J'ai entendu,*' he says. *I heard.*

'You heard *Poppy*,' I say. 'And she's a bigoted old witch.'

'You think same,' Saddam says. 'Everyone think same things.'

'Come back inside,' I tell him. 'Come inside and dry off and we can talk.'

'No,' he says, 'I can't.' He turns from me to hide a surge of tears, which his shuddering shoulders give away all the same.

'But you have to,' I tell him, thinking about how young he is to be facing all of this, and suddenly feeling genuinely sorry for him. 'It's your wedding day.'

He turns back to face me and his features contort with the effort of holding back tears. 'No one want this *marriage*,' he says, pronouncing 'marriage' the French way.

'My mother does,' I say. 'You do.'

'But you? No.'

I sigh.

'You see!' he says.

'It's ... it's difficult, Saddam,' I say. 'People are suspicious.'

'I know,' Saddam says. 'Angela is tell me. Everyone is thinking I want to live here only.'

'Yes, some people might think—' I begin.

'Look!' he shouts. 'Look at this place. Look at the rain, the cold. Why I want to live here?'

And I look out at the dismal grey of Surrey in a rainstorm and see exactly what he means.

'You think I want to . . . to *laisser* . . . Morocco for this?'

I rub his shoulder. 'Not *me*,' I lie. 'But people will think that maybe life's easier for you here than it is over there.'

'How?' Saddam gasps, choked with tears and so angry that he's forgetting to breathe. 'I done speak English. No one like the Arabs here. I can even carry a back peck any more.'

'Sorry?'

'I can carry a back peck because I look like a terrorist.'

'I'm sorry? Who said that?'

'Someone ask in London if I am terrorist.'

'Who?'

'The lady on the metro train, the time before. Here I have no job. It's raining and colding all the time. An' you people all think England's so good, and that's why I want to be here? So stupid! I *hate* here,' he says, angrily.

Saddam's head drops back into his hands and he starts to sob again, so I slide my arm further around his wet back and pull him closer to me. A big lump forms in my throat because, of course, I know exactly how feeling forced to be somewhere you hate feels.

'I thought you *liked* it here,' I say. 'Mum said you liked it.'

'I tell her I like it,' he says. 'But is not true. No family. No friend. No job. No nothing.'

'So why come?' I ask.

'*Je l'aime!*' he says, glancing up at me and looking utterly astonished that I still haven't grasped that simple fact.

I swallow hard and lean in against him and drop my head sideways so that it touches his. I sigh deeply. 'God, you really do, don't you?' I murmur. 'I'm so sorry, Saddam.'

'Everything is bloody now,' he says. 'I don't know what ... I think go home.' He starts to sob again. 'But everything is bloody there too now. I lose job. My mother done talk to me any more.'

I lean forwards to try to see his face, but he turns away, so I stand and crouch down in front of him and pull his chin towards me so that I can look deep into his eyes. He has the most beautiful eyes that I think I have ever seen on a man. I'm even slightly jealous of his eyelashes – I can't get that effect no matter how much mascara I put on.

'If you love her,' I tell him, 'if you *really* love her, then you mustn't care what anyone thinks.'

'But everyone is against,' he says, his voice wobbly. 'How I can?'

'Fuck them,' I say, and though he continues crying, he vaguely smiles too. I smile back at him. 'Fuck them all!' I say again.

'Angela says is too bad, this word,' Saddam says with concern.

'It is,' I agree. 'But between us youngsters, it's OK. Fuck them all,' I tell him. 'You say it.'

'Fuck them all,' he murmurs, and breaks into a teary grin.

'And you're sure that you love her?' I say. 'You're sure you're not confused?'

Saddam nods and swallows.

'How do you know?' I ask.

He thinks about this, and performs a wonderful Gallic shrug. But as he does so he breaks into one of the most beautiful, genuine smiles that I have ever seen. 'I don't know,' he says. But the toothy grin has said everything.

I laugh. 'My old mum really does make you happy, huh?'

Saddam nods. '*Beaucoup,*' he says, tears running down his cheeks.

'Come on,' I say, looking at him through my own watery vision, standing and holding out one hand. 'Let's go get you married.'

'You think?' he asks, looking up at me, but taking my hand all the same.

'I think,' I say, grabbing it and yanking him upright.

A LITTLE TOO RELAXED

As we head back in, huddled beneath the tiny red umbrella, Saddam asks, 'You stay with me?'

'Of course,' I reply. 'I have to go and get Mum, walk her down the aisle, but—'

'No,' Saddam says, his tone anguished. 'Please! You stay with me.'

'But—'

'You show people. You show people you are OK with.'

I squeeze his arm. 'Sure. I'll have a word with Mum.'

Back inside the manor, I drag Saddam into the ladies' and dry his jacket under the hand dryer. I check my face in the mirror, but luckily Vanessa's industrial strength make-up is holding up perfectly.

When we step out into the hallway, we cross paths with the guy with the Donald Duck tie again. He glances at Saddam, at me, at Saddam again, and finally at the sign that says *Ladies*, then winks at me, grins, and walks off.

'You know this guy?' Saddam asks.

'No, I don't know anyone who wears a Disney tie.'

He frowns at me, so I mutter, 'It doesn't matter', and drag him on down the hallway.

By the time we get to the ceremony room, it's one minute to three and everyone is seated. 'One second,' I say, prising Saddam's hand from my arm and crossing to where Mark is sitting.

I crouch down beside him and say, 'Saddam's having a case of nerves. He wants me to stay with him. To sort of demonstrate to everyone that I approve.'

'I didn't know you did,' Mark says, grinning broadly as if this is terribly funny.

'We had a long talk,' I say. 'I changed my mind. He really does love her, you know.'

'How sweet,' he says.

I frown at him. 'You're acting strange.'

'I'm a bit stoned,' he whispers rather loudly.

'Jesus, Mark!'

The registrar coughs, and when I look up at her, she taps her watch.

'It's time. Can you go and get Mum to walk her down the aisle? So I can stay with Saddam? Otherwise I'm scared he'll do a runner.'

'I can stay with him if you want,' Mark says, still grinning.

'No,' I tell him. 'Just explain to Mum. She'll understand. And she'll love waltzing down the aisle with you. I think she quite fancies you, to be honest.'

Mark stands, bumps into his chair, and then lollopingly walks from the room as I return to Saddam's side.

'He's stoned?' he asks me.

'Apparently so,' I say, surprised that he knows the signs so well.

'*J'aimerais bien,*' he says. *I wish I was.*

The registrar hits play on the ghetto blaster, and Saddam and I turn to face the door. I scan the faces present and realise that Lindsay and Jack are still missing. Giles catches my eye and winks at me, and Poppy whispers something to the woman next to her and they both shake their heads and pout. I understand entirely why Saddam didn't want to face them alone.

The wedding march starts to belt out a little too loudly from the sound system before the registrar finds the correct knob to lower it. And then once the volume is correct, Mum and Mark appear in the doorway, the two of them red-faced and giggling, and I realise instantly that Mark has got my mother stoned.

In deference to Saddam, the service is as short and sweet as it can be. The entire thing lasts about seven minutes, and other than a second fit of giggles by my mother when the registrar says, 'You can kiss the bride', everything goes off without a hitch.

Once the registers have been signed and witnessed, people stand and we start to leave the room.

I whisper to Mark, 'Tell me you haven't been getting my mother stoned.'

'She was stressed!' he laughs.

'Jesus, Mark! You're incorrigible.'

'She asked for it,' he says. 'She begged me, in fact.'

'I don't believe you.'

'Apparently she and Saddam have quite a taste for it. She says the weed is better in Morocco.'

'You fibber!' I say.

Mark just shrugs and snorts.

When we get back to the house, the caterer has, as expected, moved the entire buffet in from the gazebo to the dining room.

'I'm sorry,' he says, 'but it's like Glastonbury out there. It's a shame, but there you go.'

But the fire is flickering, the DJ in the lounge is playing sloppy love songs and the spread looks rather pretty, so I allow myself a tiny glass of champagne and decide that I'm simply not going to give a damn about anything today.

Mum floats, still grinning slightly madly, from one pair of friends to another and I notice how tight all of their expressions are and come to agree that faced with so much unspoken disapproval, stoned is the only way to be. I just wish I could join her. But as the champagne flows, even the hardest of features soften.

'So are you happy, Mum?' I ask, when we finally get a moment alone.

'Oh, perfectly, dear,' she says. 'Thanks so much for all of this. The food is *faaabulous*, as Mark would say. And those prawn thingies are gorgeous. Have you had one yet?'

'No. I'm a bit wary of prawns at the moment.'

'Anyway, it's all lovely. The whole day is wonderful. And thanks for looking after Saddam.' She touches my arm very gently. 'He told me what you did for him.'

I smile. 'It was nothing. He's quite a sweetie, isn't he?'

'He is,' she says with meaning. 'An actual angel.'

'Will you still spend the winters in Morocco?' I ask. 'Because from what I gather, he would like that.'

Mum nods, then swipes a fresh glass of champagne from the passing drinks tray. 'I think so,' she says. 'We'll see how things pan out. But yes, I expect that's what we'll do. Where is he, anyway?'

'He went off with Mark, I think.' I pull a face. 'And I know about you. You bad girl.'

'What?' she asks innocently.

'I know why you got the giggles during the ceremony. I know why you're so relaxed.'

'Oh, that's Mark,' she says. 'He's terrible. Actually, he's more of a saviour. If he wasn't ... you know ... I'd marry *him*.'

'You're unbelievable,' I say.

'I try my best.'

'But I'm glad you like Mark,' I tell her. 'He's probably my best friend. My best male friend, anyway.'

Mum nods. 'Yes. I understand that. I understand that entirely. He reminds me of ... never mind.'

'He reminds you of Waiine.'

She blinks slowly, then swallows with difficulty. 'Anyway!' she says.

I glance over at the DJ, who is in the process of mixing badly as he tries to fade from Foreigner's 'I Want to Know What Love Is' to Rod Stuart's 'Have I Told You Lately?'.

'Is he going to play this stuff all night?' I ask. 'Because I distinctly remember requesting some dance music.'

'Don't you worry about that,' Mum says mysteriously. 'We have a little surprise lined up for later on.'

'Who does?'

'You'll see. Now!' she says, scanning the room. 'I need to find that husband of mine before Mark gets him too stoned.'

I chat to the various family friends on a superficial level. They inevitably ask me, 'what I think about all of this', and I tell them as definitively as possible how happy I am that my mother has found someone she loves and who loves her. I discover that if you say it with enough conviction, people simply nod and agree.

I have a wonderful hour-long chat with Giles, Dad's old colleague. He tells me that my father would have approved of anything that made Mum happy, and goes on to regale me with tales of their college day antics, stories I have never heard before and feel honoured to hear now. Just as Giles is seemingly running out of these, Poppy Meyer comes up saying, 'I need to have a word with CC,' before she quite literally drags me away.

'Are you having a nice time, Poppy?' I ask her. She looks drunk.

'I need a word with you about that chap of yours,' she slurs.

'Yes?'

'I fear he may not be all he seems to be,' she whispers, and from the way she runs the words *hesheemshtobe* together, I conclude that she definitely is trollied.

'Go on?' I ask, intrigued and amused.

She leans into my ear and says, 'I think he may be a little light on his feet, dear.'

I frown and laugh out loud. 'Mark? Light on his feet?'

'Yes,' she says. 'I dishtinctly heard him tell Adam, or Saddam, or whatever, that he has a boyfriend.'

'Mark's gay,' I say.

'You know?'

'Yes.'

'Gosh, how modern,' Poppy says.

'I've known for years.'

'Well, believe me,' Poppy says, wobbling as she momentarily loses her balance. 'That's one kind of relationship that you'll never make work. Trust me. I know!'

I frown at her. 'What do you mean, you know?'

She flashes the whites of her eyes and nods exaggeratedly at me.

'Not *Uncle Phil*!' I ask incredulously. 'Anyway, where *is* Uncle Phil today?'

Poppy raises her hands in an 'I'm saying nothing' kind of way, but then continues anyway. 'He's with his "friend", dear,' she says, copying my mother's gesture and making the speech marks. 'So let that be a warning to you. Find yourself a man who loves you more than he loves the best man. That's all I'm saying.'

She then nods with meaning, peers into her empty glass, and staggers off in search of more.

I giggle to myself at Poppy's assumption that Mark is my boyfriend and then, desperate to see his reaction to the news, I head off to find him.

He's outside sharing a joint with Saddam, and when I

push past the flap of the gazebo, Saddam hands the joint back and jumps up to meet me.

'*Mon ami!*' he says. *My friend!*

I smile at them both and shake my head in a vaguely disapproving way.

'Am sorry,' Saddam says, more seriously. 'For before. In the rain.'

'You have nothing to be sorry about,' I tell him. '*I'm* sorry.'

He beams at me and then, as if the gesture surprises even him, lurches at me and hugs me awkwardly.

'The rain has almost stopped,' I say, breaking free. 'But too late to use the garden.'

'Inside is fine; it's cosy,' Mark says. 'So Saddam here was just asking me if you and Victor will be tying the knot now?'

'Do you know that Poppy Meyer thinks that you and I are together?' I say, avoiding the question rather deftly.

'I thought she might,' Mark says.

'She just came over to warn me that she thinks you're a little light on your feet,' I explain.

'Light on my feet?' Mark laughs, coughing out a lungful of smoke and performing a little light-footed chair-dance from his seat. 'Gosh, I haven't heard that one for a while.'

'I go find Angela,' Saddam says, giving my arm a squeeze and ducking out of the gazebo. 'But thank you.'

'Are you having a nice time, sweetie?' Mark asks, rolling his next joint.

'Yes, I am.'

'Saddam's really nice, isn't he?' Mark says. 'I thought he might be a bit dodgy about the gay thing, what with being Muslim and stuff. But he's cool with it.'

'Well, as long as he's not *too* cool with it,' I comment. 'Poppy was just telling me that the secret to a good marriage is to find someone who fancies you more than he fancies the best man.'

'Wise words,' Mark says. 'But he's totally straight, if that's what you're asking.'

'Good to know.'

I hear wheels crunching on the gravel of the drive. 'More people,' I say. 'I keep hoping Victor will turn up. I haven't heard a peep from him since eleven this morning, so I keep hoping he's on his way.'

'I'm sure he'll get here if he can,' Mark says.

'I better go out and greet them. Back in a minute.'

I squelch across the lawn and then crunch across the gravel until I reach the corner of the house, where my heart sinks. Because the car, a turquoise Matiz, isn't anything that Victor is likely to deign to drive.

But when the door opens, and a familiar hand reaches out onto the roof, and an even more familiar body squeezes itself from the driver's seat, my heart performs a little somersault.

'Ah!' I shriek, running over to meet him. 'You made it!'

Victor stretches and then wraps me in his arms, momentarily lifting me from the ground and twirling me round.

'So sorry I missed the service,' he says. 'I tried everything.'

'It's fine,' I say. 'I just can't believe you made it at all. And what's with the bumper car?'

'The only thing they had free at Stansted,' Victor says.

'I thought it was Gatwick you were flying to?'

'It's a long story ... You really don't want to know.'

'God, I've missed you,' I say.

Victor kisses me on the lips again and says, 'Me too.'

At that instant, it starts to rain again. 'Here,' I say. 'Come inside and say hi to everyone.'

'Wait,' Victor says, grabbing my hand and pulling me back. 'Is there somewhere we can go? Somewhere private?'

'Private?' I say. 'Yes, I suppose ... Why?'

Victor laughs. 'I could just do with five minutes to decompress alone with you before all that ...' He nods towards the house.

'Sure,' I say. 'Um ... wait there.'

I dash into the house and return with a half bottle of champagne and two glasses. 'Come,' I say, leading him to the side of the house. 'We can kick Mark out of the gazebo.'

As the rain intensifies, we start to jog, but when we reach the gazebo, I see through the little plastic window that it no longer contains Mark but my mother and Saddam. They are sitting face to face holding both hands and talking intently.

I raise a finger to my lips and lead Victor silently on past the gazebo to the far end of the garden. I hand Victor the bottle and glasses so that I can fiddle with the combination lock on Dad's old shed.

'Ooh, comfy,' Victor says, as the door creaks open.

'I know,' I say, pulling him inside. 'It's dusty, but ... Dad used to come here for a bit of peace and quiet. Mum hasn't touched it since.'

I pull the door closed behind us and turn to find Victor standing right behind me, waiting for a kiss. As the rain starts to drum more heavily on the roof, he kisses me on the lips and then pulls me tight and buries his nose in my hair.

'You forget how good that feels,' I murmur.

'I didn't forget,' Victor says. 'I've been thinking about this for two weeks.'

'Here,' I say, leading him over to the disintegrating club armchair, and brushing the dust away with a rag from the floor.

Victor sits on the chair and I lay myself across his lap, with my legs hanging over one side, and kick my shoes off.

'So how was the wedding?' Victor asks. 'Did it all go to plan?'

'Yes,' I say. 'Yes, it was short and sweet, but fine.'

'No drama then?'

'A bit. Saddam ran off at one point, but I talked him round.'

'That's my girl.'

'I like him,' I say. 'He really does love her, I think.'

'Well, that's good. I'm so sorry I missed the service. I brought a suit and everything. You look fab in this, by the way,' he says, fingering the velvet of my dress.

'Thanks.'

'Actually, I can still change if you want.'

'I don't think anyone cares any more,' I say. 'They're all sloshed already.'

'They look sweet together, Saddam and your mum.'

'I know. It's amazing.'

'He *is* very young. But I guess love conquers all.'

'Apparently so,' I say.

'I was thinking about us,' Victor says. 'The three of us.'
I smile.

'I was thinking about what Harrison's wife said again.'

'That the way to make a marriage last . . .'

'. . . is not to get divorced. Yes.'

'You like that, don't you?'

'Yes, I do,' Victor says, seriously. 'There's something powerful about it, about getting married and meaning it. Saying that you'll stay together no matter what happens. Making the marriage last by refusing to get divorced, no matter what.'

My stomach knots at what may be about to come. Because the truth is that though the idea of marrying Victor has crossed my mind at almost every stage of these wedding preparations, I simply haven't managed to come to any conclusion.

'So even if you don't want to get married, because you've done it all before,' Victor says, 'maybe we could still make that vow, sort of privately, to each other.'

I kiss Victor on the cheek and my vision blurs slightly. 'That's really sweet,' I say.

'So shall we?' he asks.

'What? Vow to stay together?'

'Yes. Forever.'

'Now?'

'Why not?'

'Aren't you supposed to be on one knee or something?' I say, using humour to disguise the tension I am feeling.

Victor starts to move, so I say, 'No, I was only joking, stop!', but he lifts me up, sets me back down on the chair, and then kneels before me.

He takes my hand and gazes at me. 'I want us to stay together,' Victor says, 'and any problems, we just get through them and come out the other side, OK?'

'OK,' I say. 'Me too.'

'Me too?' Victor says. 'Me too?!' and then he starts to tickle me and we both collapse in a fit of laughter.

Once recovered, I stand and fill two glasses with champagne.

'Should you be drinking?' Victor asks.

'Oh, it's only my second glass. And it's just today.'

Victor shrugs. 'Your call,' he says.

As we raise our glasses, aware that I have slightly belittled Victor's attempt at solemnity, I say, 'To us. Forever,' and Victor repeats the words.

For a few seconds, we stare into each other's eyes, and I see through the haze that his eyes are wet with emotion too, and just for a moment, I feel so happy that it actually makes my heart hurt.

'Should we go inside?' Victor asks, breaking the silence.

'Not yet,' I say. 'I've been run off my feet all week. And you must be knackered.'

'A bit,' Victor concedes.

'So we deserve this,' I say.

We manoeuvre our way back to our previous position on the armchair.

'This is nice, huh?' Victor says. 'Just you and me.'

'It is,' I agree.

414

'So, the house is pretty much done.'

'Does it look good?'

'Yeah, it does. Oh, and before you get all nervous, no, I'm not going to ask you to move back there.'

'You're not?'

'No.'

'Oh!'

'You sound disappointed,' Victor laughs.

'No, I'm just surprised.'

'Let's just say I went off the neighbourhood a bit as well.'

'Really? How come?'

'Well . . .' Victor sighs. 'Turns out Distira isn't such a nice auntie to have, after all.'

'I thought it was all Carole's fault.'

'A lot of it was, I think. But they were in it together, for the most part. And it was Distira who smashed the hole in the roof.'

'She didn't!'

Victor nods.

'But that was before we even got there!'

'I know. It turns out that Clappier's mate knows the lads who did it.'

I frown. 'I don't understand. You said it was Distira.'

'She got them to do it. Maybe even *paid* them to do it. They took some of the stones from that wall behind the house, too.'

'You're not saying . . . that's not why the wall collapsed, is it?'

'Not the house wall, but the retaining wall, yeah. That's why we had that mud slide.'

'But why? Why would she do that?'

Victor shrugs. 'I think she's a bit mad. I challenged her about it and she went off on one, saying that Mum had promised *her* the farm. So her nose was put out of joint when she found out that it was mine, I suppose. I reckon that's where most of the angst came from.'

'Is that likely, that your mum promised her the house?'

'Well, no,' Victor says. 'You can't disinherit your children in France, anyway. But anything's possible. Mum could have said anything when she was drunk. And as I say, I think Distira's probably a bit senile, if not actually barking.'

I shake my head. 'That's awful. And to do that to your own nephew. What a pair! They won't smash the place up while you're away, will they?'

Victor shakes his head. 'No. We had a big row. I kind of lost it with them. I listed everything that had happened, from the doctor who never—'

'So I was right? He *didn't* come?'

'No, I don't think so. I should have believed you. I thought it was because you were feverish. But no, I asked her for the phone number of the other doc when I got back. I told her that I wasn't feeling well. She couldn't find it, of course. Or remember his name. I was pretty angry about that one. It could have been dangerous.'

I shake my head. 'I think she wanted me dead. She kept opening the window in that bloody room. She wanted to freeze me to death.'

Victor shakes his head. 'I doubt she wanted to actually kill you. But I don't think you could say she exactly wanted you well either. I had a go at them about the tarot card nonsense too. And the keys she "lost", and the cats in the water tank ... I told her I'd call the police if anything else happens. But she'd clearly rather not have us living next door. And I think I'd rather sell the place and let someone else deal with her, to be honest.'

I exhale deeply.

'Relieved then?' Victor asks.

I laugh. 'A bit, yes. You know, I bet they took the second page of that letter I left, too.'

'You think?'

'I can't see how else, when the pages were folded up together.'

'Well, that would definitely have been Carole. Distira couldn't even have read it.'

'God, what a creepy pair.'

'So all we have to do now is decide where we *do* want to live. I suppose you want to stay in London?'

I shake my head. 'No, I don't think so. Maybe a cottage or something, but close enough to friends and—'

The throbbing baseline of 'Disco Inferno' suddenly bursts from the house. 'What the hell is that?' I ask.

'Sounds like the party is hotting up. Do you want to go back?'

'Give me a kiss, first,' I say. 'A proper one.'

I stand and Victor rises to meet me. He kisses me deeply, and when I become aware that he has a gun in his pocket, I realise that I want much more. It has, after all, been two weeks.

I turn to slide the bolt on the shed door, and then hang

the rag over the little window. Victor watches all of this with a smug grin, and then puts his glass down. 'Now there's a good idea,' he says, making a grab for my belt and yanking me towards him.

LOVE IS THE DRUG

It's dark by the time we get to the house. The music is deafening and I'm surprised that the little speakers our aged DJ set up this morning can produce such a din.

When I push open the lounge door, however, surprise doesn't cover it. My jaw drops.

About twenty people, ten from the original crowd, supplemented with a new group of people my age or younger, are dancing frantically to Kylie's 'Can't Get You Out Of My Head'.

Mark spots me immediately and comes over to join us.

'What on *earth* happened here?' I laugh.

'I got Iain to come over with some mates,' Mark says. 'It was your mum's idea, actually.'

'Are those your speakers?' I ask.

'Yes. They brought the whole lot. Simone is DJ'ing on her iPad. She's fab.'

'Sounds great,' Victor comments.

'Good to see you, man,' Mark says, turning to face him, and then hugging him tightly. 'So are you dancin'?' Mark asks, the hug over.

419

'In a mo,' Victor says. 'I need to get something to eat first. I'm starving.'

The buffet has vanished, so we head through to the kitchen where we find Mum, Saddam and a grey-haired man whose name I can't remember deep in conversation about, of all things, the pros and cons of wind-farms.

'Victor!' Mum exclaims, breaking free to hug him with unusual intensity. 'I'm so glad you could make it. I've been dying to meet you.'

'Hello,' Victor says shyly.

'Is there anything left to eat, Mum?' I ask. 'Because poor Victor here is starving.'

'Of course,' she says, releasing him. 'Will a sandwich do? Cheese? Or ham?'

'Anything,' Victor says. 'Truly anything.'

I try to help Mum as she drunkenly attempts to make Victor's sandwich, but she snappily pushes me away. Eventually, despite pausing annoyingly every time she speaks, she does manage to assemble a doorstop of a sandwich. She hands this to Victor on a plate, turns to Saddam, and says, 'Come on, let's go join the fun.'

'Do you think you'll be like that?' Victor asks, once they have gone.

'Like Mum?'

'Yes,' he says, through a mouthful of bread.

'I don't know,' I laugh. 'Probably. Would that be a bad thing?'

'Not as long as I can keep up,' he says.

Iain comes into the kitchen and asks for water. I point him, rather obviously, at the tap, and he thanks me, crosses the room, and then performs a double-take and looks back at me. 'Ah, you!' he says. His Scottish *you* sounds like *yee*.

'Yes, me,' I say flatly, a little nervous as to how this is going to unfold.

'I need to talk to you,' he says. 'I owe you an apology.'

'No you don't,' I say, trying to disguise my relief. 'It's all ...' I wave vaguely over my shoulder to indicate that it's all in the past.

'So we're OK?' he asks, filling a glass from the tap.

'Yes, we're definitely OK,' I say. 'And thanks for bringing all those people. It makes it much more of a party.'

'It's my birthday,' he says. 'Well, it's tomorrow, really. But we were all meeting today for lunch to celebrate and then Mark called. This is much more fun.'

'Well, you made Mum's day,' I say. 'Mine too.'

'I've got some E if you want it,' he says.

'God, you're terrible, you two,' I say.

Iain grins and does his best to look sheepish. 'Is that a no, then?' he asks.

'I can't anyway,' I explain. 'I'm pregnant.'

'Oh, of course,' he says. 'And you, Victor?'

Victor grins and shakes his head. 'No thanks. Not today.'

'Solidarity with the missus, eh?' he says.

'Something like that,' Victor laughs.

The music changes to Donna Summer's 'I Feel Love'.

'Ooh, I have to go,' Iain says. 'Gotta dance. Are you coming?'

I look at Victor enquiringly.

'I'll just eat this and I'll be through,' he says.

In the lounge, everyone is dancing, whooping, dipping

and diving to Donna Summer. Someone has turned the lights out, and the party is lit by the single row of flashing disco lights brought by the original DJ, who is, I now notice, sitting in a corner talking to Poppy.

All of Iain's friends are dancing like madmen, but even Giles and my mother are grooving in a disturbingly modern fashion.

A guy – wearing what can only be described as a pair of hot pants – is being swung around by a black girl with three-foot hair extensions, and when she eventually lets go, he careens off across the room and falls, rather splendidly, onto Poppy's lap. She looks frankly outraged by this invasion of her personal space.

As the song changes to Faithless's 'Insomnia', Mark breaks free and dances to my side. 'It's a great party, isn't it?' he shouts, turning and leaning against the wall beside me.

'It is. I never thought you'd get the oldies dancing to Faithless.'

'They're all E'd up,' Mark says. 'They'll dance to anything.'

'They're not!' I exclaim.

Mark laughs. 'It's nothing to do with me. It's Iain. Your mum told me she hasn't felt so good since she was twenty.'

'God, I hope she's OK. She's old, Mark. She might have a heart attack.'

'She looks OK to me,' Mark says.

Iain sees us talking and comes to join us. He turns around and leans back against Mark, who wraps his arms around his shoulders and squeezes him tight.

'CC is worried your E might give her mum a heart attack,' Mark says.

'But I didnee give her any,' Iain replies.

'She looks like you did,' Mark says.

And he's right. Mum is right now shimmying against Saddam's back.

'Ney, they're just E'd up on love.'

'Well, thank God for that!' I say.

'*He* took a quarter though,' Iain says, nodding at Giles, who has his eyes closed and is dancing, for the first time in his entire life, in time with the music.

'Giles is on E?!' I exclaim.

'Aye,' Iain laughs.

'God, Iain!' I protest.

'Look at him,' Iain says. 'He's having the time of his life.'

I look at Giles and snort. No one could deny that that is true.

'And are *you* having a good birthday?' Mark asks him.

'Perfect,' Iain says.

Victor reappears from the kitchen, still brushing crumbs from his lips. He stares a little wide-eyed at the dancers and then slides behind me so that he's holding me in exactly the same way that Mark is holding Iain.

'This is a bit mad, isn't it?' Victor says.

'Apparently everyone's on E,' I say. 'Well, half of them, anyway.'

'I thought they might be,' he says. 'Looks like they're enjoying themselves. This is a party they'll never forget.'

'It is,' I say.

'When you see what fun a wedding can be, well, it almost makes you want to have one yourself,' he says.

I twist my neck so that I can look up at him. 'Stop it, you!' I joke.

'Hey, I'm just sayin',' he says, and gives me a little squeeze.

A sumptuous mix of Hercules and Love Affair's 'Blind' comes on and I start to groove my hips against Victor's groin. 'I love this one,' I say.

Mark and Iain return to the dance floor and I watch them for a moment and think how good they look together, and what a wonderful dancer Iain is, and how much I love Mark, and how chuffed I am that they're happy together. And then I look at my mother grooving with Saddam and think the same things all over again.

Victor slides his hands down around my waist and pulls me tight, and that feeling of being so happy that it hurts returns. I glance over and see Poppy is still talking to the DJ. Even she has her arm around his back now.

And I think that there's so much love in this room right now that I feel like *I've* taken ecstasy. If Victor were to ask me to marry him right now, I don't think I could say no. In fact, I almost wish that he *would* ask.

Instead, he nuzzles my neck and says, 'So?' and I assume that he means that we should dance too. 'Shall we join them?' he asks.

'Yes,' I say, 'Let's do it.'

He pulls me in and squeezes me so tight that I can hardly breathe.

'I knew you'd cave in in the end,' he says. 'I knew when I woke up this morning that today was the day you'd say yes!